PRAISE FOR THE
HIGHLAND GAMES NOVELS

Long Shot

"A smart and thoroughly enjoyable series debut for fans
and newcomers alike." —*RT Book Reviews*

"Realistic and hilarious." —*Harlequin Junkie*

"An enjoyable read made even more so by the supporting
cast interactions." —*The Book Pushers*

"Martine is just as good with her fantasy novel as she is
with this contemporary novel. Very different from her Elementals series, Ms. Martine tackles a more realistic storyline . . . [A] light read that I highly enjoyed. I recommend
this novel to anyone who enjoys Jessica Clare, Jennifer
Probst, and Victoria Dahl." —*Under the Covers*

"What's not to love? Men in kilts showing off skills and
serious muscles equals *melt*! . . . A fun, light, and hot contemporary romance." —*That's What I'm Talking About*

D0724792

continued . . .

The Good Chase

HANNA MARTINE

BERKLEY SENSATION, NEW YORK

THE BERKLEY PUBLISHING GROUP
Published by the Penguin Group
Penguin Group (USA) LLC
375 Hudson Street, New York, New York 10014

USA • Canada • UK • Ireland • Australia • New Zealand • India • South Africa • China

penguin.com

A Penguin Random House Company

THE GOOD CHASE

A Berkley Sensation Book / published by arrangement with the author

Berkley Sensation Books are published by The Berkley Publishing Group.
BERKLEY SENSATION® is a registered trademark of Penguin Group (USA) LLC.
The "B" design is a trademark of Penguin Group (USA) LLC.

For information, address: The Berkley Publishing Group,
a division of Penguin Group (USA) LLC,
375 Hudson Street, New York, New York 10014.

ISBN: 978-0-425-26752-3

PUBLISHING HISTORY
Berkley Sensation mass-market edition / December 2014

PRINTED IN THE UNITED STATES OF AMERICA

10 9 8 7 6 5 4 3 2 1

Cover photo by Claudio Marinesco.
Cover design by Rita Frangie.
Interior text design by Kelly Lipovich.

This one is for Katie Oates Junttila,
for so many reasons.

Acknowledgments

Thanks must first be given to fellow romance authors Heather Snow, Erin Knightley, and Anna Lee Huber, who helped me plot this book. The audio recording of that session is filled with my bumbling and their brilliance. And a lot of snacking.

Alyce Anderson, cop extraordinaire, assisted me with some crime and punishment details.

The Chicago-North chapter of the Romance Writers of America gave me extremely helpful critiques on my opening chapter and a spicy scene during our annual Hot Night.

The Aphrodite Writers let me lay it all out and helped keep me sane.

My brother-in-law told me the beef jerky story . . . which apparently is one hundred percent true.

Davia Lipscher got her Realtor's license specifically to answer my questions about buying and selling property . . . which is actually *not* true.

Eliza Evans and Shannyn Schroeder were fantastic beta readers with eagle eyes, as usual, and terrific cheerleaders.

Katie and Olav Junttila fed me so many details about big-time New York financial life (and the clothes that must go with it), as well as about the city itself. They told me all about private banking and entrepreneurship. Their input was invaluable and made the book what it is. Any mistakes are my own, because those two were a godsend.

Last but not least, I'd like to thank the Chicago Scots, whose wonderful annual Highland Games prompted the theme behind this series. I also attended their truly special "Feast of the Haggis" in 2012, from which I drew inspiration for the Scottish ball depicted in this book.

Author's Note

With regard to whisky/whiskey . . .

The Scots and Canadians spell whisky without the *e*. Therefore, the drink is *Scotch whisky* and *Canadian whisky*. Drinks distilled in other areas spell whiskey with the *e*. For example, *Kentucky bourbon whiskey* and *Irish whiskey*.

In this book, mentions of *whisky* refer only to Scottish bottles. *Whiskey* means either bottles distilled outside of Scotland/Canada **or** it's a general term encompassing malted grain spirits from a mix of locations.

Chapter

1

I need a hot guy in a kilt.

Shea Montgomery snorted a most unfeminine snort as she read the text that had just come through from her best friend, Willa.

Gently moving aside a box cradling some pretty divine bottles of Scotch whisky, Shea nudged back a flap of the white tent that would be her home for the day. Down an easy slope, out in the middle of a large, open field, a group of two-hundred-plus-pound men milled about, early morning sunshine on their faces, a brisk late-May breeze kicking up their kilts. Some of the men sat stretching on the grass, some rotated their arms in warm-up, some jogged slowly around the field's perimeter.

The first throw of the Long Island Highland Games would go off in about two hours.

Smiling, Shea texted back to Willa: *Funny, that's exactly what I'm looking at right now.*

Bring one back to the city for me.

Shea peered hard at the massive guys gathering inside the flag ropes. *I take that back. Lots of kilts. None hot. Sorry.*

Take a pic. Let me decide.

Shea laughed. *I'm working. And no way to be stealthy about it when no one else is over there.*

You are dead to me.

Shea tucked her phone into the back pocket of her black pants.

"Always good to start the day off with a smile. Right, Big Boss?"

Dean, her best employee at the Amber Lounge in Manhattan, stepped into the tent, rolling up the sleeves to his white button-down shirt. She so rarely saw him outside her bar—and in daylight, no less—that she'd never noticed how much silver there was in his curling black hair.

"Hopefully it's a sign," she said, blowing out a big breath. "Help me with the inventory, will you? The master list is right there."

He read her the names of the bottles while she fingered the necks of each kind of Scotch whisky she'd curated for the day's tasting, making sure each had made it from the Amber's cellar to out here in Suffolk County.

When they were done, Dean stood back and admired her stash with hands on hips. He whistled in a high arc as he took in the bottles of port- and sherry-wood barrel-aged, and the twenty-seven-year-old single malt, and the eighteen-year-old blend.

"Nice choices," he said. "Not exactly starting at the bottom, are you?"

Shea tossed an empty box underneath a billowing table-cloth. "Yeah, well, you have to pay a hundred dollars extra just to come in here for a tasting. It was made very clear to me I had to make it special."

Dean's eyes bugged out. "A hundred bucks? No shit?"

Shea pulled her long hair back into her trademark ponytail and glanced with chagrin out at the blue velvet rope delineating the entrance to her tent. She sighed, snapping a rubber band around her hair and letting her arms flop down. "No shit."

In the distance sounded the day's first bleat of a bagpipe, a little shaky at first, but then smooth and lovely as the piper warmed up and the notes took shape. Shea recognized the tune and it gave her pause, made her smile to herself.

This was why she planned to attend and do whiskey tastings—of Scotch and others—at so many New England Highland Games this summer. Because they reinvigorated her. Because they shaped her dreams of things outside the walls of the Amber Lounge. Because they brought back memories of Scotland. Because they recalled those days, so many years ago, when she'd actually begun to *live*.

It was a perfect day for the games. For the sun and laughter, for watching powerful, kilted athletes compete by throwing around heavy implements like the hammer and the caber. For lying back on your elbows and surrounding yourself with the heartbreaking, beautiful sounds of pipes and drums, telling history through song. For cheering on young folk dancers and obedient sheepherding dogs.

Even if these particular games had its nose up in the air as opposed to right down in the peat and heather where it should be, the reminders of her Scottish ancestry warmed her heart.

But alas, she would get to do none of the fun events. Today was about the whisky.

The white tent rippled and flapped around Shea and Dean as they skillfully set out short-stemmed tasting glasses and made artistic towers of boxes and glassware behind the makeshift bar. High, circular tables draped with white linen and tied with blue bows peppered the center space, with squatter tables and cushioned chairs set outside under a canopy.

And then there was the goddamn velvet rope.

Whisky shouldn't be untouchable, relegated to only a certain level of social drinker, but that's exactly what Shea and her bottles were today, hidden away in this too-fancy tent. No one could enter who wasn't wearing the yellow one-hundred-dollar wristband. Laughable for a Scottish festival.

Shea just wanted to talk whisky, just wanted to serve what she loved. Not for the first time, she wondered if opening up such an exclusive bar had been an error in her development as a businesswoman. It clashed too much with her personality. Maybe she was better suited to running a corner pub with worn seats and scary bathrooms, but with the same access to amazing drinks. Take away the hoity-toity atmosphere, but keep the rare, good liquor.

Throughout the day, she tended to the few tasters who did manage to wander into her tent. During the long lulls in between, she gazed out at the heavy athletic field, watching the massive caber flipping end over end and listening to the excited announcer and the enthusiastic crowd's applause. She ended up sending Dean back to the city to open the Amber.

In the early afternoon, two couples ducked out of the bright sun and came in laughing. The taller husband, the one in a plaid, short-sleeved button-down shirt, was holding a set of stacked, empty beer cups. A Drinker, Shea pegged him, who'd come in here chasing the buzz. The other man, the one in a blue T-shirt, headed right for Shea, nodding as though they already knew each other. He was either a Hot Air—someone who *thought* he knew a lot about the good stuff—or a Brown Vein—someone who really *did* know.

Of the women, one wore a red visor that parked itself around her ears and extended far over her face. The other had a short, blond ponytail. Neither woman looked particularly interested in why they'd come in here, though all four people sported wrist-bands.

Shea spread her arms across the table and gave them all a welcoming smile. Didn't matter why anyone came in, when it came down to it. They were giving the drink a chance, and educating newcomers was one of her favorite parts of her job. Sometimes that was the best kind of challenge, to win over someone who'd been skeptical—a Squinter—or someone who had cut their teeth on whiskey by sneaking their parents' ten-dollar plastic-bottled swill bought at the corner bodega.

"So what do these get us?" Drinker waved his yellow wrist.

Always genial, always polite. "Tastes of three amazing whiskies and a walk-through of each, by yours truly."

"That's a big deal, my friend," added the other man. To Shea he gave a deep nod, lips pursed. "Saw you on the History Channel the other night." He didn't mention which special.

"Really? That's always great to hear. Glad you came by." Perfected responses to almost every comment from almost every type of customer.

She turned to her artful setup of bottles beneath the large banner with the Amber logo, and swung back around holding a tray of glasses. She flipped each glass over and slid it across the white tablecloth with smooth, practiced ease. One glass, two, three, four—

A fifth yellow wristband appeared at the elbow of the blue-shirted man she was leaning toward pegging as a Brown Vein. This new wristband wrapped around an arm that was crusty with caked mud. The newcomer's fingers and palm looked like he'd tried to wipe them somewhat clean, but black still clung under his nails. Shea followed that arm upward, which widened out significantly at the biceps. He wore a red-and-black-striped rugby shirt, soaked with the efforts of a recently completed match. His short, dark hair was sweat-damp and stuck out all over the place in a way that shouldn't have looked good but did. His cheeks and forehead were sunburned, and he leaned his elbows on the table with drowsy ease, leaving mud smudges behind.

Out of the corner of her eye, she saw one of the wives nudge the other.

"Welcome," Shea told Rugby.

"Hi," he replied.

She nodded at his shirt. His perfectly fitted shirt. "How'd you do?"

"Thirty-five to seventeen. We were not the higher number."

She winced. "Ouch. You at least get a try?"

"I did, actually." He blinked and straightened, looking pleasantly surprised that she knew rugby scoring terminology. "You know the game?"

"You could say that." She returned the tray to its place off to the side and set out the three bottles she was guessing this crew would like. The uninterested wives were throwing off Shea's drink-matching radar, but she'd work with what she had.

She said to Rugby, "So what I'm hearing is that you need a drink."

"Something a little finer than water, exactly." Rugby let out a small laugh. He twisted one of the whisky bottles to read the label. "Whatcha got here? What does a hundred bucks buy—wow."

"You know it?" Shea's turn to be pleasantly surprised.

"Heard of it, yeah. So that's why these things were so expensive." He waved his wrist so the loose end of the yellow wristband flopped about. "Took out a second mortgage to buy one."

Shea smiled.

The tall man in the blue T-shirt looked down his nose at Rugby and jabbed a meaty finger at the bottle in Rugby's hand. "That's made by a distiller in Scotland that still uses the original 1840 peat kilns to smoke the barley."

Shea fought for a straight face. Hmmm, maybe this guy was more Hot Air than Brown Vein. He was correct, but who voluntarily spouted off that kind of information to a stranger?

"Impressive." Rugby's eyebrows shot up exaggeratedly as he pursed his lips at Shea. Hot Air didn't get the subtle sarcasm, but she did and had to suppress another smile as she removed the bottle's cap. Customer equality and all that.

Out in the distant field, the athletes were taking a rest between events. A small contingent of pipes followed a line of old men dressed in military kilts as they marched onto the grass, Scottish and American flags whipping in the wind. The pipes started up, a wave of music drifting into the whisky tent.

Rugby cringed.

"No bagpipes, huh?" Shea teased.

"Sorry. No."

"For shame. Leave my tent immediately."

Rugby's cringe twitched toward a wan smile. And in that moment she became distinctly aware that he'd been monopolizing her attention, with four other tasters to entertain. How'd he do that?

"Why are you at the Scottish games," said Hot Air, who was tipsier than he'd originally appeared, "if you don't like the pipes?"

Rugby plucked at his dirty and sweaty shirt. "I go where the team tells me, hit who they want me to hit. Run wherever there's a goal line." He turned back to Shea. "You like bagpipes?"

Glancing out at the small parade making its way around the field, she felt the cool, familiar glass of the bottle in her hand and replied, "I do. Very much."

When her gaze drifted back to the five people standing on the other side of her table, Rugby was staring at her so hard she swore he might have been the source of all gravity.

"So," he said, throwing her a bright smile that tipped heavily to one side, "do you remember me?"

That blinked her out of that weird trance. She remembered regular faces, especially those who repeatedly visited the Amber Lounge, but with so many tastings and traveling and hired events and interviews these days, transient people tended to dissipate from her memory.

Yet there was something familiar about him. Something about his off-center smile set against the tanned skin layered with sweat and specks of dirt. But she couldn't place it right away, and she'd spent enough time away from the other four tasters.

She gave him one of her careful, noncommittal smiles. "I'm sorry. I don't."

"I'm Byrne."

A little cocky of him—but not quite obnoxious—to assume that she'd remember him based on one name. She didn't.

"Just Byrne?"

"Just Byrne." His smile widened, tilting even more to one side. Holy crap. He was far too easy on the eyes. She hadn't dared to think that about *any* guy who'd stood on the other side of her bar since Marco, and look how that had turned out.

"Shea Montgomery," she replied blandly, then turned to select a bottle. Too late, she realized she already held one in her hand.

"Yes. I know," said Just Byrne to her back. And then he chuckled.

The sound of that laugh, soft and low, slid an invisible hand around the nape of her neck, took a featherlight hold, then dragged itself seductively down her back.

Oh no. This did *not* happen to her while she was pouring.

She shook it off because she had to and turned back around to face her tasters, meeting the eyes of everyone but Byrne. She poured a shallow tasting amount in each glass, starting at the far end with plaid-shirted Drinker and ending with Byrne, who nudged his glass a little closer to her.

"Last summer?" he prompted.

She made the colossal mistake of lifting her gaze, of getting a good, long look at his eyes. Powder blue with a dark navy ring around the edge. Gorgeous. Flirtatious. Really fucking dangerous.

"At the Highland Games up in Gleann, New Hampshire." And now the dangerous eyes were smiling, too. "That cow wiped out your tent. Me and my team helped you clean it up."

The bottle slipped from her fingers. Just an inch or two, but it made a graceless clink on the table. She *did* remember him now. How he'd tried to openly flirt with her the first night after his team had won the tug-of-war competition, and then more subtly the next day after that damn loose cow had destroyed hundreds and hundreds of dollars of good whisky.

She also remembered that she'd been briefly intrigued by him. Extremely reluctantly intrigued, but intrigued nonetheless.

That damn crooked smile layered a boyish tint over his confident, intense focus on her, and she suddenly realized that his sojourn in here and all his amusing comments weren't entirely about the whisky.

Good luck with that, buster, she wanted to say. *I don't ever date tasters.*

"Oh yeah." Cool as the breeze, that was Shea. "Didn't you guys win the tug-of-war?"

"So you do remember." The way he said it, all drawn out, was packed with suggestion.

He was acting way too encouraged, like their witty banter would actually go somewhere. She shrugged. "That's about all I remember."

She turned her back on him and stepped to the center of her tasters, then poured herself her own tiny glass.

"So you do, like, a lot of these things?" slurred Drinker down at the end.

"You mean the Highland Games?" she asked, and when Drinker nodded, she replied, "Last year was my first doing the tastings. Got a couple more this summer."

"Lot more people up in Gleann," Byrne said, looking around her empty tent with an odd, thoughtful expression. Gleann's tent last year had been nonstop, from open to close.

"I am grateful for each and every taster," Shea replied carefully.

"But you wish there were more people?" he asked, meeting her eyes again.

"I always want to share whisky." God, she was starting to sound like a brochure. Throwing on a smile, she returned her focus to the two couples. "Are we finally ready to drink, folks?"

Drinker held up the small, squat, stemmed glass. "Why not the flat-bottom glasses? What do you call those again?"

"These are better for nosing the whisky," Shea replied. "Here, hold the base like—"

She didn't mean to look over at Byrne again. Habit, really, to take in everyone at the tasting table, to make sure she had their attention and that they each knew they were important to her. Hot Air was grasping the glass underneath, resting the bowl in his palm. But Byrne had the base balanced lightly in his fingertips. Correctly.

She ripped her stare from him and focused on the couples.

"Hold it like this." She showed them how to hold the base of the glass and not grip the bowl like a Viking. "What we're going to do first is nose the whisky three times, each time slightly longer than the last. One second, two seconds, three seconds. I'm going to count. Why don't you all watch me as you do it."

The women shared a glance and laughed, and Shea wondered how many of those empty plastic beer cups had been theirs.

"One."

Shea lifted the glass to her face, inserted her nose, and inhaled.

The couples followed suit and displayed pretty much the range of reaction she'd expected. Everything from I-Don't-Give-A-Shit-Let's-Drink, to Ew-This-Is-Disgusting, to dramatic, chest-pounding coughing because she'd inhaled too deeply and too long. Hot Air's expression said that this was nothing he hadn't already known.

And then there was Byrne. Nose in his glass for about a quarter second longer than was necessary. Powder blue eyes lifted just over the rim. Set solely on her.

Did he think he was the first guy to give her The Eye from the other side of the bar? This flat surface in front of her was No-Man's-Land. Quite literally.

"Should be different the second time, now that you got the shock of the alcohol out of the way," she heard herself saying. "It should be sweeter."

The corner of Byrne's mouth twitched, a hint of that crooked smile, then he buried his nose in the glass again, exactly matching her movements. Concentrating. This time *not* looking at her. Black lines of dirt had settled into the deep grooves of concentration along his forehead. He must be a few years older than her, maybe midthirties. He wore his years extremely well.

Stop it, stop it, stop it.

On cue, Hot Air started spouting off to his companions a list of all the things he smelled in the whisky. While there were never any right or wrong suggestions to specific scents or notes—whisky was an entirely personal experience—he was messing with Shea's rhythm.

"And the third?" Byrne asked Shea, cutting into Hot Air's thesaurus recitation. Hot Air shut up.

"On the third nose," Shea said, "you should smell some fruit, going deeper into the intricacies of the glass."

Her tasters followed her actions.

"Byrne! You done in there yet? Come on, let's go!"

Byrne swiveled to the sound of the chorus of male voices. Outside in the sun, the rest of his team, muddy and disheveled in red and black, beckoned to him. No other rugby players wore yellow wristbands.

Byrne acknowledged them with his glass, then took a perfect taste of what Shea had poured.

The brown liquid disappeared slowly into his mouth. His jaw worked it over for a good four or five seconds. Biting it, chewing it. Savoring it, as it should be done. Then he swallowed it back, his throat working.

Exactly like how she was about to instruct her newbies.

Byrne lifted his eyes to Shea without a hint of pretentiousness or flirting. "Excellent, thank you." Then, with a nod to the other four tasters, he left her tent.

She watched him go.

He had a long stride, masculine but oddly graceful. A leisurely confidence to his gait, contrasted by the clumps of turf stuck to the bottom of his cleats. He was built exactly how a rugby player should be with those ridiculous legs—tanned and thick and strong, with a distinct pronunciation of his quads. Might as well have *rugby player* tattooed down the side.

God*damn* it. In her mind she held one of those giant cartoon mallets and was whacking herself on the head.

Outside, the rest of Byrne's team had moved on except for one guy with a stocky build and longish blond hair. Byrne gave the other guy a "just a minute" gesture and disappeared in the opposite direction of his team.

Shea shook her head of his image and poured the next whisky for the couples, answering their questions about the Speyside distillery and the mashing process and what the years of aging on the bottle meant.

Then Byrne ambled back into view. Just a red-and-black-striped figure in her periphery at first, but her stupid brain demanded she look out through the tent flaps again, and so she did, beyond annoyed at herself. Distantly she thought she heard a nearby clearing of a throat, but she couldn't rip her stare away from Byrne.

His friend had drifted out of sight, but Byrne didn't seem to be looking for him. Instead Byrne went down the grass slope to where two couples, possibly in their forties, had spread out a blanket along the flag rope just outside the athletic field. The hammer toss was going on, but Byrne ignored the event and instead tapped one of the women on her shoulder. He gave her that incredible, crooked smile.

Toast. That woman was toast.

But then all four of the strangers were listening to Byrne say something, nodding up at him enthusiastically.

Byrne reached into the pocket of his rugby shorts and pulled out four yellow wristbands. One of the men reached for his wallet, but Byrne waved him off.

Shea gasped. Why on earth had he done that? Four hundred dollars. Four hundred dollars! Not to show off or to try to impress her, she hoped, because tossing around money was the absolute wrong way to do that.

To be generous, maybe? But still, four hundred dollars on whisky, given to complete strangers? Who *was* this guy?

As the two new couples slapped on the wristbands and stood, folding up their blanket, Byrne headed in the direction his team had gone. As he passed by the whisky tent, he turned his head and instantly found Shea. Caught her staring.

She quickly ducked her head, blindly grabbing for the third and final bottle, but not before she was blasted by the full impact of that crooked smile, far too bright in the sunshine.

That smile promised a lot. Things she hadn't allowed herself—or been afforded—to think about in a long, long time. Things that hit her right where she hadn't been touched in an embarrassing number of months.

It disturbed her greatly, to be disarmed while in uniform, so to speak. It disturbed her even more that the man who'd done it was a taster—quite possibly a Brown Vein—met while she was working, and apparently in possession of some kind of money. No-nos, all around.

He wouldn't win.

He had to know that even though he'd caught her staring,

and even though she'd looked away like a shy virgin at a bachelor auction, it didn't mean that he'd gained any sort of ground with her. She had strict personal rules to uphold, a hard-won reputation to maintain, and a business to keep at the top of the New York scene.

But when she looked up to tell him all that with her cool, disinterested expression and Stay Back eyes, Byrne was gone.

Chapter

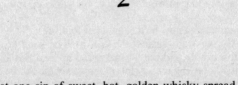

2

*T*hat one sip of sweet, hot, golden whisky spread out and tingled its way through Byrne's body. He wanted more, plain and simple, but it had been pretty clear that what he wanted wasn't exactly available.

That was a damn shame.

The day had started out with the stress of the workweek still lingering in his system, until he'd hopped into the van with the rest of his rugby team, tightened the laces on his cleats, and jogged out onto the pitch, so very ready to get physical. Every play, every scrum, every hit, knocked out a little chunk of the shit he'd had to deal with this week—the intense kissing of asses, only to lose the business in the end—so when the clock wound down today and Manhattan Rugby chalked up yet another loss, he didn't care. The game had done what it was meant to do for him, and he'd walked off the field feeling high.

Shea Montgomery had been merely a bonus. A delicious whisky chaser.

He'd been meandering through the Highland Games, trying desperately to outrun the screech of those god-awful bagpipes, when he saw the whisky-tasting tent. The names Amber Lounge and Shea Montgomery had given him a good slap across the face.

Shea. The gorgeous, intriguing whisky expert he'd met last summer. He recalled briefly trying to track her down after their chance encounter with the cow up in Gleann. But then life and work and general crap had gotten in the way, and she'd slipped from his mind for a whole year.

How on earth could that have ever happened? After enthusiastically paying a hundred dollars and stepping into her tent, seeing her standing tall and confident and utterly beautiful in front of a line of sparkling brown bottles, he really didn't know.

Then she'd shot him down, bringing the total number of bullet holes she'd given him to two, because he seemed to remember standing in front of her firing squad up in Gleann last year.

And yet . . . just now he'd caught her looking.

Now Byrne swam against the crowd as he tried to make his way toward the parking lot that jutted up against the back of the whisky-tasting tent. A lot of people seemed to be making their way over to the big field where some seriously huge guys in plaid skirts were trying to swing some sort of ball on a short pole across the grass.

"There you are. Finally." Erik was standing at the taillight of a sweet blue Tesla, tapping at his phone. "Was about to call. George is ready to leave without you."

"Sorry." Three lanes over, the van the team had rented sat idling with its side doors thrown open, George's thick body stuffed behind the wheel, the rest of the team wedged in the back. "Wanted some whisky."

Still did.

Erik peered over Byrne's shoulder, and Byrne also turned, if only to see what his friend saw. Of course it was Shea, perfectly framed by the waving flaps of her tent, standing with her hands spread on top of her makeshift bar, laughing with the four people sporting new yellow on their wrists. Her long ponytail, nearly white in its paleness, swung down her back.

"Uh-huh." Erik threw Byrne a side eye. "So what was with the wristbands?"

Byrne shrugged. "It was a great setup and no one was inside. Was a shame to let all that good whisky go to waste."

He'd loved Shea's enthusiasm, her clear knowledge, and

her patience and love for talking to tasters. More people deserved to experience that. He remembered how packed her tent had been up in Gleann. He wanted that again for her.

Erik slapped Byrne's arm. "Hey, don't suppose you'd want to stick around with me? Hire a car to take us back later?"

Someone started up on the pipes again and Byrne shuddered. "No. Why would you want to stay?"

"I don't know. I kind of love this. Feels a little like home."

"But you're German."

"Doesn't matter. I'm liking it here. I could have a couple of beers, you could try to romance the whisky chick again. Looks like some sort of band is starting up soon?"

Byrne squinted at the stage on the other side of the athletic field. More bagpipes. No fucking way.

"This really isn't my thing, man. Sorry." Normally Byrne was game for anything Erik wanted to do, but this? Besides, Byrne was champing at the bit to get back into the city.

Erik spouted something in German—he tended to do that when he got too excited or upset or frustrated—made a dismissive gesture to Byrne, and then stomped off toward the van. Byrne wove through the cars after him.

After he packed himself into the van, Erik cried out, "This thing was great! Fantastic idea, George."

"We got our asses kicked." Dan, at shotgun, sneered into the windshield. He took a sip from a flask and stashed it back into his bag. Byrne cringed.

Erik ignored Dan, as usual. "Why aren't we staying and drinking every keg they have?"

Being the last one into the van, Byrne got squeezed into the crappiest, tightest spot in the very back. Though the air-conditioning was on full blast, the odor of sweat and mud and general man pretty much ensured they wouldn't be getting back their security deposit.

"Gotta get home for dinner tonight," George said. Several other guys muttered their similar situations. Byrne and Erik and Dan were the only single guys on the team.

Byrne pulled shut the doors, George threw the van into gear, and the Manhattan Rugby Club rolled out of the Hamptons, heading back to the city.

"So you guys played a Highland Games last year?" Erik turned around in his seat to face Byrne.

"George suggested it," Byrne said. "He's from this small town up in New Hampshire that was trying to revive their games or something. One of his high school buddies called and begged that we come up and play. So we made a guys' weekend out of it."

"That was fucking *fun*," George said.

Byrne nodded, remembering playing with a hangover. "Winning that case of whisky in the tug-of-war was worth it."

"And that bartender was fucking *hot*," George added, making Byrne shift and the rest of the players nod like bobbleheads.

A string of German spewed out of Erik. He was practically bouncing in his seat. "Why don't we do that again? Find some more Highland Games, play some tourneys, make a couple of weekends out of it. Shit, it's not like we're in it for the competition or anything."

"Speak for yourself." Byrne lightly smacked the back of Erik's head.

"Well, you're the only one who can actually play," Erik added, to a chorus of loud indignation and the tossing of various dirty, rank articles of clothing.

"Anyone else up for that?" George asked from the front, eyeing the van through the rearview mirror. "I'll see what other games are going on, find out which ones have rugby tourneys, throw out some locations and dates? We can get out of town for a day or two, pound some dirt and then some beers?"

As every other player clapped or voiced their hearty approval, Byrne let his head drop back and gave it a good couple of bangs on the headrest. This was it. This was how he was going to die. Death by terrible musical instruments.

"Byrne?" A punch to his chest. "You in?"

"Ow." Byrne straightened, laughing and wincing at the same time. The whole van was looking at him. It really was true; the team didn't have any shot at competition without him. It was as much about not letting them down as needing to be out on the pitch, toes to the dirt, fingers around the ball, shoulders to another guy's body. If he wanted stiffer competition—and oftentimes he did—he could always try out for the bigger traveling teams, but it was the guys involved in this van who made it a day worth living.

"Yeah." He sighed. "Yeah, I'm in. But if you make me wear a fucking kilt I'm out of there."

Rousing shouts went up, mixed with some extrafine cursing, so it wasn't until he felt the vibration in his shorts pocket that he realized his phone was sending him a notification.

Pulling it out, his heart stopped at seeing the colored bubble on-screen. Then the organ stumbled back into beating, racing, as he swiped the screen and opened the email app.

This could be it. What he'd been waiting for, trying for, for years.

The sounds in the van descended into ball-busting and general bullshit, rehashing the match from play to play. It all faded into nothing as the private email account came to life on-screen. The inbox showed a blue *1*. Byrne held his breath.

Spam.

Spam coming in on an email account he used for only one very specific purpose, to send messages to only one other very specific email address.

Expanding his cheeks, he blew out all the air he'd been holding inside. No other emails in the inbox. Not that he'd been expecting one. He hadn't gotten a response in nearly five years.

Didn't mean he was going to stop trying. The most important people in his life needed this, depended on this. So did he.

Only one person in the Contacts folder. He tapped the address and started a brand-new email. It had been a couple of days since he'd sent one.

Elbows crunched awkwardly into his sides, he typed a short and to-the-point message, careful not to use the same subject or text so as not to get shuffled into their spam folders.

He closed the email the same as always: "Please let me know if and when the property becomes available."

He hit Send.

No one had ever accused him of giving up easily.

* * *

*T*he delightful people Byrne had sent into her tent finally left, a little buzzed, a lot happy, and with napkins scrawled with the names of several price-friendly whiskies stuffed into their pockets. Now that the entertaining hour was over—and since no other tasters seemed to be wandering in—Shea was left to wonder again about her muddy, rugby-playing benefactor.

As she wiped off the bar, her phone chimed with a text.

Still in bed. Willa.

Still? It's 3, Shea thumbed back.

Dying for a kilted man to bring me Gatorade and ibuprofen.

A big laugh bubbled out of Shea's mouth. *There was one hot guy, but no kilt.*

That'll do. Send him over.

Hmm, Shea did not know how she felt about that. About just handing over Byrne to her man-eating best friend.

Still working, Shea replied.

Still hungover.

A figure appeared at the tent entrance, fuzzy and indistinct in Shea's peripheral vision. Funny—and horrible—how she recognized the shape and stance and general oily presence of the man she deliberately hadn't seen in four years. Not wanting to, but knowing she had to, she looked up to confirm what the shiver down her spine had foretold.

Oh fuckity fuck, she furiously typed to Willa. *It's Marco. He's here. FUVCKKKK.*

Quickly she shoved the phone back into her pocket like she was in high school and not thirty-two years old.

Marco said something to the old man checking wristbands at the entrance, clapped the elderly volunteer on the back with an expansive grin, and then stepped over the velvet rope to come inside. Because such rules had never applied to Marco Todaro, oh no.

He took his time crossing the empty tent. Shea didn't move, refusing to come out from behind the bar for him. Though she was standing in her place of work, where it was easy to become who she needed to be, her ex-husband's unexpected presence threw everything out of whack, and she hated it.

"Hi, Shea." Marco's smile was blindingly, falsely white.

"Hello." She would be civil, cordial. "You look"—*orange*—"tan."

He seemed so pleased she noticed. Gross.

"Greece," he said. "Remember that yacht off Santorini?"

Yes, she did remember. And no, she didn't want to. She crossed her arms. "What're you doing here?"

He did that thing she'd grown to hate: cocking his head and making a face like *she'd* been the one to do the confusing thing, that her emotions and actions were wrong, and how *dare* she not realize this?

He spread his arms, and in one hand he held the program for the games. "Saw your name in here. Came to do the gentlemanly thing and say hello."

"No, I meant what are you doing here, at the Highland Games? You never used to let me be involved in stuff like this, and now here you are."

He made an indignant sound. "That's not true."

It was very true. She'd always wanted to get involved with the New York City Scottish Society, but every time an event had come up and she'd expressed interest in going, he'd book something else for them to do. Something obnoxious and lavish on the opposite side of the globe. Santorini, for example. Then there were the many, many times he'd taken it upon himself to make or cancel her other private social events based on whether or not he approved, or whether or not they would advance him in the New York scene.

And she'd always gone along without argument. Stupid girl. Stupid, spineless, clueless little girl.

But she wasn't that person anymore and, she supposed, when it came down to it, she had Marco to thank for that.

"You know," he said, using that syrupy, direct eye contact that had swept her off her feet as a twenty-two-year-old bartender, "I really did just come in here to say hello, see what you're up to." He swept a gaze around the tent. "Surprised to see you here. You don't belong behind the bar anymore. Don't you have employees?"

He would never understand her, what she truly wanted, why she'd left him. She sighed and let her arms drop to her sides. "Why did you really come in here, Marco?"

"Uh." He actually had the acting chops to look sheepish. "I miss you?"

"No, you don't."

"It's been a few years. Maybe I came at things between us the wrong way. Maybe things have changed."

"Nothing's changed. Believe me." At least not with him. The man had sprung from an average childhood, but his sprint up the world's real estate development ladder had wrung out his humanity.

"Shea." As he shook his head at the ground, she noticed he had a hell of a lot more silver in his hair. He would be in his early fifties now. "Listen. When you're done here this evening, why don't you come over to my place? We could have a quiet drink as old friends. I built a new house over in Sagaponack."

"Ah, I get it now. You got dumped."

"No. That's not it."

But the slack of his mouth told the truth.

"She's coming back," he added hastily.

"Of course she is." Shea laughed and turned to her precious bottles, the lovely things that had given her courage and purpose, and had finally allowed her to ask for the divorce. "New houses on the beach. Yachts in Greece. Those things don't impress me, Marco."

"They used to."

She whipped around. Stared him down. "I was young and dumb."

The sheepishness and humble pie died. Just vanished from his face. His posture straightened and tightened. "You know," he said, "Shea Montgomery served on ice doesn't taste very good."

"That's because you don't like strong drinks. You like them all watered down."

He considered her with the flat stare she'd done such a great job of forgetting. "I'll never get why you changed."

"I know, Marco. And that's the sad part. Enjoy your new house."

His nostrils flared. "I will. Enjoy your . . . bar."

Bar said, of course, like she owned a whorehouse.

"I will. Because it *is* mine. And it's more than you ever let me have."

He opened his mouth to defend himself, to say something

awful like *I let you have everything. I gave you everything*, but she held up a hand to inform him of its pointlessness. Because when she'd left him, she'd made it a point not to take a dime from him. He had nothing to throw in her face.

"Have fun at the rest of the games," she said as pleasantly as possible, knowing full well he wasn't going to stick around now that she'd shut him down. He'd come here specifically for the hunt. To him, she'd only ever been a conquest, a trophy.

Never again.

As expected, Marco turned and left.

*B*yrne toggled his keys, duffel bag, and laced-together cleats in one arm as he let himself into his apartment on East 84th. The door swung shut hard behind him, and he let everything drop in a heap. Little chunks of dried mud skittered across the slate tile in the foyer. He got out the broom and dustpan from the closet and swept everything up, so that Frances, his housekeeper, wouldn't shake her finger in his face. She probably still would, but then she'd make him cookies and all would be well.

The adrenaline from the rugby had worn off on the long ride back into the city, and now the dizzy tiredness and sore muscles started to settle in. Not for the first time, he wondered how in the world professional athletes in their midthirties survived doing this to their bodies every day. Aging sucked.

In the bathroom, he stripped off the stiff, stinking rugby clothes—*sorry, Frances*—and tossed them in the hamper, then turned on the various knobs to start the overhead rain nozzle in his walk-in shower. He stood under the soothing spray and thought about the day. By the time he'd scrubbed off the dried sweat and mud and stepped out, pulling a towel around his waist, he had a pretty good hankering for some more whisky.

After reaching into the glass-front cabinet for his razor and shaving cream, he decided against shaving. He wasn't planning on going out that night anyway. A rare, blissful Saturday night, free of having to entertain one client or another. As he pulled his hand out of the cabinet, he caught sight of the little yellow toy caboose sitting on top. A pang of warm wistfulness shot through him, and then he closed the glass door.

Going into his closet, he flipped on the switch, and rows of lights illuminated the cherrywood nooks that stored all his clothes. Frances had gone to the dry cleaners, he noted, the section with all his suits looking fuller than usual. With supreme satisfaction, he walked past the suits and the carefully pressed shirts and hanging ties. Not for another thirty-six hours would he have to think about which tie went best with which shirt, and for what client or meeting, and what that particular combo said about him. And thank fuck for that.

Instead he went for the splintering, crooked dresser stashed way in the back. The top drawer stuck as he wrestled it out, but he'd been opening it so many years that he knew its secrets. He removed his favorite pair of shorts and a Wharton T-shirt and pulled them on.

After a brief stop in the second bedroom, which served as an office—no crises had popped up on the computer he used for work, just a reminder of a late Sunday night conference call to Hong Kong—he padded out to the kitchen and found the only bottle of whisky he had. An intensely peaty one that he'd been sipping from on the rare occasions he drank at home.

Tonight seemed to call for it, however.

He brought the whisky and his phone over to where his laptop sat on the glass-topped coffee table. The sun was lowering, cradled in the tops of the buildings on the Upper East Side. No matter how much his job tended to drain him, he'd never tire of the view it had afforded him.

He stretched across the large coffee table and straightened the little green toy train engine resting in its center, then he flopped backward onto the couch.

His phone jumped, buzzed, lit up. George. A mass text to all of Manhattan Rugby.

OK. Rhode Island has a games with a rugby tourney next weekend. Competition looks loose. Who's in?

Byrne cracked his neck, then took a good earthy mouthful of the whisky, thinking too late about what Shea had said about nosing the glass first.

His phone danced with immediate positive replies going around the group, and then one text sent directly to him. From Dan.

When are we going to get real competition? We're better than this.

Byrne scrubbed his face. *Leave the team if you want. I didn't force you to join.* He'd said it to Dan a million times.

No response. Then Dan's affirmation came through, sent to the whole club. They had enough to field a team, and Byrne was already planning to bring along earplugs. Thinking about his workweek to come, he'd need a good day on the pitch, a good weekend away from the city.

Curiosity got the better of him. He opened his laptop and searched for "Rhode Island Highland Games." Next weekend's event popped up with a list of all the attractions.

His phone rang, Erik's name flashing on the screen.

"What's up?" Byrne said.

"Need your help to get into Portrait this week. Last-minute visit from a big fish and I gotta make it count. Can you call in a favor?"

"Sure." Byrne made a note to call the head of the restaurant group that owned Portrait, one of his clients. "You out for Rhode Island? Didn't see your name pop up."

"Yeah. Sorry. Looks like you're stuck with Dan."

"I'll survive." Byrne tapped his laptop screen. "There'll be whisky there again. Might give it another taste."

Erik chuckled. "Really? You didn't mention how the drink went today."

Byrne hissed through his teeth, remembering Shea's open demeanor until he'd tried to flirt. "Not so good, I'm afraid. Kind of got knocked to the dirt."

A pause. "Let me tell you a little story."

Byrne smiled, in spite of himself. "Here we go."

"There once was this German guy who believed everything his American roommate told him. This was back when the German first came to the States in college, when he was young and naive and not nearly as dashing as he is now. Anyway, the American told the German, who had a girlfriend he was crazy about, that American girls loved beef jerky. And that they loved men who made their own beef jerky."

Byrne was already laughing.

"So the German researched online how to make beef

jerky, and he ended up with a bedroom strung with drying meat and no more girlfriend."

"The moral of the story?" Byrne could barely get the words out, he was laughing so hard.

"To not try too hard, or else it looks desperate."

"Or maybe not to listen to your friends."

"I don't know about that. That was damn fine jerky. I miss it."

"Not the girl?"

"Just telling you to read the signs."

Byrne's laughter finally petered out. The little clock on the top of his laptop screen caught his attention. "Oh shit, I gotta run. Expecting a phone call."

"That's right, it's Saturday. Tell the lovely Caroline hello."

"I will. See ya."

"Beef jerky!" Erik yelled, and Byrne hung up.

Not five minutes later, right on schedule—Saturday at six thirty—the phone rang again. The picture on the screen showed a dark-haired woman with a round face holding a baby, the little girl only days old. Never failed to make Byrne smile.

"Hey, sis." He sank deeper into the leather couch, propping up his feet on the table in front of the toy train engine. "How was your week?"

"Oh, you know. Fine, I guess." Her South Carolina accent contrasted with the sounds of the New York sirens outside. "I'm exhausted. Baby K is wearing me out. I have to drag her everywhere. It's hard to get things done."

Byrne gritted his teeth. What the hell was Paul doing while Caroline had to run around with a little kid?

"Got your pic earlier this week." He looked up to the framed photo of the curly-haired toddler, which sat on his bookcase between the sci-fi hardbacks and the red toy train coal car. "Man, is she a cutie."

"Thanks. And I got the box of books." A sadness seeped through her gratefulness.

"Oh good! You're gonna love the sci-fi series. The aliens are awesome, and the captain of the garbage freighter is so tough. Right up your alley."

"A chick freighter captain?"

"Yep."

"Does she kick ass and have ten guys on the side and can just wander around the universe having adventures?"

"You know it."

Caroline sighed dramatically. "Someday. That'll be me."

"Me, too."

He loved making her laugh. It reminded him of when they were younger, taking turns softly reading chapters to each other out loud until Mom and Dad told them to conserve light, or until Alex threw something at them and growled at them to shut up. Then they'd close the battered, dog-eared paperback, stuff it into a crack in the wall that didn't get wet when it rained, and lie in the dark, whispering about the characters they'd just read, guessing what might happen next.

No wonder fantasy and science fiction were always their favorites. Even in the darkest, craziest worlds, there always seemed to be hope rippling under the worst of circumstances.

"You don't have to keep sending me books, J.P.," she said. "I do live near a library. This may come as a shock to you, but books there are *free*."

"I know, but that's not the point."

The point was to send Caroline things he knew she'd love. The point was to send her books she could sell to a used bookstore when she was done and get some money, or donate to a charity and get a little tax break.

The point was to help a beloved sister who refused any other kind of help he offered. She couldn't rip up a box of books like she—or Mom and Dad—could rip up a check.

"Kristin loves the board books, too," Caroline added.

"Good. I'm so glad." He glanced into the kitchen, where, above the microwave, sat the last part of the toy train: the blue cow car with the broken sides. The little metal cows that went inside had long since been lost to time.

"How are they?" he asked, not having to define *they*.

Caroline pulled in a breath and heaved it out. "All right, I suppose. Mom's quilting with the church, and Dad comes over to play with Kristin when she does it. He took a second job. Night janitorial stuff over at the high school."

Byrne squeezed shut his eyes, his chest hurting. "I sent them a check when I sent you the books. Can you make sure—"

"I saw it." She sighed as she said it, and Byrne knew exactly what that meant. "I can't make them cash it, J.P."

"And if I wrote you a check and told you to give half the cash to them and keep the other half for yourself?" He'd tried this avenue before. Didn't hurt to try again. Not when he pictured the broken, second- and thirdhand furniture his family ate on and slept in.

Caroline said, "I think you know the answer to that."

"I'll come down as soon as I can," he said, resigned.

"We'd love that."

Boxes of books were great, but they weren't him. He knew that. If he could package himself up and send it down to his family every month, they'd be ecstatic, but what he was doing here in New York for them was going to be even better. And soon he could tell them all about it. Soon he would be able to give them everything. He could feel it in his bones.

"Is that Baby K crying?" he asked, as the little girl squawked in the background.

"Yeah. I should go. Talk to you next Saturday?"

"I'll be in Rhode Island, but absolutely. Call and I'll make sure I'm available. Love you."

"Love you, too."

And speaking of Rhode Island, just as Byrne set his phone next to him on the couch and reached for the whisky again, a new group text came through from George: *No rooms anywhere in Rhode Island. Don't worry, I got us covered.*

That should be interesting.

Then George texted a photo of the most massive RV in existence. *Pack your sleeping bags*, it read. *We're going camping.*

Chapter

✳

3

A week after seeing Marco, Shea still had a bad taste in her mouth that no amount of whisky chasing could cure.

Now she stood happily behind the tiny card table serving as her tasting station at the "Rhode High-land Games." Cringe-worthy name aside, this event was exactly what she'd needed after a busy workweek topped off with late nights at the Amber.

The sun was setting on the Friday night opening party, and the intimate festival setup made for a cozy, fun atmosphere. Next to her table, the volunteers at the beer station were having a grand time sampling the cider and ale and were making for some interesting conversation. Across the main thoroughfare, people wandered in and out of the marketplace tents. Children giggled and squealed as their newly purchased wooden swords and battle-axes and shields clattered in play. Out on the athletic field, a reenactment of the valiant Battle of Bannockburn was taking place, accompanied by the soundtrack of bagpipes off to one side.

How could anyone not love the sound of bagpipes? Honestly.

Though she'd chatted up plenty of eager, fun whisky tasters there to enjoy the Friday night events before the fair opened wider tomorrow, the evening was almost over, and she was looking forward to food and rest.

"Just wanted to make sure everything was to your liking." Ernestine, the games' organizer, wandered over holding a plastic cup of cider. She looked a little sad-eyed with drink, even though her mouth was smiling, showing lipstick on her front teeth.

Shea grinned. "Absolutely."

And it was. Not as lovely a setting as Gleann, New Hampshire's mountains and valleys, but far better than the over-decorated, overpriced setup on Long Island. The diminished attendance in Rhode Island didn't bother Shea one bit. In fact, she enjoyed everything more because of it.

"I just wanted to thank you for contacting me about having this whisky thing," Ernestine said. She'd already thanked Shea earlier, but the woman looked like she was having such a good time it didn't matter. "What a great idea! It's been such a wonderful addition this year. Everyone who's come over here has loved you. *Loved* you." Complete with jazz hands and eyes rolled to the darkening sky.

The NYC Scottish Society had hired Shea for the Long Island games with strict specifications as to what they wanted, but coming to Rhode Island had been Shea's own idea. Here she had more accessible Scotch choices, better pricing, and a casual, open vibe. Hell, she'd even worn jeans.

As the reenactment ended and Robert the Bruce was hoisting his sword in the air, the bagpipes crescendoed over the sound of scattered applause.

Shea pulled out her phone and dialed. "Hi, Dad! Guess where I am?"

He chuckled. "I have no idea. On second thought, I hear pipes in the background. Knowing you? Scotland."

"Closer to you. Rhode Island. They're having a little Highland Games and I decided to come up for the weekend."

"Well, now how about that. Your granddad would be so pleased. And on his birthday, no less."

Tucking the phone between her ear and shoulder, she started to gather up used plastic cups with one hand, tossing them in the nearby garbage can. "I know; that's part of the reason why I came. He would've gotten a kick out of Robert the Bruce over there. Wait, I take that back. He probably would've stumbled onto the field and corrected formations and story lines."

Her dad laughed, but it sounded a little thin. Shea had always gotten along with and understood her grandfather far better than his own son.

This night, these games, made her feel close to Granddad again, but not in sadness over the fact that he was gone. More like a celebration of his life and all that he'd taught and given her. And he'd given her a great deal; she was reminded of that nearly every day.

"You're still coming mid-July, right?" Dad asked. "For our games?"

"Wouldn't miss it."

"We'll make up your old bed for you."

Ernestine's voice came over the shrill sound system, announcing an end to that evening and wishing everyone a pleasant sleep before the gates opened at nine tomorrow.

"I gotta run, Dad. Need to clean up and eat something before heading to the campground."

"Shea." And suddenly she was seventeen again, standing before her parents, telling them Granddad had invited her to live in Scotland the summer before college started. "You're not camping alone, are you?"

She'd done so well not mentioning the whisky, and then she'd gone and let slip the thing about herself being a single woman sleeping among trees and bears and axe murderers. How silly of her!

"I'm fine. I'm thirty-two and I've camped alone before. Dozens of times." That was a lie. It had only been the once—last year in Gleann—but it had turned out wonderfully. So much so that she'd gone out and bought all new equipment and had been looking forward to pitching her tent several times this summer.

"That doesn't make me not worry."

"Nothing makes you stop worrying, Dad. When I'm fifty I'm going to have to answer questions about where I'm going and with whom and whether or not I had the right jacket. Okay, I really have to go." Easiest way out of a potentially awkward conversation with him? Always have an excuse of something else to do. Otherwise he'd keep her on the line forever. "Talk to you soon."

He sighed. "Love you. You have your weatherproof coat?"

"Ha-ha. Love you, too."

By the time she put away all her bottles in locked storage and wiped down the tasting station, it was fairly dark and her stomach demanded food. She could grab a bite here, but there were only so many pasties and fish and chips and sausages she could eat. Too late to get the propane stove going and try to cook something at her campsite, so she found a restaurant along the side of the highway between the festival grounds and her campground.

The Tufted Duck Supper Club was little more than a double-wide trailer with a slapped-on deck encircling it, but all the outdoor tables were filled, and a small crowd of people lingered on the steps going in, waiting for their chance at a menu. Inside was a little less cramped. Such a perfect night—not too hot, not too cold—that everyone wanted to be out in the air, she guessed. She knew the feeling.

Memorial Day weekend near the coast on a lovely Friday evening. Anywhere in Rhode Island except a fast-food place would be just as crowded. Since she did have standards and wasn't willing to sacrifice digestion for convenience, she wedged her way deeper into the restaurant and found the bar at the back, three out of four padded seats taken by single diners. She became the fourth, sliding onto the leather.

"Lemonade, please," she told the bartender during his pause in snapping off beer caps. "And the biggest plate of nachos you have. Lots of guacamole."

The bartender grinned and nodded. She sent texts to Dean and her office manager, checking in for the night, then pulled out her e-reader.

Casual sex and violent fights and swearing—everything she wasn't allowed to read growing up—she now inhaled like a starved woman. She'd last left her dashing hero and beautiful and courageous heroine after they'd survived a car chase through the avenues of old-town Salzburg, and they were now about to get naked somewhere in the hilltop castle after having broken in to get away from the bad guys. Because why the hell wouldn't you have sex in a castle while on the run?

She scarfed down the nachos and sipped her lemonade as the book action intensified. The noise in the small restaurant dropped away, and she got lost in the most perfect alone time. As much as she liked her work, it felt wonderful to not be there right now, to have a night off outside the city.

After she scraped the last molecule of cheese from the plate with the very last crumb of tortilla chip, she reached for her drink and finally noticed how much more crowded the restaurant had gotten. It was after nine, and the vibe had shifted to a bar atmosphere. People stood crammed between the tables, laughing and clinking glasses. Even the bad rock music had gotten louder. Her cue to leave. That tent and sleeping bag were calling her name.

"Hey. I know you."

A guy with a lean, fashion-model build, alcohol-slanted eyes, and loosened tie shoved himself into her vision, practically unseating the quiet man on the next stool. The quiet man had also been reading but now looked ready to smack his library paperback over the interloper's head.

Shea, however, was a little more practiced in drunk diplomacy. She practically had a degree in it. She looked at the man in the disheveled yet clearly pricey suit, ready to send him on his way, and realized that she knew him, too. But only because he'd come into the Amber just last week, and he hadn't exactly made a good impression.

Do not engage. Repeat, do not engage. Tucking her e-reader into her purse, she took out her credit card and waved it at the nice bartender.

"What's wrong?" The new guy was beyond drunk. Quickly moving into "absolutely smashed" and "about to puke" territory. Not even worth her breath to respond. She just had to get out of there, and she could put him and about a thousand other Drinkers out of her head. What the hell was he doing *here*, of all places anyway?

"What's wrong is that you're crowding me," said the male reader on the other side.

"Sorry," Shea said around the drunk's shoulder. "He was just leaving."

"The hell I was."

Great. Before, last week in the Amber, he'd leered at her like she was bacon, like he was thinking every single sexual thing that would make her mother have a heart attack. Now he was already moving into sharp-edged, inexplicable anger, and she wasn't even three sentences into the brush-off.

As the bartender took Shea's credit card, the wasted guy actually moved in closer.

"Hey." She threw up a hand between them. "You need to back off."

"Why'd you kick me out before? I was a paying customer.

You embarrassed me." She could barely understand him. The words all blurred together.

"No, sir," she snapped. "You embarrassed yourself. Although this performance might leave the other one in the dust."

"Dan." Another voice interjected. Deeper, more authoritative, and about a million times more sober. "What's going on?"

Dan the Drunk looked down at his arm, where the newcomer had grabbed his elbow.

The newcomer. Who was Byrne the rugby player. *Here.* Was this roadside restaurant the universe's vortex for all random run-ins?

Byrne didn't look anything like a rugby player anymore. Clean face, short dark hair shiny and artfully mussed on top, not a drop of sweat anywhere. He wore gray suit pants and an expensive, pale blue shirt with the sleeves rolled to his elbows. No tie, the top button undone. His shoulders looked even wider than she remembered, the top of his head reaching even taller, his arms thick and powerful like his legs. All of that should have made buying such finely fit clothing a chore, but then the answer was obvious.

Bespoke.

Byrne the rugby player was also the kind of guy who wore bespoke clothing. The kind of guy who could afford to have shirts and suits made specifically for his body, of only the finest fabric, by highly trained tailors. Which meant he was the kind of guy who actually cared about those kinds of things. And only guys who cared about their clothes like that were guys involved in a money world that told them specifically *to* care.

The price tag for one of those shirts would probably make all of Middle America choke. She knew that because ages ago she'd almost spit out her latte when Marco had told her how much one of his bespoke shirts had cost. Now the fountain of wristbands at the Long Island Highland Games made a world of sense. He liked to show off. He wasn't Rugby Byrne anymore, but Bespoke Byrne. Greeaaat.

Byrne yanked Dan out from between the bar stools, and Dan had to clamp on to Byrne's shoulder to keep his balance. Byrne peeled off Dan's fingers. "What's going on?"

Dan grinned a liquid grin and threw up his hands. "Nothing, man. Was going to the bathroom. Saw her sitting here. Recognized her, is all."

Byrne finally looked at her, eyebrows drawn over those sinfully blue eyes. "Is he bothering you?"

"*No*," Dan said, in the tone of a fourth grader accused of stealing stickers from the teacher's desk. Cocky, spoiled men. Shea's favorite.

"Yes," she told Byrne. "He is."

"Dude," Dan said to Byrne. "I had Grant Chalmers in town last week. Took him to the Amber. And she fucking *kicked me out*. Right in front of him."

Byrne cringed, his eyes shutting for longer than a blink. "Chalmers," he muttered, hands sliding to his hips. "Shit."

Shea was a little taken aback that Byrne seemed to be more affected by this supposedly important guy's presence than the fact she'd had to kick Dan out because of the terrible scene he'd made.

None of this had anything to do with Byrne. She turned on Dan. "I don't care who Grant Whoever is. You insult me in my own bar, I tell you to leave."

Byrne's face darkened.

Dan rounded on Byrne. "She called herself a Hooters girl and *she's* the one getting pissed off at *me*?"

She waved a hand. "No, no, no. I said I *wasn't* a Hooters girl, after you came into *my* bar and treated me as such."

Byrne ground his teeth together. Nudging his chin toward the opposite side of the restaurant, where a group of ten or so men had pulled together a few tables, he said, "Why don't you get back to the team? Leave Shea alone."

"Fine, fine. Whatever."

Byrne watched Dan weave back to the other guys, but Shea looked only at Byrne. When he swiveled his head to look at her, there was soft apology in his eyes.

"What on earth are you doing here?" she asked. "In Rhode Island, at this particular restaurant, of all places?"

"Rugby." He jutted a thumb over at the raucous tables. "Playing tomorrow at the Highland Games. Can I assume you're doing the same?"

"Not playing rugby."

"Right. Of course not." A flicker of a smile.

Oh no. Not the crooked grin. *Defense! Defense!*

She raised an eyebrow at Dan's back. "You play with him?"

"Yeah." Byrne sighed. "And work with him. Listen, he's not . . . he's not as bad as he comes across."

She drew back, opening her mouth.

"I'm not defending him or anything," Byrne added, raking fingers through the side of his hair, "but he didn't used to be like that. Some shit's happened to him recently and he's, well, he's not taking it so well. I know that doesn't excuse what he's said or done to you. But if you'll let me, I'll apologize for him."

She relaxed a bit. "Thank you."

"That client he mentioned, Grant, he's kind of a big deal."

"Well, Grant is welcome back to the Amber anytime. It's Dan who'll feel my stiletto in his ass if he walks through my front door."

The bartender slid the credit card receipt in front of her, and she signed with gusto, the *S* and *M* huge, the rest of the letters a bunch of indecipherable scribbles.

"So," she said, tucking her card back into her wallet. "Where is it exactly you guys work?"

"At Weatherly and McTavish. I'm a private banker."

Of course he was. She set her purse on her lap and looked up at him, expecting to see a layer of cockiness slathered across his face. Only there was none. Just that same level of focus he'd given her on Long Island. That air of ease that was so adept at trying to trick her into falling under his spell. She wondered where he kept his wand and potions. It was some powerful stuff. She was having one hell of a time fighting it. But she *was* fighting it, and she was winning.

"You must be running a whisky thing tomorrow," he said.

"No, actually. I just like to drive up to middle-of-nowhere Rhode Island restaurants on my nights off."

He grinned. Damn it. "Can I stop by your tent tomorrow? Have another taste?"

Have another taste indeed.

Why did he have to be so charming? It messed with her head, being drawn in by his personality but repelled by the air of money that now hovered around him. And that frustrated her, too, because she shouldn't judge every single man with a thick bank account by what Marco had been like . . . except that she'd met so few men who fit that mold and had been different. Truly, honestly different. It was so much easier to stick to her guns, to avoid dating anyone related to whisky, to keep her personal life well delineated from her professional.

When she thought of Marco and the world he was involved in—the world in which she used to live—several non-complimentary words came to mind. Smarmy. False. Self-involved. And yet, when she thought of Byrne—even though she didn't know him at all—none of those words came to mind.

"Listen." She slid from the stool, and he backed away to give her room. It succeeded only in giving her a more comprehensive image of how he looked in those clothes. Like he'd been poured into a Jell-O mold lined with silk and linen, and popped out looking like a masturbation fantasy. "I have this thing about flirting with guys I meet through work. 'Work' meaning when I'm either at the Amber or doing tastings off-site. It's just a rule of mine."

"This 'thing.'" The grin cocked so far to one side it dragged his head with it. Far, *far* too charming. "Just for clarification, that means you *like* to flirt on those occasions?"

Don't smile. Don't encourage.

She hiked her purse onto her shoulder. "No, I mean I don't do it. Ever. I can't afford to make an exception."

Once he realized that she was being completely serious, his grin slowly died. He stuffed his hands in his pockets and shook his head at the floor. She could have sworn she heard him mumble, "Beef jerky."

"What was that?"

"Nothing, nothing."

"I'm sorry." Her own words shocked her. She'd never apologized to anyone she'd turned down before. It shocked her even more to realize that she meant it.

He shrugged. "And I'm sorry I'll have to endure bagpipes tomorrow without a sip of whisky."

She laughed. "Stop. That makes me sad to hear. I'm sure you'll be welcome in the beer tent."

He looked right into her eyes. What happened to the volume in the bar? Did someone magically cut it off?

"For what it's worth, Shea, I think it's a pity. I have the feeling we might've surprised each other."

With a tight-lipped smile that was a fraction of the full

wattage of which he was capable, he turned and walked away, taking his fine rugby ass with him.

*S*hea woke up the next morning to the sound of birds and a brisk wind racing through the trees. Which was completely opposite from the raucous sounds of the obnoxious party she'd fallen asleep to, coming from way on the other side of the campground. If the ranger hadn't made his quiet hour rounds and shut them up, she'd been ready to march over there and do it herself.

Normally mornings in a tent made her feel rested and rejuvenated. Not today. The solution, obviously, was oatmeal cooked over her new camp stove, dotted with sliced apples and brown sugar, and coffee dripped through a funnel percolator.

After the coffee had thawed out the chill in her fingertips, she set out on a short hike around the gentle loop through the nearby woods. A doe and her fawn were munching grass in a meadow, and by the time she got back to her campsite, she was no longer mad over the rude party.

Grabbing her clothing for the day and her small bag of toiletries, she followed the yellow signs pointing toward the shower building. Cell reception in the campground was for crap, and she spent the whole walk holding her phone out at various awkward angles, looking like an idiot, trying to find a signal. A few bars finally lit up near the cement shower house. She fired off a few quick texts to the Amber, inquiring about last night's receipts and what was on tap for today, and to see if there was anything she needed to address.

The outdoor shower experience wasn't exactly her favorite part about camping, and this one was no exception. The stalls on the women's side were frigid without heat or sunlight, and the water that came out of the showerhead was little more than a lukewarm spit that had her teeth chattering by the end.

Fastest shower known to man. Or woman.

She pulled on jeans and layered tops for when the day warmed up later, then stood in front of the mirror and put on makeup so the dark circles under her eyes wouldn't scare away tasters. Hair still damp, she left it down to dry before pulling it back into her habitual ponytail.

A few texts and emails had come through while she'd been

getting ready, and as she pushed out of the chilly showers and back into blessed sunlight, she scrolled through them. Typing a response with one thumb, her old clothes and toiletries balanced precariously in the other arm, she headed up the gravel path toward the road that would take her back to campsite 46.

A distributor was lamenting a late shipment from overseas, and she was making her one-thumbed email directly to the source in Scotland when she slammed into something so hard it not only knocked the phone and her clothes from her arms but also the very train of thought from her mind.

Dear God, had she walked into a tree? Righting herself, turning around, she saw that yes, it was a tree. A tree named Bespoke Byrne.

Only he'd gone and played another switcheroo on her. In his flip-flops, baggy jeans with pale knees, and a gray hoodie with WHARTON barely visible underneath the drawstrings, he was closer now to Rugby Byrne. And he was here. Byrne was in a *campground*.

He, too, had been taken by clear surprise at the collision. His balance off, his body having been jounced to one side, his phone bobbled from hand to hand in his attempt not to drop it.

She stood, wide-eyed with disbelief right in the middle of the path, her stuff strewn around her feet. "Holy crap. What are you doing here?"

At last his fingers wrapped around his phone, saving it from the dusty, dirty fate hers had suffered, and he turned to her, finally realizing whom he'd run into.

"Whoa," he murmured. "What are *you* doing here?"

She gestured dumbly to the building behind her. "Um. Taking a shower."

One corner of his mouth twitched. Oh hell. Who looked that good the morning, and in a campground no less?

"I mean, I'm camping," she amended. Of course she was camping. Where else were they, at the Four Seasons?

Thinking of the Four Seasons reminded her that no one but Willa and her parents knew how much she loved the outdoors. Country Shea and City Shea were two very different people, kept separate for reasons that meant her sanity. Much like Personal Shea and Professional Shea. But it seemed maybe that Byrne was revealing himself to be a man of two sides as well?

"Why are you here," she said, "and not at a hotel or something?"

"Ah, well, that's the funny part. George, the manager of our team, dragged us all up here from the city but had no place for us to stay. So he rented this huge RV, and we're crammed in there like sardines. Smells fantastic, by the way."

Her eyes narrowed. "You weren't the ones partying last night, were you?"

He winced and said nothing.

She tapped below one eye. "These bags are from you guys."

His head tilted. "What bags? You look great. We got a spanking from the ranger, if that helps."

"Kind of."

"The guys, most of them are city people and they've never been camping, never slept outdoors. I tried to get them to quiet down."

Did she read him right? Did Bespoke Byrne not consider himself a "city guy"?

Doesn't matter, Shea. You already turned him down.

"Wow. So weird to see you here," he said. "Speaking of city people . . ."

"I'm not entirely city."

"I see that." In the forest, in the morning, his eyes held a nearly impossible glint. Like something out of a cartoon.

Something buzzed around her feet. Oh, the phone. She looked down and saw it lying in the gravel. Next to the sweatpants she'd worn to bed. And the little black cotton underwear with the lace edges.

She snatched it all up, but the underwear somehow made it on top of the pile, and she had to stuff it deeper into the folds of the gray sweats. Not that that was obvious or anything.

Looking anywhere but at him, she still knew he was smiling and really wished he'd stop.

"Well, I'm going to take a shower now," he said. "First match is at ten thirty. Have to get clean before I get dirty."

Her eyes snapped back to him and she gulped. "I have to set up" was her lame response.

Neither one of them took a step to separate.

"I'd let the water run awhile before getting in," she offered. "Like, say, a half hour."

"Ouch. Thought your lips looked a little blue. I'll keep that in mind." He started to back away. For a few steps he held her eyes with his, then he turned around and disappeared behind the divider that blocked off the men's half of the shower house.

She stood there on the path lit with broken sunlight as it came down through the trees. The high windows of the shower house were cracked open, and in the quiet forest she could hear the squeak of knobs as Byrne turned on the water, the splash as it hit the concrete floor.

And then the high, hilarious shriek pealing through the trees as he stepped under the liquid ice.

Chapter

⊗

4

*G*eorge ripped open another case of light beer and tossed Byrne a new can. He accepted it but didn't crack it open, just held it to make it look like he was still going strong with the rest of them. Truth was, he'd stopped drinking two hours ago, and even then he'd only had a couple.

He was saving himself for something special and, glancing at the time on his phone, he'd give himself a few more minutes before he went after it.

The team had filed back to the campsite for dinner, high on a rare tournament victory that had quickly translated to an actual beer high. They'd each taken their turns in the glacial showers, grilled about eighty thousand pounds of various kinds of meat, and now sat around a fire talking about nothing, though they thought they were solving the problems of the world.

The games shut down at eight. It was now eight thirty. An hour and a half until quiet hours in the campground—until then, the guys would probably do their best to annoy all the families and couples within a mile radius.

He wondered if Shea was back at her site yet.

There were two things Byrne was fairly certain about: One, that Shea had very firmly shot him down last year in Gleann and once again out on Long Island. And two, something wonderful had shifted between them that morning outside the shower house. He had to believe that his seeking her out tonight wouldn't freak her out. And if it did, he'd back-pedal so fast she'd forget he was ever there.

Disappearing into the RV, he pulled on his favorite Wharton sweatshirt, the one he'd keep together with duct tape or mismatched thread or magic if he had to. Late-spring nights in the forest weren't exactly balmy.

He reached between two seat cushions and pulled out what he hoped would be his ace card, the key to unlocking the ever-growing mystery of Shea Montgomery.

By the fire, Dan was telling some overblown story about a recent business trip to Singapore, complete with full-body movement, and Byrne slipped unnoticed around the back of the picnic table, heading for the one-way road that looped around the whole campground.

He didn't know Shea's site number, but the road swerved past all the sites and sooner or later he'd find it. Away from his team, the campground turned strangely homey, like he'd been invited into a collection of warm, open-air living rooms. Fires crackled in every site. Pockets of near and distant laughter sprung up here and there, the sounds of people enjoying the pleasantly cool evening. Kids ran around with glow sticks, getting leaves all over their pj's. The raucous vibe of his own site faded, and then . . . there she was.

The *zzzrrrrt* of a tent zipper preceded her appearance. Shea crawled out of a low, beige dome tent, wearing a sleek green sweatshirt and tight jeans tucked into brown hiking boots. He stopped, right there in the middle of the road, and watched her go to the picnic table where a pot of water boiled on a small portable stove. A gas lamp buzzed and burned brightly in the center of the table, and a low fire danced in the pit just beyond. Her hair was down—pale and long and straight down her back—and the mixture of low light made it shine.

She squirted dish soap into a bucket, filled the bucket with the hot water, and washed out the dishes that apparently had held her dinner. The whole scene was so innocent, so surprising, so completely unlike the Shea he'd merely pegged as "hot" a year ago back in Gleann.

Unable to wipe the smile from his face, he ventured closer, but went only as far as the brown post with her site number painted in yellow. "Hey," he said.

Her head whipped up. A clean pot slipped from her hands and landed with a clunk on the dish towel she'd spread out over one picnic bench. He thought of how she'd dropped the whisky bottle in Long Island, and her black underwear lying on the ground outside the shower house. Seemed he tended to make her drop things.

Her expression softened. "Hey yourself."

He pointed to the dirt on the other side of the numbered post. "Can I come in? If you say no, I promise I'll walk away and you'll never have to see me again. At least until the next Highland Games."

Her eyebrows pinched as she glanced down the road. "What about your team?"

"They won't know I left until morning. Liquid ignorance. And none of them know you're staying here, if you're worried."

Her shoulders relaxed. "Okay."

"Okay about my team? Or okay that I can come in?" He pulled out the bottle he'd snagged from the RV and set it on top of the post. "I brought this."

"What is it?" She squinted at the bottle, then waved him closer. *Hallelujah.*

He set the half-full bottle of whisky on the table and turned the label to face her. She blinked at it, then looked up at him, not moving.

"Now, you have made it perfectly clear," he said, "that you want nothing to do with men when you're working or whatnot, so let me just make this argument. You're not working this very minute, there's not a bar within a fifteen-minute drive of here, and this here is *my* bottle of whisky, dragged here all the way from New York City. I was thinking that maybe you could tell me something about it, but if that's like a schoolteacher being asked to babysit on the weekends, I totally understand. I'll just go back to my animal friends."

She smiled with her eyes. Score.

Drying her hands on her jeans, she reached out and grabbed the bottle. Holding it in one palm, she read the label, her head bobbing from side to side in a *meh* gesture.

"It was a gift," he amended. "You can't insult me if it's crap."

"It's not crap." She shrugged as she set it back on the table. "Just not remarkable. Marketing did an excellent job on it once the big conglomerate bought the distillery. Fairly wide-spread, easy to come by. A lot of people love it."

"You're just not one of them?"

"Perhaps I'm biased. I knew someone who once worked in that distillery over in Scotland, and the experience when the small place was bought out wasn't the best."

Interesting.

"You know," she said, "I would've given you something better, a little more unique, if you'd come by my station today."

"You told me not to."

"No, I didn't. I not-so-subtly, nonverbally told you that flirting with me in my place of business would get you nowhere."

"Ah." He leaned a knee on the picnic bench. Closer to her. "We won the tournament, and the guys voted to come back to the campground to drink to victory instead of hanging out at the fest. I have to say I'm glad for that. We were surrounded by hundreds of bagpipes the whole day. It was awful. But it made me play better so I could get out of there faster."

She rolled her eyes and crossed her arms. "Where on earth did this hatred of bagpipes come from?"

"Undergrad at Boston College. I think they pass those things out to the locals at Starbucks or something."

"Well, I love them, and if you keep making fun of them I'm going to put you in a kilt and make you march around with the bands."

"*No*. Please no."

Her smile was incredible. Really, really incredible. And the way she tilted her head, the long stream of white-gold hair falling to one side, left him a little speechless.

"You ever wear a kilt?" she asked.

"No. No plans to, either. Ever."

Her eyes flicked down to his legs and she murmured, "Shame."

The hard part was making sure he didn't look too smug or too excited. Then she seemed to realize that she'd spoken aloud, and bit the inside of her cheek before moving to the end of the table to close the little stove and unscrew the canister of fuel.

A change of subject was due, because the last thing he wanted was for her to feel uncomfortable. He was enjoying this way too much.

"Looks like you've done this before." He gestured around the site.

She wiped down the damp dishes and stacked them in a labeled plastic bin. "First time this year. I bought myself a big Christmas present last year and splurged on all this stuff."

"Did you just wake up one morning and think, 'You know what? What I'm missing is more ice-cold showers'?"

"I was thinking that I needed more run-ins with skunks, actually." She peeked up at him as she slowly folded the layers of dish towels, but as she went on, she spoke to the cloth. "I grew up camping. They were my favorite vacations. Last year I was asked to be at the Gleann Highland Games at the last minute, and rather than stay somewhere an hour away, I borrowed a tent and some supplies and I fell in love with it all over again." She made the final fold and looked up at him. "What about you? This your first time camping?"

No. But his experience camping when he was young hadn't been for vacation, and when he thought of tents, he didn't have fond memories.

"Yes," he replied, and then inwardly kicked himself. This woman had spent her childhood outdoors and was clearly a woman with more facets than he'd originally given her credit for, but . . . the shame lingered. It glued his lips shut. And not for the first time, he hated how that made him feel.

The fire released a loud *pop*, and Shea turned to slant a big dry log over the top of the burning ones. She definitely knew what she was doing, and he found that he really enjoyed watching her. It took his mind off the past.

"So there's no Scottish in you?" she asked.

"Couldn't say. Genealogy wasn't exactly on my family's to-do list."

"I know a little." She poked at the fire. "What's your last name?"

"Byrne."

Setting down the long stick, she looked at him curiously. "Really? So what's your first?"

"My parents and sister and brother call me J.P., but they're the only ones who do."

"Hmmm. J.P. Could stand for a lot of things."

"You'll never guess." *Please, please don't guess.*

"J.P. Byrne. You sound like a bank. Like the guy I saw last night."

He was confused. "Dan?"

"No. You. Bespoke Byrne."

"*Bespoke* Byrne?"

Was it his imagination, or did a slight chill suddenly fall over them? She'd been warming up to him, too. Ah, that must be it. The fact that it *was* going well was freaking her out. She'd bent her rule about flirting with guys she met while working, but now he got the distinct sense that her retreat had something to do with his job. Or his money.

Then she gave another little shrug and it was gone, leaving him to wonder if it had been there at all.

"Just something I do, give names to people," she said. "You were Rugby to me at first. Then Rugby Byrne. Then, last night, Bespoke Byrne."

"Not Camping Byrne?"

She twisted her face exaggeratedly as she assessed him. "No. You're Rugby Byrne again. And for that, I'm glad."

He considered that, thinking he understood. "You know, I'm not anything like Dan. I mean, we have the same job at the same company, but all that showboating and drunken obnoxiousness, that's not me."

She took a deep breath. "Okay."

"I'm kind of desperate to prove that to you. If you've changed your mind and want me to go, I will, but I don't want to."

The next few seconds were endless. Then Shea sat down at the table, pulled his whisky bottle closer, and flipped her clear-water blue eyes up to him.

"So," she said, making his heart jump a bit, "do you really want to talk about Dan, or do you want to drink this?"

He sat down probably a bit too fast, but it made her mouth twitch into a smile. Reaching into her plastic crate of camping stuff, she pulled out two metal coffee mugs, blue with white flecks.

"Not exactly the fancy ones I had last weekend," she said. "Or the ones I have at the Amber."

"I've never been there."

Her hand paused slightly as she pulled out the whisky's stopper. "I'm starting to be glad about that."

"Yeah," he said, blatantly staring. "So am I."

She poured a small splash into each mug and pushed his across the wood.

"So what do I do?" he asked.

She narrowed her eyes, and he thought that he was beginning to identify her more playful looks. "I saw you last weekend. You know what to do."

"Only because I watched a video online about it last summer and remembered."

"Last summer?"

Wrapping his fingers around the mug as though it were coffee, he smiled at her over the rim. "After I met you."

"Oh." She cleared her throat. "Well, I thought you might've been a Brown Vein."

He laughed. "A what?"

"A Brown Vein. Someone who knows whisky so well it's part of their blood."

"One of your names again?"

"Uh-huh."

"Tell me some more."

"There's a Drinker, and a Hot Air."

"Let me guess. Both of those were also part of my tasting group."

She grinned. "Yep. I'd call their wives Dates, people who are just along for the ride. And then there are Haters."

"Self-explanatory."

"Exactly."

This woman was intensely amusing. He could probably sit and listen to her talk all night. If there wasn't something *else* he'd like to be doing with her, too.

"You don't think that's a little snobbish?" he asked.

She drew back a bit. "I don't mean it like that. But it helps me relate to customers if I can get the labels right. I know how to approach them or how to tailor a tasting."

"Makes sense, then." Swirling the mug, he looked at it as though it were glass and he could watch the whisky churn inside. "I think, if I had to choose, I'd pick bourbon over Scotch."

She pressed her elbows to the table. Her gaze turned inward. Dreamy, he'd dared to say. Her lips curved slightly upward. "I love bourbon, too." Then she gave a little shake of her head. "My granddad didn't, though, and he was the one who taught me all about whisky with just a *y*. Scotch whisky." When he gave her a quizzical look, she added, "All other whiskey is spelled with an *e-y* at the end, except for Canadian whisky, which is just the *y*."

"Aha."

"He claimed the *e-y* stuff wasn't rooted well enough, wasn't historical, and I get where he's coming from, but I don't necessarily agree. I love it all for different reasons."

"Historical?" He shifted on the bench, trying to scoot closer and cursing the table between them. "Explain."

She gestured to his mug. "Okay, give it a nose."

He did, using the three-step process he'd found on the Internet, which seemed to have impressed her.

"Smell that? Close your eyes."

He did.

"Picture yourself standing in a green valley, where the rain is little more than a fine mist bringing out the scent of the grass. And as you're walking along there's an old stone wall that's been there for centuries, and clumps of purple heather. It's so quiet you can hear sheep and cows in the distance, but you can't see them. If you're near the coast, you can smell the salt in the air when the wind turns the right way. Along an old road there's a pub with a thatched roof, and when you go inside, the place smells of peat fire and the polish they used on the wood bar just that morning. Everyone speaks in such a lovely accent, and as you sip their favorite whisky, you can taste their stories."

Entranced. There really was no other word to describe what he felt at that moment. Byrne didn't want her to stop describing things, but she did. And when he opened his eyes, the look on her face told him she spoke from memory. It made him want her more, and he didn't think that was even possible.

She lifted her mug in a toast. "Now let's drink."

Though he raised the mug to his lips, he didn't take a sip. Instead, he watched her drink. The moment her mug went back, her eyes fluttered closed. She worked the whisky in her mouth, at the back of her jaw, chewing it, like the random guy on the Internet video had once instructed him. There was elegance to the way she did it, however. Elegance and . . . sensuality. She looked nearly orgasmic.

Her throat worked, the whisky sliding down, and then she

opened her eyes. She glanced at his still-full cup. "You didn't drink."

I wonder why.

"Sorry." *Act casual.* "Was watching you to make sure I was doing it right."

She silently set her mug on the table. Licked her lips. "You do it right." Then she hastily added, "I saw you, remember? Last week."

Was it only last week? It seemed like they'd been doing this dance forever.

In the silence, in the stillness, just the flames behind her moved. Only the logs made sound as they popped and sizzled, and then came muffled giggles from the next campsite as a dad tried to wrangle his toddlers back into their tent.

"You did skip out before I got to the tasting part," she said. "Want me to give you the VIP tour?"

"Please."

"Okay. Close your eyes again."

He grinned. "But then I'll miss my mouth."

Jesus, her smile. A full-on, uninhibited, all-the-teeth, crinkles-under-the-eyes blast of one hundred percent beautiful.

Holding her gaze, he slowly pressed the mug to his mouth and closed his eyes. Feeling a little like Luke with the blast shield down, he trusted in his Obi-Wan and tipped back his head, letting the whisky roll past his lips and settle in the back of his throat.

"There," she breathed. "Do you taste the sun on the fields of barley? The water from the lochs? The smoke from the ancient peat bogs? The people's pride? The history?"

He swallowed. This bottle was half-gone, having been drunk by himself and nameless others back in the city, and yet he'd never enjoyed it a quarter as much as he did just then.

When he opened his eyes, she'd leaned back a bit, questioning him with a squint.

All he thought was, if this was how she did tastings at the Amber, *holy shit*, no wonder that place was so popular and that she was such a hit.

"I left out the part about the dirty men who work in the distilleries," she said. "And how rank the mash smells."

"And I thank you for that." But he still drank what was left in his mug, again tasting everything she'd just described.

She laughed and turned sideways, throwing one leg over

the back of the picnic bench. A water bottle sat at the far end of the table, and she unscrewed the cap to take a sip.

He nodded at the bottle. "Don't some people add water to whisky?"

"You can." She sipped the water again. "It cuts the alcohol and brings out the flavor. Want to try?"

The easiest thing would have been to just reach across the six inches and take the water bottle, but Byrne's life had never been easy, so why start now?

He stood up and she eyed him questioningly. But he wasn't leaving. No way. Not yet. Instead he walked around the table to her side. He straddled the bench, facing her. The fire's heat coated the right side of his body. She sat so still that for a moment he thought that time might've stopped. Maybe he wanted it to.

Taking the whisky bottle, he tipped a bit more into his mug. Shea was still holding the water bottle, and he asked for it with a lift of his eyebrows and a point of his finger. She answered with a nod but didn't make a move to give it to him, so he reached for it. Slid his hand over hers. With the tiniest of gasps, she released the bottle.

The first touch is always the best, and he let it sink in, let himself memorize how it felt.

"Just a few drops," she said, after clearing her throat.

"Gotcha." He did as the expert instructed. "Is that enough?"

"Sure." Though she hadn't looked away from his face.

Under the pretense of getting more comfortable on the hard wood bench, he inched closer to her. "Do you add water to your whisky?"

She licked her lips. *My God.*

"Sometimes."

Though he clutched the blue-and-white mug in his hand, it seemed nonexistent. Completely unimportant. The only thing he saw was Shea.

"Aren't you going to taste it?" she whispered.

He was already leaning in. "Absolutely."

And then her mouth belonged to him, her sweet whisky lips impossibly perfect, their movement open and yielding. He sank a little deeper, and her mouth let him in. Cupping a hand around her neck, he couldn't believe how soft her skin was underneath that fall of hair.

God, this kiss. *This kiss.* A whole year of anticipation had been backed up behind it, and now the taste of her rocketed through his body. The delicious whisky taste of her.

When she tilted her head more and he felt the smooth slide of her tongue against his, he made some sort of unintelligible sound. She smiled against his lips and pulled back. His hand on her neck loosened.

"I like that you're here," she said. "In this place. With me."

He nudged closer. Their legs touched. Where his whisky mug had gone, he had no idea. Didn't care.

"Not gonna lie," he said. "I straight up want you."

A small line of conflict appeared between her eyebrows, but then it vanished as she touched his face. "I want you, too, but—"

He strained for her mouth and kissed her again. Kissed away whatever *but* was about to come out. He loved the way her hand curled around his head.

"—but I have those rules," she continued, breaking away again.

He groaned. "Right, right."

"I've been thinking, though." A little tease of a kiss. A troublemaker's gleam in her eye.

"Yeah?" Suddenly he felt like a dog whose owner was dangling a leash by the front door.

"About how I've already basically bent them. And how it might be fun to completely break them. Just for tonight."

"*Yes.*" He grabbed her around the waist and hauled her up against him. She was tall but also whisper thin, and she came to him fast.

"But—"

"No buts."

She laughed. "But all I have is the tent. I don't do car sex. This is kind of a big stretch for me as it is."

"Tent sex sounds amazing. In fact, the thought of it really turns me on."

She still seemed a little worried. "I think there needs to be some sort of sign that I'm doing the right thing."

"How about this?"

Now he had her whole body up against him as he kissed her, and he felt her everywhere.

The hand on his head slid around so she had a death grip on his neck, while her other hand made a fist over the Wharton emblem on the front of his sweatshirt. Her mouth pressed harder onto his, and he wanted to tell her to go ahead and be as strong or violent as she wanted, because if she was going to stretch her rules for him, he wanted her to be as happy as he was at that moment.

The whisky taste faded, and then it was just her flavor, and she was ten times more delicious.

"Byrrrrrrrne. Fuck, man, there you are."

Oh no.

Shea ripped her mouth from his, fingers pressed to her lips, and whipped her head around to where uneven footsteps crunched on the gravel road. Shea scooted off Byrne's lap—how'd she gotten there?—and scrambled backward off the bench.

Byrne propped an elbow on the tabletop and ground fingers into his eyelids. Fucking Dan.

"*What*?" Byrne glared at the drunk leaning heavily on the numbered post.

Dan jutted a thumb back down the road, toward their own campsite. "Been walking around forever trying to find you."

"Get out of here."

Byrne looked to Shea, who was poking the fire again, her head down, her wet and swollen bottom lip between her teeth. He tried to read her mood. Pissed off? Embarrassed? What?

"Came to get you," Dan said. "We gotta go. Ranger kicked us out."

That brought Byrne up off the bench. "Are you serious?"

"You're the only one sober, so you'll have to drive us back."

"Shit." Hands on his hips, he drew a deep breath and exhaled up toward the canopy of trees that hid the stars. "Shit, shit, shit."

He gave Shea a look of silent apology. She'd stopped poking the fire and was now watching him in a way that clearly said he wouldn't get to be with her that night. So he asked for another.

"When we get back to the city," he said, dropping his voice, "can I see you?"

Her eyes flicked over his shoulder toward Dan.

"I know you stretched your rules for me here; would you consider doing the same back home?"

"Not near the Amber," she said. "That's one rule I won't break."

"New Jersey, if we have to," he added.

"Maybe," she replied.

And that was good enough for him.

Chapter

5

The elevator door slid open on the fifteenth floor of the sixties-era apartment building on the Upper East Side. Shea stepped into a small marble foyer decorated with ornate wall sconces and bursting with massive fresh flower arrangements.

This had been Marco's neighborhood. They'd lived together only two long blocks to the east. Briefly Shea wondered if it was Bespoke Byrne's neighborhood, too, but then the door to the penthouse yawned open and she was face-to-face with a short, curvy, mature woman who'd been tucked into a sparkling red evening gown.

The woman looked confused at the sight of Shea, standing alone in the foyer, dressed in a ladies' tuxedo.

"Hi, I'm Shea Montgomery. Mr. Yellin hired me to man the whiskey bar tonight?"

"Oh. That would be my husband. Come in, come in."

Shea followed Mrs. Yellin into one of the more opulent New York City apartments she'd ever been in—and back when she'd been with Marco, she'd seen a lot.

"Isaac can't stop talking about the Amber," Mrs. Yellin threw over her shoulder as her low heels clicked down the shiny wood hallway that seemed to stretch all the way to the Hudson. "Whenever I can't find him, or whenever he's been out too late, I know where he is. Or has been. I should put your hostess on speed dial."

"He's definitely a loyal customer. And a very nice man," Shea added, unsure if it was the correct thing to say. This whole being-hired-to-do-a-private-party thing was entirely new to her.

When Isaac Yellin, an Amber regular and payer of astronomically high bar tabs, had approached her months ago to do this, she'd balked. The offer was surprising enough, which was what had first given her pause. Then Mr. Yellin had named his price, and she'd been shocked into silence, which he mistook for reluctance.

Then he doubled his offer. And gave her carte blanche to choose the whiskey for the evening, as long as it was rare and expensive.

It wasn't hard to say yes after that.

The payment for her appearance fee had come through that afternoon, and she'd transferred it directly into her personal "distillery fund." The sight of all those numbers made her a little giddy, and she had to temper her excitement. There was still a long way to go before she could go after what she wanted.

Having to deal with Yellin's kind of crowd outside of the Amber for one night was a small price to pay.

The hallway emptied into a spectacular room overlooking Central Park. The masculine furniture had been clustered for perfect pockets of conversation, every seat with a view outdoors. A string quartet warmed up in the back corner. The caterers hurried about, fidgeting with mounds of hors d'oeuvres and spot-checking silverware and wineglasses. A party planner holding a tablet computer raced around, looking like one more cup of coffee might send her to the asylum.

"You'll be in here." Mrs. Yellin flicked a red-nailed hand toward a set of open double doors set off the main room. "I'll go find Isaac and tell him you've arrived."

Shea stepped through the double doors and felt like she'd been sent back in time. Or, at least, back to the country of her heart.

The left wall was floor-to-ceiling bookshelves. The entire right wall was a bar. An ornate, polished-to-a-gleam wood bar with thick columns at the corners, heavy lintels above, and gorgeous stained glass all along the back. Perfect lines of fine liquor bottles stretched the entire length of the back shelf, and on top of the bar sat her chosen bottles of whiskey, all delivered safely.

The whole room was gorgeous. Warm and inviting and

high-end without being uncomfortable. But it was the sight of that bar that had her heart thudding and a wistful smile spreading across her face. She ran a hand down the wood, then leaned over and touched the tip of her nose to a finely carved column. Inhaled. The scent of the old wood and the sharpness of the stain reminded her so much of Granddad.

"You like it?"

Shea turned around to find Isaac Yellin entering. He had one of those faces that appeared mean when he wasn't smiling and like your best friend when he was. But she'd long since gotten over being intimidated by that sort of thing.

"It's beautiful," she said. "It reminds me so much of the pubs I used to go to back in Scotland."

"It should." He grunted. "That's where I got it."

"You bought a whole bar?"

Yellin shrugged. "They were going to tear down this wonderful old hotel in Glasgow, and I couldn't bear it. So I bought what I could, had it shipped here and restored. It's my favorite room."

"Mr. Yellin," she teased. "You're not Scottish, are you?"

"One hundred percent New York Jewish." He grinned. "But perhaps Celtic by heart." He tapped his chest, sending the ivory pocket square in his fine tuxedo askew.

He went over to the bottles and palmed the Talisker 30 Year Old. "I knew you'd pick some good ones. I'd say I'm going to hate seeing the bill, but since the people coming here tonight are the reasons I can afford such incredible whiskey, you won't hear me complaining."

She smiled down at him. Even at five feet nine barefoot, she hadn't flinched about slipping into three-inch heels that evening.

"You just might be my dream client, Mr. Yellin. Most of these bottles I don't even have in my personal collection, but I've been coveting them for years and years."

One had cost seven hundred dollars, another a thousand.

Men like him liked to know they were special, and since this was her job, she was happy to oblige. Plus, she was hoping to snag a sip or three of some of the really great bottles.

"So tell me." He leaned forward conspiratorially. "How'd you get them?"

"The newer Japanese whiskeys I got through my favorite distributor. I really need to take a trip over there, taste them personally, see their distilleries. A couple of the big bourbons and Irish whiskeys I found through auctions, others through personal connections. But for the Scotch"—she winked—"I simply called up some old friends."

It was the truth. A few phone calls overseas had netted her some lucrative bottles and gave her the opportunity to hear voices she hadn't heard in a long while.

Yellin liked that. "You've made magic. Now make it special for my friends and acquaintances. Impress them with everything you've got up here." He tapped the side of his head.

"No problem." No problem at all.

Two hours later, the entire apartment was packed shoulder to shoulder with men in tuxes and women in all manner of evening gowns. The mood was lively, the food never-ending, and she'd had a steady stream of Brown Veins and Eager Beavers and Drinkers visit her little nook. Truth be told, she'd been skeptical about taking on this kind of private party, but it turned out that she interacted with Yellin's guests far more than customers at the Amber, and they'd listened to her stories of certain whiskeys with a rapt ear.

She was already exhausted, however—and so was nearly her entire stock of exceptional bottles—and there were still two hours to go. She ignored the soreness in her feet, the cramp in her cheeks from smiling so much, and the ever-increasing rasp in her voice from the nonstop talking.

She had another reason to be grateful for the busyness of the evening. It had been nearly four hours since she'd thought of Byrne.

Crap. Reset the clock.

A week and a half had passed since the campground. A week and a half of thinking about their conversation and connection. And that kiss. That spark.

They hadn't exchanged phone numbers. She'd lamented that for a good day or so, then thought that was perhaps a good thing. She knew where he worked, and vice versa, but then there were her lines. They were still there, despite how she'd tangled them all up in Rhode Island. It wouldn't feel right, contacting him at his office to start something she wasn't entirely sure about, now that time had passed. And she was grateful he hadn't called or stopped in at the Amber, because that meant he was respecting her rules.

But was she grateful? Really, truly?

Damn. Reset that clock *again*.

"Is that all that's left?" Isaac slid behind the bar and took up the same Talisker he'd held at the start of the evening, now three-fourths gone. When Shea nodded, he thrust the bottle at her and said, "Hide it. In the butler's pantry. Back of the kitchen."

With a laugh, she did as told.

When she came back into the library, the I'm-not-thinking-about-Byrne clock exploded into a thousand pieces. Because he was standing right there, next to the bar.

He didn't wear a tux, but a sleek black suit that must have cost a fortune because of the way it fit his unusual body so impeccably. Atop a brilliant white shirt lay a gorgeous tie the exact color of his hypnotic blue eyes. He looked big. He looked bold enough to steal the party away from Yellin. He looked like Bespoke Byrne.

A group of five men mingled in front of the whiskey bottles, turning them this way and that, making comments she couldn't hear over the party's noise. Byrne's profile was to her, so he hadn't seen her yet, but as she stood there, dumbfounded, one of the other guys noticed her. He pointed a questioning finger at her, then turned it to the bottles. "You? This?" he mouthed.

As she started through the crowd, Byrne finally turned. He had a glass of something clear topped with a squeezed lime already halfway to his mouth, but that dropped back down when he noticed her. His lips parted, and if she said she wasn't thinking about how they'd tasted, she'd be lying.

He smiled at her, but it wasn't one of those electrifying, crooked grins. It was with his eyes, with the warm spark and the perfect crinkle of skin around them. Then he shook his head slowly as if he couldn't believe yet another one of their random meeting coincidences.

"I'm going to start thinking I'll be running into you at the grocery store," he said, as she came up to him. "Wow. I was wondering if this"—he gestured to the line of bottles—"was you. I was hoping, I guess."

One of the other men in Byrne's group—late forties, a little paunchy—cocked an eyebrow in interest at that, and Shea started to feel a little poke of panic. This wasn't the Amber, but it was still work. Still within the walls of the professional life she'd so carefully crafted.

Byrne glanced at his companion, then back to Shea, and gave her a nearly imperceptible nod. He understood.

"It's good to see you," she told Byrne, hands clasped tightly in front of her in order to resist the urge to touch him. She longed to mess up his perfect hair so he'd resemble the muddy sin she remembered him as.

"It's"—he chewed the inside of his cheek for a second—"*great* to see you."

She reached deep inside herself and pulled out the owner of the Amber, the professional, and managed to suppress the warm-blooded woman who was still very attracted to this man.

And *this*, she reminded herself, was exactly why she never mixed her two worlds. Because it was damn impossible to keep her cool in front of someone like Byrne. The moment her customers—or tasters, or party guests—started to look at her as potential date material, they ceased speaking to Shea, businesswoman and purveyor of fine whiskeys.

"So how do you know Isaac Yellin?" she asked Byrne, the formal tone in her voice feeling so odd set against the memories of the way they'd teased and laughed and kissed in front of that campfire.

"He's my client." Byrne smiled, but it wasn't the smile she loved. Not the one he'd given to her on several occasions. "I handle his money." And then Byrne slid a sidelong look over to the paunchy man, like he was checking his reaction.

Shea took that opportunity to head back behind the bar, because even though she knew Byrne was a private banker, now that she'd been inside Yellin's place, she got a really good idea about the kind of money Byrne saw on a daily basis.

She did not want to, but she thought of Marco.

"We were out to dinner earlier," Byrne offered, gesturing to the other suited gentlemen. "Showing Gordon here"—he clamped a hand on the paunchy man's shoulder—"a good time while he's in town."

"Trying to win me over, you mean," Gordon replied with a chuckle.

Byrne's responsive laugh was so forced Shea almost made a face at him.

"I'm glad you're here," Byrne said to Gordon. "And I'm glad Shea's here, because she knows everything about Scotch. Absolutely everything."

Ugh. Byrne was using her to solicit new business? To schmooze a potential new chunk of money? This was not the Byrne who'd been at the campground *at all*.

"Bring it on." Gordon slapped the edge of the bar. "Hit me with it, beautiful."

Shea's grip on the glasses almost shattered the crystal. A glance at Byrne showed him staring at the bar, one side of his mouth twisting.

"So you two know each other?" Gordon gestured between Byrne and Shea.

"We've met, yes," Byrne said. He looked at her a second too long.

She poured out five small tastes of the Laphroaig 25 Year Old.

One of the suited guys down at the other end called out, "Oh, *now* I get it," and swung a finger between Shea and Byrne.

Well, fuck a duck. Shea ground her teeth together. The personal and professional slammed together, obliterating her carefully made boundaries.

"Shea gives wonderful notes about Scotch whisky." Byrne lifted his glass to her in what she thought was meant as some sort of peace offering, but it didn't feel very genuine. "She tells beautiful stories and makes you feel like you're standing right there in Scotland, sipping from the barrels."

What was he doing? Did he think she was going to repeat all that she'd said to him at the campground, and in the same manner, to this bunch of tipsy corporate climbers?

She trapped his eyes with hers and hoped that he could read her disappointment. Over the past week and a half, when she'd allowed herself to imagine what might happen should they ever meet again, this was not it.

"This is a peaty mouthful," she said tonelessly. "Distilled on the island of Islay. Some people say it tastes like dirt. Now will you please excuse me?"

Shea turned away, but not before she made a point to look straight at Byrne, just in time to see his face fall.

At the other end of the bar stood a woman who'd nearly drunk her way through the entire whiskey list. She'd come back to finish the grand tour. After Shea poured the woman a splash of Pappy Van Winkle twenty-three-year-old bourbon—and cringed doing so, because one should never waste such in-demand Pappy on drunkenness—she returned to her former spot to find only Gordon remained.

"Great whisky." He saluted her with his glass. "Can I have a little more before we head out? And don't be stingy, beautiful."

*G*ordon and Byrne's three Weatherly and McTavish coworkers lingered by Yellin's front door, blitzed out of their minds and ready to move on to a nightclub, but Byrne barely had a buzz and he didn't want to go anywhere. If it were his choice—if it were really up to him—he'd ditch those guys, forget about Gordon's portfolio, walk right back into that library to grab Shea, and just . . . go somewhere.

From across the thinning crowd, just a few moments ago he'd watched her leave the library and slip down the shadowed hallway leading to the bathroom. If he didn't do this correctly, it might nudge him into the stalker category.

The bathroom door cracked open, a line of light falling on the hallway floor. He headed toward her.

"Shea."

She jumped and whirled, clearly surprised. When she saw it was him, her expression changed. He couldn't stand the way she looked at him like that, like she'd rather be caught with anyone else than him in that hallway.

He kept his voice low, kept his eyes perfectly on hers. In those heels she was only an inch or two shorter than he.

"I am so sorry."

"For what?" she asked, continuing to play the you're-just-another-guest-at-this-party card.

He pulled at his tie, wanting to rip it off, to stuff the jacket down the garbage chute. "For not saying anything when Gordon kept calling you 'beautiful' like it was your job title. I could tell it bothered you, but he couldn't, and I wanted to say something but I didn't. And I should've said something to the guys I work with, when they made that comment about you and me knowing each other."

There. Her eyes softened, her body sagged a little, and she

took two steps back until her shoulders hit the wall. She crossed her arms and her gaze drifted away.

"I get it," she said. "I really do. This was work for you and you didn't want to ruffle any feathers. But it's work for me, too."

"I know it is." He put as much heart into the words as he could. "But I wish it wasn't. On both our parts."

Her eyes narrowed as she pushed away from the wall, but he decided that she looked more hurt than pissed off. "What I did for you in the campground, that tasting thing with the descriptions of Scotland, it was meant for you, Byrne. *You.* I've never said anything like that to anyone. I was telling you a little about my past because I liked you. And now it feels all oily. Like you were using that moment, that experience between us, to impress that guy Gordon."

Fuck. He squeezed his eyes shut in a long blink. "I knew that was a mistake the second I said it. I thought I was slyly telling you how much I like you, how cool that night was to me, and it was pretty much a bomb in my face."

"A bomb in mine, too. We may not have slept together, but everyone who overheard that thinks we did. And while I'm all for sexual freedom, when it comes to being a woman in a man's world, that kind of impression usually doesn't work well in my favor."

It was no wonder she'd received so much attention that night. That tux fit her like a glove, the black fabric with the subtle sheen making the lines of her body long and lean. The deep V of the jacket revealed just a peek of a white top underneath, but the rest was the creamy expanse of her chest. And he loved what she'd done with her hair, slicking it back from her face and tying it up in a big knot at the nape of her neck. She looked flawless. Intriguing. Intelligent.

But he couldn't tell her any of that. Not now.

"Do you know how excited I was to turn around and see you standing there?" he said.

Her eyes snapped to his, and he was disturbed that he couldn't read them.

"The best fucking surprise," he went on. "I had a hell of a week overseas, and I'm still jet-lagged, and my boss told me to take Gordon out, and I haven't been able to stop thinking about you, and then suddenly there you were." That might be a little of the vodka and whisky talking, but it was the truth nonetheless.

When she smoothed a hand over her hair, tucking a loose strand behind her ear, he noticed it shook a little. "I don't want to talk like that here."

"And I don't want to leave without saying what I have to say. I did not want to leave that campsite, Shea. I came back to the city, I had a day's rest before heading out to Switzerland, and I wanted nothing more than to rewind and pick up where we left off, only I knew you wouldn't like it if I showed up at the Amber."

"Byrne." One of her hands unwrapped from around her middle and she held it between them. He prayed it was because she wanted to touch him. "What happened that night—"

"Was fucking awesome. I think about it all the time. I think about *you* all the time. I wanted to kick Dan in the nuts when he showed up, because that's what it felt like he did to me that night."

She chewed her lip, and he had to focus on another part of her face because otherwise he'd lean in and do it for her.

"You're making it out to be more than it was," she said. "It was just going to be sex. I wanted to break my rules. I wanted to be a little free."

He couldn't help it—the grin poked through. "So you were going to use me?"

"Yes." Then she hastily added, "No."

That pumped up his chest a bit. "I would've been happy to have been used, Shea. Except that I knew there was something more between us. I felt it then. I feel it now."

The party rumbled on, but it seemed to be happening far, far away.

"It's different now," she said. "Here in the city. I thought I could bend my rules up in Rhode Island, but I can't in New York. And what happened in there only proved my point that I need to keep my personal and professional lives absolutely separate. I've worked far too hard to make compromises now."

"Wait—"

"I can't do it, Byrne. I'm sorry."

She turned and walked past him, veering around the corner and back into the library.

At least up in Rhode Island, it had been Dan who'd fucked up. Tonight, Byrne had no one to blame but himself.

Chapter

⬡

6

"Shea. Big Boss?"

Shea jumped out of her daze and blinked around the dimly lit Amber Lounge. Her hand, holding a damp towel, was still moving in a lazy circle over the top of the glass bar. Streaky swirls betrayed the fact that apparently she'd been standing there, wiping away at nonexistent spills, for a very long time.

"Shea."

"Huh?" She turned to find Dean at her elbow, his expression a compilation of worry, questions, and good old-fashioned humor. "What is it?" she snapped.

Dean held up his hands in a mock-defensive gesture, and she instantly felt bad. It wasn't her best bartender's fault that she'd been in a surly mood these past two weeks since Yellin's party. Actually that wasn't true. She wasn't surly all the time. Sometimes she switched that out with annoyed. Or snippy.

"I'm sorry," she said to Dean. She'd been saying that a lot, and she meant it every time. She had to do something to get out of this funk, particularly since she didn't quite understand *why* she was so down. It wasn't like she and Byrne had meant anything to each other in the first place. It had only been one kiss.

One kiss, some of the most fun conversation she'd had in

eons, an electric attraction, and a singular close-call sexual experience. Sigh.

"It's okay," Dean said. Now he looked at her with what she could only categorize as fatherly concern, and that made her uncomfortable on a whole other level. She already had one father, thanks.

"There's a couple in the Corner Pocket who requested you specifically," he said.

She peered across the sparsely filled main room—not that unusual for early on a Tuesday evening—to the private room in the far corner. To get that room, you not only had to make a reservation, but you also had to spend a minimum amount of money that had most people laughing when she told them what it was.

"Menu help?" she asked Dean.

"Didn't say." When she slid behind him to get out from behind the bar, he touched her arm. "Are you okay?"

"Yeah, absolutely." A little too cheery. It made him frown. She waved him off. "Don't worry about me. I'm fine."

But the truth was, two weeks still hadn't cured her of images of Byrne. Him, all dirty and sweaty in his rugby gear. Him, in old, worn clothes and flip-flops outside the campground shower house. Him, wreathed in campfire smoke, his face so close to hers.

Two weeks since her stupid, fragile hope—a hope she hadn't really known she'd been harboring—had been ground to dust beneath his ridiculously expensive loafers at Yellin's party.

But there was no way they could make it work. Too much crisscrossing between her worlds: personal and professional, past and present.

Focus, Shea. You've got customers now.

The Corner Pocket was an octagonal room with a similarly shaped, specially made table filling the center. Four windowed walls looked out over a cobblestoned intersection in TriBeCa. The other four walls were curtained off, separating the Pocket from the rest of the main bar. She wondered who the couple could be inside. Visiting dignitaries? Celebrities? Trust-fund babies?

But when she pulled back the velvet curtain to step inside,

the man and woman sitting three seats apart looked as not-famous as two people could be. Both in their fifties, Shea guessed, plain and unassuming. They were both dressed in dark suits, and the woman's cherry red blouse was the only splash of color in the whole room.

Shea smiled as she dropped the curtain, but the man and woman did not return the gesture. The man crossed one ankle over his opposite knee and sat back in the cream-colored, calf leather chair. The woman cocked her head, as though examining a horse at the racetrack. Odd.

Shea came to the edge of the table and rested her fingertips on the shiny wood. "Hello, I'm Shea Montgomery. What can I do for you this evening?"

After a brief pause, the man flipped closed the thick menu he'd had open in front of him and gave it a little push toward her. The thing was as thick as a Bible, and out of everything she'd done at the Amber, she was most proud of her choices and descriptions listed on those pages.

"You know the minimum we have to spend in here." Now he smiled a little, but it was more a gleam in his eye than anything else. "Why don't you bring out something really special for us? Your best. And we'd love to hear why you picked them."

Okaaaay. "Fantastic. Are you thinking Scotch or bourbon or—"

"Just Scotch. Your best," he repeated, holding up a hand and closing his eyes. Like he was used to interrupting people and telling them what to do.

Shea glanced at the woman, who folded her arms on the top of the table. Her head cocked toward the other shoulder.

"Single malts?" Shea asked. "Blends?"

"Yes and yes." The man finally smiled with his mouth.

"Will you be expecting anyone else?"

"No," said the man. "Just us."

So she could really go all out. She couldn't deny that excited her, to be able to head downstairs to the locked room where she kept the rare prizes of her Scotch collection.

"I'll be right back."

When she did return she had Dean in tow, both of them carrying trays tiled in deeply bowled glasses filled with expensive tastes of her best stuff. Just as her mysterious patrons had requested. If they drank it all, they'd be plastered by the time they left.

Dean set down his tray and departed, leaving Shea alone with the suited man and woman. They were completely unreadable. Usually she could peg a customer within a few seconds of them opening up their mouths, but these two were blank walls. Blank Walls. A new label to add to her inventory.

Shea opened her arms above the set of glasses, their varying amber liquids beautifully reflecting the dangling overhead lights. "So where shall we start?"

The man had one finger pressed vertically over his lips. "Why don't you take a look at us and give it your best shot as to what we might like? We're yours. Take us on a journey."

Hoo boy. No pressure there or anything.

Good thing this was exactly what she loved most—a rapt audience, interested drinkers, and some seriously wonderful whisky.

"All right." She set two glasses in front of her customers. "This one is aged twice, first in American bourbon casks and second in barrels once used for port . . ."

She talked for nearly forty-five minutes straight, switching out glasses and stories as easily as changing the filter in her coffeepot at home. She told them about the aging and the distilleries, peppering in some personal anecdotes about employees at each place and describing what their barrel storehouses looked and smelled like. They were spending enough that night; they deserved a little more than the average insight.

About halfway through, she realized they seemed more interested in what she had to say than the drink itself, although the man did drink every bit of his. He was a closet Brown Vein. The woman, still a Blank Wall. And a sober one, at that.

After a particular glass, he held it up to eye level and smacked his lips together. "This reminds me of this one pub in Edinburgh. On High Street, near where the old toll bridge arches over the street."

Shea brightened. "I think I know which one you're talking about. The one with the stuffed pheasant in the window, covered in dust?"

The man guffawed. "How long has that thing been there?"

"Since the toll bridge was used, probably."

"So you've been there?"

"Many, many times. I could probably be an Edinburgh tour guide at this point."

The man and woman exchanged a glance, and that's when the woman took out a pad of paper and pen. What the hell was going on?

"So what would you recommend to drink," he asked, "if I were an obnoxious twentysomething with more money than God who'd reserved this room solely to impress a girl?"

Cool. A challenge. Flipping open her menu, Shea pointed to the Pappy Van Winkle bourbon. "It's in all the movies these days," she explained, "and young, rich people like that kind of thing."

The man chuckled. "And if I were here for my anniversary?"

Shea scanned the pages for the remote Orkney Islands distillery. "This one. I'd tell them a Scottish folktale about faeries in love. Only I'd omit the end where one of them dies. Then I'd leave and let them make eyes at each other."

"Thank you, Shea. Thank you very, very much." The man looked rosy cheeked. And happy. He sat back and clasped his hands over his stomach, as though he'd just eaten two Thanksgiving meals at one sitting.

"How do you know so much about whisky?" The woman sounded exactly like she looked: tight, pinched, judicious.

Shea kept up her breezy air and shrugged. "Drinking. Talking with scads of people. Remembering everything they say and coming to my own conclusions. And I'm told I have one of the finest noses in the business." She tapped the side of it and winked. "On that, I wouldn't disagree."

The man and woman shared an indecipherable look, the woman gave him the tiniest of nods, and then the man rose from his chair and extended his hand. "Shea, my name is Pierce Whitten, founder and CEO of Right Hemisphere Media. This is Linda Watson, my director of branding and marketing."

Shea shook their hands but couldn't say what their grips were like because she'd gone numb all over. "Nice to meet you?" She was fully aware that it had come out as a question.

"We have something we'd like to discuss with you," Linda

said, also standing and setting a heavy briefcase on the table-top as she did so.

"My company owns many media outlets under the Right Hemisphere umbrella. TV stations, magazines, websites, a film production company, just to name a few. We are here because we think you'd be an incredible asset to our company. We would like to work with you."

Shea's mouth gaped open. "Me? Why? How? Doing what?"

"I've done my homework," Pierce said. "I've seen your interviews on TV specials, read pretty much every article ever written about you. I've been in here before and loved what you've done here, and now that I've met you, heard you speak, I think you have incredible spirit. It will translate so well to consumers."

Shea couldn't get her arms to move. All she could do was blink. "Sorry?"

"You're bigger than this one bar in New York City," Linda said. "Bigger than a few obscure liquor specials on the History Channel. You're a brand and you don't even know it."

"A . . . a *brand*?" Shea stammered. "You mean like those gaudy brass buckles on designer bags?"

Pierce smiled.

"The Right Hemisphere target market right now is the intelligent, successful, worldly American male. He wants to spend a lot of money and have a great time when he's not working his ass off."

"Sounds like most of the people who come in here," she replied.

"Exactly." Linda unzipped her briefcase. "You give them what they want in the Amber Lounge. We want to make you bigger than that."

Shea finally managed to move a limb, and it was to bring one hand up and rub her temple. "I'm confused. How do you propose this?"

Pierce and Linda exchanged yet another look. "Well, that's what we want to discuss with you. We have some initial ideas, but we wanted to first make you aware of our interest, and then hopefully schedule a more formal sit-down, a brain-storm, if you will. We want to open a dialogue with you."

"What are these initial ideas?"

"Well—Linda, jump in here if I forget anything—we were thinking of having you create a formal rating system for whiskey, like Robert Parker's name on wines." When Shea wrinkled her nose automatically at that, he pressed on. "Okay, then. A regular column in one of our magazines or websites. Franchising the Amber to other first-tier cities. Scheduled appearances at big-name food festivals, or on cooking shows."

"Hearing you talk tonight," Linda added, "I could see you doing a specialized travel series on whiskey-producing regions all over the world. Could be online or even on cable. I want to see you on-screen, walking us through Scotland, just like you said."

Pierce nodded vehemently.

"Wait, wait." This was too much all at once. Too much of so many things she'd never considered.

She'd had only one Big Dream as of late, and Pierce hadn't mentioned her starting her own distillery, producing her own whiskey and spirits. But that was *her* dream, and she was glad for that. She didn't want to have to answer to anyone when that finally came about. But maybe, if something like what Pierce was offering her could get her more money in order to bring that dream about quicker . . . Everything these two had mentioned scared her to some extent, if she could be completely honest, but if the end result was her finally having the means to start her own distillery? Maybe it would ultimately be worth it.

"Here are some of the magazines we produce." Linda pulled out a stack of glossies and other elegantly produced folders and brochures. "And some info about a few of our websites."

She recognized those magazines. They were on every newsstand in every airport. And though she hadn't been on the websites listed in the sales brochures, she'd definitely heard of some. And, yes, their following was huge, as far as she could tell.

She pulled out a magazine with a young starlet on the cover, wearing teeny-tiny underwear and a black blazer with no bra. "This one is like *Maxim*, right?"

"Our main competitor, yes," Pierce said.

Opening the magazine to a random page showed a headline "How to Build a Better Bookcase," illustrated by a model with impossible boobs and the smallest bra and underwear possible, wearing a tool belt around her hips.

"I see." And that was all she could say.

Pierce cleared his throat. "Right Hemisphere casts a wide umbrella. We oversee lots of different media avenues and end products."

Shea flipped through another mag, the cover a topless model, arms wrapped across her chest. "But this is the kind of thing you see me in?"

Linda replied, "It's where we see your target market."

Shea closed the magazine. It was a good thing she hadn't gotten her hopes up too high about parlaying this opportunity into her own distillery. She'd worked far, far too hard to *not* be seen as window dressing in her own bar. To become part of Whitten's Right Hemisphere seemed like such a major compromise on her part, and not in a positive way.

"Mr. Whitten—"

"Pierce. Please."

"Mr. Whitten, you're not looking for an answer right this minute, are you?"

"I meant what I said before. I was hoping to pique your interest enough that you'd come in to our offices, meet with our team. Try to find something that could be mutually beneficial." His gaze flicked to the magazine and back. "That turns you off, doesn't it?"

"It does. Those messages aren't the image of myself I want to portray."

Pierce pressed his lips together and nodded. "Everything is adaptable. We want to work *with* you. Not make you wear a tool belt."

Shea sighed. Maybe not her with a tool belt, but they'd give it to some other woman. She could just imagine them putting a model out in the middle of a Scottish field, wearing nothing but a bikini while she wielded a peat hoe.

No. Just . . . no. The answer had to be no.

"Thanks for coming to see me, Mr. Whitten." She stuck out her hand.

Several long moments passed before he took it. "I hope we've at least planted a seed in your brain and that we'll hear from you eventually." Releasing her hand, he pulled a business card out of his pocket and slipped it underneath a half-finished glass of Lagavulin.

She chose to respond to that with a nonresponse. "It was great meeting you. I'm glad you enjoyed the whisky."

For the first time since Shea had walked into the Corner Pocket, Linda showed emotion, and it was disappointment. The director of branding zipped up her briefcase, leaving all the paper goods on the octagonal table. Linda came around and shook Shea's hand. "I sincerely hope we get to work together someday."

Linda left the room first. Pierce buttoned his suit coat and said, "So do I, Ms. Montgomery." Then he was gone, too.

When the gold velvet curtain swished back in their wake, Shea fell forward, catching herself on the table. A Shea Montgomery brand? Like that hopped-up celebrity chef with the dark hair and annoying voice whose name she couldn't remember? Or Martha Stewart, without the ankle bracelet and worldwide empire? But with *whiskey*? It just seemed so strange. And potentially lucrative. But how could she make it work with that kind of company?

Reaching out, she snatched the glass of Lagavulin that held down Pierce's card. And, like she was a college freshman drinking on a fake ID, she knocked the whole thing back in one swig.

Chapter

✸

7

*B*yrne drove the edges of his thick-soled boots into the soft New Hampshire earth and pushed off with every bit of strength left in his quads and hamstrings and calves. His gloved hands moved just a fraction down the rope, his grip tightening, pulling. His body was nearly parallel to the ground, and every muscle screamed in its tautness, but he hadn't felt this energized in weeks.

On the other end of the rope, over the red flag tied in the center, burly county firemen were doing their best to bring down the reigning champions of Gleann's Highland Games Tug-of-War. But there was no way Byrne wasn't winning again this year.

It had been a really tough, shitty week. He needed this.

George crouched next to the line of Manhattan Rugby players, his hands on his knees, his head swiveling back and forth, barking orders. The firemen made a move, all heaving at once. The crowd erupted, their local guys a clear favorite to off the New York City intruders. There were three times as many onlookers as there were last year, and that pumped Byrne up even more.

The firemen's move didn't work. Manhattan Rugby was *on*, and they resisted, then countered with their own tug of herculean effort. For the past few weeks, after regular rugby practice or during spontaneous workouts, Byrne had cued up tug-of-war tactics on his phone, and the team had spent a few extra minutes on training. Looked like it was going to pay off, and it was making his blood buzz in the way that previously only rugby could.

His teammates wanted the case of whisky prize that would go to the winner, but Byrne couldn't think about that, because Shea Montgomery would be the one to award it.

No, he wouldn't think about her. Not even when he was fully aware that she was standing outside her tasting tent on top of the little hill that overlooked the athletic field. Not even when he knew she was watching the competition.

He wasn't doing this for her. He hadn't come back to Gleann for her.

George had been watching the firemen with scrutiny, and when his head snapped back to the rugby players and he shouted his command like an overweight drill sergeant, Byrne and the rest of his guys took their cue, lifted and replanted their boots, and gave it all they had.

The flag jerked to their side. The firemen stumbled and collapsed, and Manhattan Rugby was declared the winner of the semifinals. They would pull against the winners of the construction workers/teachers match, up next.

Byrne celebrated with a few back slaps and some good-natured verbal jabs, then bent to stretch his tightened legs. Getting older sucked, and thirty-five wasn't even old. As he straightened, crossing one arm in front of his chest to give his shoulder a good stretch, he felt a distinct pull on his conscious coming from the right. When he looked over, there was Shea, still standing outside her tent. Staring right at him.

A light rain began to fall. It had been spitting on and off all day and was expected to continue all through the games. Shea, however, didn't move under cover. She stood there in the mist and their eyes locked. He wondered if they were going to do this all weekend—just stare awkwardly at each other but not really acknowledge, like a pair of junior high school kids—and then she surprised him by giving him a nod and a brief smile.

A smile not at all dampened by the rain. As he raised a hand in greeting, it seemed to pull some deep muscle in his chest.

Brightly colored umbrellas bloomed all over the field, and

Byrne ducked under one that Erik popped open just as the ref's whistle blew and the next semifinal got under way.

"I'm thinking we want the teachers to win," Erik said at his side.

"Don't be fooled," Byrne replied. "Dealing with kids all day makes them mean."

Erik laughed, and Byrne stole another glance up at Shea, but she'd taken cover inside her tent.

As the teachers and construction workers battled it out, Byrne took a good long look around the grounds.

The shaggy Highland cattle were still there, secured behind a much sturdier fence this year—and looking none too happy about it. Someone had painted an enormous Scottish flag on the side of the nearby barn. The vast silver office building that had looked so neglected and overgrown last year was now lit up, and people streamed indoors to where little girls dressed in tartan were competing in a style of dance that had Byrne grasping a phantom stitch in his side just from looking at it.

The whole grounds was like Scotland had thrown up all over it. Blue and white flags were draped everywhere, with variations of plaid filling in the gaps. The rain—thank God—had kept the bagpipers away, but a band was setting up in the music tent. Families were everywhere, kids splashing in mud puddles, and even though he was a Scrooge when it came to the Scotland-heritage aspect of the games, he had to admit that the atmosphere here was wonderfully homey. Inclusive and loving and generally fun. It made him think of Caroline and his parents, how much they would enjoy something like this.

The teachers won the other semi, to the tune of raucous cheers, and after they'd been given a suitable break, Byrne pulled on his gloves, scraped off clumps of mud from the treads of his boots, and Manhattan Rugby again assumed their place on the opposite end of the rope.

Byrne had been right. The teachers were deceptively good—benefits of summers off? Extra practice?—but in the end, rugby prevailed. And suddenly he found himself exactly where he'd been one year ago: standing in the whisky tent surrounded by the deafening hoots and hollers from grown men acting like children, with Shea in front of him holding a box of six Scotch whisky bottles.

They looked at each other over the top of the cardboard, and all he could think about was how amazing she'd tasted. How good her laugh had felt in his ears. How easy she'd been to talk to.

He had to remember how many times she'd shot him down. Had to remember that she'd given him what allowance she could, and it hadn't worked out for her. He had to remember—ah, fuck it. He still wanted her. And this time for more than just sex.

As he slipped his hands underneath the box and grazed her fingertips, her lips parted. The noise of the tent clicked off. Just went mute.

Yes, the outward appearance of the scene was bizarrely familiar, but all he could think about was how different things were between what he'd wanted and assumed about her last year, versus what he wanted and *knew* about her now.

Then she released the box and stepped back, Byrne hugged the prize to his chest, and loud, nearly drunken voices slammed him back into reality.

Shea turned around and went back behind her bar. He watched her go, noticing she wore the same white shirt and black pants she'd worn at the Long Island games, only tonight she'd draped a tartan over one shoulder, like a Scottish princess.

"Get your ass over here!" George called, and Byrne returned to his team. Six of the guys immediately yanked out the bottles and hoisted them in the air, one of them launching into the rugby chant they bellowed out in the local bar after matches back home.

The tent was peppered with other rugby teams who'd be competing in the tournament tomorrow, and they took up the unspoken melodic challenge. Soon the whisky tent turned into an impromptu rugby tune sing-off that had Byrne shouting as loud as he could.

When the singing died down, the real drinking began. It started to rain so hard even the ground under the tent turned into mud. As Byrne nursed his whisky—he really didn't want to be hungover for tomorrow's match again—Dan shook his shoulder.

"She's really into you." Slurring, as usual.

"Who?" Byrne said, stupidly.

Dan rolled his eyes. "Who do you think? Did you even see the way she was looking at you over there? Don't fuck it up."

Byrne tried not to go off right then and there. "Seemed to be going pretty well between us a few weeks ago, Dan, until someone else fucked it up for me."

Dan laughed, stumbling backward into Erik, who shoved him off. Erik rarely gave Dan the time of day.

"Hey." Byrne grabbed Dan's arm, pulled him in close, and said low into his ear, "I didn't say anything then, but I should have. Shea is not Izzy. Don't try to mess with everyone else's relationship just because someone messed with yours." Dan blinked up at him with eyes that seemed to be red with more emotion than drink. Byrne gave his shoulder a pat. "Get your shit together, man. And I mean that in the best way. In a friend's way."

Byrne let that sink in and went over to Erik.

"The team's heading across the lake to some bar in Westbury," Erik said.

Byrne slid a glance over to Shea. "I think I'll stay."

Erik followed his gaze, then shook his head to himself. "Beef jerky."

Byrne grinned. "Want to stay with me? Have a low-key night here in town? This is your kind of place, isn't it?"

As the rest of Manhattan Rugby piled on a shuttle heading over to Westbury, Erik and Byrne trudged down the long drive away from the games' grounds and toward Gleann's little downtown.

"Sharing an umbrella with you is so romantic," Byrne said.

"I'm not making jerky for you."

Byrne's phone went off, and he fished it out of the damp back pocket of his jeans. He frowned down at the number. Caroline. Calling on a Friday night, outside of their long-standing conversation schedule.

"Hey there." He plugged one ear with a finger. "What's wrong? What's happened?"

"Nothing." She didn't sound so reassuring. "At least, I don't think anything is. But I'm not sure. I couldn't wait until tomorrow to tell you."

"What is it?" He realized he'd stopped in the middle of the

drive, a wet, hairy, orange cow staring at him from the other side of the fence. Erik stopped, too, and held the black umbrella over them both.

"Alex called Mom and Dad."

Byrne frowned. "What did he want, after all this time?"

"I don't know." He could hear the stress in her voice now, the sound of her shoes pacing across her kitchen floor. "He said he's been working up in Ohio of all places and now he wants to come home. To reconnect with them. And us. Says he has a car and everything."

Byrne didn't realize he hadn't said anything until Caroline added, "Hello? Are you there?"

"Yeah, yeah, I'm here. Are you sure about this?"

"I'm not sure about anything, which is why I called you. Mom said he sounded really lucid, really calm, not at all like when he took off."

"Do you think he'll show up?"

"Don't know."

"Do you want me to come down in case he does?"

"No, I don't want to pull you away for that. Especially if he doesn't show. You know Alex. I'll let you know what happens, though."

"If he does show up, don't give him any money." And then he instantly regretted saying that, because it wasn't like Caroline—or their parents—had any money to give them to begin with.

But Caroline laughed sardonically. "Yeah, I'll try to remember that."

"Love you, sis. Call me anytime," he said.

Erik motioned to hand the phone over to him. Byrne smiled.

"Oh, wait," Byrne said to his sister before she hung up. "The lover you've never met wants to talk to you."

"Who, Erik? Yay, put him on."

Byrne handed over the phone, a thing that had happened many times over the years when Caroline called while he was out with Erik.

"Hello, gorgeous," Erik said, exaggerating his German accent. "Listen, your brother needs advice. He keeps going after this woman who says she doesn't want him and has turned him down many a time, but then eye-fucks him across the room."

Byrne winced. Erik pulled the phone away from his ear and Caroline's distinct *"Ew!"* cut through the sound of the games' dispersing crowd.

"I say he needs to quit," Erik added. "What say you?"

Byrne made drastic cutting motions across his throat, but Erik was not to be deterred.

Erik sighed, then professed his undying love for the Southern woman he'd never met, and hung up. "She says go for it."

Byrne laughed. "Of course she did. Because when it comes to relationships, she's just as dumb as I am."

*E*rik looked like he'd died and gone back to Europe. Byrne also felt that way, because downtown Gleann, New Hampshire, looked like it had been carved from Scotland and transplanted into the new world. The roads curved around with little to no urban planning, the buildings were stone or beautifully carved wood, and overflowing baskets of summer flowers hung from nearly every shop front and home.

By the time they crossed through a municipal park, went over a little stone bridge, and turned down the main street, the rain had tapered off to a mist again. The huge, leafy trees arching over the sidewalks kept them relatively dry. Cars were parallel parked up and down the road, and people ambled about, either carrying passed-out kids on their shoulders or on their way to one of two open drinking establishments.

"That?" Erik pointed to a corner restaurant with a large Now Open sign hanging in one of its wide front windows. "Or there?"

The second place was a stand-alone building set a little ways off the main street, tucked between the quaint, two-pump gas station and the narrow lane that stretched back into a residential area lined with eighteen-hundreds-era houses. It was low and squat, with thick walls and small, stained glass windows. A stunning thatched roof stolen from another time and country swept up to a high peak and created deep eaves that sheltered a row of dry benches. The sign that swung over the door read *The Stone Pub*.

Byrne said, "That has bagpipes written all over it."

Erik jutted a thumb back at the newly opened restaurant.

"And that has sixty-year-old men and Pinot Grigio written all over that. Don't we get enough of that in the city?"

Just then, a couple exited the Stone, and when the heavy wood door yawned wide, a wave of beautiful, live fiddle music streamed out, underlaid by the gentle sounds of conversation and laughter.

The Stone it was.

The interior was warm and cramped, exactly like Byrne had expected it to be. What he hadn't expected was to feel so instantly comfortable in such a foreign place. Every clunky wood table in the front half of the pub was full, plates of steaming stew and lamb chops and sausages making his stomach grumble, even though he'd inhaled food only an hour ago.

He and Erik wedged and apologized their way into the back half of the pub, where a long, gorgeous bar that reminded him of the one in Yellin's apartment lined the whole far wall. People gathered around tall tables, and on a small, triangular stage in the corner stood a lone fiddler. The guy, whose brown hair grazed his chin, barely looked old enough to drink. He tapped his foot and played with his eyes closed, and seemed to be as lost in the music as most of the people in the pub.

Erik tapped Byrne's shoulder with a twenty. "What do you want?"

"Something cold and wet and alcoholic."

"Bartender's cute."

Byrne looked behind the bar that gleamed with old wood and rows of polished brass taps and laughed at the sight of the old man drawing a black stout. "What got you? The yellowed teeth, the hunched back, or the fact that his balls probably hang down to midthigh?"

"Not that one. Her."

An adorable brunette with a pencil stuck behind her ear was chatting up two old ladies at the far end of the bar, one of whom had her silver hair pulled into pigtails and had quite possibly the largest boobs he'd ever seen. Byrne felt it appropriate to call the bartender adorable because she didn't look much older than the fiddle player.

As Erik moved in, preparing to turn on the foreigner's charm, Byrne went to the side of the room near the dartboard, where there was an open table. The table, however, had a hand-scrawled sign sitting on it. "Reserved for the Most Important People in Gleann," it read.

So Byrne instead claimed an empty spot along the wall where there was a ledge for drinks, and waited for Erik.

And then Shea walked in.

The Stone was a dark place, its shadowed corners filled with the ghosts of old cigars and pipes, but when Shea stepped into the bar, it was like someone had taken a spotlight and magically transformed it into a woman.

A fucking gorgeous woman.

She'd pulled out the ponytail, and the rain had clumped together pieces of her long hair, making it look darker. The tartan still hung over one shoulder, tied down at the opposite hip, but she'd rolled the sleeves of her plain, white button-down shirt to her elbows.

A man and a woman flanked her: a classically pretty woman with thick, dark hair and a really big guy in a Red Sox cap, both of whom Byrne vaguely recognized. The guy knocked his forehead on the low, heavy ceiling crossbeam that divided the back bar from the front restaurant area, and the three of them laughed.

Many people called out to them, specifically to the guy, as they made their way over to the "reserved" table. Red Sox snatched the table sign and pointed at the old man bartender, who winked in return. Shea was chatting animatedly with the dark-haired woman as she pulled out a chair to sit. Who knows what drew her attention to the specific part of the wall that Byrne was currently holding up, but she paused with her hand on the back of the chair and found him. Caught him staring at her the way he'd caught her staring at him after he'd bought those strangers the whisky-tasting tickets.

With his eyes alone, he told her he thought she was beautiful. He told her he didn't want to stop what they'd started.

So of course Erik chose that exact moment to stumble back to Byrne and spill the Stone's inky porter down Byrne's arm.

"Sorry," Erik said, pushing the sloshing pint glass into Byrne's hand. "Here. I'm going back in. Forecast is looking really good."

Byrne looked down at the wasted teaspoons of fine beer

sliding over his forearm. If it weren't for the layer of tug-of-war mud slathered on his skin, he might've licked the porter off.

"Forecast for what?" Byrne asked, but Erik just clinked glasses with him, gave him a vague thumbs-up, and then pushed back toward the bar. And the young bartender.

In the far corner, the fiddler ended his song with a flourish and the bar applauded.

Shea's friend cupped her hands around her mouth and yelled, "Yeah, Chris!" while Red Sox put two fingers between his lips and released an earsplitting whistle. It was then Byrne remembered where he'd seen that guy before. He'd been in the whisky tent last year, hanging out with Shea, and then the next day he'd been one of the competitors in the throwing events in the games.

Onstage, Chris lowered the fiddle and shot a shy smile out to the crowd. He looped his hair behind his ear, gave a shallow bow, then tucked the instrument back under his chin and started a new song. Something slow and lovely and full of the history Shea had talked about in the campground.

At that moment, Shea turned sideways in her seat and shifted her brilliant blue eyes to him. As though she was thinking the exact same thing.

And then all of a sudden the spotlight was shining right on him, because she'd gotten up from her chair and came to stand not two feet away.

"Hi," she said.

That's what he found most fascinating he supposed, that there was never any shyness about her. No hunch of the shoulders or awkward shuffling of her feet. She said what she meant and she acted because she wanted to.

"Hey, I know you." He leaned his elbows on the drink ledge behind him.

"Did you guys drink all that whisky already?"

"It's somewhere over in Westbury," he responded, "with the rest of the team."

"Congratulations on winning. I don't think I said that. Earlier."

"You didn't. You didn't last year either, as I recall."

Her head tilted to one side as she gave him a lightning-fast once-over. "You're all muddy again."

He remembered how he'd looked on Long Island. "That I am." He took a long drink of his porter, as an excuse to look but not speak, because, strangely, he had no idea what to say. *She'd* approached *him* for once. This was uncharted territory.

She sucked in her cheeks, then said, "We seem to have better luck when you're covered in muck."

He thought about that for a moment, then nodded. "Seems like we do."

The couple who made up the "Most Important People in Gleann" sat at their table, engrossed in each other. The woman was talking and gesturing wildly, and Red Sox eyed her with a hungry expression that only another man might appreciate. When she was done, all he did was grab her chin, pull her in for a kiss, then say something against her mouth. Byrne had to look away. When he glanced back, the couple was moving toward the dartboard, leaving their important table vacant.

"Who are they?" he asked, to fill the hole. "They look familiar."

"I know Jen from the city. She's an event planner and she organizes the games here. Last year was her first, and she asked me to come here as a favor."

"And you came back this year for the camping." He hid a smile behind his porter.

"Exactly. Just the camping." She glanced at Red Sox. "His name is Leith. He grew up here and he competes in the heavy athletic events. The caber and the hammer and such."

"Oh, right, right." Now he remembered. Leith was the name of George's friend from Gleann, the one who'd called last year and begged Manhattan Rugby to come up to compete.

"Do you want to sit?" Shea asked.

He almost choked on his beer. "Sorry?"

She gestured to the empty table. "It took a lot for me to ask, J.P. Byrne. Please don't make me say it again."

Hell yes. He grabbed the back of one chair and sat, before she could change her mind. As she took the seat next to him, he had to ask, "What's changed, Shea?"

The cool thing was, he didn't have to clarify. She knew exactly what he meant. Sweeping a long look around the

Stone, with the drifting notes of the fiddle twining around them, she replied, "Being here. Feeling comfortable." Then she looked right at him and said, "Seeing you again."

"Well, I'm glad." It went a little deeper than that, but he couldn't show all his cards at once.

At the dartboard, Jen and Leith finished arguing about something or other, and Leith looked over at his now-occupied table. Byrne raised his glass, and Leith smiled and nodded. An understanding between two men who'd never met, like a ribbon tied around a dorm room doorknob.

He pointed to the plaid Shea wore. "Is that your family's?"

She fingered the edge of the sash. "It is. My granddad moved back to his homeland after my grandma died when I was a little girl, and he gave this to me when I was over there visiting."

"When was that?"

"Five summers running, starting after high school. He died the winter after I was last there." An old pain crossed her face, but then a wistful smile erased it.

"Still miss him?"

"He changed my life. Made me who I am."

People didn't say things like that unless they wanted to talk about it, so he bit. "How so?"

The rigid way she'd been perched on the edge of her chair broke, and she angled her legs toward him. "He gave me whisky, of course. He started it all."

"Plying young, impressionable girls with alcohol. I like him already."

"Hee, yes, you would've liked him. So my first summer there, after I graduated high school, I turned eighteen. He brings me to a pub, and not to have dinner."

"Wait, you graduated high school at seventeen?"

"I did."

Byrne whistled. "Smart cookie."

Shea let out a little snort. "Not really. Strict parents."

"But they didn't do your homework for you, and you went to college, and now you own your own highly successful business, so if I want to call you a brainiac, I believe I'm in my right."

"We're getting off topic. Do you want to know about my granddad and the whisky or not?"

More than anything. "Absolutely. Sorry."

"Okay, so Granddad thinks he's going to get me innocently wasted on Speyside whisky on my eighteenth birthday, but the moment they gave me my first taste, I was completely in love."

"Who was 'they'?"

"Granddad and the bartender, this twenty-year-old guy who asked me out a few weeks later. I ended up dating him that whole summer."

"I hate him. Continue."

She laughed. "So they thought I was just going to toss the thing back, and cough and gag, and then I'd have to be carried home. But I was so utterly fascinated by the drink. It was like my whole head had been awakened after being asleep for eighteen years. The bartender worked part-time in a distillery, and he showed me how to nose the whisky and then properly taste it. And I could smell and taste *everything*. The two of them just kept pushing little samples of all these different whiskies in front of me. I remember them staring at me as I described what I was experiencing, and Corey, that was my ex-boyfriend, told me everything he'd learned working at the distillery. By the time we'd tasted all the bottles in the pub, he'd exhausted his knowledge and told me he wanted to introduce me to his bosses." She shrugged. "And that's how it all began."

"So the bottom line was, you did end up getting drunk that night after all."

She giggled. Actually giggled, with her hand over her mouth and everything. "I did. I was eighteen and I'd never had a drink before that."

The beer, which was halfway to his mouth, came back down with a slam to the table. "How is that possible? You said you went to high school."

"Freshman year only. But my parents pulled me out because they said it was a bad influence. Homeschooled me."

Well, there went his horribly wrong judgment about homeschooled kids, out the window. "No way."

She seemed to enjoy his shock. "Yes way."

He had to throw back the last of his beer at that. He wanted another, but didn't want the slightest break in this conversation. Just then, another glass slid in front of him.

"Just passing through," Erik said, as he set a pint in front of Shea, too. "You didn't see me."

Byrne laughed. "Then thanks for the invisible beer."

Erik melted back into the crowd, heading for the cute bartender again.

"One of yours?" Shea asked.

Byrne nodded. "The best of mine."

Shea flashed him an uninhibited smile. "I have one of those, too. Makes you fear for life without them."

The new beer felt welcomingly cool between his palms. "So. Strict parents. Homeschooling. So they must have *loved* that you went over to Scotland and drank with Grandpa."

"Oh, yes. They *loved* it." Sarcastic eye roll.

"So what do they think of what you do now?"

Her eyebrows lifted in resignation. "They don't. Or if they do, they immediately put it out of their minds. If I bring it up, which I've learned not to do, they change the subject."

"Which I will also do now, in case it might be a sore subject."

Another shrug. "Not really. I deal. They're too precious to me to fight with them over it, and it won't change anything anyway."

The second beer tasted better than the first, because he got to watch her drink, too.

"Did you use Corey for his distillery connections?" he asked.

She laughed. "I totally did. He didn't catch on until the second summer, when I told him I didn't want to date him, and that I just wanted to work in a distillery and learn everything I could."

"Did you?"

She grinned wickedly. "What do you think? I learned everything and more. Made some incredible connections with people in the industry who saw promise in me, who told me that I had one of the best noses they'd ever been exposed to. I still keep in contact with them. But not Corey."

"Thank God for that. Tell me what happened after college, how you got to the Amber."

Her first uncomfortable pause. The only reason he noticed was because she finally looked away from him, and the only cheesy thing he could compare it to was like when the sun ducked behind a cloud for a second.

"Well, I was on the plane home for the last time, that final summer, and I was crying because I knew what I wanted to do with my life and didn't have a clue how to go about it. Or what sort of jobs were available to me."

She was, quite literally, the most fascinating woman he'd ever met. He didn't want her to ever stop talking. He wanted more. Wanted to sit here at this ugly, clunky table with the hard, uncomfortable chairs and talk to her until the place cleared out. And then start all over again.

"I majored in business, since there was no whisky tasting degree."

He barked out a laugh. "You sure about that? Depends on where you went to school."

"You know what I mean. I was a good student, but business really wasn't my thing. It's not even about being book smart. To make it in New York City in that arena you have to have this take-no-prisoners, go-get-'em attitude, and I just didn't have it. I didn't want it either, to work in that high-rise world. So I did what any recent college grad does who's questioned what the hell to do with their life: I waited tables during the day and tended bar at night."

Another odd glance into the crowd, toward where Jen and Leith were arguing over a dart's placement. Shea twisted her glass between her hands. "I saved money. I was loaned some more. The rest is history."

There was more, he knew, but she'd given him so much already that he didn't want to push. He was already insanely happy over how much she'd said. He was, he dared to think, encouraged.

"Did you know," he said, "that the most I could find on your background was that you learned to love whisky in Scotland?"

She arched an eyebrow. "You looked me up?"

"Not really. Just what's on the Amber website." He took a drink. "How come you shared that story with me?"

As she stared at him, the look in her eyes changed. The cool, aloof Shea vanished and in her place sat the affable, interested Shea he'd kissed on a picnic bench.

"The campground," she replied.

He leaned forward. "The kiss?"

She considered that. "No. Everything else about it. Seeing you there, first of all, in your jeans and sweatshirt and flip-flops, looking all normal and well . . . you know."

He smiled. "No, I don't. Do tell."

She swished a hand at his face. "*That.*"

Good enough for him.

"But I have to know something," she added.

"Okay."

"Who the hell was that guy at the Yellin party?"

He frowned. "You mean Gordon?"

"No. I mean you."

A ton of air whooshed out of his lungs, and he scratched at his head, feeling where the mud from the tug-of-war had dried along his hairline.

"The suit, the smirking, the obnoxious talk with those guys—"

"I know." He stared into his beer. "I know."

"Because I liked the Byrne who came into my whisky tent on Long Island. And I really, really liked the Byrne who surprised me at the campground. Rugby Byrne is who I'm into. But Bespoke Byrne, the Byrne who was at Yellin's, was most definitely not that guy."

"Bespoke Byrne, huh?" He tried to push a smile to his face, but it felt forced, and probably looked all wrong, too. "It's the suit," he said. "Sometimes it gives the wearer super-powers of being an asshole."

Shea shook her head. "I wouldn't go so far as to say 'asshole,' but definitely different. Even after you assured me at the campground that you weren't at all that kind of guy. I was ready to bend more rules for you, and you threw me off guard. Confused me. It was like you were two different people."

"I was. I am. I have to be. The nature of the job I picked. And most days I hate it. I hate it because it's who I have to be to survive in that world. But I'm finding that the longer I have to be that guy, the harder it is to shake him off."

Her turn to lean forward, pressing her elbows into the table. "So how do you do it? How do you shake him off?"

"Rugby." Instant, easy answer. "Rugby on the weekends,

working out, training, practicing during the week. Whenever I can, even if it's the middle of the night. Let me hit, let me run, and I feel like myself again."

All her focus was on him. Good and tight. It felt amazing.

Chris ended another song, the last note strung out and buried under applause.

Byrne hadn't realized he'd been staring back at Shea, silent, until a woman said, "Hey, you guys."

Both he and Shea startled like they'd been caught with their pants down. He looked up to find Jen standing between them, her mouth cocked in a knowing grin.

"Sorry," Jen said.

Shea drew casual fingers through her hair. "What's up?"

"Leith and I are heading out now."

Leith grabbed Jen from behind, one of his hands sliding around her stomach. He looked a little red-faced, a little antsy. Byrne knew that look very, very well.

"You lose, Leith?" Shea poked.

"No," Leith said, his face angling toward Jen's neck but not quite touching. "I won. And I want my prize."

Jen pried Leith's fingers from her body, only to wind them together with her own. "I just wanted to come over and tell"— she touched Byrne's shoulder—"sorry, what's your name?"

"Byrne."

"Byrne. Right. Hi. I recognize you from last year." Jen shot a sidelong glance at Shea. "Anyway, I saw you take the shuttle into town, and I just wanted to let you know that the last shuttle going around the lake is leaving in fifteen minutes."

Worst timing ever.

Leith pulled Jen out of the pub, Jen's throaty laugh trailing behind.

Byrne looked back at Shea, who was already watching him. She stood up quickly. "I should get going, too," she said. "The tent's all set up, but I have to throw the sleeping bag inside. Going to be a little damp."

Then she bit her lip, as though she, too, was remembering how enthusiastic he'd been about potential tent sex. He didn't want her to be embarrassed, though, and didn't want to make a big deal out of it, so he stood and gestured for Erik's attention. When he got it, he pointed to an invisible watch.

Shea was still staring at Byrne with those big, gorgeous, sunny eyes. When her lips parted, he almost injured himself restraining the urge to kiss her.

"I can't stop thinking about that kiss at the campground," he blurted out.

Her head tilted back. It was slight, a minuscule movement, but it was an invitation if he'd ever seen one. A temptation that he knew he couldn't take right then, even though he was salivating for her, his mouth anticipating the press of hers. He wanted to taste all the stories she'd just told him, the whiskies of her past, and just . . . her.

"Neither can I," she said.

"I want another. Hell, I want a lot of them."

To that she said nothing. He hoped it was because she wanted him as badly as he wanted her, and she was just as clueless as he how to go about it gracefully.

To hell with grace.

"And fucking," he added. "Fucking would be great, too."

She was a big girl with a commanding presence, a confident woman who knew exactly what she wanted, and he was pretty sure he was reading her vibes correctly.

He felt his cheeks tighten as his grin broadened, and he loved the slow smile he got in return.

The breath she drew in was choppy, even less steady on the way out. "It would, wouldn't it?"

"But not tonight."

She shook her head. "No, not tonight."

He bent forward at the waist, getting close enough to touch but not actually doing it. "See you tomorrow then?"

"Yes."

And it was the most beautiful word he'd ever heard.

Chapter

⊗

8

The morning was hot, and so was the paper coffee cup in Shea's hand. She locked up her car where it was parked in the lot between the big silver building that used to be some company's headquarters and the fairgrounds' sprawling field. Her whisky tent was on the building's front lawn, just one part of the tiny, temporary town of white tents where she'd make her home for the day.

The games wouldn't open for another hour, and she wouldn't be serving whisky until noon, but she'd arrived early because she found herself in the mood to watch a little rugby.

The fairgrounds teemed with players grouped together by the color of their uniforms, all getting ready for the day's tournament. Red and black, that's what she recalled Byrne's team wore, and she stopped on the sidelines to scan the pitch for him.

There he was, jogging across the grass at midfield. He was moving away from her, but she'd know his body anywhere, which was strange because her exposure to it had been extremely limited and had been hindered by those pesky things called clothes. Black shorts showed off those killer thighs, and the red-and-black-striped shirt fit snugly around his waist and chest and biceps. The blond guy from last night ran next to him. Byrne was talking, telling a story with big arm gestures, and his friend was laughing.

Then Byrne flipped around to jog backward. Still talking, he happened to look over and see Shea standing next to a family setting up lawn chairs. He did a double take, which probably wasn't too smart considering he was also running backward and talking, and he tripped.

Stumble, thud, ass in dirt, amazing legs flying up in the air.

His friend doubled over, arms wrapped around his waist, and didn't make a move to help Byrne up. Shea snorted coffee out of her nose, which, as it turned out, didn't feel good at all. She choked, pounded on her chest, and then when she looked up, Byrne had come up to his elbows on the grass and was laughing at *her*.

She turned around to clean herself up, but she was going to have to live with a coffee stain down the front of her white shirt all day. Looked like she'd be sporting a strategically placed Montgomery tartan.

When she faced the field again, Byrne had popped to his feet. Still at the halfway line, he kicked one foot back, held his cleat in his hand, and stretched his quad. His crooked smile, aimed directly at her, was a lightning bolt that zapped her squarely in the chest.

He looked too clean. Like Bespoke Byrne had just changed uniform. But the rain yesterday had made the pitch all muddy, and just a few minutes of play would fix that. Shea thanked the graces above and below and wherever the heck they all were that his first match was before she had to get behind the bar, because she was going to love watching him get all messy.

She could admit that now, after last night. Which was funny to think because usually you said "after last night" in the context of something sexual.

Even though they hadn't touched once, it had been exactly that.

A whistle blew somewhere and the teams cleared the field, fading into their spots on the opposite sideline.

Manhattan Rugby played first, the opposing team from somewhere an hour south of Gleann, and when the red and black took the field, Shea couldn't deny the little kick of excitement that zipped through her body.

Byrne was a forward, of course. He was easily the biggest guy on his team, the one in the best shape. The one who looked

like he'd been made to play this sport. The forwards were the
players who got into the thick of the tangle of bodies during a
scrum. They did the rucking and mauling—that hard, physical
contact, that pushing and shoving and scrambling—when a
guy was tackled and the ball had to come loose.

She'd watched enough rugby in her life to know that all of
that fulfilled exactly what Byrne had described last night: that
intense need to run, to hit. To be hit. And to get right back up
and start it all over again.

She watched it all happen. His face shifted to an intensely
focused scowl. His whole body went tense and loose at the
same time, the ripple of readiness and preparation mixing
into a buzz that Shea could feel across her own skin, even
fifty feet away. He glared at the yellow team, hands on his
thighs, and just like that, he transformed into the Rugby
Byrne she hadn't been able to get out of her mind for weeks.

Watching him now, she didn't think she ever would.

The whistle chirped to start the match, and the team in
yellow kicked over to Manhattan. Erik, a back—one of the
fast guys, a runner—caught the ball and took off, weaving.
When he was tackled, his knees hit the field in a splash of
mud. Byrne was there, diving in, going after the ball, then
passing it backward to another back.

It didn't take long for Manhattan Rugby to get the first
try. It was Byrne who made it, too, as he took a backward
pass, tucked the ball close to his chest, and dove behind the
posts. His whole body hit and then rolled across the wet grass
for the five points. Their kicking player made the conversion,
which added another two points, and Shea heard herself
shouting and clapping along with the sparse few strangers
standing nearby.

The yellow team got the next try then followed it up with a
conversion, and then a very quick penalty kick, which put
them ahead by three points. It made Shea chew her fingernails, but in the end, the New Hampshire team didn't stand a
chance. Because they didn't have Byrne. He played intensely,
incredibly. He was all over the field, the clear leader, so
spot-on and direct in his tackles and passes. He made the
sport look effortless, even though she knew how much work it
took to give focus to such beautiful brutality.

Manhattan Rugby quietly celebrated their first tournament victory, and even from across the field Shea could see Byrne's smile. Could feel the weight of everything he wanted to throw off as it lifted from his shoulders and drifted away.

The sounds of Gleann's Highland Games coming alive drifted up from behind her. When she turned away from the rugby pitch, a sea of cars had filled the parking lot, and streams of people walked up the long drive toward the gates, past those dastardly cows. The smell of the food stands hit her nostrils, and the *rat-a-tatta-tatta-tat* of an unseen snare drum pinged her ears. She'd been so engrossed in the match she hadn't even realized the day had started without her.

*S*hea had packed up, marked the boxes for Jen to ship back to New York, and was rolling down the tent flap to close the whisky-tasting area, when she heard him behind her.

"Hi."

She loved the breathiness of his *h*, how he drew out the sound. When she turned around, she really loved the curve of his smile. And the way he stared. And stared.

"You're still here," she said. "I take it you won the tournament?"

"We did. Winning the tug-of-war was far more lucrative, though."

"Both events? You may not be invited back next year, you know."

"Competition for the tug-of-war was stiffer, if that tells you anything."

"You all set?" called Jen from over by the heavy athletic field where the sheaf toss was just finishing up—Leith was on deck, a pitchfork in hand, ready to stab it into the bag of hay and toss it over the high bar.

"Yep!" Shea waved. "See you back in the city!"

"So," Byrne said after Jen had given Shea a thumbs-up and Leith's name blurted over the loudspeaker to the sound of great applause.

"So." Shea removed the Montgomery tartan from her shoulder and stuffed it into her bag.

He pointed to the coffee stain. "Kind of looks like Scotland."

She laughed. "It does, doesn't it?"

"Thanks for watching this morning."

"I haven't watched a match in a long time. It was my pleasure." Oh yes, it was. "You know, you're really good. If I can say so, way better than any of the other guys. On either team." He seemed pleased at that but didn't respond. "Can I ask you something?"

"Sure."

"What you said last night about playing—if you wanted a bigger challenge, why wouldn't you join a more competitive league?"

He bobbed his dark head from side to side. "Sometimes I wish the competition was stiffer, but this is my team. George and I have been playing for a long time, and we brought on the other guys, taught them how to play and such. I couldn't just leave that, turn my back on them."

A loyal man. It made him that much more attractive. "Have you always played?"

He shook his head. "Football my whole life, up through college. Then in grad school a buddy introduced me to rugby. Since my football days were over, I got hooked."

"You played college ball? For what school?"

"Boston College." There was an odd finality to his answer, but she had no time to dwell on it because he asked, "How do you know the game? Wait, let me guess. Your grandpa."

She remembered the old tube television in Granddad's sitting room, how the nearly constant sound of the matches would fill the whole cramped house, how the TV's picture would jump and waver, and Granddad would spend as much time pounding the top of it as he did cheering on his teams.

"Exactly," she replied.

The sun was starting its descent down to the hills and trees on the other side of the lake, and the light was very, very kind to his tanned skin and sky-blue eyes.

"That field was pretty muddy," she noted. "How are you so clean right now?"

He chuckled. "We hosed each other off. There's a spigot on the back of that big building."

Oh my. "How did I miss that?"

Applause over on the athletic field marked the end of the

sheaf toss and the athletic events for the day. A huge crowd
had gathered around the grass, and a fog of kilted pipers and
drummers lingered on the far side, preparing for the massed
bands conclusion to the games.

Byrne cringed. "I see an army of bagpipes lining up. You
wouldn't want to get out of here, would you?"

Shea stuck her tongue out at him, then glanced at her
closed whisky tent. Her work here was done for another year.
She wasn't holding any bottles, and Byrne wasn't on the
opposite side of the bar from her. She was free to do whatever
she wanted with him.

"I would. Very much."

As she walked past him, still avoiding his touch until they
were well away from the grounds, she caught a glimpse of his
hot, impish grin, and it made her shiver.

He followed her to her car, a small white two-door with
windows you actually had to roll down by hand.

"So where are we going?" he asked as she stuck the key
into the ignition.

"Away," she said. "Alone."

"Perfect." He reached for her.

She leaned away and he dropped his hand. "Sorry. Trained
response," she said with a glance out the windshield to see if
anyone had noticed. "How about a deal? How about you don't
touch me until I say it's okay?"

The dip of his head, the heavy look at her from underneath
his lashes, was wildly flirtatious. "Sure. Forbidden fruit. I like
that kind of expectation."

"So do I." She started up the car and put it in reverse, then
veered out of the lot and onto Route 6. "Can you imagine the
kind of sex people must've had in Victorian England? All that
restraint? All that buildup?"

"I was half kidding. Usually I'm more of a go-for-it kind of
person."

"Me, too." She licked her lips, kept her eyes on the straight
line dividing the two-lane road ahead, and took a chance.
"But if it weren't for the restraint, when you fell on your ass
this morning, I probably would've crawled on top of you."

He huffed out a sound that was something between an

exhale and a laugh. She snuck a sideways glance and saw how his jaw worked beneath a grin.

"If you're going to play it that way," he said, "when I saw you standing there, all I wanted to do was shove you up against the goalpost."

"Sounds like that might hurt."

"I'd make it better."

She was having a devil of a time trying to suppress her own smile. "Yeah? How?"

"I'd lick your neck as I opened the zipper of those pants."

Her turn to release some sort of garbled, involuntary sound. The weight of their mutual desire made the interior of the car warm, and she turned on the air-conditioning.

He slammed his head against the headrest. "Please say we're going to your campsite. I'd never fantasized about tent sex before, but ever since I met you it's vaulted to the top of my to-do list."

The straightaway of Route 6 ended as it followed the valleys and hills of the increasingly mountainous land. The forests thickened, the light turned dappled above. She adored this area.

"We're going to my campsite," she said.

"Thank *God*."

"We're going to have to be quiet, though. Think you can do it?"

"I . . . fuck, I don't know. If I have to be. Not going to let it stop me." His voice dropped. "You?"

"I'll give it a try. I like a good challenge. Although"—she slid him a look—"I might need something in my mouth."

"*Jesus*, Shea." He shifted in his seat. "Such a dirty mind on that homeschooled girl."

"It's years and years of repression coming out. Lucky you."

There was a long pause before he murmured, "Yes. Lucky me."

Then they drove in silence for a time, the lovely New Hampshire summer evening passing by on the other side of the windows.

"You know," she finally said, because she was in an honest mood, "you intrigued me last year. I told Jen I wasn't interested in you and managed to convince myself of the same, but I secretly was."

He sighed. "I'm kind of glad I didn't know what I've been missing this whole year."

Out of everything he'd ever said to her, that made her shiver with warmth and also bow her head in a twinge of regret. Because she'd been the one to turn him down last year. Just look at what she could've had.

And it was only the beginning.

Up ahead, Route 6 veered southwest into a little piece of New Hampshire where old trees and quiet evenings made for a beautiful state park campground. A green sign with an arrow even pointed toward it. But another road, a narrower lane without lines, forked off to the right and disappeared around a bend. When she saw it, she caught her breath.

Releasing her foot from the gas, the car slowed to a stop on the shoulder of Route 6.

Byrne turned to her. "Something wrong?"

She stared out the windshield at the right-hand fork and felt the tug on her heart. "No, nothing's wrong." Hands still on the wheel, she turned to him. "When are you going back to the city?"

"First thing tomorrow. Ass-crack of dawn, most likely."

"Me, too. Are you up for a little detour? I'd like to show you something."

She hadn't known she wanted to do this when they'd climbed in her car back at the games. It was a big deal—to her, at least. But the thing was, she *wanted* to share this with him, and she wouldn't get another chance if she drove past it now.

"Now I'm the one who's intrigued," he said. "I'm yours tonight. Wherever you want to go."

She smiled, released her foot from the brake, and accelerated off Route 6 and onto the unmarked road.

The countryside was beautiful along the state highway, but the area that opened up along this one particular hidden road was breathtaking. Green hills rolled up on either side, the road skirted gracefully around them, and her car was like a surfer negotiating waves. They drove past little glens, golden with wildflowers, green with new grass, and haphazardly divided by meandering white fences. The lowering light made everything rosy and hazy and lovely.

"Wow," he breathed next to her. "It's gorgeous."

"And that's not even the half of it." She steered with her left hand and held up her right index finger. "Wait for it . . ."

"Wait for what?"

Up ahead, the road narrowed to one lane as a stone bridge arched over a creek and entered a pass sheltered by two silver cliffs. She smiled to herself when she saw the bridge and slowed the car.

"Wait . . ." she whispered.

The car rolled over the stones on the bridge and entered the shadowed pass. When they came out the other side, the cliffs abruptly dropped away, sunlight hit the windshield in a glorious burst, and she turned into the secret valley that she'd been dreaming about for a year.

"*There*," she said. "Did you feel it?"

"Feel what?"

"The portal into another world. Going over that bridge and coming through those rocks, that's what it feels like to me. We're not in the lake valley or anywhere near Gleann. We're . . . here."

"A portal, huh?" He slowly turned in his seat to face her, a strange smile ticking up one corner of his mouth. When she glanced at him, his eyes were shining. "You don't read science fiction or fantasy by any chance, do you?"

"Sorry, no."

"Damn. For a second there I was attracted to you."

Her heart did a somersault.

"Where's this portal lead? Alien world? Human settlement on the moon? Faerie castle?"

She loved how she could hear him smile, even though she couldn't turn to look.

She came around a familiar curve—butterflies of excitement turning in her stomach—then went up a high hill. Once she reached the crest, she slowed the car again and pulled over to the side of the road.

"It leads to here," she told him. "Get out and I'll show you."

As she came around the hood, he exited the car. Only ten feet off the road rose a set of rotted, slanting steps leading up to the decrepit front porch of quite possibly the smallest house ever built. The windows were boarded up, the grass overgrown.

Byrne scratched his head. "What is this place?"

"Not the house." She nodded to the side where a rusted swing set stood. "Follow me."

And he did. She skirted around the abandoned house and stepped into the sprawling, sloped backyard that opened up into the most gorgeous valley she'd ever seen on any continent.

Layers of gentle hills stretched back toward the sunset. Low stone walls divided the land into trapezoids and lopsided pentagons. In the distance, where two hills dipped down to the valley floor and touched like lovers, rose an immense stone house. Vines crawled all over the facade, five chimneys popped up from the right and left wings, and a porte cochere stretched over a circular gravel drive. The double front door was massive, rounded at the top, and to Shea, it looked like the perfect entrance to a perfect home.

Just beyond the house rose the peaks of an old barn, also made of stone. Several other, smaller buildings were scattered around the grounds, like children milling about a mother's skirt. The driveway that branched off the main road was blocked by a chained, iron gate.

Shea opened her arms, encompassing the whole valley, the entire farm. "The portal leads here."

Byrne stood next to her on the rise overlooking it all. "It's beautiful. Really, really beautiful."

She took a deep breath. "It's my Scotland."

He turned to her. "Your Scotland?"

"Yes. It reminds me so much of over there. The stone walls, the way the mist settles in the early morning. That house is exactly like some of the huge manor homes that are all over the country. I even looked up this one's history. It was built by Gleann's founders, so the place is Scottish to its core. It's like they scoured the whole New Hampshire mountain range to find the one place that reminded them most of home."

A rusted metal bench sat in the long grass near a dried-up pond, and she went over to sit. When Byrne sat next to her, the thing gave a groan and they both laughed nervously, but it held.

"Isn't the campground the opposite way from here? How'd you find this place?"

"Driving around last year, after the cow destroyed my tent and I served what little whisky was left. I was mad and needed to cool off, so I went exploring. When I came out from between the rocks and saw this view, I almost got in a wreck, almost hit that tree back there. I must've sat on this bench for hours, but it still wasn't long enough, because I came back early the next morning. I saw how the dawn fog made everything even more perfect."

She pointed to the drive that circled around the back of the house toward the barn. "There's a huge amount of open land that stretches beyond. Old servants' quarters. A pond."

He nodded at the chained gate. "You bad homeschooled girl, you."

She rolled angelic eyes toward the sky. "It's been empty for a while now. I didn't hurt anyone." She sighed contentedly. "This is the best view, though. You can see everything from here."

Pulling one leg up next to her on the bench, she clasped her hands around her knee. The sun kept dropping, the shadows getting longer and longer, the temperature going down as the wind picked up.

"It's for sale," she said.

He said nothing for several long moments, then asked, "Do *you* want to buy it?"

That was the question of the century, wasn't it?

She stared at that front door and imagined herself pushing the key into the lock and walking inside. In her mind she saw smoke curling from several of the chimneys and a border collie hopping gleefully over the low rock wall.

"I've been dreaming about buying it for a year now."

"Really?" It wasn't incredulity, not laughter, that he responded with. As he searched her face, he did so with what she could only describe as a dazed wonder.

She nodded, hugged her knee closer. "Uh-huh."

"For what? What would you do with it? Start your own Von Trapp clan?"

Could she tell him? The question lingered in her mind for only a breath, because the answer was apparent. Yes, she could tell Byrne. *This* Byrne. The one with the dirt under his fingernails and the quiet understanding.

"I want to start my own distillery. Bourbon, rye, blends, specialty liqueurs, you name it. I've been wanting to do it for years now, I just didn't know I wanted this to be the location until I stumbled upon it last year."

Faintly, far in the distance, came the rumble of thunder. Erratic clouds over the hills and house made for the beginning of a dramatic sunset.

Shea swept a finger across the landscape. "The barn is perfect for the stills, plenty of room. The outbuildings could hold the barrels for aging, and there's enough room to get trucks in and out. With all this land I could eventually grow my own grains. Wouldn't that be cool, to have a closed loop like that?"

Holding up both hands, framing the house between L's made with her thumbs and forefingers, she said, "I could live in and run my business from the house. And then, when the distillery picked up, I could turn one wing into a B and B or a hotel, like some of the old manor homes in Scotland have done. Help Gleann attract more visitors. There's enough room for a restaurant, too. Something like a farm-to-table place that I could pair with my own whiskeys?" She let her hands drop, let her back sag against the bench.

"Shea, I . . ."

She shouldn't have been scared to find out what he thought, but she was. A little.

He braced one hand on the back of the bench. An excited light danced in his eyes. "What on earth is stopping you?"

She laughed. "Money, first of all. Do you know how much all this land and all these buildings cost?"

"How much?"

She told him. It had a lot of zeroes.

"That's a steal. This valley is wheezing. It's coming back to life, but it's still pretty sickly. Grab it now, while you can."

She cringed. "Of course it's a 'steal' for someone like you."

He rolled his eyes. "Take my job out of this. That doesn't mean anything. I know the price of dreams very, very well, believe me. The meaning of a dollar or a thousand or a couple of million is not lost on me. Not when dreams are on the line."

She desperately wanted to ask about the passionate way he

stabbed a finger into his knee with each word, but he kept going.

"What are you doing to work toward it?"

Grabbing her hair, she twisted it over one shoulder. "Right now, I'm saving like crazy. I guess I'm going to try to get preapproved for a mortgage and then apply for a business loan, but I don't know if I can get what it will cost to buy this place, fix it all up the way I want, and also get the distillery going. In the end, it may be easier to start a boutique distillery back in the city. Something I don't need a mortgage for. Something that doesn't require as much up front. I could hold on to the Amber that way, too."

"Would you let the Amber go otherwise?"

"For this place? Yes. I'm growing out of it. My dreams are bigger than it. It was a stepping-stone that I'm very grateful to have found, but I want more."

"You could sell it."

She answered carefully. Slowly. "I could. I could use the money to start up the distillery, but then I'd lose my only source of guaranteed income." When he cocked a questioning eyebrow, she added, "After getting everything up and running, which will take a lot of time and serious overhead, and then after distilling and barreling, I couldn't even *begin* to think about selling any whiskey for at least two years while the first batch ages. And that's just for the younger bottles. I'd go at least three."

"Ah. Right." He gazed out at the house. "But you're also Shea Montgomery. Judging by my very limited exposure, I'd say a good portion of your customers, and a lot of others in the liquor world, would climb over one another to get at your own brand of whiskey."

Brand. That word again.

Pierce Whitten's business card flashed in her mind. Followed by the image of a bikini-clad model holding Shea-brand whiskey bottles by their necks.

"Are you scared?" Byrne asked.

She thought about that. "The last time I felt like this, I was just about to open the Amber."

"See? There you go. Look how perfect that turned out."

She pressed her lips together, remembering that time. "Circumstances were . . . different."

He gave her a look that was clearly a prompt for more, but she couldn't tell him all about that. Not yet, anyway.

"That's fine." He slowly rose, smiling down at her. "I like a woman with a little mystery." He breathed on his knuckles, then rubbed them on the front of his shirt. "Got a little mystery going myself."

What was he doing to her, this man? How did he manage to be so intelligent and charming and ambitious and really fucking hot all at the same time?

She wanted to ask him so much. She wanted to know about his life and his dreams. His mystery. But she also just wanted *him*, and their time here—on this side of the portal, in this quiet little world so far removed from the city—was shrinking by the second.

How did she want to spend the time with him that was left?

Standing, she found herself close within his space. Close enough to touch again, though neither made a move to do so. When she inhaled through her nose, his scent was this incredible mix of the turf he'd rolled around in all day, and the wood polish from the Stone Pub the previous night, and the sweet water he'd hosed himself off with.

"I like that you showed me this place," he said, sweeping a long look over her valley. The beautiful house felt both fantastically posh and wonderfully homey at the same time. Kind of like Byrne. She didn't know if she'd ever be able to come here again and not see him standing on this rise, the spread of her dreams unfolding over his shoulder.

His eyes came back to her, and this time they were unmistakably hot with desire. His voice was low and rumbling, like the encroaching clouds.

"I like *you*, Shea."

The humor, the lightness of their moments together here in Gleann, slipped away.

Weeks ago she'd considered one night of sex with him and thought that would've been the end of it. Maybe it would have, had it actually happened. But now? What exactly did she want? Him, yes. Absolutely him. Byrne naked and between her legs, no doubt about that.

But after? What then?

He was staring at her mouth with hunger, the speed of his breathing doing its best to catch up to hers.

And then she realized she didn't want to think anymore. She just wanted to say *yes*.

Could he see the way she was already shaking, already vibrating? Surely he could. Her vision was actually blurring with the force of it. So why wasn't he touching her?

Then she remembered how she'd made him promise not to touch her until she said it was okay.

"Sorry. Okay. *Now*."

Breath whooshed out of him. He grabbed her. No, she grabbed him. There was a messy tangling of arms as they each tried to figure out where to put theirs, whose limbs went where, what they both wanted to touch, to feel. His chest went hard with tension, his arms tight with movement as they wrapped around her back. She didn't know where to go first, and in that brief moment as they pressed together, all was chaos.

And then their mouths met and there was instant peace.

Utter and complete heaven. A burst of taste and heat and light that translated quickly into a full-body shiver. It started where his lips moved across hers, a gentle claiming of her senses, and then the moment his tongue came out and licked hers, her entire body reacted. She was powerless to stop the shivering, the wave upon wave of adrenaline that coursed through her and made her arms into vises around his neck.

She wanted him to feel what he did to her. To know it. To know her.

When he pulled away, his own lips slack as he wildly searched her face, she knew he did.

Taking his head, she pulled his mouth to hers again. It was the antithesis of the campground kiss, which had been all innocence and tentative seeking, uncertainty and careful exploration. This kiss was a dive into a pit of half-crazed vipers. Of absolute lust, stolen from the atmosphere, sucking it out of the world. She wouldn't doubt if every lover everywhere suddenly looked down at themselves, wondering where their libido had gone, because she and Byrne had stolen it *all*.

Fuck, it was amazing, this high. To be kissed and grabbed with such untamed need.

The pulse between her legs made her weak, and when his big hands shot upward into her hair, yanking her head back, so he could attach his lips and tongue to her throat, her legs completely gave out. He held her up by sliding one of those ridiculous rugby thighs between her own.

The cry that came out of her mouth shot high and shocked over the valley—a direct response to the unexpected burst of pleasure that raced across her clit.

His head snapped back, and she barely recognized him for the slack-jawed desire that had taken him over. He breathed hard, an animal just after the attack, ready to devour.

"I want to hear that again," he said. "Only with you naked. And underneath me."

All the words that came to her mind would sound so dumb spoken: *Wow. Yes. I want that, too.* So instead she spoke with her body, her tongue darting out to lick his bottom lip while her hand slid down the cotton stretched over his flat abs. The nylon of his warm-up pants made the hard length of his dick impossibly smooth and alluring, and as the heel of her hand pressed down it and dragged back up, they both made low sounds. Raw want in vocal form.

In the distance, more thunder, louder and bigger, echoed what she felt. An impending storm.

"Trying to torture me, eh?" His sideways grin, all slow and sure.

"Trying to make you want me even more."

"Impossible."

He kissed her again with her hand wrapped around him, and never had the promise of sex felt so good.

Just then a sharp, terrible sting stabbed at her ankle and shot down the top of her foot. "Ow!"

He yanked back, eyes dancing with worry. "What? What'd I do?"

"Nothing! Ah, damn it!" She folded herself in two, stretching for her ankle . . . and saw some sort of giant flying bug out of the prehistoric ages taking off. Giggling.

"Did you see that thing?" She pointed.

He laughed, but it was a pained sort of laugh. The kind of laugh guys do when they're turned on and it's the only sound blue balls will let them have.

"You okay?"

Holding on to his shoulder, she balanced on one leg to rub the ankle. "I'll be fine." She glanced at him wryly. "A bug bite? Seriously? That's what interrupts us?"

"You allergic?"

"No, but it—"

"Good." With a sudden sweep of his arms, he tipped her off her feet and cradled her close to his body.

She pushed at his arms—holy cow were they strong—because she felt like she had to, but secretly she loved it. "I'm not helpless, you know."

His eyes twinkled. "You've got that She-Ra power woman thing going on. Which I love, by the way. But this feeds me testosterone. Let me do it so that evil bug doesn't steal my hard-on." He started kicking through the long grass, back toward her car. "Plus, I want to kiss it better."

"You want to kiss my foot?"

"I want to kiss something else."

She was spaghetti in his arms, so when he swung her back down and her shoes hit the gravel on the side of the road, her legs didn't hold her. Again. But then he was pressing her hard up against her car, the door not giving her any quarter. Not that she wanted it.

And when his mouth took hers again—just absolutely claimed it, ruining it for anyone else's mouth ever again—she distinctly felt that the damn prehistoric bug had done absolutely nothing to kill his erection. *Praise be*.

He was between her legs now, pressing in, the fabric of his pants slipping and sliding all over where it felt the absolute best. She could tell, by the way he had his hand pressed into her throat and his fingers on her face, and by the slow curl of his hips as his hardness tried so eagerly to get into her softness, that he was going to be so, so good in bed.

"Tent sex," he murmured as a particularly good undulation of his hips brought out stars behind her eyelids and a mini-orgasm everywhere else.

The wind picked up without warning, tossing the trees in the distance, coming down upon them like a gathering wave and carrying with it the sweet scent of impending rain.

"Mmmm," she said, because every sense of hers was on

fire and it was all she could get out or think to say. His ass felt incredible under her hands, especially when he curled against her, that flex of muscle, and she couldn't wait to feel skin on skin.

The first drops of rain hit the top of her head and dripped down her cheeks. She held on to Byrne for dear life, kissing him and kissing him as the rain echoed their intensity, until all of a sudden the drum in her ears wasn't her hormones or her consuming desire but the drive of rain on the hood of her car and the beat of the drops as they slammed against the nearby abandoned house.

When they took a breath, when she could finally drag herself away, Byrne was soaked, water sluicing down through his dark hair and heading right for his wicked grin. The wet rugby shirt sealed itself to his body, and the wet pants showed exactly what she'd felt and wanted so desperately.

He peered up into the rain, and it made his eyelashes clump together. "Damn," he said. "There goes tent sex."

"What *is* it with you and the tent?"

He shrugged. "Because you're in it?"

Shea futilely tried to wipe water from her face as the rain drove down. Steam started to rise from the heated pavement. "Wow, that came fast."

A possessive hand on her hip, fingers digging in. "So might I, the second I'm in you."

She scrunched up her face. "You know that's not exactly good for a girl, right?"

So many white teeth as he laughed. "I meant the first time. Then a lot of time for you. I mean, *a lot.* And then a good, long second time."

"That's more like it. Get in, Quick Draw McGraw."

They piled back into her car, the rain making blurred sheets down her windows.

"Your seats are going to be soaked," he said, patting her crappy upholstery.

"That's okay. The eventual mildew will remind me of you."

"Excellent." He flicked pointed eyes at her chest. "That boring, proper shirt doesn't look so wholesome right now."

The rain had made the white cotton translucent, showing the pale pink bra underneath. She wasn't well-endowed by any means, but the image was still rather salacious. And she found she liked it, looking like this in her work clothes. She exaggeratedly pushed out her chest, hard nipples and all.

"We small-chested girls need all the help we can get."

He slowly shook his head. "You need no help at all."

Her hand holding the key paused halfway to the ignition. "Um, I just remembered. Hope this isn't awkward or anything, but I'm not on the pill and my . . . stuff . . . is back at the campsite."

"Would you consider coming back to my hotel room? I've got"—oh that smile—"stuff."

In her pause, he turned serious and added, "It's one of those motels out on Route 6. The kind with the doors that open to the outside. I have my own room, you can park right outside, and no one on the team will see you run in. If that's what you're worried about."

"I'm not embarrassed or anything about being with you. You get that, right? It's not *you*."

"I do. It's all good."

"It's just, I came here for work. People know me. I can't give out the wrong ideas—"

"Shea, it's cool."

"Of course it's cool. You're about to get laid and—"

He leaned across the center console and kissed her. Close-lipped. The pressure lovely. The length longer than a peck but shorter than a kiss that could quickly morph into something desperate and never-ending.

As he pulled back, the smile was no longer on his lips but in the warmth of those pale blue eyes.

"You, my dear," he whispered, "are the best kind of surprise."

Chapter

✴

9

As Shea did a U-turn on the narrow access road, Byrne couldn't stop shivering. And he wasn't entirely sure it was because of the rain-soaked chill.

Shea turned on the heat, even though it was still easily eighty degrees outside. "You okay over there?"

The best kind of surprise. One hundred percent.

"I will be," he said.

The headlights speared through the darkness, the windshield wipers flapping back and forth.

"What?" The wickedness in her voice came through loud and clear. "No more talking?"

He barked out a sound of frustration. "Time for telling you what I want to do to you is past, I'm afraid, unless you want a big mess in your car."

"Ew!" Laughing, she slapped him on the arm.

It was an oddly intimate gesture, one that might've happened between two people who actually knew each other. Who had had more than a few random encounters among the screech of bagpipes and strange shaggy cows. Peaceful campgrounds. And random rich men's apartments.

And it felt completely natural.

He caught her hand as it slid down his biceps, her fingers cool and damp from the rain, and brought her palm to his mouth. He hadn't planned to do that. The urge just came to him, this need to taste her in this way. His lips fit perfectly into the little cup of her hand. The rain against her skin was delicious.

The sound that came out of her mouth was a musical mixture of surprise and desire. For a millisecond she tried to pull her hand away, but then she gave in. And inside that millisecond, he knew there was a very real possibility that she could become more to him than sex. There was a chance she could be part of his future and exist in his world outside Gleann, New Hampshire.

Maybe he should stop now before he got too lost in this woman. She'd built such formidable structures around the sections of her life, but now that he got a peek inside, he saw what a funny, warm, smart, sexual creature she truly was.

Fuck it. No way was he stopping. He was going for it. And not just for the sex. He was going after *her*.

When his tongue pushed through his lips and slid up her palm, the car swerved to the left. She yanked her hand from his grasp and righted the steering wheel.

"Thought you said you were in pain over there." Her chuckle sounded strained, her voice tight.

"I am. That wasn't for me."

She gripped the wheel hard at ten and two. "No more distracting me if you want me to get us to your motel in one piece."

But the way she slipped a long, sultry glance in his direction was such an open dare, such a clear invitation to distract her more.

He cleared his throat, ready for the challenge.

"You have the best legs," he said. "I want them around me. On my shoulders. All that skin. I want to be tied up in you."

She coughed, then blew out a long breath between tight lips. "Calm down, calm down."

"Sorry. Can't."

She glanced at him. "I meant me."

He reached for her. She jumped when his fingers smoothed over her knee and ran up the inside of her thigh. Underneath those wet black pants, her leg clenched hard.

"What are you—" A tiny gasp came out of her lips—so high, so wonderfully girly—as he dug his hand between her legs, pushing down slowly, his thumb rubbing just *there*.

"No distractions," she whispered, even as she stamped her left foot against the running board and lifted herself up a bit, letting him further in.

He dragged his hand back out, lazily, as though they had all the time in the world. Even though he'd done this to tease the hell out of her, it was making him absolutely insane.

Aside from Mary Alice who'd worked at the Dairy Queen back in high school, he'd never wanted to get a woman out of a uniform so badly before. And if Mary Alice had once been the gold standard for girls wearing plain, dictated clothing, then Shea was fucking platinum. There was an entire mine of treasure buried underneath that boring white shirt and those black pants.

She moaned a quiet complaint when he pulled his hand away. He sat back, satisfied. For now. The look she slid him—full lips parted, eyes glassy—made his knee bounce in anticipation.

The ride back to his motel should have taken about twenty minutes, but Shea did it in about four. He might've feared for his life on the bending, dipping backcountry road except that his mind was soaring somewhere in the sexed-up cloud of imminent possibility. The real world sped by him in a soundless blur.

She swerved into the parking lot outside his motel and shoved the gear into park so hard he thought it might come off in her hand.

"Anxious, are we?"

"There's been a lot of buildup, Mr. Byrne. You don't even want to know all the incredible things my mind has been promising my body."

"Of course I want to know." Door open, one foot on the asphalt outside. Rain slicked down his exposed leg. "I'll make it all happen."

"Can you read my mind or something?"

"No. Your body. It'll tell me."

Starlight hit and burst in her eyes. A gorgeous smile ticked at her lips, but only for a second. She tried to wipe it away, but the remnants were even more beautiful, even more intriguing. "Just so you know, I hate cocky men."

He responded by getting out, shutting the door, and jogging through the rain over to room 134, the second-to-last door on the ground level. She remained in the car until he got the card-key in the lock. A gentle jiggle. Then a hearty jiggle. Then a jiggle that rattled loudly up and down the row of doors. He thought, *No, no, no. I am* not *going over to the office to talk to some greasy-haired late-night desk clerk about getting a new key now.* Then, green light. Thank fuck. He stepped inside as her car door slammed. Then Shea appeared at his heels, slipping into the warm, dark room behind him.

The curtains were pulled nearly closed. The lamps out in the parking lot burned brightly, and a hard white stripe of light divided the room, lying crooked across the circular table under the window and traveling over both double beds.

A vision flashed in his head. Shea, lying back across the bed, her body perfectly framed in that stripe of illicit light, all that pale skin completely uncovered and moonlit gorgeous.

"I thought you were more of a Four Seasons guy," she quipped.

"Clearly you need to get to know me better."

She'd been teasing, but he was not.

As he turned to secure the deadbolt and the chain lock, she snapped the curtains closed with a screech of rings across a metal bar. He was ready to protest the loss of light and his fantasy, but then Shea went to the standing lamp in the corner and clicked it on the lowest setting.

Much warmer, much more intimate.

Her shoulders rolled back and down as she turned to him. He loved how the rain had clumped together long portions of her hair.

"I want to see you," she said.

Yes.

"Back to the 'I wants,' I see." Never being one to disappoint, he took the hem of his rugby shirt and peeled it off before she could say anything more.

As the shirt came off and hit the circular table with a wet *splat*, the air-conditioning swept a chill across his damp torso, tightening his skin. But then the look in her eyes and the gentle lick of her lips heated him up rather nicely.

As her fingers rose to the buttons of her wet shirt, he closed the space between them and pushed aside her hands. "I want to do it."

The first button, right above the crease between her breasts, popped out of its hole. The second button came free and he peeled back the wet fabric, exposing the pink of her bra and the hard nipples pushing up against it.

"You'll be the death of me," she said all hushed, her chest pumping with breath.

"No, not death." The third button. "Life. Pleasure."

"That's what I mean"—her head lolled back on her neck, and now he could see how evenly creamy and pale her skin was all over—"the death of me."

The final button. "Sounds like you need more pleasure."

He had to pull the wet sleeves of her shirt hard down her arms, and when he got to her wrists, the dampness of her body wasn't giving up the fabric so easily. If there was one thing he could identify in life, it was opportunity, and this definitely was one.

Pressing right up against her until they both shivered with the contact, he used the shirt to trap her arms behind her. It arched her back, pushing her chest against him, and even through the bra the feel of her nipples on him was absolute heaven. Holding her like that, motionless in his arms, he kissed her.

It started out slowly, the prodding of his lips to open her mouth, the tentative, deep penetration of their tongues. But the second she moaned, the very moment that she wordlessly told him how much she wanted him, how much she was ready, the kiss turned hard, stinging, unrelenting.

When he couldn't breathe anymore, when her taste and the passionate way she kissed simply became too much, he edged back and finally yanked the shirt from her arms.

She swayed on her feet, looking dazed, drugged. He loved it.

Reaching behind her again, he unlatched her bra, feeling the tickle of the wet ends of her long hair. At last she was exposed, and if the bottom half of her body was anywhere near as pretty as the top, he might claim that she'd be the death of him, too.

As he bent to unlace and discard his cleats, and to pull off his socks, she toed off her own black shoes. And since he was already down there, he kneeled, reached out, and thumbed open the button of her pants. Her breath hitched when he went for the zipper, drew it down with more patience than he thought himself capable of. He looked up at her.

"Death," she murmured. Her head slowly shook back and forth, long strands of hair falling down over her shoulders, swishing across those perfect tits. She must like how it feels, he thought, because she kept doing it.

"The way you're looking at me is pure evil," she drawled.

"Yep."

Fingers curled over the top of her wet pants, he pulled them down to her knees. He'd meant to unwrap her slowly, to enjoy the rain-soaked present of her, but her underwear came down with the pants, too. Vaguely he was aware she wore a pink thong that may or may not have matched the bra. But then he didn't really care because, good lord, she was definitely as lovely below the curve of her waist as she was above.

Bracing one hand on his shoulder, she let him pull one pant leg off, then lifted her knee and allowed him to do the other. The pants discarded, she stood before him, her feet set far enough apart to give him the best view of something else in a beautiful shade of pink. He leaned forward—he was powerless to do anything else—and drew a long, slow lick up the seam of her body.

It elicited a full-body shiver from her and drew a low groan up from deep inside his own chest. Underneath his hands, her thighs quivered. He held on and pressed in tighter. Kissed her there. Licked in a little deeper. Swirled the wonderful taste of surprise around with his tongue.

Pressure on his shoulders, then the tangle of fingers in his hair. "For the love of God." She shuddered. "Get naked."

Reluctantly, with the mental promise that he'd be back for more later, he removed his lips from the warm, wet, delicious spot.

Rocking to his feet, he pulled out the string to loosen his warm-up pants.

"My turn to help." With a mighty swing of her hips she came forward, sliding her hands down his chest, then shoving them into his waistband.

Just as he was getting lost in the way she simultaneously moved her mouth across his and her hand up and down his dick, she released him. Stepped back. Left him gasping and brain-dead.

Then she dropped down.

Oh, Jesus, she was naked and on her knees in front of him. Taking off his pants and underwear. Licking her lips again. Like he was a three-hundred-dollar bottle of whiskey or something.

The moment he was fully naked, her mouth was on him. She tangled her tongue with his cock. Rolled him around in her warm mouth. Sucked him down her throat. Suddenly he was insanely jealous of every single whiskey she'd ever put in her mouth. Then she pulled off him with a *pop*.

She sat back on her heels, knees slightly apart. Panting, she asked, "Where's your . . . stuff?"

He grinned. Couldn't help it. "My 'stuff' is over here."

On shaking legs he swiveled and dove for the hastily packed gym bag sitting on the far, unused bed. There they were, stuffed into the inner side pocket. Emergency condoms. *Hallelujah.*

As he got one open, he felt her slide up behind him, pressing her front to his back. The chill of her skin was gone, her body now fantastically warm. Right before he was ready to roll on the rubber, she snaked her arms around his waist and took him in hand. Stroked him with impeccable skill. He couldn't move for a while. Couldn't think. Just felt.

Then . . . *enough.*

There was a frenetic switching of places, of him regretfully extricating himself from her sweet-hard strokes and turning his body around. He took her elbow and pivoted her so she faced the brown dresser with the chipped edges and loose handles. She bent forward, placing her hands over those edges, widening her legs just a bit.

He stood there, captivated by the graceful bow of her back, the way her delicate triceps muscles popped out as she held herself up, the perfectly generous swell of her ass tilted up to him and the long, long, *long* stretch of her pale legs.

The condom on, he came forward but did not enter her. Not yet. Instead he covered her with his body, kissed down and then back up her spine, to end with his mouth against her ear.

"I think you're so beautiful," he whispered.

There was no tease in that sentence. No joke. That simple declaration of truth was intense. Thrilling. A promise to her. A promise for more. If she'd let him give it to her.

And then he was inside her. He didn't know if her reaction—the buckle of her spine, the drop of her head, the high moan that streamed out from her throat—was because of his entry, or because of what he said.

She felt . . . God, now was not the time for words. Really. It was time for feeling and moving and experiencing and enjoying. His head went psychedelic, spinning and colorful, as the feel of her body around him—tightening, clenching, taking—obliterated any and all else.

The shock of something cool against his hip forced his eyes open. He looked down to see her reaching behind to grab him. *Move*, demanded the pressure of her hand on his hipbone.

Who was he to disappoint?

He pulled out, not completely, but enough for the slow burn of pleasure to squeeze along his dick. Enough for him to crave going back in. When he thrust again, her hand left his side, swinging around to slam hard into the edge of the dresser. She gripped it, knuckles going white, her ass nudging out even more.

She'd tossed her car keys onto the dresser, and every thrust jerked the big, poorly made piece of furniture. The keys rattled in time to her tiny, feminine grunts. The soundtrack to heaven. Still, heaven wasn't enough. He wanted more.

He'd wanted her for a long time. Since that first glimpse of her last year, right in this town. He realized that all the one-night stands and other flimsy, doomed-from-the-start, half-assed relationships he'd embarked on over the past twelve months had failed because he'd been holding out for her. Waiting for the surprise of her reappearance.

Too much thinking, Byrne. Not enough doing. This woman is finally yours.

It was already fucking fantastic for him, but he wanted to make it even better for her. Claiming her waist with one hand, he reached around with the other and found the hardness of her clit buried in slick softness. The feel of her had him swearing under his laboring breath. He strummed her easy compared to how she seemed to want the sex to go, because she was that kind of woman. One who loved those kinds of contradictions.

One of her hands slapped the top of the dresser again and

again, and he could feel her legs going a little liquid and shaky. He kept going, never relenting. She was getting close, and he was so pleased to be able to read her body like that, on their first time.

Only after she came—loudly, perfectly, with abandon—did he worry that maybe one of his teammates could hear through the walls. And then he didn't really care. He could feel her coming—on his dick and with his hand, where her thighs had clenched around him—the little contractions, the teasing pulses, and he stayed still inside her, just *feeling*.

When she finished, she collapsed to her elbows on top of the dresser, panting. The picture was incredible, this satisfied woman whom he himself had panted over for what felt like forever. He couldn't take the restraint any longer, and just let go. Let himself fuck her as he remembered this entire weekend. Let the memories of their words and touches, glances and experiences, take his physical sensations and crank them up to a level he'd written off as the fodder for romantic movies and story lines in books—impossible things. Like aliens and unicorns.

Like portals to other worlds.

He swore when he came. A grinding, drawn out "Fuuuuck." When he bit off the last of the *k* and he was still pulsing inside her, the rubber not diluting a single damn thing, he was vaguely embarrassed for having spewed out such a porntastic exclamation during orgasm.

Shea turned her head then, her profile as gorgeous as ever, and smiled over her shoulder. No embarrassment was necessary, he realized, because even now, in perhaps the most awkward moment of any kind of sex, he felt perfectly comfortable with her.

They both made sounds of regretful sensation as he pulled out, and it took her a few moments to straighten. When she finally turned around, her skin was no longer pebbled with chill but glowing with a sheen of stunning sweat.

The only way the sex could've possibly been any better was if he could've seen her face. Now, however, he could look at her straight on, and what he saw there stole his words. There it was, written in the perfect circles of her eyes, the O of her lips—the very same intense connection he felt toward her, reflected back at him in her expression.

Then she blinked. Gave a little shake of her head. And he knew what she was doing by pushing it all away. Sometimes, when things got to be too much, it was easier to try to ignore them.

Then, true to her surprising nature, she took his face in her hands and kissed him. When she smiled against his lips, he thought, *That's exactly what I wanted.*

But as she drew back, he didn't know if he'd meant the kiss, the sex . . . or just her.

She glanced over at their random piles of wet clothes. "Don't suppose this is the kind of place that has free bathrobes."

He shook his head. "Can I interest you in a towel the size of a washcloth, though?"

"Tempting."

"I could sew a few of the towels together," he said. "Something chic to wear back to the campground. No one would ever suspect where you'd been or what you just did."

"Or who."

They both laughed. As the sound died, they continued to stare at each other. "Or," he offered, "you could stay with me until they were dry. I did promise you a second—"

"I'm not staying, Byrne." Her brow furrowed as her eyes flicked to the door. "I can't stay."

"Yes, you can."

She gave him a sad, conflicted smile and went over to her clothes.

He had to get rid of the condom, and dashed into the bathroom. Those five seconds in the fluorescent-lit, generically tiled room gave him a momentary sense of panic that she'd slip out without saying anything else. Jesus, was this how it felt when you really, really didn't want to let someone go?

Wrapping one of those washcloth towels around his waist, he went back out into the bedroom to find that she'd pulled on her damp bra and underwear, her skin was goose pimpled again, and she was holding her black pants and grimacing at them like they were vegetables and she was a three-year-old.

The sight of it created a sharp pang in his chest, the meaning of which he couldn't quite figure out. Was it because she was covering up? About to leave? Or was it the uncertainty about what would happen to them after she walked out that door?

What *would* happen? What did he *want* to happen?

She shoved one long leg into the wet pants and shivered exaggeratedly. It was terrifically cute.

He had to try another angle. "You can't sleep outside in a tent in wet clothes."

"I've got dry clothes at the site, a rain tarp over the tent, and a good sleeping bag."

That was his last bullet, and it missed its mark. "Okay." He ventured a little closer.

She had her pants on but not her shirt. She took her time putting it on, her teeth chattering as she buttoned it. When she finished she looked up at him. "I'm sorry, Byrne. I feel like—"

He waved her off. "Don't apologize. No need." Another couple of steps closer. "So, I know that since you're here in Gleann under the Amber Lounge–Shea Montgomery banner you don't want patrons to know about your wild sex night with the mysterious rugby player"—she gave him a wry, amused grin—"and I get that. But what if I said I wanted to see you again? Back in the city. What if I wanted to try to be with you? To figure out a way to fit into your life for longer than a night?"

"Well." Her eyes warmed as she drew a long, slow look over his body, just barely covered in that stupid towel. "As long as you wear that."

It was enough, and it made him smile.

She grabbed her keys from the dresser, undid the chain lock, and threw the deadbolt to the side. The doorknob turned in her hand, and right before she walked out into the rain, she looked directly at him and winked.

It was only after he listened to the whir of her car as it pulled out of the lot did he remember that he still didn't have her phone number.

Chapter

✹

10

They said bad things happened in threes, but that day Byrne chose to change the word "bad" to "good." Two pretty terrific things had already occurred, which made him pumped up and confident that the third was just around the corner.

Early that morning, as he'd been on his way to work, Caroline had called. A Wednesday ring so soon after an off-schedule Friday night phone call. He tried not to let himself read too much into it, but he couldn't help but be on guard.

"To what do I owe this early-morning pleasure, sis?"

"You were right about the ship captain. Badass. Love her."

He laughed. "Told you."

"No, seriously, I think I'm in love. I might leave Paul for her."

He stopped at the corner of Lexington and East 86th, not caring about the press of commuter bodies in the summer heat. "Or you could just leave Paul period," he said. "Ditch the deadbeat. You could leave him for me and the city. I could—"

"Not an option, J.P. Baby K is his, and I have to look after Mom and Dad."

He sighed, biting his tongue. Was worth another shot anyway.

"So I know you're probably walking into your high-rise filled with fancy suits and piles of money as we speak," she said, "but I wanted to call and let you know something."

The Walk sign clicked white and he crossed, heading for

the gum-spotted cement steps leading to the 6 subway that
would take him all the way down to the Financial District.
"Uh-oh."

"No, it's good. At least, I'm choosing to believe it's good."

"Okay."

"Alex came back."

Byrne almost tripped down the stairs. He stumbled and
caught himself on the railing, and a guy hauling a giant guitar
case swore as he had to swerve around Byrne.

"When?" He hopped back out onto the sidewalk so he
wouldn't lose the signal underground.

"Late last night. Pulled into Mom and Dad's, and they let
him in."

Holy shit. Caroline had told him this might happen, but
Byrne never actually *believed* it.

"They let him in." He shook his head, trying to absorb that
doozy. "Has he asked for money yet?"

"No, that's the thing. He's *got* some money. He says he's
been working odd jobs around the Midwest, saving up. The
piece-of-shit car he's driving even has his name on the title."

"Wow."

"But then he said he'd had enough of wandering and just
wanted to come home, to try to make it up to Mom and Dad,
to mend fences and all that stuff. He says he wants to get a job
here in South Carolina and try to, and I quote, pick up the
pieces of his life."

Byrne's suit coat was starting to make him swelter, and he
wriggled out of it, stepping under the awning of a corner
bodega. "And you believe him?"

"You know, I think I do."

"There was a pause before that."

"He looks good, J.P. Well, good for him. Better than when
he last took off."

"Anyone looks better when they're not drunk and beat up
by bookies and angry townies they've hustled."

"Hmmm," she said, and he couldn't tell what kind of *hmmm*
it was.

He swiped at the back of his neck, pulled at his collar.
"Mom and Dad are good with this?"

"They're thrilled he's back. He's out this morning looking for work, and he said he's going to pay them rent until he can get a place of his own. They're actually a little thrilled with the help."

Byrne gritted his teeth. Alex shouldn't be the one helping their parents with rent. Byrne should be building them a house. On the parcel of land he was so desperate to buy.

"I'll call them at lunch. See how they're doing."

"Alex should be back then. You can talk to him."

"All right," he said, but the response was automatic, like most placating things said to his family.

"Go into it with an open mind, J.P. I think you'll be pleasantly surprised."

So at midday Byrne had called home. His mom answered, pretending to be surprised at the contact. After the charade was done and he cycled through his typical check-in questions—"Are you eating well?" "Are you getting fresh air?" "Are you sleeping enough?"—Mom cleared her throat, and he knew what was to come.

"Those books you send your sister make her so happy."

"Good," he said.

"And we, um, we got your check, too."

Here we go.

"We can't cash it," she said.

With his mom on speakerphone, he'd turned to the bank of windows in his office and stared without seeing at the buildings on the other side of the glass. "Can you just deposit it then? Save it for a rainy day?"

"It's too much, J.P." Her voice shook. "And we'll be fine. We've always managed."

"Mom—"

"I told you not to send any more money."

"No, you said you didn't want to see any more checks. I addressed it to Dad."

She'd sighed.

That's when he brought up Alex, because he simply had to. "Caroline said Alex is back."

Mom brightened. "He is. And he looks so good."

Byrne ground fingers into his eyelids. "Can you do me a favor then? Can you make sure the check is voided and ripped up?"

In the awkward pause that followed, he worried his mom

might actually protest. Then she said, "All right," and Byrne guessed that Alex was standing nearby.

"That J.P.?" came Alex's low twang in the background. "Can I talk to him?"

Mom handed the phone to Byrne's lost little brother— gone for five years after gambling away the last bit of money Byrne would ever give him.

"Hey, man." His brother's voice. A stranger's voice. "How are you?"

Byrne made small talk around the erratic beating of his heart and the whirring of his brain as he tried to figure out the reasons behind Alex's sudden reappearance.

"Things are going to be different." Alex's sincerity sounded so very real, his voice not slurred, his thoughts lucid. "I'm ready to change. I'm really ready, J.P."

"You understand," Byrne replied, shuffling through papers on his desk to hand a specific one to his waiting assistant, "that I'm the kind of person who needs more proof than your word."

"I understand. I do." Alex sounded sheepish, humble. "I haven't had a drink in six months. Haven't gambled in eight. I'm a changed man since we last spoke. A determined man. I feel the best I've ever felt. I got a job today, too. Third shift at the cotton mill."

If it weren't for the distinctive accent Byrne remembered so well from their childhood, he might've thought he was talking to an impostor. But it was Alex Byrne, most definitely.

"Good for you," Byrne said.

"Hey, maybe someday soon I'll save up enough money to come visit you. See how you live, what you've made for yourself."

"I'd like that," Byrne said, surprised to realize that he truly would. Maybe, if Alex came to New York, Caroline and his parents would follow. Maybe this was the spark the whole family needed to move forward. It was exhausting, constantly being disappointed in your own brother. Constantly worrying about him and his effect on their parents.

Yet as Byrne hung up with his brother and parents, he found that he wasn't worried. Not for the first time in years.

That was Good Thing Number One.

The second was even better.

He got a return email. At last. After years of unanswered

questions and offers and outright pleas, the landowners in South Carolina had finally gotten back to him.

The single sentence read: *Thank you for your continued interest in one of our properties, Mr. Byrne. We may have some news for you shortly.*

Hot damn. What perfect timing.

Good Thing Number Two.

Now, with just an hour left before midnight, he was standing in his kitchen, drinking a bottle of beer and hoping for the third.

Four days of waiting to contact Shea was okay, he thought. Four days for them to readjust to their individual lives back in New York. Yet every night he sprawled across his big, empty bed, closed his eyes, and pictured Shea's face as she talked about that old farm. He pictured the sun going down behind her as it had that evening, the gold light painting her hair.

Then, with a shiver of sensory recollection, he'd remember the curves and lines of her body, the way it had felt being inside her, and he'd have to get up and jack off in the shower, wishing it was her wetness around him instead.

It had nearly killed him to wait four days, but work had been insane, and that was great for keeping his mind from thinking about her at highly inappropriate times.

He knew today would be the perfect day to contact her, because the stars had aligned. Great things came in threes, he convinced himself, and the first two had come and gone.

Shea had to be three.

On his way home from work that day, he'd taken a chance and called her office at the Amber. Voice mail.

"Hey. It's me," he'd said.

It's me? Already he was saying that? Every guy who'd ever tried to get ahold of her probably said that, so he quickly added, "It's Byrne. Since I know you'd like me to stay away from the Amber right now, I'm hoping that I'm allowed to *call* you at work, since you left me standing there in a towel without your personal number. So with that, I'm going to be all cool and casual and completely non-stalkerish, and ask you what you're doing next week. Maybe Tuesday night? I'd love to catch up."

I can't stop thinking about you.

"Maybe some dinner?"

More sex would be fantastic.

"Anyway, let me know. Here's my number."

That had been three hours ago. It was probably high serving time at the Amber right now, the place filled with people like Bespoke Byrne on a work night, entertaining clients and such. If he heard back from her, it probably wouldn't be until tomorrow, and he'd be in meetings all day.

The phone rang. Dropping the beer bottle from his lips, spilling a little on his favorite Boston College T-shirt, he lunged for his cell phone where it sat on the black soapstone counter next to his open laptop. He didn't recognize the number, though it had a Manhattan area code.

Could it be?

"Hello?"

"Hey."

Good Thing Number Three.

Her voice was friendly, with the perfect amount of emphasis, not too much enthusiasm. Like she'd practiced the single word before dialing his number. That made him smile.

"It's kind of late on a school night," she said, and he could picture her wry expression so vividly. "I took a chance and thought you'd still be up."

"Always up at this hour," he said. "Usually working. When I was just out of grad school, I'd still be at the office now."

"Wow, really?"

He didn't want to talk about that. "I had no other way to reach you. Hope it wasn't a big deal, leaving that message at your office."

"No, but I'm calling you back from my cell."

Translation: *Here's my number, for future reference.*

Good Thing Number Three Point Five.

"I'm saving it," he said.

"I'm still at the office, too," she added.

"At least your job is fun. Interesting."

"You don't love your job?" Genuine surprise.

He considered that, leaning against the counter. "It's not a matter of love or hate. It's what I do. It gets me where I want to be."

"That's a lot of effort, a lot of time and stress, for something you don't love."

"There's a method to my madness."

"Which is?"

Money.

She filled in his silence with a drawn-out, "Ahaaaa. So, let me ask you this: When will it be enough?"

Glancing across the breakfast bar, into the living room, he stared at the green toy train engine on the coffee table and thought about the mysterious email he'd received from South Carolina earlier that day.

"Soon," he said. "I believe soon." He shifted the phone from one ear to the other, suddenly feeling like a teenaged boy calling a girl for the first time, not a grown man who had clear chemistry with the grown woman on the other end.

"For someone with such a wildly successful business," he said, "why are you so mistrusting of money?"

"I have reason," she replied dryly. "Good reason."

It seemed they both had little stories tucked away inside. And that was okay. This thing between them, whatever it was, was new and sparkling clean. No need to rush it or muddy it up. Nothing to do but enjoy it. Speaking of which . . .

"So," he said. "Tuesday. Are you available? Can I see you?"

"I actually have plans that night."

"Oh. Well, maybe—"

"But I was wondering if you'd like to meet me there?"

He started to pace, something he never did, as hopeful adrenaline coursed through him. "Sure."

She chuckled. "You don't even know what it is."

Right. "So what is it? I reserve the right to refuse now if you throw out something like . . . something like polo. Or painting pottery."

She snort-laughed, and it was totally adorable. "Don't worry. Not anything like either of those."

"Are you going to tell me?"

"No, I'll keep you guessing. I'll text you the address at eight on Tuesday night. Can you get there by nine?"

"Is this some sort of dating test?"

"Something like that. I'm seeing if I can do this, go out with someone I met through work. This place is nowhere near the Amber, nowhere near my apartment. It's neutral territory, but it means a lot to me, so yes, I guess it is a test. I'm sorting it all out."

"I'm dying of curiosity now."

"But it's not really a date-date. Bring a friend if you want." She quickly added, "Just not Dan."

Byrne rolled his eyes. "No problem. Not looking to fail your test on the first try, thank you very much."

A group date, then. He was totally fine with that. He just wanted to get to know her better.

"Oh, and you can leave Bespoke Byrne at home, too," she said.

He grinned. "Want me to throw on my cleats and go roll around in the dirt before I show up?"

"Now we're talking."

He put her on speakerphone and scrolled through his appointment calendar. "You know, I may not have a choice. I'll be coming straight from the office that night, so I'm afraid a suit and tie is what it'll be. Would've been perfect for a proper date."

"Who says what's a 'proper date' or not, Byrne? You and I have hardly been proper so far."

Mischief, that's what this woman was up to. He could hear it in her voice. He loved it. Wanted more.

There was something profoundly comforting about having her on the other end of the line, even when several moments came and went without either of them saying anything. They inhaled at the same time, as if to speak, and then exhaled at the same time, too. God, he loved her laugh.

Byrne crossed his legs at the ankle and relaxed against the counter. Damn smile wouldn't go away.

"Byrne." Her voice was sunset warm. "I'm really glad you called."

A memory came to him. The sight of her face, lips parted, eyes dreamy, just before he kissed her.

"I'm really glad you called me back," he replied.

"See you Tuesday, then." So hushed, so lovely.

"Bye." His own voice was barely more than a breath itself.

And for a guy who spent eighty percent of his day either on the phone or talking, talking, talking, he found he did not want to hang up with her. He could've kept talking to her until daylight.

Now how about that.

* * *

*F*or the next six days, Byrne filled his mind with images and memories and fantasies of Shea. The odd thing was, they weren't all sexual. So many of them involved only words.

By the following Tuesday, Byrne had pretty much reached the end of his patience rope. But it was the best kind of expectation, the best kind of anticipation.

The day had been nonstop, without time even for a proper lunch, so by the time he stepped out of the cab at the Upper West Side address Shea had texted him forty-five minutes earlier, he was more than ready for his "not really a date" date. The suit felt like chain mail, and he wanted nothing more than to strip it off and throw on some jeans, but if he'd gone home first to change, he'd have been late. And Shea had requested nine p.m. sharp.

He checked and double-checked the address on his phone against the one on the building in front of him. And groaned.

The place was an old movie theater, a semicircular marquee extending over the sidewalk. A mannequin wearing a hazmat suit sat inside the foggy-windowed ticket booth. The black block letters on the marquee spelled out: "Karaoke. Every Tues."

The people heading into the bar—or was it a club? A nuclear waste site?—were hipsters to the nth degree, at least ten to fifteen years younger than he and dressed about twenty years older.

The cab pulled away from the curb, and he was half tempted to call it back.

Karaoke. Wow.

Not three seconds later, Erik pulled up in his own cab after having taken some Canadian guys out to dinner. His phone was pressed to his ear as he got out, but it dropped from his face as he looked up at the marquee.

He abruptly cut off his conversation by saying something in German. Then, to Byrne, "No fucking way."

Erik swiveled around as if to leave and Byrne grabbed his arm. "Come on. I think she brought a friend. Might be fun."

"I'm not singing."

Byrne pressed a hand to his chest. "Hell no. Neither am I."

Erik loosened his tie. "What if that's what she wants in order to sleep with you again?"

"In that case, you just might get the most spectacular version of 'I Will Survive' you've ever heard in your life."

Erik laughed. "Let's get the hell inside, then."

A five-dollar cover, paid to a girl who was dressed like a seventies-era movie star. She didn't look at them as she checked their suit coats, her gum snapping.

A short hallway led them to an open space with a vaulted ceiling painted with chipped murals of vineyards. The old theater seats had been mostly removed, except for a nostalgic row along the very back. Byrne stopped there, scoping out the scene, looking for Shea. The slanted floor had been reconstructed into crescent-moon-shaped levels, dotted with high tables and delicate chairs on spindly legs. The bar curved around the right side, with padded booths forming a VIP section on the left.

There was a guy onstage, microphone in hand, singing something by the Beatles . . . and he was *good*. Really, really good. Byrne knew only enough about the Beatles to discern their sound and a few songs, but this man, who was about as unassuming as the person who got you coffee every day but whom you would never recognize on the street, was owning the song. His body moved all over the stage, and his voice filled the auditorium. He played to the crowd, but not in that cheesy, reality-show way.

Every table was filled, and each person watched the singer with rapt attention and clear appreciation. This was no two a.m. drunken karaoke night.

"Didn't scare you off then."

Her.

Byrne turned, and he was glad a drink ledge was right in front of him to grab on to, because the sight of her almost knocked him over.

A dress. Shea Montgomery was wearing a dress. It was black. And small. The thing only went to her midthigh and, damn, her legs were incredible—so pale against the dark dress, and too strong and long to be real. Big, shiny jewelry decorated her wrists and neck, and she'd done something to her hair to make it a little curly and crazy. The heels on her sparkly shoes made her as tall as he, and he found that he really liked that.

As he stepped closer, he shoved his hands into his pockets because suddenly he felt like she was a priceless painting that he shouldn't touch. Even though he desperately wanted to.

"You look," he said, "incredible."

"Thank you." Her nod was the same brief, professional one he'd seen her give her tasters and customers, but the smile was all genuine. All for him. "So do you."

"Even in the tie?"

She let out an overly dramatic sigh. "I suppose it will do."

Erik cleared his throat and Byrne was jostled out of his staring. "Oh. Sorry. Shea, this is Erik."

Shea was the first to hold out her hand. "Saw you in Gleann. Nice to put a name with a face."

"Nice to have a name," Erik said with a smile. "Great to meet someone who makes Byrne here leave the office at a decent hour."

A ten-dollar bill waved in front of Shea's face, and Byrne blinked at the short brunette who was holding it. Her smile dug two dimples in her cheeks.

"I bet her," the brunette said to Byrne, "that once you saw it was karaoke, she'd get a text saying you had to cancel."

Shea snatched the ten and slipped it into her tiny handheld purse. Her eyes twinkled as she glanced at Byrne.

"Thanks for the vote of confidence," he told her.

Shea shrugged. "It was more hope than anything."

Fantastic. The night was incredible already.

"This is Willa," Shea said, dragging the brunette closer to her side.

Willa saluted the men with two fingers. She was voluptuous and heavily painted with makeup, and kind of fascinating to look at. She was dressed like she'd stepped out of a nineteen-forties war movie, with big rolls in her hair.

"Hello, I'm Erik." Erik thrust out his hand to Willa. "Your conversation partner for the evening."

"Oh, hey, wingman!" Willa shook Erik's hand vigorously. "I'm the wingwoman. We need call signs or something."

"I'll be the German Gigolo."

Willa raised her empty drink glass. "Excellent. I'm Wonder Tits. We're going to be very happy together."

Erik burst out laughing, and Byrne knew his friend had met his match. "You look dry. How about I buy the first round?"

"Absolutely."

They peeled off, arm in arm, and Shea watched them go, saying, "Well, at least we know how their night is going to end."

Byrne was entranced by the gloss on Shea's lips. "I should warn you that Erik is the biggest flirt on two continents."

Shea laughed. "Willa hasn't been into anything more than casual sex for over a decade. I should probably warn Erik about her instead."

Byrne grinned.

Shea met his eyes, and hers did that thing where they seemed to glow, like they'd done when she'd been kneeling in front of him, taking off his pants.

The way she bit the inside of her cheek to repress a smile was both adorable and wonderfully hot. "Hope you don't mind the friend thing. Thought we both might need an escape route, if need be. You're not offended by that, are you?"

"Not at all."

"Good. Because this is where Willa and I come every Tuesday, and I couldn't cancel on account of a *boy*."

She pivoted to head for the bar, and even though he'd seen her naked, had spent most of their time naked staring at her ass from behind, he couldn't help but stare at it again.

A tiny black dress was far, far more preferable to boring black pants.

"What are you drinking?" she asked over her shoulder as she rested her hands on the edge of the bar.

"Beer. That one." He pointed to a tap capped with a giant anchor. "Can I buy?"

"I asked you here. Let me."

Onstage, the guy singer finished on an incredible note, the music ending on a strong guitar chord. The whole place erupted in applause and whistles. He caught a towel thrown to him and wiped off his forehead, then left the stage.

"For the record, I asked you out first," he said. "Up in Gleann and also back here in New York."

"Potato, potahto. Just let me buy the first round, Byrne."

"Here you go, Shea." The bartender pushed Byrne's lager and Shea's drink over to them. "You lose Willa already?"

Shea laughed. "This is Byrne. We're not on a date."

"That's right," Byrne said. "I'm still just in test-drive mode."

The bartender volleyed a look between them, not quite getting it. "Okay."

As Shea guided them back to the drink ledge, she said, "I've never brought someone who wasn't Willa here before."

Byrne wouldn't be a true guy if that didn't make him stand a little taller, didn't make him want to grab that microphone and growl out some sort of prehistoric sound of satisfaction.

"Vodka?" Byrne guessed, pointing to her tall glass filled with clear liquid and a bunch of sparkling ice.

Her lips fastened around the straw. How she could sip and smile and look like she wanted to devour him all at once, he didn't know. And he didn't really care.

"Water," she said. "I'll want a dirty martini after."

He took a drink of his beer. "After what?"

"Next up onstage," came the drawn-out boom of an unseen announcer, "Shea."

A new smattering of applause.

Byrne almost choked. "You *sing*?"

"Don't sound so shocked! Or I'll make you get up there, too."

The beer sputtered in his mouth, and he had to lean forward so it wouldn't dribble down his shirt. "No." He dabbed at his chin with a napkin. "No, I'm not singing. At all. And I'm not bad-shocked, I'm good-shocked."

She fiddled with her straw. "Good. Because I'm a little nervous myself."

"So why do you do it then? You don't have to—"

"Oh, but I do. I'm always nervous before I go up, but I know how awesome I'm going to feel after, and it makes it all worth it. Kind of like rugby."

He nodded, completely transfixed.

She pointed over his shoulder. "Why don't you go stand by Willa and Erik? You don't even have to watch."

"Why on earth wouldn't I watch?"

Was it even possible to look away from this woman?

She looked honestly perplexed. "Well, I'm not doing this for you," she said, and then handed him her water. She skirted around the back part of the crescent-shaped auditorium, heading for the wood stairs on the right side of the stage.

Byrne didn't go up to Willa and Erik, because he simply could not get his feet to move. They came to him, standing on either side.

"She's really glad you came," Willa said, "even if she doesn't come out and tell you."

Shea reached the top of the stairs and met a wiry man who smiled genially as he handed Shea the microphone. They talked for a few seconds, Shea gesturing and the man nodding, and then he disappeared.

Shea walked to center stage and said into the mike, "This is called 'The Last Day of Our Acquaintance.'"

The music started, a sole acoustic guitar making quiet, slow, melancholy strums.

"Can she sing?" Erik stage-whispered to Willa, as though Byrne couldn't hear.

Willa shushed him.

When Shea opened her mouth, out came this throaty voice that had Byrne tightening the grip on his beer glass so hard he thought it might shatter.

She sang with the microphone set on the stand, her torso loose and flowing, accenting the words in perfect time.

She didn't make eye contact with the audience, but sang to some unseen ex-lover far past the heads of everyone who watched and listened. The song built and built, her tone controlled and sad in the beginning, but then as the emotion grew, the lyrics echoing frustration and loss and heartbreak, she just . . . let it loose.

That voice. That *voice*.

He thought about all that she'd revealed to him up in Gleann about her dreams of the distillery. At the time he thought he'd learned so much about her, but she'd still held back. He'd just cracked the surface with her, and it was like he was a treasure hunter who'd broken down a wall to find a vast cavern filled with jewels beyond.

To see her up onstage—that presence, that clear passion— dear God, he didn't know if he'd seen anything like it.

She loosened up as the song went on, the release coursing through her body and voice, just like she'd said it would.

By the time the song finished and she was gripping the microphone stand in both hands, her legs braced apart, the power of the finality of her voice ringing through the club, Byrne knew it. Was absolutely sure of it.

This was not mere attraction. It was complete and total infatuation.

Chapter

✦

11

The trance ended the second Shea bit off the final sound of the final word of her favorite song. She walked offstage dimly aware that the room was enthusiastically applauding, but it was the buzz in her mind that fed her the most joyous sound. She came off the last step onto the main floor, feeling rubber-legged, weightless, and deliriously happy.

Everything from that week—the late shipment from Juniper Imports, the canceled interview that had completely messed up her schedule, the contact from her "silent" partner Douglas Lynch badgering her about profits at the Amber and future strategies she didn't quite agree with, and nervousness over seeing Byrne again—dissipated from her soul.

She wove through the maze of cocktail tables. Byrne still stood at the back of the auditorium. He looked almost as dazed as she felt.

Willa snagged her before she reached him, however.

"Thought you should know," Willa said, "that he didn't stop staring at you the whole time. He didn't drink, didn't talk, didn't do anything. Just watched. I wiped drool from his chin when you were done."

Over her shorter friend's head, Shea caught Byrne's eye. One side of his mouth ticked up, as though he'd heard what Willa had just told her.

"Excellent job, by the way," Willa added. "You practice that one in the shower?"

Shea tore her gaze from Byrne. "In the kitchen, actually. Better acoustics. You sticking with the usual?"

Willa peered out over the tables set with their singular little lamps and the irregular polka dots of various drinks. She shrugged. "Of course. It's my thing."

"Next up onstage," cried the wizardly announcer from behind the curtain, "Willa!"

Willa's "thing" was wartime melodies. Old tunes backed by big brass and tinny drums that fit her high, slightly nasal vibrato perfectly. Shea pinched Willa's butt as her friend waltzed off toward the stage steps.

Shea finally went up to the guys. She'd forgotten Erik was there, too.

"Great job," Erik said.

Shea nodded. "Thanks."

Byrne just kept grinning.

"So, um." Erik rattled the ice cubes in the bottom of his glass. "Yeah." He ducked away and bellied up to the bar.

Byrne bit his lower lip. "Remember what I said in your car, about you surprising me?"

"Sure."

"Well, that was nothing. Holy shit, Shea. Had no idea you could sing. I mean—holy shit."

"Stop. You're going to give me a complex."

He gestured to the stage. "Not that I'm an expert or anything, but you could do that professionally."

"Don't want to."

"But you're amazing."

"If I wanted to do it professionally, I would. But I don't want it to be something I'm paid for. It's more than that to me, if that makes sense."

He nodded slowly. "You know, I think I do. Sometimes I want more when it comes to rugby, but I wouldn't want to do it professionally. To have that kind of pressure would take away the joy part."

"Exactly."

"Who sings that song?" he asked.

"Sinéad O'Connor. Probably my most favorite female voice ever."

He crossed his arms and raised an eyebrow at the same time. "An Irish singer? Will they revoke your Scottish heritage for that?"

"Oh hush."

"It's a sad song." He cocked his head, eyes warming. "A gorgeous song."

"I think so, too. I love the way it builds, the emotion in it."

"Should I be worried that you sang a song about the end of a relationship on our first not-a-date?"

"Not remotely."

He stared at her for a second. Or five.

"Here." He nudged a dirty martini toward her. "You earned this."

"Oooh thank you." She took out the swizzle stick and plucked a big olive off the end with her lips. Byrne watched her intently.

Onstage, Willa was joking back and forth with one of the audience members. If they had the Willa Show here every night, the place would clean up.

"How do you and Willa know each other?" Byrne asked.

"We used to wait tables together, way back when. When she learned I loved to sing, she brought me here and we've become regulars. It's an escape for both of us, but for different reasons."

"Makes sense. You're different people."

"She's a freelance graphic designer now. Insanely talented."

"And you're Shea Montgomery, whiskey expert extraordinaire." He sipped his beer.

"Shh." Shea put a finger to her lips. "I want to watch her."

Willa brought down the house, as expected, her schtick hitting this crowd right between the eyes. With her beautifully curled hair and bright red lips and subtle hip shaking, matched to the upbeat song, there wasn't a single person in the bar who wasn't tapping a foot.

"Wow," Byrne said over the raucous applause as Willa finished. "You have to try out or something to be able to sing here?"

"Kind of. You have to send in a tape to the owner for vocal

approval, and you have to submit your songs beforehand. It's not for drunks or bachelorette parties or anything."

"So what you're saying is that if I got up there and opened this hideous mouth, I'd be run out?"

"Probably with a pitchfork in your ass, yes." She took a sip of her martini. "And I wouldn't call your mouth hideous at all."

Willa came off the stage, negotiating the steps sideways in her tight, unforgiving skirt, and then crossed the floor. Erik intercepted her and gave her a stinging high five. Shea and Byrne bowed repeatedly, arms raised, as she came up. Willa was laughing so hard she dabbed at the mascara beneath her eyes.

And then her laughter died. Just fell off her face like melted makeup.

"What?" Shea asked.

Willa's wide, unblinking eyes darted to the left, over Shea's shoulder. And then again.

Confused, Shea turned and—*oh shit.*

Seriously? Not again. Not tonight. Not *here.*

There was Marco, descending upon one of the curved VIP tables in the back row. He was touching the back of a puss-faced girl with a sleek brown bob. Had to be ten years younger than Shea, which didn't surprise her at all. The way they interacted clearly said they had some history.

Seemed like the girl who Marco had said was "coming back" actually had.

"What is it?" Byrne beside her, his voice low near her ear.

How the hell had *Marco* ever heard of a place like this? Wasn't it far beneath him?

Onstage a very large man with a very large voice started in on a Pavarotti. Any other night Shea would've appreciated it, but right now everything sounded sour.

Marco gestured for the bobbed girl to slide into the booth and, with two fingers, turned to summon a waitress. He found Shea instead and did a double take. Then he did that thing where he moved his head on his neck like he was cracking it, going in for a boxing match.

Byrne stood close to Shea and followed her line of sight. "Him?" he asked.

"Yeah." Shea sighed and took a giant gulp of martini that burned down her throat. "Him."

Marco leaned down to say something to his date, who immediately swiveled and caught Shea in a laser-beam stare. One hand tipped in bright pink nails folded into a fist on top of the table. Her eyes narrowed, and then Shea couldn't see her anymore because Marco blocked the way as he weaved his way toward Shea.

"Want me to take him down?" Willa made a karate chop move.

Shea snorted. "Nah, I'm good." And really, she was. "Erik, would you mind taking Bruce Lee here for a drink refresh?"

Willa gave her arm a comforting squeeze, then disappeared with Erik.

Byrne stayed right at Shea's side.

Marco reached them. "Hi, Shea." Some of his tan had faded, but he still looked so *fake* compared to Byrne. Even his laugh sounded manufactured as he let it loose, shaking his head. "Twice in one summer. What are the chances?"

"Pretty slim."

"What are you doing here?" Unlike at the Long Island Highland Games, he seemed honestly shocked to see her.

Shea glanced at the stage.

Marco's head snapped back on his neck. "Really? You sing?"

"Really." She'd never sung for him. It had always been something she'd done in secret, only for herself. Even when they'd been married, she'd always felt that he'd never understand how it fed her. And he'd never really been all that interested in knowing what made her tick.

That should have been a big fucking clue they were doomed from the start, but at that age she'd never been big on anything but fairy tales.

Marco said, "We came here—that's Sabine over there—because we heard the singers were always great."

And Shea could never, ever come here again. Her weekly release, her unadulterated joy, gone. Bastard.

Beside her, Byrne stuck out his hand. "How's it going? I'm Byrne."

"Sorry," Shea said. "Byrne, this is Marco."

Marco blinked at Byrne, as though finally realizing she'd been standing there with a man. He shook Byrne's hand, and in that space he put two and two together, his gaze flicking back and forth between them. Shea didn't feel like making any sort of explanation aside from introductions. She didn't know what she'd say anyway—she had no idea what she and Byrne were, couldn't put a label on it.

A not-a-first-date, but they'd already fucked. They'd already fucked, but they'd laughed first, in the way you would on a great first date. It was all so very convoluted, standing there with her ex-husband looking on.

"You seem familiar," Byrne said. "You're not Marco Todaro, are you?"

Marco puffed up, as was expected. "I am."

Byrne turned a little white, which was completely not expected. He recovered quickly, but casual, friendly Byrne disappeared in a short second, replaced by a stiff, awkward impostor.

"You in real estate?" Marco asked Byrne. "I'm developing the new building on East 47th. Biggest deal in that area since 2008."

Of course he wasn't going to miss an opportunity to spout off about his properties, especially if it involved mentioning tons of money. Shea didn't bother to resist the roll of her eyes.

"No, not in real estate." Byrne replied, throwing back his shoulders. "I'm with Weatherly and McTavish."

"No shit." Marco raised both eyebrows. "As?"

"Private banker."

"Oh, really." Marco looked smugly at Shea then, and she knew what he was assuming: that she'd gone from one big-money guy to another, while shouting to the heavens that she'd never do such a thing.

"Then you must know Ren Aaldenberg," Marco said.

Now Byrne looked really disturbed. It probably went right over Marco's head because Byrne was doing an excellent job of smiling to cover it up, but Shea knew well enough now when Byrne was smiling for real . . . or when Bespoke Byrne was doing it for him.

"I do," Byrne said. Though his mouth grinned widely, his eyes were tight and flat.

Then Marco responded with his own insincere smile, the one that made her skin itch. "How funny. We're meeting Ren and his woman here tonight."

His woman. Ugh.

Byrne looked over to Erik then, but Erik was telling Willa some story, making her laugh. Byrne shifted on his feet and crossed his arms, his fingers tapping impatiently. Shea wondered if she should go over to grab Erik, but then the thought of leaving Byrne and Marco alone together was nauseating.

"I'll be sure to look for you next time I'm in your office," Marco said to Byrne.

"Do that." Byrne's reply was smooth enough, but he took a long drink of beer directly after, and Shea distinctly felt that some sort of guy challenge had been issued, in some sort of nonverbal man code.

Marco tossed another look back and forth between Shea and Byrne. "First date?" he asked bluntly.

Oh, for fuck's sake. *Leave, you jerk.*

Then she realized: she'd walked away from him before. She could do it again now.

Reaching out, she laced her fingers through Byrne's, making him jump. "Not exactly," she purred to Marco, then smiled up at Byrne in a way that couldn't be mistaken for anything other than *Yes, we've already fucked and we're about to do it again.*

It had the exact effect she desired. Marco's whole body went tense, the slimy confidence wiped from his face.

She should have known, however, that he wouldn't just throw up a flag and admit defeat.

"Don't make too much money, Byrne," Marco snapped. "And watch her with your friends."

In her hand, Byrne's grip slackened.

Shea's stomach dropped, but the hole was quickly filled in with anger.

Marco gave them a dismissive, cold nod, not even looking them in the eye, and said, "Have a great night."

He left. Went back to Sabine.

Shea started shaking. She tried to extricate her hand from Byrne's but he held on, shockingly, and gently tugged her around to face him. She didn't want to know what her face looked like, all scowling and twisted. She was having a hard time keeping her breath under control, a very old fury having resurfaced.

"Hey," Byrne said, giving her fingers a squeeze. "You okay?"

"That was my ex."

"Yeah, I kind of got that." His gaze slid over her shoulder, in the direction Marco had gone, but came immediately back.

"I didn't fuck his friend when we were together. He made it sound like that, but I didn't."

Byrne gave her a small smile. It was a flicker of the Byrne she knew—the one she liked. "Okay. Doesn't matter, but okay."

"Jesus, why does he always have to—"

He leaned closer. "Can we get out of here? Let's go somewhere else you love."

Looking deep into his eyes, she saw that he was still disturbed by something, but that it didn't seem to have to do with Marco.

"That sounds fantastic," she agreed. "Let me grab the other two."

Byrne turned to watch the door, and Shea realized the whole thing had to do with that Ren guy Marco mentioned. Marco knew someone at Byrne's company? What were the awful, icky chances of that?

At the bar, Willa threw back a good amount of vodka in shotlike form. Erik said, "A woman after my own heart."

"We're changing venues," Shea told them, dragging them back to Byrne.

"Where to?" Willa asked when they were all together.

"How about that terrible corner pub in Hell's Kitchen? The first karaoke place we tried years ago."

"Sounds lovely," Erik said.

"Do they have beer?" Byrne asked, already stepping backward toward the door.

"Absolutely," Shea said. "And not even the good kind. I'm talking light beer. Colored water. In pitchers."

Byrne circled a finger in the air impatiently. "Let's go. It's calling my name."

He led the procession toward the door, then stopped so suddenly Shea ran into his back. She struck a solid wall of muscle, clad in an exquisitely fine suit.

"What is it?" She took her time peeling away, enjoying too much the feel of him.

"*Shhhhhit.*" He turned his face to the side, grimacing, then jutted a thumb toward Marco's table where a man of his similar age and a woman who was close to Sabine's were just arriving.

Erik pushed next to Byrne. "Fuck, is that—"

"Yeah." Byrne did not sound happy. At all.

Just then, Marco pointed over at them, and the newly arrived man—Ren Aaldenberg, presumably—raised a hand. Beckoned them over.

"Way to ruin a perfectly good night." Erik sighed.

Willa asked, "Who is that with Marco the Asshole?"

Byrne met Shea's eyes as he said, "Our boss. I tried to get us out of here in time, Erik."

"How does he know Marco?" Willa pressed.

"He's got Marco's portfolio."

This was not happening. Way too many wires crossing tonight, too many connections Shea found far too thin and shaky to try to balance.

Byrne plastered on his best Bespoke veneer and turned to give the quintessential guy nod to his boss, the kind that was all chin and machismo. Then he said to Shea out of the corner of his strained smile, "I won't make you go over, but we have to have a drink. I'm so sorry. I tried to escape."

Erik was already on his way over, all teeth and open arms.

"Do what you have to do," she told Byrne. "It's work. I understand."

He scratched at his chin. "I do have to. He saw me, their table is on the way out, he's my boss, Erik's already over there . . . *Fuck*. I don't want to. Tonight was supposed to be no work, all about you."

"It's fine." She touched his arm. "Really."

"Come on." Willa took her elbow. "Let's wait by the door."

"All right."

Byrne touched Shea's waist as she walked past. No, not touched. *Took.* Slid his arm around her lower back until his hand grabbed her hip in a way that distinctly reminded her of how he'd worked behind her in that Gleann motel.

"A few minutes. Ten tops," his lips promised, while his eyes promised something else entirely.

She smiled in return, then avoided Marco's table as she walked out to the lobby, Willa in tow.

But then ten minutes turned to twenty, and twenty turned to thirty, and the little buzz she'd gotten from her dirty martini was slowly ebbing, and her craving for light beer was only getting worse.

"What's the holdup?" Willa snarled as she tapped something out on her phone. "Want me to go find out?"

"No, I'll go."

Shea had to fight the crowd as she made her way back into the auditorium. Bodies pressed around the table Marco and Ren had commandeered. Erik and Byrne were smashed into the back of the booth listening to Ren talk, who was red-faced and using gestures worthy of opera.

Someone—probably Marco—had gotten bottle service, and the half-empty bottle of vodka sat in the center of the table. The party wouldn't be going anywhere for a while, especially if Marco was intent on using Ren to keep Byrne from hooking up with Shea that night.

For a moment it looked like Byrne was trying to sidle out of the booth, but then Ren clamped a hand on his shoulder and pressed him back down. Bespoke Byrne let out a short burst of forced laughter. Shea turned away.

She took out her phone and texted him the address of the Hell's Kitchen karaoke bar.

Dying here, Byrne texted back. *Meet you there ASAP.*

"No guys?" Willa asked as Shea returned to the lobby.

"Doesn't seem like it."

"You okay with that?"

"Sure." Shea shrugged. "It's not like it's a date or anything. He got trapped. It's happened to all of us. Let's go. He'll meet us there."

She ignored Willa's sympathetic expression as they went out to the street and hailed a cab.

She hoped Byrne could extricate himself soon and they could turn their not-a-date into something more. She hoped and hoped and hoped.

But at midnight, after she and Willa had drunk their share of a terrible beer pitcher and sang all the good songs in the terrible bar's terrible karaoke catalog, Byrne still hadn't shown up.

Chapter

✴

12

*S*hea was sitting on a bench in Washington Square Park, picking at a takeout Cobb salad, when her phone rang. The sound and vibration jolted her out of a daydream so deep she might have actually been asleep. The plastic fork flew from her hand and landed in a pile of what she guessed to be dog hair.

"Hello," she snapped into the phone, not looking at the number calling but instead sneering at the befouled, only means with which to eat her lunch.

"Ah, shit." Byrne sighed. "I deserve that."

His voice sounded like his throat had been stuffed with hot coals. It unnerved her how attractive she found that.

"No, no. The phone surprised me and now my fork is lying in what I think is the remnants of a Bernese mountain dog."

He laughed. "What?"

"Never mind."

He took a deep breath. "Shea, I'm sorry about last night. I really am."

Setting aside the plastic salad container, she leaned into the bench and let the dappled sun coming through the trees flicker across her upturned face. "You don't owe me an apology. It wasn't a date. You ran into your boss."

"But I told you; I didn't *want* to be with him. Not after

work hours, not when I hadn't prepared to be *that guy*. That bespoke guy you talked about before. And I definitely didn't want to be with *Marco*. What a fucker. I can say that, right?"

A tingle spread through her. "Yes, absolutely. Did he talk your ear off?"

"Didn't talk to me at all. Talked around me. But stared at me."

"I know that look. What did you do?"

"I stared back."

"Good boy."

"Shea." Another sigh, her name sounding like a ragged breath that reminded her all too well of how he'd sounded when he'd been inside her. "I wanted to be with you last night. A lot. I wanted to drink bad beer and laugh some more. I wanted to talk, have a great time."

"Huh. And I was just looking for sex."

"God, you're incredible." He cut himself off. "By the time my boss had gotten so wasted and his girlfriend—or mistress, or whatever they're calling those things these days—had to carry his ass out, it was almost one a.m. It was like the worst fucking movie that wouldn't end and I couldn't leave the theater. I wanted to meet you, but it was late and I wasn't sure if you'd still be out or up or—"

"You sound like you had a rough one."

"Feeling like it, too. I'm almost too old for this."

She crossed her legs, considering how to respond. "Willa and I had a good time. You missed out."

"I should've called or texted or something. I feel like shit for doing that to you."

"You're calling now, aren't you?"

"I am. And I'm sorry."

Secretly, she was ecstatic he was apologizing. She was thrilled to hear the regret in his voice, the honesty in his feelings.

"When can I see you again?" he asked. "Just you and me. Or do I need to go through another test?"

"You don't." She smiled, having to look into her lap because the sun on her face suddenly got too bright. "You passed loooong before Marco popped in."

"So good to know. I'm yours, you know, for whatever kind of date you have in mind. You could take me to a bagpipe convention if you wanted and I wouldn't put up any kind of fight."

"Wellllll . . ."

"I was kidding."

"There's this thing next month that the Scottish Society puts on, their big formal ball. I've volunteered to do the whisky tasting during the cocktail hour, but afterward there'll be dinner and music. They cut a haggis, and everyone is in formal Highland dress."

Absolutely no sound filled the pause that followed. "What exactly is 'formal Highland dress'?"

"A really smart kilt on the bottom, black tie up top. It's very elegant, very sexy on a man. I love it."

Another few seconds passed before he cleared his throat. "Okay. If that's what you want. I gave you my word."

She burst out laughing, could barely speak. "I'm kidding. Clearly it's not your thing. I wouldn't do that to you."

"Oh." Now he was laughing, but in more of a thank-God way than a ha-ha way. "So what's your schedule look like this week?"

She didn't have to glance at her phone to know. "Tonight, a big private event at Amber. Tomorrow I'm headed out of town. Be back Monday."

"Someplace fun, I hope?"

The slight note of disappointment in his voice wasn't supposed to give her a little flutter of delight, but it did.

"Should be fun, yes. I'm visiting my parents. Sort of an annual tradition, this weekend. I'm looking forward to seeing them, spending a couple of days hanging out. Should be nice and quiet. You?"

"I was hoping you'd be available, because George is dragging the team to yet another bagpipe fest over the weekend. I don't know if I'll go. I may just stay in the city."

Shea sat up, the Cobb salad sliding off the bench to join her fork in the dog hair. "Not the Highland Games near Philadelphia."

Another big pause. "Yeah. Why?"

"Because that's where I'll be. I grew up outside the city. The Montgomerys never miss those games. We have our own tent and everything. Granddad would turn over in his grave if we didn't show. I won't be working or anything, just watching and seeing family, but I'll be there."

"Well now." She adored the throaty, hoarse quality to his chuckle, the way she could picture that freakishly handsome smile cocking to one side. "Suddenly I have the urge to be surrounded by bagpipes."

*M*anhattan Rugby didn't have a chance in hell of winning this match—and the Philadelphia team they were playing now wouldn't ever let them live it down—but Byrne ran, ball clutched tight to his body, as though there was still a possibility.

The warm wind pushed past him. No, he pushed past it. His legs were on fire. All sorts of new bruises and strains that should have slowed him down only made him feel more alive. He wove around the Philadelphia players decked out in green, thinking he had a clear shot to make a try, but then he got taken out. Tackled from the left side. His knees hit the ground and he released the ball.

Erik snatched it up, leaped over the top of Byrne's body, and rolled in for the five-point try.

The final whistle blew, and the Philadelphia team whooped up their win. Erik came over to help Byrne up.

"Wish that would've been for the win," Erik said, breathing hard. "You don't care, do you?"

Byrne lifted up his shirt to wipe his face. "Nah. Felt amazing. Good and hot, too, just the way I like it."

"That wouldn't have anything to do with your audience, would it?"

Byrne didn't have to turn in the direction Erik indicated to know who was standing on the sidelines, but he did anyway because he loved the way Shea looked that afternoon. He loved that she'd come to watch; it made him play that much better.

He grabbed a water bottle and headed across the grass.

She was wearing this long blue dress that fit tight across her chest and waist and skimmed her ass so well he wondered if she could wear underwear with it. They didn't manage to connect last night. He'd arrived late with the team, and she was busy with extended family. But now . . . now she was all his.

"Did I just see you lick your lips?" he teased as he went up to her.

"No."

He shrugged exaggeratedly. "I'm pretty disgusting right now, so I thought you and Rugby Byrne could—"

With a roll of her eyes she peeled away, but not before he caught the twinge of a smile. He laughed and jogged to catch up with her. She let him catch her quite easily, which was good because his quads were just about done.

"How'd I do this game, coach?" he asked.

She shaded her eyes from the sun. "You know very well how you did. For the millionth time, you should find a better team."

Behind him, the official's whistle chirps called the next two teams to take the pitch. The new teams were going through their chants and songs, voices rising, pumping themselves up. In the distance another pipe band started to play, the punch of the drums filtering over to them.

"I'm really glad we're both here this weekend," he said. "Away from the city."

"Me, too. It's my last games of the summer, and I'm a little sad. I've got that black-tie ball back in the city next month, but it's not the same." She scanned the grounds and breathed deeply. "Want to walk around?"

"If you're not embarrassed to be seen with me before a shower."

"Not one bit."

They meandered around the Highland Games, which were larger than Gleann's and much more fun and laid-back than Long Island's. They stopped by the heavy athletic field, where Shea described the hammer toss and the caber toss and scads of other throwing events. Byrne had never known the rules, so he hadn't appreciated the strength and skill involved, but as he watched the athletes now, he was greatly impressed.

They watched black-and-white border collies corral sheep, and Byrne noticed Shea's trancelike smile. He recalled what she'd told him once about wanting to see a dog on that farm up north.

Moving back toward the rugby field, there was a long alley of smaller tents dedicated to various Scottish clans. They were draped with flags and banners, their tables laden with big books where you could look up your heritage.

"Didn't you say your family had a tent here?" he asked.

"Yeah, down at the end. My dad'll sit there all day, but my mom—"

"Is right here, honey."

An older woman with Shea's coloring but not her height, wearing a shapeless dress and huge straw hat, was coming toward them from the direction of the rugby field.

"Oh," Shea said. "Hi. Mom."

Shea Montgomery, the woman who could throw a wasted Dan out of her bar with a stern look and a few carefully placed words, was now tossing awkward glances between him and her mother.

"You said you'd be watching rugby," her mother said, "and I wanted to come find you to tell you I'm getting a ride home from Ingrid now so I can start dinner."

"You could've just texted me," Shea said.

Her mom waved an elegant hand. "The walk around was nice. Never watched the rugby before. It's very violent, isn't it?"

Byrne took his cue. "It can be. Hi, I'm Byrne." He stuck out his hand, hoping it wasn't too dirty. "I'm only violent on the field." He smiled.

"I'm Peg. Shea's mother." When Peg smiled in return, he saw where Shea's came from.

Shea pressed fingertips to her forehead. "Right. Sorry, Mom. This is Byrne. He plays rugby."

Byrne laughed. "Yes, ma'am. I do. I'm also friends with your daughter."

Recalling what she'd said about having conservative parents, he hoped he'd said the right thing.

"Yes," Shea added quickly. "Old friends."

Technically that could be true, since "We Fucked Once and Are Really Into Each Other" wasn't exactly a description either of them could give her mother.

"How nice." Peg waved to someone behind Byrne and mouthed, "I'm coming." Then, to her daughter, "Okay, I'm off. See you back at the house?" She started to walk away then turned back. "Oh, Byrne?"

"Yes, ma'am?"

"Would you like to come for dinner? Any friend of Shea's is a friend of ours."

Byrne looked to Shea, searching for a clue on how to answer. She lifted her shoulders as if to say, *It's up to you*, so he responded to Peg with an "I'd love to."

"Fantastic! We're having lamb." Then she walked away toward the waiting Ingrid, who was sawing at the air with a hand fan.

He watched Peg go. "She's very nice," he told Shea.

Shea was grinning proudly. "That she is." The smile faltered. "You *sure* you want to come?"

"The team is just grabbing burgers later, and Dan is here, so I really don't want to be responsible for him tonight. I'd rather be with you."

"But at my *parents'* house? We haven't even had a date yet."

He quirked an eyebrow at her. "As long as we can make out on the couch after they go to bed."

She laughed, but there was wide-eyed panic behind it.

"Why don't I head back to the hotel with the team," he added, "and take a shower, change clothes and all that, and you can pick me up when you're ready?"

"All right. Sounds fine." But she still looked a little spooked.

"I'm serious about just wanting to spend time with you," he said. "Unless you think it's going to go badly? Is your dad a horrible monster or something?"

"No, not at all. He's great, actually. I guess I just . . . I mean I'd like to . . ."

She trailed off, her gaze meandering over to the rugby match that had just started, and a new splotch of color appeared on her cheeks. *Aha.*

"Yes?" he teased.

"I'd like to be naked with you again."

"Deal. After the lamb. I won't even touch you at your parents'. They won't have a clue how much I like you."

"They'll know what we are. They just won't ever say it out loud, won't ever admit it."

"And what are we?" He was enjoying this far too much.

She opened her mouth to respond, but then her face wrinkled in confusion. "I'm not sure?"

He laughed. "Good enough for me. I don't have a clue, either."

"Good." She smiled. "So . . . lamb? And then naked?"

"Lamb," he said, an intense excitement blasting through him. "And then naked."

*S*hea's childhood home was everything Byrne had never had. The parents were similar, if only for the fact they loved their children and wanted the best for them, but the house stuffed with furniture, the dining room table laden with home-cooked food, the overall warmth . . . *everything* was different.

It was all he'd dreamed of growing up, the very reason he'd taken that football scholarship. When he'd left for college, his dreams were humble. A house like the Montgomerys' had at first felt like more than enough. But then he'd gotten a taste of what more there could be, seen what so many of his classmates already had, and his dreams got inflated. By a couple of million notches.

It should have been stranger, having dinner with Shea's parents, except that it wasn't. Peg and Fergie Montgomery were as witty as they were wholesome, joyous as they were pious.

Byrne sat there at the oval table with the lion-claw legs and plastic apple-themed placemats, drinking his sparkling water and listening to Shea and her parents recount stories. Didn't matter that he had no idea who or what they were talking about, they had an easiness to their relationship that made Byrne happy to just sit back and listen.

"Will you say the blessing, Byrne?" Peg asked after she'd set out the lamb roast.

He fish-mouthed for a few seconds; then, remembering what his own mother had told him about meal blessings ages and ages ago, he said, "I'd love to."

His parents, long since having gone bitter over religion, had told him that blessings before meals were less about praying to something or someone, and more about giving thanks for what you had.

Holding hands with Peg on one side and Shea on the other, he said, "Thank you for family. Thank you for health. Thank you for fine company and thank you for love. And thank you for allowing me to be here tonight."

Peg squeezed his hand once and reached for the carving knife. Shea was positively beaming.

Once he'd left South Carolina, meals had taken on a whole new definition, meaning he actually ate food three times a day, often more. After college and grad school, once he was thrust into the financial world, meals often meant cramming in food at his work desk at ten thirty at night. Or eating out with coworkers, or entertaining clients.

To sit at a table with family—even though it wasn't his family—was an eye-opener. A welcome change from his life in the city, a welcome addition to his life experiences. He could sit here for hours, listening and soaking it all in.

And watching Shea.

She was lovely as she interacted with her parents, but it was interesting how she held back. How her speech patterns changed, how carefully she chose her words, and how perfectly that serene smile stayed pinned to her face.

"You sure you can't stay through tomorrow night?" Peg asked Shea as they were finishing up the homemade cherry pie, almost half of which was sitting in Byrne's belly.

"Can't," Shea said, folding her napkin. "Sunday nights are really busy at the Amber, if you can believe that."

Just like that, the mood in the dining room shifted. Not chilled exactly, but awkward in its silence, when the rest of the evening had been filled with conversation.

Fergie frowned into his water glass. Shea met Byrne's eyes for a moment as if to say, *See?*

Byrne cleared his throat and asked into the silence, "Did you happen to see Shea on the History Channel the other night?"

He could say he'd been bored and was flipping through the channels only to stumble upon the whisky special, but the truth was, he'd searched it out and recorded it especially.

Fergie's chin lowered as he looked at his daughter over the top of his glasses. "History Channel?"

"She was really fantastic," Byrne said. "It was about bottles of Scotch whisky uncovered in archaeological digs. Cool

stuff. The things she knows, they're amazing. That one inter-
viewer said you should get your nose insured." Byrne smiled
at Shea and she smiled back, but it was strained.

"You never saw it?" Byrne asked her parents.

Shea gave him a weird look, and then Byrne glanced into
the front living room, where all the furniture had been placed
for conversation. No TV.

"No, I'm sorry," Fergie said. Only he didn't aim the apology at Shea.

Shea closed her eyes a beat longer than a blink. Byrne
instantly felt like a complete shit.

Peg rose, gathering the dirty dishes and stacking the pie
tin on top.

"Can I help you with the dishes?" Byrne asked, thinking
he had to smooth things over somehow.

Peg looked perplexed. "Oh, I wouldn't dream of it."

Fergie followed his wife into the kitchen, and Byrne whispered to Shea, "I'm sorry. Did I fuck up?"

She shook her head. "No. But thank you for trying."

How he wanted to bend in closer, give her a kiss of encour-
agement. "You okay?"

A little roll of her eyes and a genial twinge of a smile.
"Sure. We're used to talking about everything but my career.
Ignorance is bliss in this family. I can handle it. It is what it
is." She threw a pointed glance at the kitty-cat clock hanging
by the archway leading into the kitchen. "You ready to get out
of here?"

"Only if you are."

"Oh, yes."

"Mom," she called, "I'm going to take Byrne back to his
hotel."

They went into the kitchen to say their good-byes, and as
Peg gave Byrne an unexpected hug, she asked him, "Will we
see you again?"

He hesitated, glancing at Shea. "I certainly hope so."

"I'll meet you outside," Shea told him. "Just let me talk to
my parents for a sec."

He ducked into the lamplit front hall, looking for the door.
Earlier that evening they'd come in through the back because
Shea wanted to show him the patio she'd installed with her

father during one of her high school "classes." On the right, the hallway was bisected by a staircase heading to the second floor. The green-striped wallpaper was covered with family photos. Immediately drawn by framed images of baby Shea, he stopped to look at them all.

Plump, tiny toddler Shea. Big-toothed little kid Shea. Awkward, stork-legged teenaged Shea. College-aged Shea standing in what could only be Scotland, an older man who was clearly Fergie's father draping a sweater-clad arm around her shoulders.

By the stairs hung an ornate frame, heavy and silver. The photo inside was of Shea and Marco—him in a perfectly tailored tux that gleamed with money, and she . . . in a wedding gown. They stood on the steps of St. Bartholomew's Church in Manhattan, the train of her dress swooping around to spill in carefully placed folds down the steps.

Shea looked impossibly young, all baby-faced and glow-eyed, and Marco like one of those creepy old men who just swapped out girls when they aged too much.

They looked like models, photographed for some dramatic magazine spread meant to highlight lavish city ceremonies. Only they were not models. It was absolutely real.

Shea came out of the kitchen, jingling her car keys. "You ready to—"

Byrne whirled, but she'd seen him leaning toward the picture. Her face turned as white as that wedding dress. As she slowly came toward him, her eyes locked on the photo, her lips curled in a sneer.

He said the only thing that came to mind. "You were *married* to him?"

She reached out, took the frame off the wall, and tossed it onto the stairs. The glass cracked.

"Yes," she said. "I was."

Chapter

✦

13

Shea took Byrne's elbow and guided him out to the small front porch. At the height of summer it was still light at this hour, though sunset was approaching. Words escaped her. For what felt like a whole minute, she couldn't remember how to speak English. That fucking photo. Why the hell hadn't her parents taken it down?

Byrne slipped his hands into his jeans pockets. "For the record," he said, "you don't have to tell me anything you don't want to. I'm not reacting this way because I feel like you should've told me, or that I'm owed any sort of explanation. That's not it at all. I'm just wondering why you didn't say anything more at the club the other night. You said 'ex' and I assumed boyfriend."

"That was kind of deliberate. I don't like admitting I was married. Especially to him." She tugged on the ends of her hair. "I'd say I'm shocked he didn't tell you himself, except that he'd eventually have to admit that I was the one to leave him, and he wouldn't show that kind of weakness to someone like you."

Byrne cocked his head to one side. His expression filled with compassion, and it made her heart squeeze for unknown reasons.

"Want to tell me about it?" he asked softly. "You can say no."

She took a deep breath. "You know, I think I do. Want to tell you, that is. I think you should know since . . ."

Since what? She had no clue what they were to each other, where they were going as a couple. Only that there was *something* there between them that was over and above just sex. She realized that she wanted more than a physical relationship from him, and keeping secrets probably wouldn't help her in the long run.

He smiled at her from under his lashes. "Will this require the terrible light beer kind of courage? Or maybe something fancier? I do know a bit about wine."

Why did he have to be so awesome? She laughed nervously and continued to tug at her hair.

"Nothing right now." Liquor was for enjoyment, for celebrating. Not for dulling. "We seem to drink a lot together and I don't want to tonight. I know where we can go. To talk."

He swept a gesture toward her car parked in the driveway. "Lead the way."

She drove to a lake on the outskirts of town. A wide dock stretched out into the water, and on the opposite side two hills dipped low—similar to the hills around the Gleann farm—perfectly framing the impending sunset. It was nearly eight thirty, and the sun was already a huge orange ball settling into the green basin. The benches nailed to the dock were full of families waiting for prime picture-taking time. Little kids ran around, excited to still be awake.

Shea went all the way to the end of the dock, took off her sandals, hoisted the hem of her long dress up and over her knees, and sat down on the edge, her toes skimming the cool water. Byrne kicked off his flip-flops, rolled up his jeans to midcalf, and did the same.

Hands perched on the lip of the wood, they turned to each other at the same time. He was so incredibly gorgeous in the sunset light, and she fought a powerful urge to tell him so. His lips parted under the force of a short, sharp inhale, like he was going to tell her something. He merely smiled. With his eyes. Sometimes that was the best kind of smile. Then he turned his face to the water, his bottom lip rolling between his teeth.

"It was four years ago," she said. "The divorce."

He nodded to no one in particular. "You looked really young. In that picture."

"I was. A baby. Barely twenty-four."

"And how old was he?"

She had to think about that. "Forty-three or something? Remember I said I used to tend bar? After college?"

"Yes."

"Marco used to come in there. A lot. He talked to me. A lot. Tipped me. *A lot*. I fell for it. Really hard and really fast."

"I noticed you said 'it,' not 'him.'"

It hurt, even to laugh at herself. "Exactly. I fell for everything he wanted me to. The big talk, the big show, the big gestures, the even bigger money. All those things I didn't even know about growing up, and my naivete just ate it all up with the spoon he was using to feed me."

Byrne swallowed, still staring out at the water, which had turned the most vibrant shade of gold. "Did you love him?"

"I sure thought I did. We had one of those weddings you only read about in magazines, the kind with a thousand guests and five-course dinners and . . ." She flitted her fingers toward the sunset, as though she could erase it all with a gesture. "And I thought that *was* love, all that stuff. He made me believe it. He made my parents believe it."

"I was going to ask you about them, why they still had that photo up."

"Marco always knew exactly what to say to them. All lies, of course, about his religion and how much he loved and supported and protected me. All of that was bullshit."

"So you loved him but he didn't love you."

"I don't think he knows what love is. He just wanted—" She couldn't say it. It sounded so unbelievably dumb and egotistical, coming from her own mouth. She could say it to Willa, could bitch about it between martinis and karaoke songs, but not to Byrne. Not another man. Not a man she actually cared about.

"He wanted arm candy," Byrne finished, looking over his shoulder at her.

Still so awkward to admit, but he said it so naturally, so matter-of-factly, that she strangely didn't feel put on the spot. She gave the tiniest of acquiescent nods.

He responded with a little roll of the eyes. "Don't worry," he said. "I know his type all too well. Did he cheat on you?"

She shook her head. "Don't think so. He always wanted me with him. Constantly going here, traveling there. A party, work thing, benefit, vacation, whatever. I don't know when he'd have had the time, honestly."

"Arm candy." Byrne scowled. "So what did you do during that time? Not work at the same bar, I take it."

She let out a humorless laugh. "No. Noooo. He made it very clear once we were married that I didn't 'need' to do that anymore. And because I was stupid, I agreed with him. So I didn't do anything. Nothing he didn't have me do anyway."

Byrne leaned back on his hands, and she had the hardest time in the world not staring at the flat of his belly, the way his T-shirt stretched across his chest.

"Are you sure we're talking about the same Shea?" He squinted against the sunset. "Not your doppelgänger or anything?"

It still hurt to be reminded of who she used to be. Or, more accurately, she *didn't* used to be.

"Because," he went on, "I can't think of anything you'd like less than to be sitting in some rich older guy's apartment, waiting for him to snap his fingers. I know I don't know you all that well yet, but I can't believe you ever put up with that."

Yet. She clung to that single word. Held it close to her heart. Used it to create hope.

"But at that age I didn't know any better," she said. "Not really, anyway. My parents taught me until I went off to college, and even then it was to a school smaller than many high schools. I spent a lot of time in Scotland, yes, which was the first thing ever to crack open my eyes to the world around me, but it did only that. I was still a baby, scared to be bigger than I was, if I can be honest. I graduated college and I knew nothing. Nothing, Byrne.

"I carried around this fairy-tale view of life that my parents had woven around me. They wanted me to go to college and find a career—preferably in something they approved of, naturally—but they talked about marriage all the time. Like it was the end-all, be-all, to find that perfect man and marry him and all would be right with the universe. I didn't date all

that much—Corey in Scotland was my only really big boyfriend, and I still shouldered this embarrassment and shame
about sex—so when Marco came along I literally thought he
was my prince, come to complete the fairy tale that had been
woven into my subconscious.

"I was so weak, so pliable. And my parents were thrilled.
It wasn't about the money so much as knowing that I would be
taken care of, packed away in my own castle, kept safe and
cherished. And I thought the same thing, for a really long
time."

She'd told the story while gazing out at the water, because
it was easier to voice that way. But when she turned her head
to look at Byrne, he was studying her in a way that immediately put her at ease.

"So what changed? How'd you know you were trapped in
this . . . life? It sounds to me like it should've been quicksand.
You know, the more you struggle the deeper you fall in.
Marco doesn't seem like the kind of guy who'd let you go so
easily, especially if he didn't fuck around with other women.
How'd you get out?"

She pushed her hair back. "The Amber. The Amber got
me out."

A light of understanding brightened his face. "You said
you'd been divorced four years. When did you buy the Amber?"

"Five years ago. And I'm not the one who bought it."

That, above anything, felt odd to say. To anyone and everyone peering through the windows, Shea Montgomery was the
owner/operator of the Amber Lounge.

Byrne went a little slack-jawed. "With Marco's money?"

"No." A kick at the water. The splash rippled like yellow
diamonds. "Remember that friend he so smoothly mentioned
at the karaoke club?"

His chin rose and he made an "ahhhh" sound at the back
of his throat. The same sort of sound he'd made when she
took him in her mouth.

"So Marco didn't like his friend bankrolling your bar, I
take it."

"No. Especially since Douglas and I didn't tell Marco
about it until after it was pretty much a done deal. By then I
knew I was leaving Marco. The Amber was my new love. I'd

found my freedom, my life, my personality, and I didn't want or need my husband anymore."

"How'd you tell him?"

"I just"—she lifted her shoulders—"did. I said that I was divorcing him, that I didn't want a single dime of his, that I'd leave with what I'd brought in, and that I'd found my calling. I never looked back."

"Wow." He gazed at her with a hint of his crooked smile. "So how'd you hook up with this other guy? Douglas, you said?"

"Just to be absolutely clear, we never, ever 'hooked up.' Not in that way."

"Didn't say you did. Never even thought it, actually."

"Good."

"So how'd that come about? I mean, I remember you said when you were over in Scotland that you had that epiphany about wanting to work in whisky somehow. How did that translate to the Amber?"

"We were having drinks one night, me and Marco, Douglas and his wife, and Marco had to leave for some reason or another. I ordered a whisky—a twenty-three-year-old Laphroaig, as I recall—and Douglas seemed impressed. You don't generally drink Laphroaig if you're a beginner. He started asking me about my background, what I knew about whisky, what I smelled and tasted, all that stuff. I then got a few more whiskies to have the other two try them. I was a little tipsy and just having a good time, babbling on about the drinks, but Douglas was a little blown away, if I can say that about myself."

Byrne grinned. "You can. By all means."

"He kept asking me all these detailed questions, even had me take out the menu and point out things about bottles I remembered, distilleries I'd visited, what I'd recommend to certain kinds of drinkers. I knew more than any of the staff in the place. He came to me a week later with the idea of us going into business together."

"Owning a bar."

"Not just any bar. A whiskey lounge. Fairly exclusive, high-end, with premium spirits from all over the world backed by solid knowledge. He would be the money but I would be the face, for lack of a better word. He put complete faith in my ability to run a business."

"Is he still involved? Do you have to report to him?"

She licked her lips. "Yes."

"An angel investor."

"Exactly."

"Gotcha. Those money guys. It's hard to let go."

She nudged him playfully with her shoulder, and it felt entirely natural.

"So what's he want?" Byrne asked. "More say? Change?"

"Yes to both. Things that don't really appeal to me. But I think I'm also done answering to someone else. I want my own thing—"

"The distillery."

"Well, yeah, that would be great. But before I found the farm I was just kicking around the idea of buying him out. I don't have the money for that, either. It's all a big circle I need to figure out."

"What are your other options?"

Chewing at her lip, she considered whether or not to tell him about Pierce Whitten and the nebulous, scary, and quite possibly extremely lucrative offer from Right Hemisphere. She decided not to, because she really didn't want to get into a detailed discussion about her business right now.

"There might be some . . . stuff . . . going on," she told him. "It may help me get closer to the distillery thing. Or I may be right back where I started. I don't know. It's still too early to say."

She turned her face to the lake, into the brilliant light.

The sunset had reached its peak of gorgeousness, half below the water and half above, huge and glowing, its gold and orange diminishing by the second. All sorts of romantic. Around them, cameras were going off, families posing at various points on the dock, kids running around, oblivious to the miracle right in front of them.

She and Byrne sat there, watching the sun disappear in silence.

Then she felt something on her hand. A gentle brush against her right pinky. She looked down to see Byrne had edged closer. He slid his palm over the back of her hand, interlacing his fingers with hers.

"I think I get it now," he said quietly. The words carried like a breeze, wrapping around her.

She flipped over her hand, curling her fingers up into his, and it might have been the most lovely, most peaceful moment she'd had since returning to the States after that final Scottish summer.

"I dream of the distillery," she said, "because I dream of having something of my own. It's my idea, my thing. It's what *I* want. Not something someone else brought to me or gave me or wants to be a part of. My own. My dream that I can work on every day. I don't want to answer to anyone else. I want to be responsible for my own failures, my own triumphs."

Byrne's hand tightened around hers, slowly and lightly at first, then ending with a hard squeeze. He tugged at her until she looked up into his face. Those incredible eyes, all pale against his sunburned skin and the darkening sky, searched hers.

"Sometimes I look at you," he said, "and I think I know everything that I want to say. And then I open my mouth and nothing comes out."

"And then everything you thought you wanted to say sounds dumb? Yeah, I know that feel—"

He kissed her. Shut her right up with the soft, soft pressure of his lips against hers. It felt like it had been forever since they'd done this. And never exactly like this, because every time with him had been distinct.

He tasted . . . beyond description. Those words he mentioned before just flitted away on wings of utter bliss. She loved this kiss, the undulation of their mouths, the wetness of it, how they barely touched.

Then he swiveled toward her. Wrapping one hand around the back of her neck, he deepened the kiss. She let him, even though there were people still mingling around. Which said something about him right there.

She told herself it was because they weren't anywhere near New York City or the Amber or a bottle of whiskey, but really it was him. Him. Byrne. The way he looked, the way he listened, the way he touched her and, God yes, the way he kissed.

She was getting dizzy, buzzy . . . and impossibly turned

on. Maybe even embarrassingly so, considering they were still in public, sitting on the dock of the town in which she'd grown up. When he let out that deep groan in the back of his throat, she lost it. Became this puddle of boneless desire that he could form to whatever shape he wanted.

Somehow she got her head straight and pressed a hand to his chest, pushing him away. It took some strength, too, to stop the kiss that neither of them wanted to end. But it did end, as they peeled themselves apart and breathed heavily.

He blinked down at her, then dragged a slow thumb across her bottom lip. They smiled at the same time, and as she started to laugh, she buried her face in the warm, smooth, incredible-smelling crook of his neck, the bristles of the short hairs along his nape tickling her nose. She inhaled and tried to get herself to cool down.

Wasn't working. She was gripping his clothing now, wanting it off.

"Nothing to see here, folks," he told no one in particular. "Go about your business."

"Can we go about ours now, too?" she whispered in his ear.

He stilled. Tilted his head. "Which is?"

"Lamb. And then naked, remember?"

"The sunset detour is over?"

She pulled back, took his face in her hands, and kissed him soundly. "The detour is definitely over."

He was on his feet so fast she barely saw him move.

Chapter

14

"Another hotel room." He sighed as she pulled her car into the parking lot of the Bluebird Inn, a remodeled old chain motel that was trying to be a quaint little bed-and-breakfast but really only looked like some grandparents had barfed all over a Motel 6. But it was on the opposite side of town from her parents' house and she was with Byrne, and really those were the only two things that mattered at this point.

"Someday," he added, dramatically shaking his head. "Someday."

"Sorry. I know you were holding out for a tent again." She shifted the car into park and turned off the engine.

He was peering into the brightly lit lobby. "No outside access rooms this time. And I'm on the third floor with the rest of my team. You can take the elevator while I take the stairs, if you want. I'll meet you up there."

"Wouldn't dream of it," she said, and leaned across the handbrake to kiss him.

A big kiss. One with really good pressure and lots and lots of tongue.

"Ah, stop." Though he shoved her away, the lopsided grin was all *come here*. "I need to get you inside."

He all but pulled her across the parking lot and through

the lobby, their hands twined so much they were just a ball of fingers. He was practically running, and still she found the pace lacking. Wasn't anywhere near fast enough.

The short elevator ride was interminable. The hurry down the baby-powder-smelling hallway a marathon. The blood that surged and pounded through her body was saturated with desire. All she could think was: *now now now I must have you NOW.*

He jiggled the cardkey in the lock and flung open the door. They tumbled inside. The door clanged shut and she was diving for him, blinded by need.

He thrust out a hand between them. "Wait."

Oh God, her clit was pulsing, her breathing all erratic, every stitch of clothing rubbing her skin raw. "What? Why?"

"Uh." He ran a hand through his hair, making it stand up in ways that shouldn't be as hot as it was.

"Oh no." Her stomach sank as a realization hit her. "Don't tell me you didn't bring . . . stuff. Because I forgot, too."

That same nervous laugh, that brain-scrambling glance at her under those lashes that really should be outlawed. "Oh, I brought stuff," he said. "Lots of stuff. So much stuff you better prepare yourself for what's to come."

"I'm prepared. Let me touch you. Or you touch me. I really don't care which at this point."

"Yeah. Um." He coughed out a shaky sound. "I'm really hopped up, Shea. Just barely holding on here."

"So am I."

"And I'm—" He dragged a hand over his face. "I'm really, really into you."

She sucked in a breath. Stared deep into his eyes. "I really like you, too."

Apparently they were both sixteen now.

His smile was brief but full. "I don't want it to be like last time, in Gleann. I mean, that was incredible and I loved it, but there's no rush tonight, is there? I don't have to get you back by a certain time? Your dad isn't going to be waiting up or anything?"

She grinned. "No."

"So let's . . . take our time."

She could have sworn he was saying something else entirely

with those eyes. They were worlds in of themselves, and she was losing herself in them.

Taking their time sounded perfect. Taking their time sounded amazing. And even though they were standing in a darkened room, completely alone, less than three feet apart, with sex practically being fed into the room through the air-conditioning unit, the anticipation between them made the atmosphere sparkle.

Byrne blindly reached behind him and flipped over the security deadbolt. The sound shot loud through the room. The only thing louder was her breath, and then the quiet shush of his footsteps as he closed the space between them.

One step. Two. The final third. He seemed so tall to her just then, with his chin tucked into his chest and his eyes blue circles of fire. She stared up at him, her lips parting, begging without words. When he finally touched her, it was with both hands. They lifted slowly, sliding simultaneously across her cheeks. The light skim was electric, and when his fingers dug into her hair and he held her face and finally kissed her, the whole thing went from electric to combustible.

In terms of kisses, it skewed toward chaste. There wasn't even any tongue. Lips barely apart, a feather touch. But when it came to meaning, to promise, it was the dirtiest gesture in existence. He ended the kiss. Started another one. Nudged her mouth open, took just a little bit more.

But silly her, she gave him everything.

Then she was being walked backward toward the bed. Or maybe she was leading. She didn't even know. Did it matter?

When her calves hit the edge of the bed, it paused the kiss. Byrne's hands slid from her neck and face, skimming across her shoulders and down her arms. He pulled his mouth away at the same moment he drew her in for a tight embrace—a simultaneous abandonment and intimate enclosure that got her mind all mixed up. She tucked her face into the crook of his neck. It wasn't just a hug, but a hard, desperate clinging that distinctly felt like the beginning of something huge.

Byrne rubbed his cheek against her hair, and maybe he was saying her name, but she couldn't quite be sure. The whole world had been concentrated into this generic little hotel room. It was so dangerous, to be feeling this much for one particular person. She knew this, had warned herself the same a million times. But there was absolutely no stopping this, no matter how she scolded herself now. She'd once, jokingly, thought of him as the source of all gravity, pulling the planet together with his force.

Now she knew it to be true.

With an easy push, she stepped away from him. Keeping her eyes lifted, she slowly lowered herself to the bed, sitting there with hands pressed to the edge like she'd done earlier on the dock. His eyes and forehead took on that pained expression again, as though she was too much for him, too. A single finger reached out to tuck a piece of her hair behind her ear.

As he bent over her, fingertips to the duvet, she pushed herself up and across the bed. He came over her, filling her vision with his wide chest. He settled his knees between her legs as she opened for him.

She could have counted to one hundred for all the time he took to fully lay her out on the bed, to align his body with hers, to come down on top of her and give her all his perfect weight.

It had never been like this between them before. That first kiss in the campground. Then another in the open field in front of her dream farm. Then up against her car. Then— *shiver*—from behind over a cheap dresser. They were all sexual actions and positions that didn't speak so much to intimacy or connection as much as rabid hunger. She'd done so well, playing off the Gleann motel night as something she could leave behind when the door closed and the cardkey was turned in. Who the hell was she kidding?

This was what she'd wanted. What she'd been dying for. Because there was nothing like having the man who you wanted more than breathing to give you all his weight and then to actually take your air.

Gently, slowly, he pressed her body into the mattress. Instinctually, her thighs closed around his hips, and when one of his hands came around to wedge underneath her knee and pull her leg higher, she tilted up her hips and gave him even more.

His chest felt rock hard beneath her palms, and she realized it was because he was still holding back. Still hadn't given *everything*, every pound and every sigh, to her. Dragging her hands down his arms, she pulled away his support system.

When he sank into her, burying her in his delicious weight and surrounding her with his scent and feel, he groaned and finally—finally—kissed her.

To take her mouth in that way, laid out like lovers, slow and steady and wet and open, cemented her sole desire. The way he clung to her hands, pulling them above her shoulders and pinning her down, made her high. Higher than an addict. The lick of his tongue sent her crashing back to earth. Sent her back a changed woman. She'd never be the same. Would never be able to attain again the current soar of her mind and the hypersensitivity of her skin.

He released her mouth with a groan and a ragged breath. Lying there, still pinning her down with hips and chest and hands, he stared into her face. He looked as hopped up as he'd claimed.

The word *no* had absolutely no meaning for her now. Only *yes*. Yes yes yes.

So she said it. Whispered it to him as she stared at his slack lips. "Yes."

He just kept looking down at her, and in that moment she didn't know which unasked question she was responding to.

Yes, I am yours.

Yes, you can do anything you want to me, at any pace you like.

Yes, I want you.

Yes, I want more of you.

Yes, I want it all.

And when he lowered his mouth to hers again, he whispered that word as well.

The kiss that followed was filled with *yes*, and it was the most luscious word in existence.

For someone who'd been so insistent at keeping Byrne at a careful arm's distance, she couldn't get close enough to him now. The pressure of his kiss wasn't enough, the entirety of his weight wasn't enough, her hands weren't full enough.

He rolled off her, holding a fistful of her dress on her belly. Forget what she'd thought about going at whatever pace he wanted. He was *killing* her. She conveyed her frustration with a little nip of her teeth on his bottom lip.

"Patience, patience," he murmured.

"Don't have any anymore. For the love of God, please touch me."

He grinned against her lips, and then nipped back. "Slowing things down, remember?"

But just as she rolled her eyes and moaned in disappointment, he yanked her dress up higher, skimming a hand over her breast. Fingernails scraped lightly over the nipple that pushed against her bra, sharp as a blade.

"I want to know you," he whispered, moving his mouth to her neck, her ear. "I want to test you. To figure you out."

Peeling back her bra, he pinched her nipple. Light and teasing, and she sucked in a shaking breath.

"Yes." And this time it was Byrne who said it. The one word, full of satisfaction and longing, slithered into her ear and down her spine.

"I want to know you, Shea. What makes you crazy. What makes you wet. What makes you beg."

This. *This* was what made her crazy. His deep voice in her ear, the length of him pressed against her body, the feel of his hands on her, and the absolute, desperate need for *more*.

But what she said was, "It's you."

He went completely still the same second in which she realized what she'd admitted.

It was a key in his engine, though, because when he moved again, it was like she'd revved him up and released him on a free track.

With a low, feral groan he pressed even closer, consuming her mouth with his. Grabbing her hip, he rolled her to her side so they were face-to-face, mouth to mouth, and then, with complete skill, silent and stealthy like a ninja, he had her bra undone.

She was a doll in his arms, letting him bend her and move her as he pushed her dress over her head and peeled the bra down her arms. The arch in her back was involuntary, an offering for him.

"Figured something out," he murmured as he bent his mouth to her nipple and licked it, "that we both love this."

She loved it so much she thought she might be able to come just from that.

"Harder," she said, the syllables spread out.

He bit her, lightly closing his teeth. It bowed her off the bed, and he held her down. Did it to the other nipple. And again.

"Okay, okay," she panted.

He looked up at her between her breasts, and maybe she'd been expecting a look of the devil, of mischief, because the intense focus and dreamlike desire on his face almost undid her.

"Okay what?" His voice was like campfire smoke.

"Okay." She licked her lips, felt the quiver in her thighs as she spoke the words he wanted to hear. And that she wanted to say. "I'm wet."

Just a slight tic of his eyebrow. Just the gentle roll of his lower lip as he briefly gnawed on it. And then he moved, nudging his body up higher on the bed. One hand found the top elastic of her underwear, a wonderful threat.

His tongue dipped in her ear. "I need to make sure."

She whimpered. Actually whimpered.

Achingly slowly, he slipped his fingers beneath the satin. The wait for him to touch her, for him to finally feel the proof of her arousal, to know what he did to her, made her shake beyond any measure of control. Still, he didn't touch her.

Pushing up to kneel, he held her eyes with his as he drew off her underwear. She lifted her hips to help him.

His gaze slowly meandered over her naked body. She'd never felt so exposed and so beautiful at the same time. He looked huge and unbearably hot above her, his jeans-clad thighs bracing hers, his shirt pulled tight over a pumping chest. She deliberately stretched her arms above her head, making her back arch and her legs part.

"I learned something else," he murmured. "You like me to look at you."

Yes, she did. Very much. Because to be that wanted, to know she was that desirable and that attractive to another person, was the greatest turn-on she'd ever experienced.

Then he leaned forward again but didn't give her his weight, didn't cover her. Supporting himself on one arm, hand planted on the mattress by her shoulder, he slipped his other hand between her legs. No warning, no pausing. Just a quick, easy slide into where she wanted him most.

His gorgeous blue eyes squeezed shut. He turned his face away. "*Fuck*."

She opened her legs a little more and he went in a little more, then dragged his fingers out, bringing her wetness with him. Over her.

His eyes shot open and he faced her again. Came down a little closer. His fingers slid up and down, over and inside her. So easily, so perfectly.

"My God," he kept whispering in what she could only categorize as awe. "My God."

He was making her twitch, her whole body spasming, and it wasn't even an orgasm. Like she was a marionette, and every tiny, wonderful movement of his fingers created a greater, more exaggerated movement somewhere else inside her.

Had he figured it out yet? That all he had to do to make her come was touch her and look at her as he did it?

He must have, because he kept doing what he was doing, rubbing her with increasing intensity. And she kept opening for him, kept rocking her hips, encouraging. Showing him that she loved it all.

And when she did come, a spiraling crescendo that seemed to take forever to rise, he was still staring at her, whispering, "There it is. There it is."

Keeping her eyes open was nearly impossible, her eyelids heavy, wanting to close under the weight of the pleasure shuddering through her center, but she wanted to look at him more. Wanted to see how her orgasm looked through his eyes. And just when she thought it was over, that she'd reached the top of the wave and that the pulse inside her couldn't get any more intense, Byrne's lips parted, he increased the pressure and speed of his hand, and she exploded.

No keeping her eyes open anymore. But the second they fluttered shut, her cries got louder. She felt him cover her again, and then his mouth swallowed her sounds. She let her screams go, releasing them into the kiss, and her throat went raw from the force.

When she finally came back down, finally fell over the back side of the wave and into the gentle lull of the dip, he removed his hand and his mouth, and she opened her eyes.

He was smiling, his eyes brilliant. The more crooked his

smile, she was learning, the happier he was. And, baby, that thing was cocked so far to the left it was practically in his ear.

Her thighs shook as she lowered her ass to the bedspread, her quads tightening up.

"Oh my *God*," she said, and then laughed, because that's what you did sometimes when you were too overwhelmed to say or do anything else.

He kissed her again, still wearing the smile, and laughed against her mouth. "Never been called anyone's god before."

"Was that slow enough for you?"

He pretended to consider it, pursing his lips. "Not sure. The real test comes now."

Impossible that she still didn't feel fulfilled, but sometimes fingers just weren't enough. Sometimes you needed a much bigger part of a man than his hand and his grin and his ultra-sexy words.

She stretched up to kiss the column of his throat at the same time she reached down for his belt buckle. *Slow*, she had to remind herself. *Painfully slow*. As she tugged the leather out of the buckle and let the faint clink of metal upon metal fill the room, he pushed back up to his hands and knees above her, staring her down. The smile gradually faded.

Shea pulled the buckle loose and wrapped the metal square in her fist. Byrne's shirt hung down, ballooning off his chest, and the knuckles of her free hand grazed his bare belly. The touch made him suck in a breath, his stomach muscles contracting. Flipping her hand over, she pressed her palm to all that smooth skin over hard rugby muscle. She pushed her hand up his chest as she pulled out his belt from his jeans.

One plodding, prolonged belt loop after another.

Throwing the belt to the side, she took fistfuls of his soft cotton shirt and pulled him down against her. When she kissed him, opening her mouth and giving him her tongue, she made sure it was nice and unbearably slow.

The erection that rose behind a wall of denim and a too-cold zipper called her name. A deep undulation of his hips made her a wordless promise.

First, he needed to get naked. Releasing his mouth, she pushed his shirt higher, toward his chin.

In a movement that definitely couldn't be considered as

"taking his time," he shoved off her. Knees on either side of her thighs, rising above her like the dark god he was, he stripped off his shirt and threw it down to keep his belt company.

Before, in the other hotel room, she hadn't taken the time to appreciate how he looked without a shirt. That night had been about satiating a driving need, about finishing something that had been building between them for days and days. Now, however, she was starting to understand what he meant by taking it slowly. If it weren't for the wet emptiness between her legs, she could've lain there all night, just staring up at the round, strong shoulders, the sculpted shape of his pecs, and the firm lines of his waist.

Taking her hand, he pulled her out from under him to join him in kneeling on the bed. When he slid a hand around her head again, fingers pushing into her hair, she could feel how tangled he'd made the fine mess, and she couldn't care less. The sensation of the gentle tugs against her scalp, mixing with the careful, soft strokes of his lips on hers and the feel of his jeans' snap and zipper in her fingers was . . . well, worth it.

Making it last, drawing everything out so she didn't miss a sensation or a sigh, ensured that she would remember absolutely every detail about right now tomorrow or next week or, hell, when she was eighty. She couldn't ever recall another sexual experience like this—when she wasn't so much as interested in the end, the big finish, as all the little tiny stuff in between.

She couldn't recall ever having a partner with whom she'd *wanted* to.

She opened Byrne's fly and skimmed his jeans down and around his ass.

She'd always loved guys' underwear, how their pants had give and bagginess to them, but that they sometimes wore those ass-hugging boxer briefs underneath that showed everything. She wondered if this was what men liked so much about seeing women in little underthings—peeling off that tiny, last barrier for a perfect revelation.

The tightness of his ass as she shoved down his underwear—*slowly, Shea, slowly*—elicited her own smile. And when she moved her hands to the front and finally felt him, enveloped him, knowing that incredibly smooth, iron length was all for her, she felt her own smile go crooked.

His breath stuttered. Though she adored the feel of him in and against her palm, she knew she'd adore it even more someplace else. So she folded her legs beneath her and lay back down, slipping her legs on the outside of his this time, opening herself up. He looked away from her face, all the way down her body, and the sound he made was like he'd been punched in the chest.

The flurry of movement that followed—the awkward shifting of his body as he tried to roll off the bed and shuck his pants and underwear, and then get back on the bed with grace, taking out a small square of "stuff" from his bag, no less— had her smiling with satisfaction and amusement and pure joy.

"Patience, patience," she murmured as he inserted his knees between hers again.

He glanced over at his hurriedly discarded clothing. "That doesn't count. I wasn't touching you."

"Hmmm. You owe me a striptease. A nice, long one."

He came down over her again. "You really want that?" he asked.

"No." Again, she reached between them, taking his cock and giving it a nice, long pull. "I want this. I just want you."

All teasing dissipated, just left the room on silent feet. Shea lay there, staring up at a suddenly very serious but always exceptionally gorgeous Byrne. A breathtaking want filled her, pouring from her heart and streaming into every available space in her body, digging in to make room where there wasn't before.

She reached up to skim fingers across his cheek and around his chin, then raked her nails through his hair. It was a powerfully intimate caress, and he closed his eyes against it.

Then he rocked forward, the bed releasing a creak underneath them that echoed the deep, gradual movement of his body. The tip of his cock grazed her wetness and they both gasped, eyes locking with the meaning of what was to come. And there was definitely meaning. Something far beyond just getting off. Something more than scratching an itch.

She let him see that on her face, tried to let him know how much further than fucking he'd taken her, and hoped that he would understand.

He reached down between them, fitted himself into the perfect, slippery spot, and . . . pushed. Not even all the way in, just the beginning, but he was staring deep into her eyes, and then she saw it, too, what he was feeling.

All that this could be.

Another push, a longer thrust, and then another and another, until he found a stroke that was utter perfection in fluidity, in timing, in the way it filled her. And then she had to close her eyes and just feel. Just let it all go.

Her arms dropped from Byrne's shoulders, going limp at her sides. She dug her heels into the bedspread and lifted her hips, angling them in a way that had him voicing his appreciation. God, he was going sooooo slowly, and the desire for more—more power, a faster pace, no concentration whatsoever—made her absolutely insane for the want of him.

She wrapped the bedspread around her hands, holding on like it was rope. She cracked an eye, caught a glimpse of his gritted teeth and shadowed eyes, and knew that his vow to take it slow was wearing him down.

With a groan and a little sag of his torso, he bent down to slam his mouth against hers. Such a brief, powerful kiss, and it broke something in him. Pushing back, he took her legs over each of his arms and pushed her knees up into her chest. The power of him inside her pulled a sharp cry out of her throat and sent her hands flying involuntarily above her head.

He was really moving now, a crazy, driving rhythm and force dragging deliciously inside her, and she needed something to hold on to. Something better than sheets or pillows. Something she could *grab*.

Her fingers scraped along the underside of the fake headboard that was attached to the hotel wall. There was a little bit of lip to the wood, like it had been made for this exact purpose, for women like her who were being driven out of their minds with pleasure. She grabbed the wood, fingers curling under it, held on tightly, and just *felt*.

It seemed impossible that anyone could be fucking her this well, but then all she had to do was slit open her eyes, watch Byrne's body move in and out of hers, watch the serious ecstasy turn his face flushed and intense, and then she was lost all over again. When she looked at him, her physical pleasure slammed into her emotions and they got all tangled up.

And yes, it was more than a little scary, but it was also, hands down, the greatest feeling in the world.

He shifted a little, just a nudge of his knees closer, just a slight change in angle, and then he hit some phenomenal spot inside her. She gasped, a great sucking in of air that made her lungs ache. He pulled out, did it again, and her hands clenched on the headboard, her arms bursting with a brand-new strength. She yanked hard on the board, an involuntary reflex, holding on for dear life.

And then the headboard came off the wall.

With a crack of cheap wood, it just peeled off. One whole side of the thing thumped down onto the mattress, which at sometime had been swept clean of pillows.

Startled, she craned her neck backward toward it and laughed. "Whoa. That's never happened before."

Byrne was grinning again, still inside her. "Love it. That's the way it should be."

Slapping a hand to his shoulder, she dug in her fingernails. "Don't stop. Keep going."

The smile took on an impish curve, and he began to move again. Slowly at first, working back up to his previous pace. The little break did wonders for her ability to feel, and it was like the first thrust all over again.

When he moved, the mattress jiggled the broken headboard against the wall, and the soundtrack couldn't have been more perfect.

She watched in awe as he came, realizing she'd never seen it before. He'd been behind her the last time. She loved the clench of his teeth, the deep lines that gouged between his eyebrows. But she especially loved the way he said, "Oh, *fuck*," like he'd been thrown from a cliff and was falling into nothing, elated and excited and terrified about what was to come.

Because she knew exactly how that felt.

Chapter

✸

15

*T*he whole week after Philadelphia, Byrne kept trying to find the perfect word to describe the connection between him and Shea, but the best he could come up with was *awesome*. He was a numbers guy, so he didn't sweat it too much. Because everything about it had, indeed, been awesome.

He'd even stopped covering up his emotions when he thought about her and just let the shit-eating grin take over whenever it felt like it. Sometimes it appeared in the office, and he didn't even care. Sometimes the laughter that came out of him during client dinners or on conference calls was actually genuine. Even Dan called him out on it, but Byrne wasn't about to open up to him.

Erik, however, had just clapped him on the shoulder and gave him an encouraging nod. No mention of beef jerky at all.

Byrne and Shea had returned separately to New York from Philadelphia on a Sunday. Monday night he begged her to come over to his apartment after she'd finished closing up and he was done with an overseas call. And in the wee hours of Tuesday morning, long after normal people went to bed—and just hours until he was to depart for the Caribbean—he tried his damnedest to get her to destroy his headboard, too.

The shakes and shivers of her body, and the gorgeous sounds she made during orgasm, turned out to be enough.

But then he'd left for Grand Cayman Islands for four days to entertain two different clients and meet with three different banks. Still, every day he found a way to call her. She told him about her schooling with her parents, and the Christian girls' college she attended, and how Scotland had started her rebellion, but the divorce from Marco had finished it off.

He told her the basics about his full-ride football scholarship to Boston College, and his Wharton years. It was hard to tell the story without mentioning money, but he did it.

Her favorite movie was *Being John Malkovich*. His was *The Terminator*. She even sang him some more Sinéad O'Connor.

If someone had told him a decade ago that he'd like talking to a woman as much as, or possibly more than, fucking her, he would've laughed in their face. But Shea was different in almost every way.

Now he was back in New York after a flight that had been delayed twice, making him nearly five hours late. He was utterly beat, tired of talking, tired of being Bespoke Byrne, and yet all he wanted to do was see Shea in person, talk to her face-to-face, and curl his hand around a fine glass of bourbon.

Stripping out of his suit and tossing the whole thing into the hamper for Frances to take care of, along with the rest of his dirty travel clothes, he dove into the shower.

Beneath the spray, he recalled his second-favorite moment in that Philadelphia hotel room. After he'd managed to reattach the headboard, he admitted to her that that was about the extent of his handyman skills. He didn't even know how to use a power drill. Hearing that, she'd pretended to get out of bed, disgusted. He pulled her back down, and then he stretched out beside a naked Shea to learn every curve of her body with his fingers.

She'd laughed and kissed him and said, "I like this Byrne a lot."

And as he'd gazed into her face he remembered thinking, *Funny. I love this Shea.*

Really, he should learn that smiling in the shower got you a mouthful of hot water.

All clean, towel wrapped around his waist and skin still damp, he dialed her cell. She didn't pick up and he left a message.

"I'm home. I really want to see you. I'm coming to the Amber. I hope it's okay. Call back if it's not."

It was ten o'clock on a Thursday and she'd definitely be at the Amber. He just couldn't wait until she was off, and since he still didn't know where she lived, a good old-fashioned stalking wasn't possible.

He chose to believe that showing up at the Amber would be okay. So many things had changed between them since their first meeting. Not-first-dates and long conversations and mind-blowing sex. Encouraging words with hidden meanings and other little things that told him he was different to her. Special. Not a—what was that term she put on men who came into the Amber and thought she was entertainment? A Coyote Drunkly.

He padded into his closet and hit the light switch, illuminating the rows of Bespoke Byrne's stupidly expensive uniforms.

He couldn't be Bespoke Byrne tonight, not when he knew Shea liked Rugby Byrne. But he couldn't walk into the Amber in a holey frat T-shirt and ratty jeans, either. Yet that was the only other kind of clothing he owned. It seemed those were the only two lives he lived, and one was clearly so much larger than the other.

With a sigh he reached for the silk shirt with the wider stripes because it felt more casual, grimacing the whole time at how that sounded in his head, even to himself. He made a mental note to go shopping.

Snagging his wallet and keys, he hurried down to the lobby of his building. The doorman called him a cab, which dropped him off in front of the Amber.

It was a hot, sticky night, and some brave customers were hanging out in the narrow, fenced-off sidewalk garden. The windows were tinted, but the lights inside backlit a sizable crowd. When the door opened to let out a couple holding hands, a blur of voices and the low, sexy thump of music streamed out.

Byrne entered and was instantly impressed. The feel of the place was hip without being exclusionary, comfortable without being overly casual. The seating was strategically placed groups of cream-colored leather chairs around stone tables, and the bar was made of gleaming glass set with rows upon rows of bottles.

The lighting made everyone beautiful. Or maybe it was that everyone inside actually *was* beautiful.

The pretty hostess asked if he had a reservation.

For a bar? "No, but can I grab that last chair at the end of the bar?"

She tucked a Bible-sized menu under her arm and led him to the chair in question.

Shea was standing behind the bar three chairs down, hands spread out in that way that gave the impression she was listening to every word, that you were the center of her attention.

He'd been on that end before, and he understood why she insisted on keeping those strict boundaries between her and her customers. The men in suits at the bar—and they were all men, only a scant few women were scattered around the main room—were all watching Shea talk as she lifted a bottle and pointed to something on the label.

None of those guys knew what she looked like with her hair down, all messy on the sheets. None of those guys knew that sometimes she snorted when she laughed, that she had a mouth like a sailor on occasion. That she could sing like nobody's business.

That she was into Byrne.

Smiling to himself, he edged his way along the wall, following the hostess to the very last bar seat, getting all warm and excited the closer he got to her.

As he slid onto the leather chair, Shea said automatically, without looking over at him, "Be with you in a second."

"Hi," he said.

She stopped midsentence—something about the peat smoke process—then did a double take as she finally noticed him sitting there. Her eyes went wide, her gorgeous lips parted. Then she gathered herself, cleared her throat, and threw Byrne the most genial, most bland, most universal smile possible.

But her hot eyes shot him a look all their own—one he knew very, very well.

"Excuse me." She nodded to the four other men she'd been talking to and sidled over to Byrne. "Hello there."

She was good. There was definite playfulness behind her eyes, but her posture and her expression were incredibly cool and disaffected.

She flipped over a silver napkin in front of him. "Can I help you pick something out?"

"Not sure." He, on the other hand, couldn't keep the smile from his face. The very telling, very excited smile. "Looking for something wet."

Next to Byrne, two of her previous customers whipped their heads toward him. Another coughed into his whisky and the fourth had to clap his buddy on the back.

The glint in Shea's eye hardened. Her ears turned pink. Uh-oh.

She pursed her lips, pulled the whiskey Bible around, and flipped open to a specific page. She swiveled it back to face Byrne, one fingernail tapping a listing in the middle of the page. "How about this one?"

Seventy-five dollars for a single glass. Probably not even all that big a pour, either.

Ah, shit. He didn't know which had pissed her off more. The surprise visit? (Didn't she check her phone? He never got word from her to not come.) Or was it the joke he'd meant for her ears only?

Suddenly he felt like he should be the one being wrangled by a border collie. Nice and sheepish.

He slid a finger down the page even farther, to the one-hundred-and-twenty-dollar glass. "How about this one instead?"

I'm sorry, he told her silently.

The man at his elbow leaned over, saw where Byrne was pointing, and let out a high whistle, his bushy eyebrows shooting for the ceiling. Byrne realized that his conciliatory move had made it look like he was showing off for her. Or showing off for other men he didn't even know.

Double shit.

Shea blinked at him, then her eyes narrowed. "Gladly," she said. Her flat voice smacked of the tone she gave every other one of her customers. The men he wasn't anything like. "An excellent choice. Let me go get the bottle from the back."

As she turned without a glance in his direction, Byrne refused to slump. That had backfired. Big-time. How had his genuinely good intentions gone wrong in the span of thirty minutes?

Now she thought he was back to being Bespoke Byrne. In

her own bar. She probably assumed that he'd come in here intent on planting his flag in her territory, thinking he could break her rules, that he was different. He was, yes—at least, he wanted to believe he was—but this wasn't going at all the way he'd intended.

He'd just wanted to see her face. He'd wanted to show her how much he missed her, how much he wanted to spend time with her. Waiting one more night just wasn't going to cut it.

And he couldn't tell her that now, not here. He couldn't try to pull her away—that would make it exponentially worse. He couldn't try to explain or backtrack or apologize—not with the rapt attention of the guys to his right.

So he'd wait it out. Have his expensive drink, and not try to chat her up again. He'd leave quietly and call her later. Maybe leave a message that would make her smile. Something about ripping headboards off walls.

A big hand clamped down on his shoulder. "Thought that was you, Byrne."

Byrne startled and looked up into the shrewd but affable face of Pierce Whitten. Byrne rose and shook the man's hand. "Pierce. Good to see you. What a surprise."

"I can say the same. How've you been since Yellin's party?"

"Can't complain. You spending time in Hawaii this year?"

But Pierce didn't get a chance to respond, because Shea was back, setting a gorgeous bottle of Scotch next to Byrne's elbow. The label was decorated with curly script and all sorts of numbers that didn't make any sense to him. Only a third of it was gone.

"Hey now." Pierce pointed at the bottle, puffing out his cheeks.

Shea finally noticed Pierce standing there, and her gaze darted back and forth between the two men. If Byrne didn't know better, he'd say she was shocked to see them talking. Like she already knew Pierce or something.

Eyes widening, she said, "Mr. Whitten. Hello."

"Pierce. Please." He leaned a hand on the bar. "I came back hoping for a word with you."

She swept an almost nervous look around the packed bar. "Um . . ."

"Okay, maybe fifteen words."

Her grip on the neck of the expensive bottle tightened. "I may have a minute in a little while."

Pierce patted the bar. "Great."

Byrne was still trying to decipher Shea's odd expression and ramrod-straight posture when he realized she still hadn't poured his drink, and that the man standing next to him was not only one of the most powerful men in entertainment but also one of the most decent.

Byrne tapped the lip of his empty glass and asked Shea, "Can you pour one more of those for my friend?"

"Sure," Shea replied after a moment. "Absolutely."

As she slid another glass in front of Pierce, the media magnate eyed Byrne. "You came here alone?"

Byrne cleared his throat, shifted on his seat, and made a specific point *not* to look at Shea. "I did. But I'd love it if you joined me in this. I felt the need to celebrate coming home after a long trip. Got anything you want to drink to?"

Pierce glanced at Shea. "Not yet. But hopefully soon."

Now Byrne was really curious.

Shea popped out the cork stopper on the bottle and carefully splashed two hundred and forty dollars' worth of whisky into two heavy-footed glasses.

"It's kind of a strange coincidence I ran into you here, Byrne, considering you were the one who told me about Shea here."

"You did?" she said to Byrne.

"I knew he loved whisky," Byrne replied, "and I thought he'd appreciate what you knew."

Pierce was eyeing them, a finger wagging back and forth. "And you two know each other?"

Byrne stayed silent. He'd let Shea answer that one. All she said was "yes."

Pierce's hand dropped and he said nothing more. Byrne had always liked that about him—his tact and decorum, the politeness that made you want to open up to him.

"Will you two excuse me?" she asked, and then turned away before either of the men could answer. She went to a middle-aged man with a tattooed neck and pointed to the bar, clearly asking him to take over.

"What's all this about?" Byrne asked, throwing a glance at Shea as she moved deeper into the crowded bar.

Pierce picked up his glass. "I want her to work for me."

Byrne couldn't hide his surprise. "And you two have talked about that before?"

"Once."

Why hadn't Shea mentioned this? Not that she was required to or that she owed him anything, but when she was talking about wanting to expand beyond the Amber and dreaming of opening her own distillery, wouldn't something like this have come up? Then he remembered her going all quiet at one point, and him getting the distinct impression that she was glossing over something.

"She turned you down?" Byrne asked.

Pierce's lips flattened as he nodded. "But I don't give up. Not when I know I'm right."

And the CEO hadn't sent one of his executives or middle managers to do the pitching. This hunter was going after the deal himself. It was one of the many reasons why Byrne respected him so much.

Byrne didn't want to prod. This was Shea's thing, and he hoped that if she wanted to tell him, she'd do so when she was ready.

Byrne raised his glass to Pierce. "To new deals then."

Pierce took his first sip of the whisky. "Holy shit. That's good stuff. She pick that out for you?"

"Not exactly," Byrne mumbled into the glass, then swallowed his own taste. *Holy shit* was right. He chewed it for a bit at the back of his tongue and pictured Shea doing the same. Pictured her drinking this in some secret, dusty warehouse filled with barrels, and then being equal parts smug and gleeful over having snagged such a special bottle.

"So." Pierce took another mouthful, teeth bared in appreciation. He nudged his chin over to where Shea was weaving through the tables. "You two are together?"

Would be dumb of Byrne to deny anything was going on. He and Pierce knew each other too well. Resting his elbows on the bar, Byrne considered how to answer. "I hope so."

Pierce smiled with his eyes, a restrained expression that reminded Byrne of his own father, who smiled so very little.

"It was great until I walked in here," Byrne added, not really sure why, only that he felt the need to explain to someone. "I think I fucked up."

"Why would you think that?"

Byrne swirled the brown liquid in his glass. "What you and I have, what we work for every day and what we've earned, it makes her uncomfortable."

"You're talking about money."

"Yeah."

"Huh." Pierce regarded him over his glass, then pulled the drink away and considered the whisky sloshing inside. "Huh," he said again, and Byrne could practically see his brain gears churning.

"She'll talk to you," Byrne said, beckoning to the tattooed guy behind the bar for the check, "after I leave."

Byrne scrawled his signature on the bottom of the outrageous check, tipping twenty percent.

He looked out over the bar, filled with people dressed to the nines, many of them drinking drinks just because they were expensive, to say they could. To buy them for other people they wanted to impress: a date, an investor, a client, a family member.

"Huh," Pierce said yet again.

"Listen, it was great to see you. I hope it goes well for you tonight."

Pierce nodded sagely. "And you, too."

Byrne laughed, though it sort of hurt.

As he slid off the bar stool, he found Shea in the very center of the main room. Four guys in their midtwenties—investment bankers, most likely, entry-level by the cloud of cockiness and impending drunkenness hanging over them—had commandeered the big armchairs surrounding a low stone table. One was holding the Amber's giant menu with one hand and trying to snake the other around Shea's ass, to the lip-smacking, obnoxious glee of his friends.

Byrne's blood began a slow boil, but then he watched Shea easily step away from the touch. Shoulders back, she established a new position. She shot the asshole a coolly professional stare and said some words to him Byrne couldn't hear. The offending little shit looked appropriately abashed.

And Byrne suddenly got it. Why she didn't like him coming in here, all smiling and flirting so openly. Because she probably had to deal with that crap nightly, and encouraging one man—even if it was a man she'd been sleeping with, laughing with, talking with—could send the absolute wrong kind of message to anyone else even considering hitting on her.

She started to walk away from the center table, her expression darkening, but then she caught sight of Byrne standing near the door, and she stopped.

Apologizing across a loud room of people wasn't possible. Neither was telling her how he felt. So he did what came naturally, and that was putting his hand over his heart, and giving her a nod to convey his regret over having come.

Hopefully she would know what he meant.

*S*hea watched Byrne leave the Amber, the fine clothes he likely thought were "casual" disappearing into the crowd packed near the hostess stand. And then he was out the door. Gone.

She wanted to chase after him, grab him right there in the middle of these tipsy strangers and throw her arms around him. Which was the complete opposite of what she'd wanted to do after he'd come to the Amber without notice when he knew her personal and professional boundaries perfectly well.

You name it, she'd felt it when she'd looked over and found him sitting there at the end of her bar. Shocked. Off balance. Excited. Mortified. Confused. Frozen.

Earlier that day he'd texted to tell her that his plane from the Caribbean had been severely delayed and that he wouldn't see her until tomorrow. Sighing in disappointment, she'd removed her cell phone from her pocket and stashed it in her office.

Now, instead of delivering the center table's order to the bar—the obnoxious little prick who'd grabbed her ass could wait another five minutes—she went down the back hallway and ducked into her office. She spun the combination on her desk safe and dug into her purse for her phone.

There it was, a voice message from Byrne, time-stamped not even an hour ago: *I'm home. I really want to see you. I'm coming to the Amber. I hope it's okay. Call back if it's not.*

Hell and damn.

She stared down at the phone, wondering if she should call him right now, but then decided against it. The conversation she wanted to have with him deserved more than a quick ring between toting around trays and glasses.

Tossing her phone back into her purse and then locking the safe, she headed back out to the noisy bar, thinking of Byrne and wanting the work night to be over.

Pierce Whitten had commandeered Byrne's former seat. He was enjoying the expensive whisky by the looks of it, too. She felt conflicted. On one hand she was extremely curious about why Whitten had returned. On the other hand, her conscience was telling her that no amount of money he offered could get her to compromise her principles, and that she should just ignore him tonight.

The first hand won out.

"Stick around behind the bar, Dean," she told her employee. "I need to talk to someone."

Dean nodded, and Shea blocked out the expressions of disappointment coming from the four suits who'd previously been so eager to eavesdrop on her interaction with Byrne.

"Hello again, Pierce." She stretched out her hand. "Sorry about before. You caught me by surprise. More than your first visit."

"Hello." He shook her hand briefly. "I see you're rather busy tonight, and I suppose it's my fault for dropping in unexpectedly on a Thursday, so I won't take up much of your time."

He didn't ask if they could go someplace quieter, which would've meant that he really did want a lot of her time, so she said, "All right. How can I help you?"

He smiled, and it was professional and warm, not remotely oily or contrived. "I'll just say it. Hell, I'll just admit it. We did a shitty job before. I did a shitty job of selling my own product to you."

"No, that's not—"

"Now that I've talked to you more, Shea, now that I've done even more research on you, and now that I've really watched how you interact with your customers"—he raised dubious eyebrows at the obnoxious center table—"I've come to the conclusion that I took the wrong approach before. I went home that night after leaving here and thought about your reaction to and what you had to say about my media outlets. I talked with Linda about the doubt we saw in your eyes, and we came up with something else. So here's my new sales pitch—"

She held up a hand. "Wait. But you're still proposing the same thing?"

"Same proposal, along with anything else you feel we could collaborate on under the Right Hemisphere umbrella. I still want a sit-down with you, hear what you have to say. I want to know what you want and how we can help make that happen."

An image of the Gleann farm, captured in sunset with encroaching rain close behind, came to her so strongly she could smell the sweet grass and the pungent tang of the whiskey's sour mash seeping out from the barn distillery. She inhaled long and slow.

"Go on," she said.

"I want to expand our market beyond the upper-class male demographic. I want to appeal to women as well. I also want men to respect powerful women and realize how knowledgeable, interesting women make their lives better. I want them first to be shocked as hell that a woman knows as much as you do about a subject that is so typically male, and then I want them to bow down in worship. I want women to turn an eye to my products because they applaud you and because they want to expand their own horizons. That's not going to happen if all I have is a bunch of guys spouting off to more guys. I want intelligent, determined, strong women at the core of my new arm of business, and I want you to be my queen, so to speak."

He clapped his hands together once like he was finished, but then quickly added, "Oh, money. You probably want to know about money. There's the potential for a lot of it. And you'll benefit just as much as I will." Now he nodded and crossed his arms. "There. I'm done."

She looked around the Amber, the place she built with her own hands but with someone else's bank account. For the first time, the dream of the distillery felt tangible and achievable.

When she looked back at Pierce, she saw the ghost of Byrne sitting on that chair.

"So . . ." She chose her words carefully, not really knowing how to address this. It was yet another blurring of the lines between personal and professional. "Byrne told you about me?"

"He made me aware of you, yes."

And Byrne knew of her dream, knew how much it would cost and that she was nearly desperate to break away from the Amber. How much of a hand in all this did he have?

"I have to ask. Did Byrne put you up to this proposal?"

"No one puts me up to anything, Shea. You don't get to where I am by following someone else."

Made perfect sense.

"I'm trying to get my timeline straight," she said. "When did he tell you about me?"

"At Yellin's party."

"You were there?"

He smiled. "I was. I even got a drink from you, at Byrne's suggestion."

"I'm sorry. I come across so many faces, it takes a lot for me to remember one or two."

He waved her off. "It was late at night, but I'd only just arrived. Byrne and I hadn't run across each other in a while and we got to talking. I said I wanted a good drink and he pointed to where you were, said you really knew your stuff, that you were famous. So of course, as a Scotch whisky lover, I had to see for myself."

Shea dropped her gaze to the bar top. This had all happened *after* she'd gotten annoyed by Byrne's behavior at Yellin's and had turned his begging eyes and pleading words away. And before she'd ever even told him about the farm and the distillery. Before they'd reconnected in Gleann. Before they'd ever really talked.

And yet he'd still brought her to Pierce Whitten's attention.

"Is Byrne your banker?" she asked. Because that connection would just be too weird.

Pierce laughed low. "No. We met through mutual business acquaintances five or so years ago at some boring event or another. Let's just say we had a very interesting conversation in which we discovered some personal similarities, and the whole thing may have involved a hell of a lot of this." He hefted his now-empty glass. "Only not nearly as fine."

Ah, male bonding. Couldn't be called such if it didn't involve alcohol.

"I feel like it bothers you," Pierce added, "that he told me about you?"

"No, it doesn't." It would have, if Byrne had secretly asked Pierce to do her some sort of favor, knowing how she had her own dreams and wanted to break away from Douglas Lynch and the whole "silent partner" thing. But because of the timing, it didn't sound that way at all.

Still, she was confused by Byrne's motives. He'd been frustrated and angry at her rejection of him at Yellin's party, and yet he went on to be gracious toward her in front of Whitten.

Because he hadn't wanted to let her go, and he'd known what the two of them could be long before she'd allowed herself to believe the same.

God, she was such a shit. Assuming all men were vindictive and ill-wishing after getting dumped. Assuming that all men had ulterior motives and said one thing while doing another. Assuming all men were like Marco.

"Will you think about it, what I said tonight? Will you try to picture everything I told you?" Pierce pushed his glass toward her, indicating his departure.

What Shea pictured was a possible means to finance buying that farm up in Gleann. All on her own. What she saw was a way to keep bringing in money without having to be in New York to keep an eye on the Amber. What she saw was a reliable source of income while she was building the distillery, and letting the new whiskey age in barrels before it could be sold and actually bring in revenue on its own.

What she saw was her well-earned, clawed-for, respected name being associated with something so tits-and-ass like Whitten's current ventures.

Why couldn't there be a middle ground?

"I will think about it, yes," she said.

She realized she was staring at the two empty glasses, one with Byrne's thumbprint, when Pierce said his good-byes.

"Huh?" She looked up. "Oh. Sorry. Good-bye."

He looked at her for a long moment. "Can I just add one more thing before I go?"

She nodded.

He pressed his lips together, and it was an expression of earnest. "There are very few people in this world who I trust."

She blinked. "Really? That's surprising, considering the size of your company."

"I mean *really* trust. As in, I know they stand on a good, firm foundation, and if I blow in their direction they aren't going to immediately fall over because I'm the one coming at them. They fight honestly for their position and they hold their ground with enviable strength. Do you understand what I mean?"

She thought of Willa, of course. How her friend had been the only person to stand up for, and next to, Shea when she'd decided to leave Marco. When a world of false friends had left Shea, Willa had remained. "I think so, yes."

Pierce buttoned his sport coat. "Good. Because you should know that I find Byrne to be one of those people."

"Because he's good at what he does?"

Pierce shook his head. "Because of that foundation I mentioned. You know that conversation he and I had five years ago? Funny thing about alcohol, it tends to bring out the truth in some people, and let's just say that Byrne and I realized that we are both standing on very similar foundations, if you know what I mean."

"I'm sorry, I don't think I do."

Pierce smiled genially. "Maybe you'd like to ask him. I get the feeling he'd tell you, and then you'd know that he didn't come to me with any sort of hidden agenda, because somehow I get the feeling that's what's bugging you. He's not anything like those assholes." He nudged his chin toward the Amber's main room.

"I know he's not."

"Good." He checked his watch. "I should go. Told my wife I'd be home at a reasonable hour, and I appear to be stretching that definition. I'm looking forward to hearing from you, to setting up that meeting." Then he slid another business card onto the bar and gave it a tap.

She watched him leave. Apparently he'd paid the valet to keep his sleek, black Mercedes sedan parked right at the curb out front.

Dean ambled to her side. "Everything okay?"

"Yeah, it is. Oh crap, I forgot to tell you center table's order." She rattled off the youngsters' desired glasses from memory. "Try to push bottle service when you bring it over. I think they're in for the long haul, and they're good for it."

"Sure thing." Dean started to reach for new glasses, setting them on a tray.

She turned once more to the front door, as though Byrne might reappear any second.

"Dean, I think I'm going to head out for the night. You good to close up? The party in back is all done and the check signed, they're just mingling, finishing their drinks. The Corner Pocket is empty, unless our show-offs out there want to pony up."

Dean laughed through his nose. "I'm all good. The others have got the main floor covered. You sure you're okay?"

"I'm fine. Just want to go talk to somebody."

Dean smiled knowingly as the first drops of a Kentucky bourbon hit the bottom of a glass. Little got past Dean, but he would never say anything to embarrass Shea or threaten his employment here. He'd told her many times it was the best job he'd ever had or could ever dream of.

"Go," Dean said. "I got it."

Shea ran to the office, grabbed her things, and headed out to the curb. The valet whistled for a cab and she gave the driver Byrne's address.

Chapter

✬

16

The phone rang—the one that only the doorman called. Wishful thinking had Byrne shooting off the couch so fast he might've pulled a hamstring. He did some sort of awkward hurtle over the leather ottoman and tripped, stumbling over to the kitchen island, where the small white phone hung on the wall.

"Hello?"

"Good evening, Mr. Byrne. Sorry to bother you so late, but I have a Ms. Montgomery downstairs to see you? Should I send her up?"

Byrne pounded a silent fist of victory on the soapstone counter. "Absolutely. Yes. Send her up."

Hanging up the phone, he swept a glance around his place, making sure there wasn't anything embarrassing lying around. He'd shed his clothes the second he'd returned from the Amber, like they were poisoned and had ruined his whole surprise. Maybe they were, because whenever he wore them, things seemed to go not-so-right when Shea was around. His belt lay in a loop in the hallway, but he'd kicked his pants and the striped shirt into his closet.

Now he wore cotton drawstring pants and a T-shirt from the last Rugby World Cup he'd bought online. He plucked at it, thinking how Shea would love it. How it wasn't poisoned.

When he heard the shush of footsteps outside his door, and saw a wink of shadow in the light that came under the crack, he jogged across the foyer and stretched for the knob. He threw open the door, unable to hide his happiness. His relief.

Shea stood in the hall, arms folded loosely at her waist, shoulders curved in, her expression unreadable.

Okay. Not what he expected. Or hoped for.

"What a nice surprise." He opened the door wide. "Not like mine earlier. I'm really sorry for that."

"I took a chance that you wouldn't be in bed."

He glanced at his arm that never wore a watch. "It's not midnight yet. Wouldn't even consider it."

That got her lips to twitch. "Can I come in?"

"No, you have to stand out there and we can pass notes underneath the door." He stepped to the side, and liked how she glanced up at him as she passed.

She entered tentatively. It wasn't the first time she'd been here, but she was acting like it, looking all around, moving slowly, not stepping on the area rugs. He closed the door.

"When I saw those guys," he said to her back, and she turned around, "the ones at the table when I was leaving, I realized what you have to face there at the bar. What you fight. I didn't lump myself into that category." He went to where she was standing motionless next to the kitchen island. The lights were low in the apartment, and the artificial stars of the city created a gorgeous backdrop for her.

"How we were in Philadelphia got me energized," he went on, "and then I was gone for what felt like forever and I was missing you. And, well, I got cocky. I couldn't wait until tomorrow to see you, and the Amber seemed like a good idea. I thought if I showed up you'd, I don't know, give me a pass or something. I assumed I was different from all those others, and you know what they say about assuming."

"You are different." Her arms dropped to her sides, her eyes meeting his. "You surprised me, is all."

"But if you encourage one guy like me, who seems to think he's better and different than all the others, then I see how it takes down your entire wall. You told me that before, but now I've seen it with my own eyes, and I'm sorry for putting you in that position."

She slipped her purse onto a bar stool, which meant she was staying, giving him a jolt of anticipation.

"It's okay," she said. "I was looking forward to seeing you, too. I was torn when I looked up and saw you there. Really, really torn. I wanted to climb onto your lap and kick you out, all in the same second."

He nodded.

She added, "I'm sorry for pushing the expensive drink on you."

He shrugged and then realized how callous and egotistical that might have looked.

"I'm sorry for being aloof," she said.

That surprised him. "You don't owe me any kind of apology."

Though she nodded, there were still questions behind her eyes, and he didn't know if he was in the doghouse or not.

"So Whitten said something odd to me after you left." She peeled away from the kitchen island and wandered into the main room, the L-shaped couch set up to enjoy the amazing western view. She trailed a hand over the back of his favorite chair.

He curved around the opposite direction, going to sit on the far end of the couch closest to the windows. The leather cushion let out a *whoof* as he dropped into it. "He did?"

"He said something about trusting you. How he had faith in you because you guys had the same foundation or something like that."

A little ball of nerves in his stomach grew spikes and started to roll around. "That's what he said?"

"Yes." She fondled the edge of a blanket draped over the back of the armchair.

"He told me he wants you to work for him."

The lines across her forehead deepened. "He does. He wants to build me into a brand. Writing articles and a travel series and a bunch of other stuff. He asked once before and I turned him down. He came back to beg for a meeting."

Byrne sat up, scooting to the edge of the cushion. "Wow. That's really exciting. A huge opportunity, Shea."

"It is. A huge amount of money, too."

Byrne could only imagine.

"You weren't thinking about that, about me possibly working with him, when you told him about me, were you?"

"No, not at all. You'd just shot me down—again—but it didn't make me think any less of you. Just the opposite, in fact. I ran into him shortly thereafter and realized he'd probably get a kick out of you."

That seemed to relax her a bit, though he couldn't say why.

"What're you thinking?" he asked.

She sighed. "I am . . . intrigued by his new proposal, but I have a lot of doubt about the products his company puts out, what sort of image he's selling."

"Ah. Of course." Byrne rubbed his hands together.

"This is going to sound terrible, but the second I heard that you'd introduced us, I had images of you two making some sort of cigar- and booze-filled deals in the back of a strip club about me—"

"Shea, my God. I would never—"

"I know." She held up a hand. "I know that now, and I feel shitty for ever thinking that."

Suddenly he understood the sadness and doubt etched into her face. "Marco really fucked with your head," he said.

"He did. I'm just cautious now. And maybe a little paranoid."

"Not every guy, or business deal, is like that, you know."

"I'm slowly learning that, but I've been burned so badly before." She draped one thigh over the arm of the chair and settled her weight onto it. "Pierce knows my doubts surrounding the other things his company does and made mention that he is willing to branch me out under a new umbrella, taking that into consideration."

"That's good. That's a start."

"After you left he made these cryptic remarks about how I shouldn't judge his proposal based on the fact that you made the introductions. That's where the foundation thing came in. He said you guys bonded over something, and what he learned about you made him label you one of the good guys. That he trusted you when he trusted so few people."

Oh boy.

"Can I ask you about that?"

Byrne blew out a breath and had to look away from her. Of

course his gaze hit the green toy train engine straightaway, and it made his heart hurt. "You really want to know?"

"I do. I'm curious, Byrne. I'm curious about you."

"You are?"

"Yes." She rolled her eyes exasperatedly, but it had shades of the fun Shea he knew and adored. "We've spent so much time talking about me, I feel like, and so little time talking about you."

Foundations. That's how Pierce had put it, huh? If what the two of them had had could actually be considered foundations. And Pierce had thrown it out to Shea as part of his sales pitch, it seemed, pulling Byrne into it. Pierce saw no shame in that, but Byrne was mightily uncomfortable. He scrubbed his face with dry hands.

When he pulled his hands away, there was the train engine again, filling his vision.

Really no other way around this situation than to just say it. Shea had told him all about Marco and the divorce and the partner involved with the Amber. She'd told him about Scotland and her start with whisky, and had even brought him to meet her parents. And he'd, what, busted on a few rugby guys out on the pitch for her? Made a few jokes and got her naked? Ogled her while she sang karaoke?

As she slid from the arm of the chair into the seat, he knew that if he wanted her in his life, if he wanted *more* from her, *more* between them—he'd have to tell her. If he wanted to give himself to her, he couldn't do it piecemeal.

Boom. So here he went.

"When Pierce said that we—he and I—had the same foundations," Byrne began, "he meant that we both grew up poor."

Shea's head tilted a little, but she said nothing. Did not recoil or make an otherwise disgusted face.

Inhale, Byrne. Exhale.

"And when I say poor, I don't mean like we clipped coupons and shopped at Walmart and couldn't go out to eat that much. I mean like, we got our clothes through church donations and at the Goodwill if we were lucky. My family ate at the homeless shelter once a week, showered there, too. Until I got to junior high and I could shower at school, which I did in secret until I got caught one day by the wrong kid with the worst mouth. Speaking of school, I got free lunches and all other sorts of stuff that made for a couple of really awful years. Kids can be evil, and it's hard to rise above shame and embarrassment at that age."

There. That was the expression Byrne had been waiting to see on Shea's face. That openmouthed shock that straddled the line between pity and "I totally see you differently now." The expression he dreaded so much growing up that he'd trained himself not to look into people's eyes so he didn't have to see their reaction to his hygiene or clothing or free lunches.

But he was on a roll, and if she wanted to hear it all, then he was going to dump it all at her feet.

"We lived in a train car, Shea. An abandoned, rusted train car sitting on an old set of tracks that ran through a tobacco field. Me and my younger sister and brother, my mom and dad. We lived in a fucking rotting piece of metal in the middle of a field because my parents had had me when they were in high school and got kicked out of their homes. They never finished school and had seasonal jobs at the tobacco farm because we didn't have a car and couldn't drive anywhere."

Her eyes immediately traveled to the green engine in the center of the coffee table. And then over to the red coal car on the bookcase in the corner.

"Reminders," he said, following her gaze. "Where I came from, and all that."

"What about family services?" she asked, her voice quiet.

He stared at the engine. "My parents avoided that for a really long time. They wanted to keep us all together, to make us the best family they could, to not give up. They were good parents. It may sound strange to say, but they were. They are."

The couch cushions dipped, startling him out of his daydream. Shea had moved next to him. He blinked over at her. He was waiting for her disgust to show. The pity. The recoil. Except that she'd moved *closer* to him.

"Where?" she asked.

"What do you mean?"

"I mean, where was this? Where did you grow up?"

"South Carolina."

She gave him the tiniest of smiles. "What happened to your accent?"

"Lost it. On purpose. After I got out of there and went to college, I let it all go."

"Byrne, I—" She cut herself off, her eyes ablaze with something he didn't know how to name. "Wow. And you got into college on that football scholarship. Full ride, you said."

"Yep." Absently, he rubbed his knee that tended to ache whenever he thought about this point in his life. "The second I left South Carolina, I realized I'd been given a fresh start. I could make up my whole past life, lie about my childhood. So I did. No one knew. I learned how to leave it all behind and become someone new. I learned how to push forward and never stop." He waggled his eyebrows. "I learned how to talk to girls. How to talk to people, period. How to look them in the eye."

"And then Wharton."

He nodded. "More scholarships. Financial aid. Jobs out the ass. I had absolutely no life."

She pressed fingers to her lips and whispered, "Oh my God, Byrne."

She scooted closer. Now their thighs touched. He was starting to get a little dizzy from the proximity, combined with the feeling like he was bleeding out from the mouth, his gut empty but his heart fluttery and full.

"I'd say I can't believe you did all that on your own," she said, "except that I totally do. I completely believe that you made all that happen. And now look at you."

"Now look at me," he echoed, thinking of the clothes he'd kicked into the closet barely an hour earlier.

She gasped. "You look, I hate to say it and I really can't believe it, ashamed. Like you're actually ashamed about all that you've accomplished."

"No, no. I'm not at all ashamed of that part. But the beginning, where I started off, my childhood . . . it hangs over me. How we lived, what I didn't have, what I had to endure. I can't shake it, no matter what I do. I'm trying, but I just can't. You don't understand what it's like, hearing about where all these guys I went to school with and now work with came from. And it's not even that they all grew up with money, although most of them did, but just to have, say, running water was a hell of a lot more than what I had."

He could feel his heartbeat kick up. His knee started to bounce. "And the culture I work in, Shea, it's crazy. It wants wealth alone and tends to look down on those who don't have it. So I keep my background private, close to me, because I don't want to be judged for it. I've worked my fucking ass off to get where I am, and I can't afford to be looked at any differently."

She regarded him for a thick moment. "I think you've got it all wrong. I think people would respect you even more because of where you came from and what you've accomplished. I think that's what Pierce was trying to tell me."

"Yeah, but Pierce grew up an orphan, passed around foster homes, taking handouts his whole life. He knows me. He gets me. It's different."

She looked down at her lap, and he knew he hadn't convinced her. "I didn't know that about Pierce," she said. "Are your parents still alive? Your brother and sister?"

He swallowed. "Yep. Still in South Carolina. Mom and Dad are still doing the odd-job, minimum-wage thing in their fifties. I don't even think they have insurance. They don't live in the train anymore. They've got a small apartment above a pizza place, but money is only slightly better than it used to be. Caroline just had a baby, well, not a baby so much anymore, but she never got beyond high school either, and her slacker boyfriend just barely supports them. Caroline works part-time as a cashier, but she's smart, capable of so much more. My brother, Alex . . ." Byrne blew out a breath and scrubbed a hand through his hair.

"Trouble?" Shea filled in.

"You could say that. Never did anything his whole life, and then the gambling and drinking took over and we lost him. He's destroyed my trust, but not my love. Not my hope for him. He's actually gone home now, says he's clean and wants to start over. I want to believe he's better. Caroline tells me to. I'm trying to hold on to that hope."

He watched her eyes flicker around his apartment that even he knew was large and quite nice, even by New York standards.

"They won't let me help them," he blurted. "At all. They are far too proud. They've told me they want to work, to earn whatever they have. I respect that, but it frustrates the hell out of me, this limitation. I could support them all, it's all I've ever wanted to do since I went away to college, but they won't let me. They don't want to be given anything. They want to prove themselves."

Shea's smile was golden. "Like you."

He sighed. "Like me, I guess. The checks I've sent them have actually gotten ripped up. I've learned my lesson."

Shea's gentle, warm hand reached out and slowly unfurled his fingers where he'd unknowingly made a fist in his lap. When she flattened his fingers, she threaded hers through his and edged her body closer. Her stunning face, all shining understanding and pale beauty, was right there. Right there in front of him.

"I'm sure you've done all you could," she said.

"No." Man, his hand really wanted to make another fist, but Shea held it fast, and he found he was grateful for it. "They won't take my money, so I'm trying to do something else."

Now this he'd never told anyone. Not Pierce. Not even Erik. Not anyone.

"What?" Her other hand slid up his arm and rested where his shoulder curved up to his neck.

He licked his lips. "I'm trying to buy the tobacco field we used to live on. The land is gorgeous, right near a river. My parents were so upset when we got kicked out. New owners came in when I was in junior high and told us to get off. I mean, we were squatting and it was their right, but they displaced a family, and my parents finally had to go apply for aid and all that. It destroyed them. Killed their pride. We lived in this box of an apartment in a terrible neighborhood where it wasn't safe to play outside, and every night we talked about the sunsets we used to have over the fields. Caroline and Alex and I missed running over the land, playing in the river. That fucking train was actually a good memory compared to where we'd been carted off, if you can believe that.

"So I thought that I could buy it back from the company who took it over all those years ago. Give it back to my parents. Maybe they'd let me slip in a house without them knowing."

Shea's eyes glimmered. "My God, Byrne."

"It's a huge parcel. Massive. A shitload of money. I've been after it for years. Ever since I graduated. But I finally have the money for it. Finally. And there are whispers that it'll be on the market soon."

She gasped. "Is *that* why you do this?"

"This" meaning being Bespoke Byrne.

He looked into her watery blue eyes. Licked his lips. And nodded. "Yes. That's why I do everything. For my—"

He didn't get any further. Shea's mouth was on his, her lips wet and warm. She threw a leg over his lap, pressing his body deep into the couch cushions. And he gladly let himself be buried.

*S*hea actually tasted more of Byrne as she kissed him this time. More of his life, more of his desires, more of everything that made him *him*. His story had been salt, bringing out the flavors of every aspect of his personality.

"It's so great to hold you," he whispered.

"Are you kidding? It's incredible to hold *you*."

Her tongue slid across his. Slow, gentle strokes that had her losing all manner of strength in her legs and arms. She could taste the truth of him, but also the reluctance of him having to voice it. He really was ashamed of himself, of where he came from. She could feel the power of that emotion in the clutch of his hands at her back, and then the way his fingers bit into her ass.

She regretted ever naming him Bespoke Byrne, for labeling him based on how he dressed. For assuming what kind of person his appearance made him. It was almost as bad as what he'd endured as a kid, only in reverse, and it made her feel ashamed.

And then all of a sudden it happened.

It happened when his kiss grew incrementally more insistent, his lips nudging open her mouth painfully slowly. It happened when he shivered beneath her, when she heard the sound of his desire get trapped in his throat.

It happened as all their prior conversations suddenly came rushing back to her—their jokes, their pure, true connection. It happened as she remembered the contentedness on his face as he'd said grace at her parents' dining room table, and when she'd sat on the dock telling him about her past. When she'd realized that he was no storybook fairy tale, that he was anything but false.

She fell in love with him.

It was not: *Oh shit, I'm falling, what the hell is going on?* Not: *If I'm not careful, I think I may fall in love with you.* But: *I'm already a goner. I've fallen. Whoops.*

Shea tightened her hold on him, as though his body were a lifeline and she could use it to hoist herself up and out of trouble. But it was too little, too late.

She needed a breath, because the stilted ones coming through her nose weren't enough. She pushed against the couch cushions, removing her mouth from his with a final lick.

"No, no, no, no, no." His eyes were at half-mast, his erection at full. "Where're you going?"

She ran a thumb over his bottom lip. "Don't want to take advantage of you in your fragile, exposed state."

A bit of the amused gleam returned to his shadowed eyes. "No advantage. None whatsoever. Come back here."

He reached for the button on her pants, got it popped out before she scooted off his thighs and somehow found her feet. He looked up at her questioningly.

"Did I scare you?" he asked, taking her hand. "You look a little spooked all of a sudden."

He had scared her, but not in the way he thought.

"I like your bed," she said. "I'm an old-fashioned girl like that."

"Old-fashioned you are not." He rose to his feet, dragging his body against hers.

She reached up and pulled out the band of her ponytail with one hand. As she led him down the hall toward his bedroom, he said, "I love your hair. Have I ever told you that? I love it down."

Something that simple made her shiver all over again. It was almost as big a turn-on as straddling the hottest guy in existence on his mortgage-payment sofa. As she turned into his bedroom—a corner room, of course, with the mosaic of the city spread out just on the other side of the glass—she smiled at him over her shoulder. Turning back around, about to pull him over to the bed, she caught sight of an open door, the light on inside. His closet. Shooting him a sly grin, she dropped his hand and headed toward the sumptuous space done in deep cherrywood shelves and racks.

"Now where are you going?" he asked behind her.

"Another detour."

"Now?"

"You got somewhere else you need to be? My detours are good, remember?"

When she tossed a wicked look over her shoulder, she was rewarded by a flash of white teeth.

"Oh my," she breathed as she stepped into the closet. It was larger than her childhood bedroom. "You sure you're not a girl?"

"Pretty sure."

She kicked off her shoes and dug her toes into the plush carpet. The uplighting was soft and subtle; there was no harsh glare from a fluorescent bulb connected to a swaying string. Rows of suits and shirts and perfectly folded stacks of sweaters made her feel like she was in the middle of some upscale men's store.

It was official: she had closet envy.

A full-length mirror occupied the whole far wall, and next to it, strangely, was a pressboard dresser with a huge chunk of white laminate gouged out of the side. The front was covered with stickers for bands. Bands she liked. A lot.

Running a hand over the top of the out-of-place dresser, she saw how old it was. It was the kind of thing a kid would have in college. Something cheap, generic, utilitarian. The kind of thing an honest, hardworking, corporate-climbing clothes hound of a guy would keep around to remind him of where he'd been. Like the toy train.

She didn't have to crack open a drawer to know what was inside. "Rugby clothes?"

"You got it."

She walked back toward him, down the length of the closet. "Which is your most expensive shirt?" She thumbed through the hangers of perfectly ironed button-downs, one by one.

"Keep going. Keep going," he directed. Then, when her fingers dragged into a section of pastel colors she'd never imagined him wearing, he said, "That one."

She pulled out the hanger. "This? This is your most expensive shirt?"

He smiled.

"It's . . . purple."

He shrugged and leaned against the doorframe, arms crossed. "It's Italian. Got it in Rome during a client thing. And, you know, when in Rome . . ."

"Ah, yes. European peer pressure. 'Here, dress like us so American males will look at you funny when you get home.'"

He chuckled. "Exactly."

"I've never seen you wear it."

"You haven't seen me wear a lot of this stuff in here. That's kind of on purpose."

That made her pause.

"I actually had a bit of a fashion crisis before heading over to the Amber tonight. I didn't want to look like the guy I know you don't like, but I didn't really have much of a choice."

She thought of how she'd internally commented on his clothing earlier that evening, and cringed. "This stuff's like your anti-Superman outfit," she said.

"I know how you like me. Nice and dirty, remember?"

That crooked grin was veering toward an entirely different definition of dirty.

"You're pretty clean right now," she said. "But I kind of want to fix that."

"You do, do you?"

He'd already undone the button on her pants, so all she had to do was lower the zipper and let the things fall to the floor. He stilled, watching intently as she did just that. She reached up and unbuttoned her shirt. Deliberately. Teasingly. Then the fine white cotton joined the pants in a puddle.

Byrne's jaw worked. His fingers made heavy indentations in his upper arms.

Shea stretched behind her back and unclasped her bra, peeling the straps off her arms. She reveled in his stare for a moment, then, rolling her palms down her hips, she pushed down her thong, and gave him her back as she did it.

Byrne made a choking sound. "Jesus Christ, Shea."

Part of her wanted to make a joke about how a good home-schooled girl with conservative parents wouldn't like that language, but the time for one-liners seemed to have passed.

His eyes were all over her naked body as she walked back

into the closet; she could feel them on her like the best kind of summer breeze. She returned to the section with the pressed, button-down shirts and touched the purple Italian one.

"What are you doing?" His voice had gone a little breathless.

The fabric was sinfully smooth underneath her fingers, and it came off the hanger with a whisper. Draping it over her shoulders, she slipped her arms into the sleeves and let the cuffs dangle past her fingertips. Turning back to Byrne, she kept the buttons open, letting him see a whole naked strip of her, right down the middle.

He dragged a palm across his face, and he looked as pumped and ready as if he were about to jog onto the rugby field, but also as worn out as though he'd just played the match of his life.

She sauntered toward him as he slowly pulled away from the wall, arms dropping to his sides.

"What am I doing?" she whispered. "I'm going to show you that I don't care about clothes or money or the fact that you never had any. Just that I care about you. And also, I'm about to get this ugly, expensive shirt really, really wrinkly."

*B*yrne had never loved that Italian shirt, but he'd fallen in love with Shea as she'd worn it.

He didn't tell her, but he gave her his heart as they had sex on the floor of his closet. Later, after they'd moved to his bed and did it again, he could've sworn that he suddenly felt heavier. Like she had given him her heart in return.

The next morning, he cursed the blare of his alarm clock, until he realized that the sound that had awakened him was actually his phone ringing. Naked, he ran for where he'd left it in the kitchen, then padded back to where a sleeping Shea was taking up more than half his bed.

"'Lo?" he said, his mouth dry, voice scratchy.

And then he sank onto the edge of the bed and listened.

What he heard was something that vaguely resembled Caroline's voice, telling him something so awful he only caught key words. As she cried, his bedroom turned into a sea of red, and every muscle in his body bunched so tightly he started to ache from head to foot.

"Okay," he heard himself say into the phone when she was done. "I'll be there as soon as I can."

"Thank you," Caroline said between sniffles. "Thank you."

"What is it?" Shea whispered behind him, after he'd numbly said good-bye and tossed the phone onto the night-stand. It struck the wood and spun to hit the wall.

Shea's hand slid up his spine. Though her palm was warm, it gave him very little comfort.

"What's happened? Where are you going?" she asked, her hand making a slow, light circle around his shoulder blade.

Hands on his knees, his head sagged. "Remember Alex, that brother I told you about? The one we all wanted to believe was better and all that?"

"Oh no." There came the *shush* of bedsheets as she sat up, her hand dropping away.

It took several tries to tell her, but he finally got it out. "He stole most of my parents' money and disappeared. I'm on the first flight out to South Carolina."

Chapter

17

*B*y the time Byrne landed in Atlanta and drove halfway across Georgia to just over the border of his home state, he was no longer sad. Just plain angry. He could barely see the lines in the road, he was shaking so badly. Wherever Alex went next, Byrne would follow. And his brother better hope that the police found him first, because Byrne couldn't be sure what he would do when Alex was within arm's reach.

His parents still lived in the one-bedroom apartment above the disgusting pizza place where they'd moved after Byrne left for college. The only thing sadder than the seventies-era strip mall that housed it was the surrounding town that had died since the dog food manufacturing plant had closed over a decade ago.

Byrne parked his rental car, a green something-or-other sedan, on the street opposite the pizza place and apartments. No meters or thirty-dollar-per-hour garages here. He looked up at the too-thin drapes covering his parents' window and recognized Caroline's shape pacing back and forth, holding her fourteen-month-old daughter.

This didn't feel like coming home, not like he knew it should feel, not like he *wanted* it to feel.

The staircase going up to the second-floor apartments was unlocked, and the hallway at the top smelled like garbage. The

door to apartment 3 was also unlocked because his parents had
been expecting him, and he turned the knob with trepidation.

The kitchen looked exactly the same as it always had, only
more worse for wear, the small living room just beyond. Caroline slid Kristin onto the couch, then rushed into Byrne's arms.

She'd always been a rounder woman, but she'd lost a lot of
weight, most apparent in the rings beneath her eyes and the
feel of the bones in her shoulders as he hugged her.

"How are they?" he whispered into her ear. She answered
by pulling away and letting him see the pain on her face. He
walked around her and went into the living room.

"Dad," Byrne said, as his father came down the hall. The
two men forgot their usual handshake and went in for a
mutual embrace that had Byrne rocking in the smaller man's
arms. Then Byrne turned to his mom, who was pushing up
from the orange armchair.

"Hi, Mom. Came as soon as I could."

She tried to hide her wet eyes before she hugged him, but
he saw them all too well.

"Sit. Sit," Mom said. As she patted Byrne's arms and smiled
up at him, she successfully evaporated the impending tears.
She'd had a lot of practice doing that over the years. "Do you
want anything? A sandwich? A soda?"

What was she doing, offering him food at a time like this
when they probably couldn't spare any extra? "No, thanks."

"Coffee at least, then. I know it's a long trip to get here.
You must be exhausted."

"Mom, no." Byrne took her hand, pulled her back around
to keep her from going for the kitchen. "Come sit with me.
Tell me what happened."

His parents sat on the couch, one on either side of their
only grandchild. Baby K got tired of the toy plastic keys she
was holding and started to fuss. Caroline blew a piece of
brown hair off her forehead and went for her kid, but Byrne
hadn't seen his niece in months and she'd practically doubled
in size and adorableness. He got to her before Caroline, knelt
down in front of the beautiful little kid, and smiled.

"Hey, cutie. It's your Uncle J.P. You're going to be seeing a
lot more of me."

Kristin smiled back. She already had teeth. Byrne let the

kid play with his fingers, not even wincing when she pinched and pulled at the hair on the back of his hand.

The little girl satisfied, he swiveled his head between his parents. "So? Will you tell me what happened?"

"He found where we keep our savings," Dad said. "In an old Monopoly box in the closet."

God forbid they trust a bank. Byrne clenched his teeth, making his whole jaw ache.

"He stole our social security numbers, too," Mom added. "He didn't come home after work one night, and the next morning we realized that he wasn't going to. When your father saw the money was gone, I went to the sock drawer in my bedroom where I keep a notebook with all that important stuff written down. The cards were tucked in there the day before. And then they were gone."

Byrne blew out a long, forceful breath and hung his head. "The good thing is he can't do anything with those without leaving some kind of trail. Tell me you've at least called the police."

"Yeah, we have," said Caroline behind him.

"How much did you have? How much did he take?"

Dad chewed his lip, glanced over at his wife. They both looked twenty years older than their actual ages.

"How much?" Byrne pressed, careful to keep a tight rein on his frustration. It wasn't directed at them, and he didn't want to make them feel worse than they already did.

"Close to a thousand dollars," Mom finally answered.

A thousand dollars they'd likely been saving for years and years. For an emergency or a better place to live or gifts for their only grandkid or even retirement. And fucking Alex had appealed to their hearts, convinced them he'd changed, and snatched it out from underneath them for . . . what? Another gambling loss? To make another bet? Drugs? Or just to disappear somewhere else?

Out of all those options, Byrne really hoped it was the last.

Alex had to know that this was the final straw. This was the absolute last time their parents would welcome their youngest son back into this family. And maybe that's why he'd done it. Maybe he'd come back after a long time away, guessing that their parents had squirreled away every penny possible and would have a stash worthy of plundering. In all the time he'd been away, he'd lost all sense of family and only saw his parents as a means to an end. But an end to what?

Byrne gently tugged his hand away from his niece, and Caroline came to take over. Byrne stood before his parents. "You know what I'm going to say, right?"

Mom looked to Dad, but Dad just stared at Byrne with hands fisted in his lap.

"Give me your bills," Byrne said. "Your rent, electric, water, everything, for the next couple of months. Caroline and I are going grocery shopping, filling your fridge and freezer. And I'm getting y'all some gift cards, something generic with a long expiration date, that you can use whenever you need something."

"J.P. . . ."

"Mom, this is *not* a discussion." Damn it, he hadn't meant to sound so pissed off. But guess what? He was. "I'm not taking over for you, I'm not supporting you. I'm helping you until you can get back on your feet. Until we find Alex and see if we can get back what he took. If he hasn't thrown it away already."

His parents threaded their fingers together. Mom nodded. Dad's eyes filled and he turned his face away.

"But if we don't," Byrne added, "if it's all gone, at least let me put a thousand bucks in a proper bank for you. Please."

Neither of his parents responded to that.

Byrne turned to Caroline. "You, too. I'm doing the same for you—the shopping, the gift cards—because I'm sure you've dug into your own pockets since this shit's happened, and I want to make sure you and Baby K aren't hurting."

"Your mouth, J.P.," his mom said numbly.

When a stab of guilt flashed across Caroline's face, Byrne's stomach dropped.

"No," he said to Caroline. "No way. You didn't give him any money, did you?"

Caroline looked sheepishly at her baby as she replied. "Paul did. Alex took right to him. You know how Alex is, all charming and smooth when he wants to be. He made Paul think he was this great guy, that he had his act together and that they were these close brothers-in-law or something. Paul hasn't gotten off that couch for me in months, but they were going out all the time. Alex would even pay for the beers. But

I guess he pulled some sort of scam and Paul ended up giving him around two hundred bucks over the course of a few days."

Byrne couldn't speak. Couldn't think. Didn't even want to move for fear of what his body might do. That wall above the couch would look pretty good with his fist going through it. But he'd never been violent like that, not even when it came to Alex, so he swallowed it all down and stared at the stained and nappy rug, hands on his hips.

"Then I'll put two hundred dollars in Baby K's college fund," he said quietly. "All right?"

"Thank you," Caroline said.

The four of them just looked at one another. Kristin flopped onto her belly, then scooted awkwardly off the sofa to immediately plop on the floor and play with a spongy yellow ball. It was a strange and awful thing to realize, but at that very moment, he'd never felt closer to his family.

"So." Byrne clapped his hands and rubbed them together. "Can you tell me where the stores are? I'll start with the house stuff and go grocery shopping closer to dinner."

"I'll go with you," Caroline offered, standing.

"Why don't you stay with them for now?" he countered. "Since I just got here?"

Their parents looked grateful. He loved those expressions. Wanted to see more of that. Wanted to *do* more. Maybe this was finally the thing that would allow him to do it. It sucked that it had finally come to this.

He whipped out his phone and wandered through the kitchen, bathroom, and bedroom, tapping notes about everyday items they needed. Not extraneous, frivolous things, but things like new toothbrushes, and pillowcases without stains or holes, and forks with straight tines.

A couple of hours later he felt like Santa Claus, hauling in giant bags of bed linens and towels, soap, and kitchen gadgets. Mom looked at him for a heartbreaking moment, her hand on her chest, and he hated the shame he saw there. Hated her embarrassment. It reminded him of when he'd had to go pick up donations from the church when he was younger. When she came forward to help him put everything away, she thanked him in a small voice. He let her boss him around about where everything went, and she was smiling again.

Dad made coffee and Byrne told them about rugby, how he'd been playing in Scottish fest tournaments all over the northeast. As Caroline put Baby K down for a nap, he told his parents a story about trying to find a good hamburger in Switzerland that had both of them laughing without having to think about his reasons for being in that country. After Caroline came out, holding a finger to her lips for quiet, he ushered her out the door, and the two of them raided the grocery store.

An hour and a half later, he was once again heading down the garbage-smelling hallway. His hands were full of plastic grocery bags, his fingers close to being sawed off by the handles, when his phone rang in his back pocket. He hadn't had a chance to tell all his contacts overseas that he would be out of the office. If he had to be honest, it wouldn't have mattered, since he was technically available 24-7 anyway, and it was early morning in many areas in which he had client money.

"Crap. Caroline, can you grab my phone? See who it is?"

They were halfway down the awful hallway, and Caroline was carrying only a giant package of toilet paper. She dropped it in front of apartment 3 and made a face as she pulled out his phone.

"Weird, going into your big brother's back pocket. Okay, the name on the screen says . . . who's Shea Montgomery?"

If Byrne's heart wasn't already pounding from the hike up the stairs, carrying his weight in food and sundries, it pretty much jumped out of his chest at the sound of his sister saying Shea's name. Of course a plastic bag strap chose that moment to break, and cans of green beans and soup rolled down the sloping hall.

"Oooo, she's pretty," Caroline crooned, dangling the phone in front of her face. It was the old Caroline, the happy one he remembered from their nights lying awake in the train car, making each other laugh away the teasing they'd both gotten at school that day. "You take photos of all your clients looking all come-hither?"

"Caroline!" He couldn't drop the rest of the bags. Had to stumble, drunk-like, the rest of the way. He tapped the door with the toe of his shoe.

As he strained, his biceps muscles two seconds away from popping off his bones, Caroline peered harder at the phone.

"Not just pretty. Gorgeous. This the woman Erik was talking about? Is she your girlfriend now?"

He'd taken that photo of Shea the morning after the first time she'd come to his place. From the neck up, you couldn't tell that she only wore a bedsheet. Her pale hair was messy and wild and all around her face, down in the way he loved it. Her mouth was lipstick-free and her eyes these deep pools of blue. The morning sun was coming through his bedroom windows, and he'd wanted to capture the moment.

She didn't look come-hither, just . . . stunning.

The phone stopped ringing.

Mom finally opened up the door and he waddled in, dropping the bags onto the linoleum, hoping he hadn't cracked the eggs.

He whipped around to Caroline, holding out his hand for the phone. Of course she held it hostage.

His sister arched an eyebrow. "Do you have a girlfriend?"

In the ensuing pause, the chime went off to indicate Shea had left a message.

"Do you not know or something?" Caroline teased.

Byrne had to laugh. "Actually I don't. We've never talked about it. But I guess she is. I like to think she is."

"Well, that's good news, J.P.," Mom said from the floor, where she was picking through all her new food.

"Mom." He cringed. "I'm thirty-five. I'm not talking about this in my parents' kitchen." He grabbed a giggling Caroline around the waist and snatched the phone from her hand. "I'll put this stuff away in a minute. Just give me a sec."

As he ducked out of the apartment, he even saw his dad grinning at him from where he sat in the armchair. So glad the slightly awkward moment could bring a bit of happiness to this sad, sad room.

Back out on the sidewalk, next to the pizza place window with the flickering neon sign, he looked at Shea's photo for a long second before tapping the Call button. She picked up quickly, and he sank against the brick wall.

"How's it going down there?" Her voice was soft and sympathetic, and he was really grateful she didn't ask how he was.

"Better, now that I can talk to you. I feel very far away. From everything."

She sighed. "Any news?"

"They're letting me pay their bills for a couple of months. I just bought out Walmart and need to find a way to store it all in their place. I never want to see my brother again. My sister's kid is cute as hell. I miss you."

She gasped. And then he could tell she was smiling. He couldn't really explain how he knew; he just did.

"It's been less than twenty-four hours," she said.

"Doesn't matter. A lot can happen in that time."

"True. Very true."

He came away from the wall. "You say that like it means something."

"Welllll. I did a lot of pondering today, and I—"

"Pondering, you say?"

"Yes, pondering. And I think that I'm going to take that thing with Whitten and Right Hemisphere. I mean, I'm at least going to sit down to a meeting with him, hear his ideas in detail. Throw out some of my own. We've got a meeting set for a few weeks from now."

That made him incredibly happy for her. "You feel good about it?"

"Yeah, I do. It could extricate me from the Amber. It could give me money to put away for the distillery. There are possibilities."

"And you'd have more time for kilts and those hideous bagpipes."

She laughed. "Exactly."

The following pause was filled with things he sensed she wanted to say. "What is it?" he asked.

"I just realized I feel awful for telling you this good stuff when you're, well, you're down there, feeling not so good."

"Oh, believe me, when I'm *down there* I feel very good."

"Byrne!"

He laughed, and it felt like it had been days and weeks since he'd done that. How did she always do that to him? This woman who he'd once sworn was made of ice?

"Tell me more," he prompted. "About Whitten, what you're thinking."

"I think I'm excited. I'm a little scared, which tells me I'm probably headed down the right track."

He took a deep, deep breath, nodding to no one. "That's

what I've always thought. I wouldn't have gotten where I am without that kind of thinking. I wouldn't have been able to help my family in this moment if I hadn't thought that exact same thing so long ago, and if I hadn't lived it every day since."

"Really?"

"Leaving them, leaving South Carolina, scared the hell out of me. But I knew it was right. Just had to take that first step."

He loved the silence that followed, because it was filled with her breathing.

"Any word on that land?" she asked.

He gazed down the totally deserted main avenue, where a lone streetlight directed no traffic whatsoever. "Not since that odd email. I'm going to go do the pushy, obnoxious thing and stop by their offices on Monday."

"But you said there might be movement on it, right?"

"Yeah, that's what they said. Or hinted at. I'm taking that as license to do a drop-in, wave my checkbook around if I have to."

"You have a checkbook?"

"A virtual one. Can I wave my phone? Does that have the same effect?" She laughed, and so he felt compelled to say, "I love your laugh." And then, before she could reply, "I should go. My parents and sister were way too interested in the fact that your picture popped up when you called. I'm afraid I had to tell them about you."

"And what did you say?"

"That I hoped you were my girlfriend."

"Well, I am, if you're my boyfriend. My older boyfriend by two years."

"I knew there was a reason I was feeling guilty and awkward at your parents' house."

Another sigh. "Call me when you get back, okay?"

He turned and slowly lifted his eyes to his parents' window, desperately wanting to get them out of that apartment. Out of this town, this state. "I may call you before that. I can't promise anything, though."

"Whenever you want. I'm here. Or at the Amber. But I run the place so it's not like I can't pick up the phone or anything."

"Okay. Bye."

I think I love you.

"Bye," she said, breathy and lovely, and in his imagination she said those three words back.

*B*ut six days later, Byrne returned to New York without the land.

His decade-long dream lay dead and buried in a South Carolina tobacco field, there was still no sign of the brother who'd ruined everything, and he had *no fucking land*.

Because the land, it turned out, wasn't actually for sale, and there were no plans for it to enter the public market.

He'd gone into the company office, as promised, only to find out that there had never truly been movement. The threat to sell had been some sort of internal politics bullshit. Byrne tried to make a counteroffer, but it was useless.

Byrne got it. The situation was business. But this time it was business to them and personal to him, and it hurt in a way he'd never experienced before. He thought of Shea, how she liked to keep those clear lines between the two worlds, and how she hated when they got smudged.

He settled deep into the airplane seat and sipped vodka the whole flight back from Atlanta. Didn't matter that it was mid-morning. Two of those little bottles, splashed with soda. The buzz stuck with him as he deplaned and retrieved his bag. It followed him to the taxi stand and rode along with him in the whining, rattling cab as it crawled from LaGuardia into the Upper East Side. It made the city a little blurry, a little bit easier to take.

He'd called New York home for almost a decade now, but was it?

At least his parents and Caroline were situated for a while. At least they'd allowed him to help temporarily, even though they'd refused—again—to let him move them somewhere else. To let him take care of them.

At least he was coming back to Shea.

It had been days since they'd spoken. After the disappointment about the land, he couldn't bring himself to call her. Couldn't force himself to do anything but be with his family, playing cards or shopping or taking Baby K to the park or helping Caroline organize her shithole of a house while Paul sprawled on the couch doing nothing.

They'd never known about his dream to get back that land—and now they never would—but Shea did. Byrne had no idea what he was going to tell her. His heartbreak was almost too great to voice. But she would ask and he would have to open up to her. Before, there had been such great hope, a reason to keep putting on those clothes every day. Now? Now what?

For the first time since leaving for Boston, he felt hopeless. Dreamless.

His body ached all over like he'd just finished the hardest rugby match of his life, one in which he'd played the entire time at a hundred percent and they still lost by fifty. He could actually sense gray hairs poking their way to the surface.

He entered the lobby of his building in a daze. It took two tries to press the button up to his floor because he was just so drained. As he exited the elevator, the hallway with the plush carpeting seemed as ugly and long as the one leading to his parents' place.

Byrne inserted the key into the lock of his front door, thinking dismissively that it felt a little odd, a little loose. In the foyer, he unceremoniously dropped his suitcase and tossed his keys onto the little table underneath the wall mirror. He must've been really out of it, because the keys completely missed the table and clattered to the tile. Odd, considering he'd been doing the same thing every day for years. Whatever.

He wandered half-blind down the hall and into the main room. Frances must have pulled the drapes to keep out the sun, and the place was remarkably dark for morning. With him gone, there'd been nothing for her to do, so he'd given her the week off with pay. She'd probably been grateful to not have to lug his suits to and from the cleaners, to not have to grocery shop. What a dumb thing for him to think about now, but it was literally all the space he had left in his brain.

He flicked on a couple of light switches. The cans in the kitchen came on, as well as the lamp that sat on the long table just behind the couch. Only the lamp wasn't on the table anymore. It was lying in pieces on the floor, the shade askew, the circuitry keeping the bulb alive.

It threw a sickly, dying light on the war zone that was his living room. His heart punched out of his chest.

His entire apartment was destroyed.

Chapter

18

*T*he cops had been over and through his place for the past few hours. The doorman had been questioned and questioned, but he'd seen nothing, had nearly cried with disappointment over this happening to Byrne. The security footage showed no one suspicious or out of place coming in the front doors.

Which meant it had been some kind of inside job, with the perpetrator coming in through the service entrance or the garbage chute. Something like that.

Byrne stood near the kitchen island, gazing with detached numbness at the slashed couch, the shattered coffee table glass, the shredded books. The kitchen floor was a pile of broken dishes and glasses.

Every article of clothing in his closet had some kind of jagged hole or rip. Byrne's own serrated bread knife lay in one of his torn shoes.

The only shirt that hadn't been touched was the purple Italian one. It was still rolled into a tight ball under a pillow near the headboard, where it had been left after he'd peeled it away from Shea's body in what now felt like an eternity ago. He pulled it out and brought it with him back to the kitchen.

A female cop, the one in charge, came into the apartment,

her short legs stepping over the suitcase where he'd left it in the foyer. She approached him with a grim face, and though she addressed him, she scanned the disaster.

"A recently hired maintenance guy with a criminal background that he hid from the building owners took a pretty huge bribe from a stranger who said he wanted to surprise his girlfriend who lived here. Maintenance guy said the man was charming and young, late twenties maybe, dark hair. Gave him close to a thousand dollars for access. Fingerprints are all over this place and we've sent them off to the lab. We should have a name shortly."

Byrne's stare traveled to the shattered coffee table. Then his eyes gravitated to the bookshelves where the books he and Caroline had loved were now in shreds. Then to the framed Boston College and Wharton diplomas that had been ripped from his office wall and smashed to bits.

"Pretty sure I already know the name," he told the cop, the words hurting his throat.

She turned to him, removing her hat and managing to look both frustrated, pissed off, and impressed all at the same time. "How come you didn't say anything to me before?"

"Because I didn't see it. I mean, I saw it, but I think I was just in shock over the whole thing. I just now pieced it all together."

"See what?"

He pointed to the coffee table. Once a large square of mahogany wood covered by a thick slab of frosted glass, it was now in tiny pieces, the rug underneath peppered with shards. The green toy train engine sat right in the middle, as though someone had lifted it up high and slammed the metal thing down into the glass . . . and then had gone through the apartment taking every other piece of the train—the coal car, the cow car, the caboose—and tossed them together in the mess.

Everything else in the apartment had been destroyed where it stood. But the train had been gathered and pulverized all in one place. To make sure they were seen together.

"That," Byrne told the cop. "When those prints come back, I can already tell you they'll belong to Alex Byrne. My brother."

* * *

*M*uch later in the day, Byrne wheeled the same suitcase he'd brought to South Carolina back out of his apartment. The only difference was that he'd added a couple of things: the crumpled purple shirt and the green engine.

The toy was unrecognizable now. The whole side had been bashed in, the wheels unturnable, like Alex had held it in his hand and smashed the thing down repeatedly on the edge of a table. Or stamped on it with big, thick boots.

Byrne would've given just about anything to be out on a rugby field just then. Not in practice, not going nowhere on a treadmill, not lifting weights, but powering across the grass with another guy's mug in his face and all Byrne's muscles focusing on the attack.

Instead he pulled the suitcase to the curb, stuck his hand out, and waited for a cab to swerve over.

The other hand pulled his phone out of his pocket and pushed the button to call Shea.

"Long time, no talk," she said, chuckling upon answering. The sound of a cash register chimed in the background. "Are you home?"

Home. That concept seemed even more foggy now that everything he owned was in tatters.

"I'm in New York, yeah."

"I've been thinking about you, wondering how you've been."

The way those words made him shiver confused him even more.

"What're you doing now?" she asked.

"I'm, ah, heading to a hotel."

"Why?"

His heart jackhammered and his breath came up short. "Because while I was gone my brother broke into my apartment and destroyed it. It's crawling with cops."

She gasped. "Oh my God. Byrne, I . . . holy shit. You're not going to a hotel. Come stay with me. Please."

A cab finally swung next to the curb and Byrne opened the door. "I don't know—"

"I insist. Don't be alone right now. The thought of you staying in a hotel when I'm right here . . ."

He was torn. He desperately wanted to see her, to hold her, to just sink into her—and he didn't even mean sexually—but he was balancing on a very fine edge, and he had no idea which way his mood was going to go.

"You can stay as long as you like," she said. "I'm at the corner bodega right now, but I'll be home in a few minutes."

"Yo!" shouted the cabbie as he rotated in his seat to glare at Byrne. "You gettin' in or not?"

Byrne couldn't guarantee that the fury he was feeling wouldn't be taken out on an innocent hotel room à la a nineteen-seventies rock star, so he said to Shea, "Is this what it takes to finally get an invitation to your place?"

It was a bad attempt at levity, grasping for their usual easy rapport, but he was strung out and desperate to feel anything else.

"Is this what it would take," she replied softly, "to give you a little peace?"

He sighed, climbed into the backseat of the cab, and pulled the suitcase in. The cabbie raised his eyebrows and turned an impatient hand, silently asking, *Address, you dumbfuck?*

"Where's the secret location?" Byrne asked her.

She told him and he directed the cabbie to Chelsea. Then Byrne sank deep into the seat, closing his eyes.

Shea's studio apartment was on the top floor of a prewar townhome on a tree-lined street. He tugged the suitcase up the cement steps and let his finger hover over the buzzer, noting that his hand still shook. Inside, he heard a door open above, and he climbed two sets of stairs to get to her.

She wore jeans with hems that curled, worn and soft, under her heels. Her white T-shirt looked like it had been cut into a tank top over ten years ago. Bright blue bra straps peeked out from underneath the cut cotton. Her hair was down, streaming over one shoulder.

She was a sight for sore eyes, if there ever was a true definition of the phrase.

Though she smiled, it was strained and sympathetic, and it made him feel strangely uncomfortable. One thumb hooked into the back pocket of her jeans, and she sat into a hip, waiting. Waiting for him to move, to give her an idea of how to act.

The second he stepped into her warm, sunny apartment,

she grabbed him with one hand and shut the door with the other. His arms wrapped her up good and tight.

"Hi," she murmured into his neck, taking a big inhale.

He already knew that she smelled divine.

As her grip on him tightened, he realized what he was doing. He was leaning on her—figuratively and literally—and he found it profoundly disconcerting. He, who had always been the pillar for others, specifically his family.

Gently, he slid his hands around her rib cage and pushed her away.

She chewed a thumbnail as she studied him. "The only thing I can think to ask is 'How are you?'" she said, "but I know it's the stupidest question in the world."

He released the suitcase handle and ambled farther into her apartment. It was long and narrow, with a set of two windows overlooking the street in front and two others in the doorless bedroom in the back. The small kitchen sat right in the middle. She'd done the place in overstuffed furniture draped with blankets and printed pillows. Lots of color, very cozy and eclectic. The antithesis of the stark, modern, masculine Amber.

He loved it.

He stood there, looking over the place she'd kept so private it had taken several not-a-dates, a healthy dose of amazing sex, and several Byrne tragedies in a row for her to invite him into.

She came up next to him, slid a hand over his shoulder. "What happened?"

The whole past week slammed into him. Took him out at the knees. He collapsed forward, catching himself on the back of one of her two gray couches. He took a moment, trying to breathe around the stumbling block that was the bass drum of his heart.

Pressing his hands heavily into the couch back, he said to a bright, striped pillow, "Best I can figure? Alex stole everything my parents had and used it to get up here, knowing that I'd fly down there to be with them and Caroline. He bribed some new employee in my building, and broke in to destroy my apartment."

He pushed away from the couch and faced her. One hand covered her mouth. "Destroyed?"

"Completely. As in . . ." He couldn't say any more. Just went over to his suitcase, kicked it onto its side, and crouched to rip open the zipper, exposing the mangled train engine lying on top of all the dirty clothes he'd hauled back from South Carolina. He grabbed the green metal in a tight fist and held it up to her. She didn't take it, just stared in horror.

"Jesus. Is that . . . ?"

"Yeah." His voice died. Still crouching, he dug two fingers into his eyes, grinding away the sting. "Everything I had in that apartment. Everything I own, even down to my shampoo and old DVDs. And the train. Especially the train."

"But *why*?" She lowered herself to the floor next to him. "Did he steal anything?"

He shrugged. "A watch I never wear, some cufflinks. Little metal things he'll probably try to sell. But it wasn't about that for him."

"So what was it about? I'm kind of lost here."

Byrne set down the green engine on the hardwood floor between them. "This. It was about this."

Understanding clouded her eyes.

"Saying 'fuck you' just wasn't enough for him," Byrne said. "I kept trying to help my family, would've given them everything I owned if they'd let me, but I cut him off because he took advantage."

"So he's bitter. Even though it's his own fault."

Byrne nudged the toy engine farther away like it had just stung him. "Bitter doesn't even cover it. This is his hate. His jealousy. And it came out of something I was trying to do to help them, help him. I'm so fucking angry. If this is what he wanted from me, this breaking down, this rage, then he fucking won."

She reached out to touch his knee, but it suddenly felt like too much and he stood, moving out of her reach.

"At least you could help them out when you went down there. That's got to feel somewhat good, right?"

Shea's voice was full of hope, of positivity, and even though he knew she was trying to help him, it made him feel false. Because he hadn't truly been able to help, in the end. Maybe temporarily, but everything would go back to the way it was for them very soon. And he'd be piling the bits and pieces of everything he'd ever owned into a Dumpster.

He scowled and scrubbed a hand through his hair.

"What happened with the land?" she asked.

He laughed, because he couldn't think of anything else to do besides scream.

"Oh no," she whispered, and he heard her rise from the floor.

" 'Oh no' is right."

"You didn't get it."

"No. Wasn't ever for sale in the first place and doesn't look like it will be anytime soon. Fuck it."

"Byrne, I'm so sorry."

He said nothing. Not a single word came to mind.

"You can stay here as long as you like," she said, straightening her shoulders. "Bed's not as big as yours is—was—but you can have your own side and everything."

He glanced all around her apartment, finally knowing what it felt like to be overwhelmed by someone wanting to help you when you believed you should be helping yourself. It wasn't a good feeling. It made him uneasy. Like he was a burden.

"I can go shopping with you," she offered, pushing a smile onto her face. "I can introduce you to the freedom of buying clothes off the rack. I could carry bags or lamps or new pillows or whatever you need."

He just stared at her.

"At least it was just stuff, right?" Her smile kept trying to expand.

His eyes dropped to the toy engine and he frowned. "But it's not just stuff. My mom gave that train to me for my tenth birthday. It can't be replaced."

"I know, I know."

She was being as gentle as possible, her sympathetic eyes briefly closing, but it still bothered him for some reason.

"At least you can afford to replace all the things you need. And you've got insurance?"

He just looked at her. "That's not the point, replacing them."

"I know. I know it's not. But at least you can, is what I'm saying."

Ah, okay. He got it. He could replace all that pricey stuff

because he was Bespoke Byrne, and she had a pretty good idea about how much money he had to have stowed away for land he'd now never get.

"Right." His head bobbed in a nod, but it felt like it was moving through sludge. And that was literally all he could say, because he couldn't be certain about his tone, should any other words come out.

"Maybe"—she stepped closer—"maybe this could actually turn out to be a good thing for you."

His head snapped up. "*How*?"

She winced but didn't back down. *That* was the tone he'd been trying to avoid, but he was wire-strung and he couldn't possibly believe that what she'd said was true. Or that she meant it. His dream had just been stolen out from underneath him, his parents basically had to start over, his brother had destroyed Byrne's apartment and everything he owned . . . and this was supposed to be a *good* thing?

"Just hear me out, okay?" She licked her lips and edged even closer, hands up and fingers splayed. "Do you want something to eat or drink?"

"No, I don't want anything. I'd like to know what you meant."

Biting the inside of her lip, he could see her gathering up the strings of her control and holding on tight. But he couldn't seem to stop himself. He felt really, *really* on edge, and a stiff wind was coming up fast on his back.

"I'm not attacking you, Byrne. Let's just get that straight right now. What I'm trying to do is make you feel better. That's why you came over here, wasn't it? So you could be with me and tell me what's up and let me try to help?" She didn't let him answer, which was probably a good thing, because what was on the tip of his tongue was to say that he didn't want to talk anymore.

"What I meant," she said, "and I'm thinking out loud so bear with me, was that all that stuff you had in that apartment— that incredible furniture and all those clothes and, yes, even that toy train—was somehow connected to your past. You bought all that expensive stuff because you could. Because you felt some kind of pressure to. Because it was the opposite of how you'd been raised and what you'd had growing up, and you wanted to make a point. But maybe you've grown past that."

"Grown past it?"

"It was Bespoke Byrne, all the way, even though I don't like to use that name anymore. But think about how you are with me. You're Rugby Byrne. You're my Byrne. That amazing guy who has absolutely nothing to do with all that stuff in your apartment. You are not connected to it. It doesn't define you, but you seem to think it does."

"*That* does." He thrust a finger at the engine. *Shut up, Byrne.*

"No. It doesn't." She slowly shook her head. "You're using it to cling to your shame, that embarrassment you told me about. Those emotions you said you escaped when you left South Carolina. You said you've used the things in your apartment, like the train, to remind you of your past in a good way, but maybe they're really an anchor. Maybe that train was holding you back instead of pushing you forward."

"That's dumb. Every day I look at the pieces of that train and I'm reminded of what I'm doing and who I'm doing it for."

Jesus, Byrne. Just shut the fuck up. She's trying to help.

Yet he couldn't get himself to listen. Or obey.

"All right. I get that," she said. "But don't call me dumb."

Weariness seeped into him at the same time this disagreement—fight?—was making him all hopped up. Far too many emotions chased one another through his brain. He sighed. "You're not dumb. Not at all. I'm sorry. I just don't agree with you."

"Fine." She crossed her arms. Stared him down. "But—"

So she wasn't going to drop this. He lifted frustrated eyes to her ceiling.

"—I think perhaps that this had to happen," she continued, "for you to finally be able to let go."

His chin came back down so fast he got dizzy. "Let go of what?"

She opened her arms. "Everything. All that stuff you told me about your past. All the things you hate. All the things that frustrated you and ate at you for years and years. All the shame. All that bad shit was in the atoms of your furniture and the apartment's incredible view and every piece of clothing in your closet. You convinced yourself that the things you bought were good things, that they healed you on some level, that they proved you'd risen above where you'd started, but they really didn't. *I* know there's no reason at all for you to be ashamed of what you've lived through, but sooner or later you need to realize that, too. And maybe this is that time."

"My parents and sister won't let me do what I want for them, to make their lives better. My brother broke into my apartment and spit in my face. I'm fucking angry and I want him gone from my family. I came to you for comfort. That's it. You're reading far too much into this and it's starting to piss me off."

"Good," she said with a firm nod.

He recoiled. "*Good*?"

"Yes, good. I think this is the world's way of telling you that you need to start over. Erase your goals—because you've reached them, or you've done all you can—and start over with new intentions. Or adjust your old ones into something you actually can do, and not focus on all that you haven't. Because I've got to say, Byrne, you are completely shackled to that train, and everything it means."

"Wait a minute. That train means my family. Who I would do anything for. Who I *want* to do everything for. You realize that, right?"

"Yes, of course." She rubbed her forehead, like she should be the one in pain right now.

"And you want me to just leave them behind? To forget all that's happened and 'start over'?"

"That's not what I said *at all*. I never said to forget. All I'm doing is suggesting that you use this as an opportunity to reevaluate. Take a step back and figure out a new life going forward—one that makes you feel good in every way—as opposed to trying to drive in the tracks that train already gouged out for you. I think that this horrible, awful, nasty event could actually allow you to be who you were meant to be. What I meant was that you aren't like so many people who get handed this kind of setback and have no way of climbing out of the hole. You have the means to rebuild your apartment and your life at the same time."

"'The means.' Right. You keep talking about being able to 'afford' things. I don't know who you want me to be, Shea. Poor Byrne or Rich Byrne."

"I don't want you to *be* anyone. No one but yourself. I don't think you're either of those guys, not deep down. Not anymore. I'm just saying that even though the world seems really dire right now, that you do have the means to help yourself. You're not helpless. And that you could manage to skew this into something good. But maybe I should've just kept my mouth shut."

"Maybe," he muttered.

Good God, Byrne. You're an ass. She's not Alex.

She drew a sharp inhale, stared at him for a long moment, and then dropped her chin. "I see," she whispered.

As she looked down at the train still sitting in the middle of the floor, he almost lunged for it.

That inconsequential thing that really did feel like an anchor now.

When she tilted her face back up to him, her pale hair hid one eye. The other carried a great deal of confidence, frustration, and severe intelligence.

Deep down, he knew she was only trying to help. He *knew* this. He unclenched his hands from where they'd unconsciously dug into his upper arms. "Listen, you don't deserve any of my anger. It's because I'm wired, and you just happen to be the one standing right here, not Alex. I kind of hate myself right now, for saying what I have." He inhaled. Exhaled. "I think I'll stay in that hotel tonight. Try to clear out my head."

That one visible blue eye softened. "Byrne, you don't have to—"

"I know. But I probably should."

And then he turned and left.

Chapter

✦

19

It was extraordinarily rare when Shea rued the day she'd grown a backbone and learned how to voice what she felt and wanted, to express her beliefs. And today was not one of those days.

The look on Byrne's face as he'd backed out of her apartment—the pain over his situation, the regret over his impassioned, reactionary words to her, the helplessness and the anger—played over and over in her mind. She wanted nothing more than to clear them all, to smooth the lines from his face.

She wanted nothing more than for the two of them to pick up where they'd left off before he'd been called away to South Carolina. She longed to be with him, to lie tangled in his sheets again, the light from his closet falling across his bed as they talked about nothing and everything. She wanted to rewind.

He'd come to her place yesterday looking for a shoulder and an escape, but she'd felt in her heart that he needed something more to pick himself up. He was a man with such grand plans that to just roll over and play dead was completely unlike him. For him to move forward, he needed to see the larger picture. He needed to see that this wasn't an end, not after he'd worked so hard.

She couldn't take back anything she'd said to him, and she didn't want to. He'd been unnervingly emotional, and yes, maybe her timing had sucked, now that she looked back on the whole exchange. But it didn't make what she felt in her heart any less truthful, any less powerful.

The words he'd said to her, his visceral reactions, had been fed by his terrible situation and exacerbated by his confusion and anger, and she understood that none of it had truly been focused on her. But she'd happened to be the one in his presence, and she hadn't conformed to what he'd expected. It had been easiest to use her as a conduit for everything he was feeling. As a scapegoat.

Yes she was a little uncomfortable with that, but she was also willing to forgive since she understood the circumstances. And . . . she was dying to see him. Dying to talk to him. To know how he was. If she could do anything for him.

Her couches were the complete opposite of Byrne's firm, leather-covered pieces of furniture. She'd picked them out for the very reason that they were huge and soft and that you could burrow between the massive pillows and get lost when you wanted to. Like this morning. But it seemed that she couldn't burrow deep enough, because she could still see Byrne's suitcase propped up next to the front door, the toy engine sitting on top.

For when he came back.

The message she'd left him late last night had been short and sweet: "Please call me. I need to know you're okay." *I think I love you.*

Picking up her phone yet again that morning, she saw that he'd neither texted nor called.

Sitting there waiting would just about kill her, so she jumped off the couch and hit the shower. She'd go to the Amber early and drown herself in work. The trip to Kentucky for a VIP bourbon tour and a meeting with the distillers needed to get off the ground, there were some inventory issues to address, and she still had to approve the tasting list and check bottle availability for the upcoming Scottish Society ball.

Showered and fed, she marched to the 1 train, rehashing the whole scene with Byrne for the umpteenth time. Wondering how she could've put things differently to make him see that this could be a spectacular new beginning, not a disastrous end. Wondering what he might say to her, once he had time to sleep on it.

Coming out of the subway at Franklin Street, she was still mooning about it. Then she turned onto West Broadway, and the sight of the Amber sign, a short block away, slapped clarity and focus into her mind. Until she noticed a man standing on the sidewalk outside the Amber. Normally it wouldn't have made her stop, except that he was alone, holding a big, professional-looking camera. And he was taking pictures of her bar.

Her first thought? That something had gotten leaked about her impending meeting with Right Hemisphere. But who would do that when nothing had been signed or even formally discussed?

The photographer finished clicking at the old brick exterior and slung his camera over his shoulder, then pulled out his phone. As he talked, he took out a little notebook and set it up against the Amber's door, writing and nodding at the same time.

It became very clear that he was waiting, quite possibly for her. She couldn't say exactly why that made her uneasy. Maybe because she was usually notified about interviews or photo ops, not surprised or ambushed like this.

Just then her phone rang, and before the reporter could look up and notice the sound or her, she ducked back around the corner out of sight. Leaning against the fire station, she saw it was Willa calling. Shea exhaled in relief. She'd tried to call Willa last night after Byrne left, but the crazy woman had been out, of course.

"Hey, girl," Shea said to Willa. "It's a bit early for you to be up, isn't it? It's only nine thirty."

The pause on the other end was completely un-Willa-like. Even for a hungover Willa. She let out a strange sound that might have been a laugh. "Yeah. It is. Are you okay?"

"Sorry I didn't leave a message last night, but things were just so weird and I knew you were out having fun. God, I don't even know where to begin. Byrne came back yesterday and I think we got in this fight but I'm still not sure, and he left all mad. Things were so great before he left for South Carolina and now . . . now I have no idea what's happened and it's driving me crazy."

Normally Willa would've jumped in by now. Normally she would've made a joke or ripped on the entire male species or even asked Shea for all the details. But Willa still said nothing, and a chill skated down Shea's spine.

"Wait," Shea said. "What exactly are you asking me?"

Willa gasped. "Oh, honey. You haven't heard? You haven't seen?"

Shea pushed away from the wall. "Seen what?"

"Oh, shit." She let out a long breath. "Maybe it's better you found out from me."

"Found out *what*?"

Another deep breath. "Sweetie, it's that shitty society gossip website. The one with all the anonymous, passive-aggressive jabs at the rich people. The one that follows Marco's crowd to restaurants and the beach and takes really ugly photos and posts them online."

Shea knew exactly which site that was. It had covered her own wedding with disgusting vigor, speculating about the people in attendance and making up all these petty things she may or may not have said about the whole event. It had chosen the most unflattering photo of her in her wedding dress, taken when she'd sneezed or something, and put up a caption of something along the lines of, "Billionaire bride hates the fifty-thousand-dollar flowers!" It was a despicable, gross publication . . . that apparently a lot of people looked at. Whether for purposes of schadenfreude or just for a laugh, Shea never understood.

She rubbed her temple. "What did Marco do now?"

Another pregnant pause. "Maybe something really bad this time."

Shea suddenly started to feel sick. "Tell me."

"Um, remember that trip to Santorini he took you on? With that other couple? The heiress or tycoon or something like that?"

It had been another real estate developer from Monte Carlo, and it had been six nonstop days of drinking and parties and a continuous loop of obnoxiously wealthy people she didn't know and would never see again. "Yeah, I remember."

"God, I hate telling you this. There are pictures. Of you. Up on that site. Right now."

"Pictures."

Her mouth dried up as some specific events of that trip came back to her. It was shortly after their wedding, and at the peak of her complicity, of her doing whatever Marco told her to.

"It looks like you're on the bow of this massive yacht, and one of the photos is of you kissing a guy who isn't Marco. The caption is speculating you cheated on your husband, who was somewhere else on the boat. And that it was the beginning of the end to your marriage."

Shea knew exactly which picture that was. "But that's not true! It was all a game. Marco was sitting right there the whole time. He even took the picture. We were all laughing and the kiss wasn't even any more than a peck!"

"That's not the worst of it," Willa added. "There's another of you draped across the front of the yacht. Topless."

Fuck. Shea went dizzy and had to fall back into the wall. Marco had taken that photo, too. They'd been alone for that one, but it had been between them. A private moment.

"And they're online?" Shea squeaked out.

"Yeah. I mean, they pixelated your tits on the official page, but . . ."

Shea got it. It was the Internet. If there were pixels on one site, there were actual nipples somewhere on another.

What the hell was going on? How did this happen? Her hands started to shake.

She and Marco had taken a million pictures on that trip, most of them typical vacation shots. Nothing salacious. But those photos had been picked out of the whole lot and deliberately sent out.

Goddamn vindictive, jealous bastard.

"I . . . I have to go," she told Willa.

"No wait, Shea. Stay on the line. I'll come to you or you can come here."

"Sorry. I can't . . ." Couldn't what? Talk? Think? React? Understand? "I'll call you later. I need to figure some stuff out."

"Don't go online, Shea. Whatever you do, don't go—"

"Bye, babe."

Shea ended the phone call. And then found the website.

There she was. Twenty-four and half-naked, the sparkling Mediterranean stretching behind her. Tiny blue bikini bottoms, suntan-lined chest thrust out, showing off for the camera. For Marco. Her new husband, whom she'd once thought was her fairy-tale prince.

And there she was again, playing drunk truth or dare with the Monte Carlo couple. Marco had dared her to kiss the other man. She did it—without tongue, no more than a half second long—and then all four of them had collapsed into laughter and poured more Cristal.

Why would he even have these pictures still? Why would he *do* this?

Of course. Running into her twice recently—once with her new boyfriend—only reminded him that he'd lost her. And it wasn't even her as a person that mattered. It was that he'd lost *at all*. She'd proven to the world she didn't need him, and he didn't like it. In his crazy mind, he felt like he still had to get even somehow.

The posting of the photos had been time-stamped at the crack of dawn that morning. Just below them, in obnoxious, half-bolded, half-italicized type, was a declaration that the photos were sent from an anonymous source, followed by speculation that Shea herself had done it to give her and the Amber a boost. As though this were all part of a horrific marketing plan.

That, above all, made her fighting mad. Made her want to pound brick and then pound Marco's face. She had not spent the last four years fighting to be acknowledged as being at the top of her industry, only to have everything canceled out by one man's fucking ego.

Marco did this. Marco would have to fix it.

She wheeled away from the Amber and the photo hound who was waiting to ask her nosy questions and take hideous reaction shots. Where would Marco be right now? Did she even still have his contact info in her phone? She scrolled through her address book as she barreled down the sidewalk without looking where she was going. Crap. No number for Marco. She could call his office—

The phone rang in her hand. The photo that popped up on-screen was of a bushy-bearded bagpiper, Byrne's name in white type across his forehead.

Shea gaped at the image, debating whether or not to answer. Of all the times for him to call back. Then she realized she kind of needed to hear his voice to calm her down so she could plan her attack. There was a good chance he didn't know what had happened that morning. The Byrne she knew wouldn't go anywhere near those kinds of websites.

"Hi," she said, but she was a terrible actress, and her voice sounded as flat and unenthusiastic and hurt as she felt.

"Shea." He let out a deep, aggrieved sigh. "I saw . . . I saw the photos. I'm so sorry."

She stopped dead in her tracks. "You saw them? How? I just found out five seconds ago."

He cleared his throat. "Do you even need to ask? Dan."

Shea filled the following pause with deep breathing worthy of a yoga instructor.

"What can I do for you?" he asked. "How can I help you? Do you want me to come over?"

That stopped her. What could *he* do for *her*? After he hadn't allowed her to try to help him just last night? It was all so confusing, another layer she didn't know if she could handle just then.

"I'm not at home," she said. "You don't need to . . . I'm fine. I'm just trying to figure out what to do."

"How did this happen? Where'd they come from and why are they online?" He sounded slightly out of breath, like he was pacing, getting riled up.

"Marco," she replied. "Marco took them. Years ago."

"Mother*fucker*." Byrne kicked something. The crash was faintly metallic. A file cabinet, likely. "I want to kill him."

"There's no reason for that. Then I can't do it myself."

Byrne released a growl of frustration, but it was muffled, like he'd covered the phone so she couldn't hear.

"I can't believe this happened to you. Tell me what I can do."

She took a deep breath of exhaust-filled New York air and had never wished to be camping in the middle of nowhere more.

"Nothing. You can't do anything, Byrne. This is my embarrassment and I'll deal with it."

He paused. "Tell me this resistance isn't because of last night."

She was curious if he'd apologize. When he didn't, she

simply said, "It's not. Byrne, look, I'm glad to hear your voice, I really am, but I am fighting a full-on rage meltdown here, and I have to figure out what I'm going to say to Whitten after I've murdered Marco."

Byrne's voice deepened. "You're not going to see him, are you?"

"Who? Whitten or Marco?"

"You know who. God, I can't even fucking say his name."

"Oh, hell yes I'm going to see him. Theoretical guns blazing. Or maybe even real ones. Look, I have to go. I have to do something to put out this fire. I can't just stand here on this corner thinking it will go away on its own."

"Wait." It sounded like he was scrambling, shuffling things around on his desk. "Let me come with you."

"What? Why? No, thank you, Byrne. This is my thing. I don't want you anywhere near this bloodbath."

"Shea, please—"

"I really don't want to argue right now. I don't want to argue with you at all, if you must know."

She knew she was acting similar to how he had last night, pushing him away when all he wanted was to help, but this was her problem and he couldn't do a thing about it.

And that was probably exactly what he'd thought about her last night.

"Okay." His tone softened, resigned. "Okay."

"I'll try to call you later."

"Shea."

About a thousand layers of emotion filtered through the way he said her name. Regret. Frustration. Longing. And something else, something far, far deeper. None of which she could afford to think about right now. He muddled her brain on her best days, and she needed all her faculties at hand.

She told him good-bye and leaned against an empty newspaper box.

Suddenly she thought of her parents. Once upon a time they used to troll the New York City social pages for mentions of Marco and her. Maybe they'd stopped since the divorce. Hopefully they'd stopped. The liquor business, to them, was disappointing enough.

Her phone buzzed in her palm. It was Pierce Whitten, and

she stared at his name with a dry mouth, wondering if she should pick up. Right before the final ring, the one that would kick the call into voice mail, she tapped Answer. She was a business-woman above all and would conduct herself accordingly.

"Good morning, Pierce."

"Shea. Hello." He sighed in a completely different way than Byrne had. "I'm so very sorry this has happened to you."

Of course he would have seen. The Internet was his world.

What was she supposed to say to that? *Thank you*? Instead she remained silent. A bus rumbled past, the jet of its hot fumes kicking up around her.

"Are you still there?" he asked.

"I'm here."

"Look." Another sigh. "I'm just calling to let you know that my offer still stands. That Right Hemisphere is behind you."

"You've got some pretty deep reach," she said. "Can you erase parts of the Internet and wipe human memories?"

"I wish I could, Shea. I wish I could." That fatherly tone again, the one he'd used when he'd described Byrne. "What I can do, what my company and I are really damn good at, is marketing. Targeting. Spinning things our way."

She narrowed her eyes. "What do you mean, exactly?"

"I know we haven't signed any papers, but call me an opti-mist. Just give me the word and I'll put my PR people on this. We can misdirect people's attention, we can turn it in your favor, you name it."

Shea started to sweat. Even when she ducked out of the direct sunshine into the shadows outside an art gallery, the heat was still oppressive.

Turn private, naked photos in her favor? Use the scandal to somehow boost her name or her business? And do it under the umbrella of Right Hemisphere, thereby linking herself with the company whose current direction she didn't care for? Declare herself for Whitten before they'd ever come to mutu-ally beneficial terms?

"No," she told him. "Don't go near it. Please."

"All right," he replied after a pause. "I had a feeling you'd say that, but I wanted to offer anyway."

"It was just gossip, but they made accusations that I was doing this to be in the spotlight. If I did anything like that, with your company, I think it would only prove them right. And they're not."

"I understand. Is this affecting how you're looking at our meeting?"

How could he even ask that right now?

Just yesterday she'd thought she'd had everything under control, thought she'd had the steps to her future all set up and she was ready to climb. Now they were crumbling, and it hadn't even been her engineering mistake. It was someone from the side, lobbing bombs at her foundation.

Just yesterday she'd allowed herself to start putting in writing all her ideas for the distillery.

"As of right now?" she replied. "Yes. It does. This is going to take a while to sort out in my head. And in the public eye."

"I'm not canceling the meeting, Shea. Nothing has changed on my end. In two weeks my team and I will be waiting for you in my conference room, and I sincerely hope you'll show."

The thought of doing something to splash her name even more across the media made her shudder. The thought of having to face obnoxious strangers at the Amber with this hanging out there made her want to pack a tent and disappear into the mountains. Forever.

"Can I just say one more thing?" Pierce asked.

"Sure."

"You can lift your chin and soldier on and turn this into something you own. Or you can let it rule you. It's your choice."

Shea hung up, feeling more confused than ever about her professional direction but very, very clear about her personal one.

She found the number to Marco's office and stabbed the numbers on the screen like they were his eyes.

"Shea," Marco said when she'd finally worked her way around his assistant and got through to him. "I had a feeling I'd be hearing from you today."

"Don't say anything more. Not a word. Meet me in front of the horse in Union Square."

"When?"

She was only momentarily thrown off by his quick acquiescence.

"Now, jackass."

Chapter

20

*B*y the time Shea came up out of the subway and marched around to the statue of George Washington on his horse, Marco was already standing in front of the pedestal. Waiting for *her* for once.

His suit looked slick, his silvery hair even more so, but the troubled look on his face was so unlike the Marco she'd known that for a second she questioned whether or not it was the real him.

As she stamped up to him, his hand came out of his pocket and he watched her approach with wariness. Damn right he should. He should be glad they were meeting in public, because she wasn't sure what she'd do to him if they were alone.

She got right up close so that he couldn't ignore her fury. Her hurt. "*Why?*" Her voice sounded like she'd smoked a carton of cigarettes on the way over.

"Shea, I didn't—"

She stabbed a finger in his chest and he actually backed up a step. "Don't even *think* of trying to deny those photos aren't yours. Because I remember when you took them, you piece of shit. Unfortunately I haven't been able to forget everything."

His shoulders slumped a bit. "Of course they're mine. You know they are."

"So *why*? Why?" She couldn't help it, she was shouting

now. "Why would you do that to me? I left you years ago. *Years.*"

"That's what I'm trying to tell you. It wasn't me. It was Sabine."

"Who?" Right. The dark-haired child with the bob from the karaoke bar. The one who looked like she wanted to shoot fire from her eyeballs at Shea. The girlfriend who'd come back. The girlfriend who'd had to watch her slimy lover mow people down to get to his ex-wife and then had to sit there while he kept Byrne from getting back to Shea.

"She got into my computer or my phone, I don't know which, and found these. She was pissed off about you. I mentioned you more than once. She knew I'd gone to the Long Island Highland Games to see you and hated it, even though we'd broken up. And then we had a huge fight after the karaoke bar. She sent the pics to that website."

"Are you *kidding* me?"

He opened his hands and shrugged. "I wish I was. But she's jealous and—"

"Immature. Vindictive."

"Now wait a second—"

She cut him off with a sound of disgust.

"I had no idea she did that until this morning, Shea." Marco actually put his hand to his heart, the corners of his eyes turned down. "I honestly didn't. And I hate that she did it."

"That doesn't help me. Not at all. Do you have any idea what this has done? Do you have any idea what this has ruined?"

He sniffed and shifted his stance, stuffing his hand back into his pocket. She'd watched him lather up and schmooze many an acquaintance with that stance, and she wasn't going to let him use it. He was looking everywhere around the park but at her. "You look amazing in those pics, if that's anything. And they're just tits."

"It's my career!" she shouted. "My name. The respect I'm due. But of course you would never get that."

"I think you're making a bigger deal out of it than it needs to be."

On one hand she couldn't believe this. On the other, it was exactly what she'd come to expect from him.

"What are you going to do about it?" she demanded. "Because you have to, you know. Do you know the kind of shit I could tell the press about you? The kinds of things I've kept to myself all these years?"

He paled. "Like what?"

"By the look on your face, I think you can guess." She folded her arms across her chest. "How are you going to fix this, Marco?"

He wiped at the corners of his mouth. "I'll issue a statement, saying I had nothing to do with it. Telling them about the game, that you didn't cheat on me. That it wasn't the reason behind our split. That those were private photos and that they were stolen and posted without my knowledge."

They stared at each other. None of those words made her feel any better, but they were the right words to say. It was exactly what she'd wanted him to do.

"Why the hell do you still have those pictures?"

He gave her that look again, the one that said she was the crazy one for not being able to read his mind or not knowing him inside and out. "I told you that day at those stupid Highland Games. I miss you. I've wanted you back since the day you came to me with the papers. But you left and I've been pissed off ever since." He sneered. "I had to watch you go behind my back with Lynch, do your own thing without even telling me. And then I found out you're dating *that guy*—"

"Stop."

The way he'd brought Byrne into this, just slipped him in there like her relationship was some kind of excuse for him hanging on to those photos, forged a whole new blade of anger that stabbed into her head.

"Byrne has nothing to do with this. And we've only just started to see each other. You've held on to those photos for years, Marco. *Years*."

Marco looked pointedly over her shoulder. "Where is he? Shouldn't a man be with his woman in her time of distress?"

"I don't need a man to hold me up."

"You keep telling yourself that." He hiked up the sleeve of

his suit coat and checked his gold watch. "I have to go. I'll make the statement, Shea. Because those photos were never meant to be found, and I do hate that strangers can see you like that."

"And you'll delete them."

One of his eyes twitched, and he said nothing to acknowledge her demand.

"Delete them. Do you hear me?"

Reaching into his coat pocket, he took out a pair of sunglasses and slipped them on. "You have to understand how much I hate the fact that you left me." Then he turned and walked away, pulling out his phone to make a call.

She wondered if his making a statement would actually make a difference in anything except making him look better. Making him look like the victim. The pictures had still gone up. People had seen them. The Internet was forever. The damage was done.

Shea headed down one of the bowed paths through the center of the square and found a bench.

Byrne called two minutes later. "I'm sorry. I know you said you'd call but I just had to know how you're doing, what's happened. I'm worried."

She sank back against the bench. "I just saw Marco."

"And?"

"His mouth said he regrets what happened with the photos—which his lovely daughter, I mean girlfriend, stole and then leaked, by the way. He told me he's going to issue some sort of statement denouncing them. But his eyes and the rest of him basically said that I had it coming because I left him. And I think he's going to keep them anyway."

"Mother*fucker.*"

"I'm starting to think that should be my line." She looked back toward the statue. "He's still standing over there near the curb. I want to go push him into traffic."

"Don't. Then he won't be able to fix this mess."

She sighed and had to look away from her ex. "I don't think anything is going to fix it except time. Time and me staying out of sight for the rest of eternity."

She heard the squeak of an office chair. She pictured him

behind his desk, his feet propped up, a row of glass at his back, framing the East River.

He cleared his throat, and when he spoke his voice softened. "Would you have pushed me into traffic last night? After what I said? After the way I walked out?"

"Yes," she said. "But not because I hated you. Because I thought you needed a wake-up. I thought you could benefit from listening. I thought I was helping you."

Another, deeper squeak of the chair. "Yeah. Okay."

But that was all he said. No more explanation. No apology. No other acknowledgment of what they'd said to each other. Fine. She didn't think she had the energy to rehash it now anyway.

"What are you going to do now?" So heartfelt, so true, so warm. It was the Byrne she'd come to know.

"I'm going to sit here for a few more minutes. After that, I don't know. There was a reporter outside the Amber earlier. I don't want to go there. I have reliable employees who can hold down the fort for a while." There was a spot of pink gum ground into the pavement near her feet, and she toed it absentmindedly. "Pierce says I should own it, that I shouldn't let it rule me."

"Oh? You talked to him?"

"He called. Told me his offer still stands, that he's not canceling our meeting."

"What do you think you'll do?"

"My gut says not to take it. To keep hanging with the Amber but to avoid the main room for a while. To work in the back, in the office, until I feel comfortable again."

"What about the loan you were looking into? For the farm? Wasn't it contingent on the income from Whitten's proposal?"

She turned her face to the trees. Little bits of blue sky poked through their rustling tops. "Byrne, the farm is such a superstar dream. I can start something in the city, something smaller, for much less money."

"Or you could take Pierce's offer and get what you've always wanted."

"Jesus. Does no man think this is as big a deal as I do? My boobs are out there for everyone to see!"

A dad and his junior-high-school-aged son wearing Miami

University baseball caps, who were ambling through the square, looked up sharply at her. The dad frowned. The kid grinned.

Byrne sighed. "That's not what I meant and you know it."

"What did you mean?"

"That there's no excuse for not going after what you want, or what can *get* you what you want. Only impossibility should stop you, and that farm is a very real possibility. You once said you should do it because it scared you. Don't try to talk yourself out of it because of a new fear."

She flashed back to their argument in her apartment and how it seemed like he was saying similar things to her now to what she'd said to him then. They were going around in circles.

"This is something shitty that happened *to* you," he said. "I know it's hard right now. I know it's humiliating and awful. But you would be rising above it. I think most people would see that. And think about how many other people would visit your distillery or drink your whiskey, and either won't know or won't care about all this."

"But right now I feel like whenever someone will be talking to me or working with me from now until the end of time, they'll remember that they've seen my boobs."

The kid in the cap giggled now. The dad gave him a shove and ushered him toward Broadway.

"Sorry," she called to their backs. Then, to Byrne, "I need to stop saying 'boobs.' "

He laughed, but it was strained. "What you need is to take that meeting."

How come she couldn't tell him what to do, but he could tell her? "I don't think I'm going to. I need time."

"All right. Okay." But she could tell by his tone of voice that he didn't agree.

A blaring ambulance whisked around the square, having to stop and start again and again as clueless people in the crosswalk tried to slip in a chance to get across the street before the emergency vehicle, and bumper-to-bumper cars couldn't make space. It created a big pause in the conversation, so after the noise died down, she asked, "Where did you stay last night?"

"The Gramercy Park."

Not too far from where she sat right then. "What did you wear today?"

"I went shopping. In a store. Off racks."

The exaggerated glee in his voice made her smile, and suddenly she missed him so much she couldn't see straight. "Would liked to have seen that. Did you figure out the labels and such?"

"I did. I'm not completely hopeless, you know."

Another drawn-out pause, and the sun hit her hard on one side of her face, feeling far too much like the spotlight she wanted to get out of.

"I have your suitcase. And your train."

"Oh. Right."

"Would you want to come over tonight to pick them up?" A note of hope snuck its way into her voice. "We can talk. Wallow in each other's misery. Or maybe we could finally go on that first real date."

"Shea, I—" A growl of frustration. "I want to. Yes, absolutely. To all of the above. But, shit. I'm leaving tonight for Switzerland. I'll be gone for a week."

That did not disappoint her or make her sad. Not at all. But someone should probably try to explain that to the sinking feeling in her stomach and the hard press of tears against the back of her eyes.

"God, I'm so sorry," he said. "This thing has been planned for ages. Since before you and I even met. I probably should've told you before, but running off to South Carolina threw so much out of whack. I'm going with Aaldenberg, my boss. Remember him?"

"Uh-huh."

"I should be here for you. Shit, shit, shit." The chair squeaked big-time, like he'd jumped up and the thing had snapped back into a wall or desk. "You know something? I never questioned my travel before. I would head to the airport on a moment's notice, not step foot in my apartment for weeks, and I didn't care. Until I met you. Now I care. I want to be with you tonight and I can't cancel. This timing couldn't be worse."

He hadn't owed her this information. They hadn't reached that point in their relationship, she told herself over and over and over.

"I understand," she said automatically.

"I want to see you the second I get back," he said.

"Yes. Please." She tried to inject enthusiasm into her voice, but it just came up flat.

She didn't need him with her, but she sure as hell wanted him.

"I should go." She stood up. "I should call my staff, get some things straightened out. Let them know I likely won't be in to the bar for a while."

"Shea, I—" He cut himself off, and the world seemed full of all the possible things he could say.

"Yes?"

"I promise I'll come to you when I get back. I promise I'll make it up to you. Call me anytime you need me. Please."

"Okay."

But as she hung up, she knew that she was on her own for the next week, telephone calls or not. And maybe, as she considered the hazy images of her future, that's the way it had to be.

Chapter

✪

21

*T*he world was full of numbers.

Seven days gone from the Tits Seen Round the World. The photos had been taken down, but the Internet's memory could string out forever, and there were online caches left that still showed her smiling at Marco's camera—some with black bars slapped over her nipples, some without.

Seven days since she'd stepped foot in the Amber. She'd been in constant contact with Dean to deal with issues and the books and orders and the like. His last email, sent just that morning, read, "Take all the time you need. The gawkers will eventually die down." Looking at each night's receipts, she could tell that her tables had been consistently full.

She hadn't heard from Douglas Lynch, but that didn't surprise her much. Usually she only heard from him when he had an issue or idea, or wanted to suggest a change. He was being smart by avoiding this whole thing, as well he should. It wasn't public knowledge that he'd backed the Amber from day one and that Shea's marriage to Marco had died shortly thereafter. Who knows what sort of bold and italicized caption could be crafted from that?

Six days since Marco's promised statement, which had been surprisingly conciliatory and regretful and truthful . . . which meant a PR person had written it. Whatever. It was done.

Five days since a phone call from her parents. Her mom had been tearful, her father gruff and embarrassed and disappointed. Both had been shocked—shocked!—to learn that adults behaved like that. All Shea could do was express her anger over the whole thing and make it clear that while she'd willingly taken the pictures at the time, what had happened since was unfortunate. She got the feeling they wanted her to apologize for something.

She wouldn't.

And then she added the whole mess to the list of things they'd never be able to bring up again. The unexpected bonus? She'd been on the line while her father carried out her old wedding photo to the trashcan. The sound of shattering glass had made Shea smile for the first time in what felt like a long while.

Three days since her last email from Byrne. He wasn't the greatest or most enthusiastic typist, so they'd been short. Things along the lines of "Just checking in" and "Hope you're okay" and "Hate that I'm not there." Her replies had been just as succinct.

If anything, the chopped-up communication served to remind her that she'd never taken a photo of him and wanted one desperately. The random bushy-bearded bagpiper wasn't doing what it should.

More numbers . . . Seven days until the scheduled meeting with Pierce Whitten at Right Hemisphere headquarters. Five days until the Scottish Ball, where she was supposed to make her first public appearance since the scandal. She hadn't canceled either event, but she hadn't made up her mind yet on whether or not she was actually going to show.

"I'm sorry I'm not Byrne."

The sound of Willa's voice jolted Shea from her sad trombone musings. Shea looked up from where she'd sprawled paperwork from the Amber across her coffee table. Willa had taken over the dining table with a giant sketchpad, a huge laptop, and a colorful array of pencils.

"I'm sorry you aren't, either. My mind started wandering, and you don't exactly have the correct equipment to fulfill what I was thinking about." She smiled weakly. "I'm kidding. I'm so glad you're here. I needed my friend this week."

Willa grinned. Her phone buzzed where it rested by the sketchpad. She picked it up, looked at it, then tossed it away.

"Go," Shea ordered, finger pointing to the door. "Go out. Stop ignoring all your admirers and take back your social life. I'm okay now."

Willa shrugged. "I'm good here. They can wait."

"You've been here five days. I love you, but come on."

Willa folded her arms on the table and eyed Shea hard. "They mean nothing to me. You mean everything. And you called me for a reason. When you leave your apartment, I will, too. Besides," she said, as she picked up a black pencil, "do you even know how much work I've finished here this week? My clients are going to be thrilled. I'll actually beat several deadlines and deliver early. I'm thinking I should start paying you rent. Maybe make this table my permanent office."

Shea rolled out of the couch that was trying to eat her and wandered over to the table. It was reclaimed wood, and she'd bought it earlier that year because she thought that someday it would look wonderful in a rural farm.

Willa was sketching a logo for some new restaurant opening up near the High Line in the Meatpacking District.

"You're really good," Shea said. "I know I've told you that a million times, but I love your eye, your style."

Another phone went off, and this time it was Shea's. She pulled it out of her back pocket and stared at the text next to the little pic of the bagpiper.

Landed. When can I see you?

She flipped the phone around so Willa could see. "It's him. He's back."

Willa sighed dramatically and looked forlornly at the spread of design work. "And I was getting so much done." She winked at Shea. "Just kidding, darling. I'll get out of your hair. That is, if you want me to. You're looking a little, I don't know, doubtful?"

Shea stared at the silly bagpiper. "I'm . . ." The suitcase still sat by the front door, the train teetering on top. "I'm excited. I'm nervous. I guess I am a little doubtful. It's been a week. Things were so . . . weird . . . when he left."

"So you *don't* want to see him? That's the vibe I'm getting."

"No. I mean, yes. God, yes. I want to see him." Shea wiggled the phone. "But this whole thing is so strange. Right before he left for South Carolina things were . . ." She sighed. Actually sighed. Like she was in a nineteen-fifties sitcom or something. "And then that shit with his brother and family happened, and then his apartment, and then Marco and the photos, and—"

Willa shoved a hand at Shea. "Stop. Those are nothing. A stutter."

"A *stutter*?"

"None of those things had anything to do with the two of you." She tapped a pencil on the table in time with her words. "I wish I could videotape you guys just so you could see the way you are together. Maybe you two could be the first couple in history to skip the whole 'I don't know how he or she feels' step in a new relationship. You're crazy about each other. End of story."

"That argument we had after his apartment got broken into was pretty bad. He was really frustrated with me, and I was with him. And then he went to Switzerland without us really talking about it. I could've told you where we stood or what I thought two weeks ago, but now?"

"Oh, for heaven's—" Willa snatched Shea's phone from her grasp.

"Give that back."

Willa typed something at lightning speed. "There. Done." She held up the phone. She'd texted: *Now.*

"Why did you—" Shea began over the sound of steam pushing through her ears.

Her phone buzzed. Byrne.

Be there in an hour. I have something for you.

Willa gathered up her things, gave Shea a kiss on the cheek, and left.

Fifty-seven minutes later, the sound of his knock on her door made her heart ride a pogo stick. She jumped up from where she'd been sitting, anxious, on the couch. She threw open the door and suddenly there he was.

He'd been wearing a little smile as the light from her apartment fell across his body, but as he took her in, it faded. But in one of those good ways, like what he was feeling was too much for his expression to hold in. She knew exactly what that was like, because she was just standing there, staring at him.

Then his head sagged to one side, his crazy-gorgeous eyes turned to starlight, and he whispered, "Oh. Look at you."

The sound of his voice lit a fire in her and she reached out, grabbed the front of his shirt—not silk, cotton—and yanked him inside. He kicked the door closed and his big arms came around her. She buried her face in the crook of his neck and, good lord, his scent invaded her, made her dizzy.

"You feel amazing," he said into her hair. "I wish I could've done this for you the day I had to leave."

That managed to pull out a few of the tears she'd been resisting for a week now, but she sniffled them back before he would know.

Slowly he released her, only to take her face in his hands. His lips parted as if to kiss her, but then he asked, "Anything new? Anything since Marco's statement?"

The call from her parents, but she didn't want to mention that just then. "They took the photos down but the Amber's still swamped, apparently. I haven't gone in. Willa's been keeping me company."

His thumb grazed her jawline. "I wish it had been me. Can you forgive me for leaving?"

"There's nothing to forgive. It's work. There are things you can't get out of. Believe me, I understand." But she felt her eyes start to fill up again, and this time he did notice. His face softened and she started to extricate herself from his hold. "I think I need a tissue."

He let her slide away.

When she came out of the bathroom, he was still standing in that spot by the front door, hands in the pockets of his flat-front gray pants, looking around her place. A small leather airplane bag hung from one shoulder. He looked different. Good different. Amazing different.

"Thank you for that." She gestured to his arms, stupidly. "I needed it. I don't think I knew just how much."

He gave her a wonderfully warm smile, not remotely crooked. "Of course."

She stepped closer, gazing up into his face. "I really wish I could've done that for you, when you came back from South Carolina and found your apartment the way it was. I really wish I could've helped you like that."

His smile sagged. "Well, you came at me with words, not with arms."

Her mouth dropped open.

"Oh crap." Blood drained from his face, his eyes growing wide. "That didn't come out at all the way I wanted. I'm so sorry. That was a shitty thing to say."

"Yeah, it kind of was. I was trying to read you that day, and you had this barrier up like I probably shouldn't touch you—"

He kissed her. A brief, hard meeting of just their mouths that reminded her of their very first.

"You can always touch me," he said.

She blinked at him, a little thrown by the sudden change. "I, um—"

He grinned. "Come here." With a gentle tug on her fingers, he pulled her over to a couch. Right before he sat down, he unhooked the bag from his shoulder and set it on her coffee table. He unzipped it but didn't take anything out. Looking up at her, he patted the cushion next to him.

She sat not because of some outside force, or some invisible magical woo-woo that belonged in a storybook, or because he was gravity, but because she wanted to. Because she'd missed him, and she needed to know about him. About where they stood right now and where they went from here.

He looked bottled up, she just realized. Like he had something he wanted to tell her but couldn't get it out, so she asked, "Any news on your brother?"

"Yeah." He scratched lightly at the back of his head, but it quickly turned to a rather violent scrubbing, his face all scrunched up. "They caught him hopping a subway turnstile in the Financial District. Dumb shit. Almost like he wanted to get caught. Maybe he did."

She came to her knees on the cushions. "And your apartment?"

"As soon as they found out it was him, they charged him with—what was it?—burglary, criminal damage to property."

"Is that something you get sent to jail for?"

Byrne sighed, and it sounded soul deep. "Yeah. Stealing my parents' money isn't going to help him, either."

"Will you get to see him?" When he didn't answer right away, she amended, "Do you *want* to see him?"

"Yes. And no."

She nodded, thinking that if she were in his position, she'd think the same thing.

He turned his head to meet her eyes. "Are you going to take that meeting with Whitten?"

The answer lodged in her throat. A hard, small word that felt like a pill swallowed the wrong way.

"Can we just not talk about that right now? I've been not talking about it for a week and it's been great."

Pressing his lips together, he glanced at his bag. "I have to say, that really doesn't seem like you."

"What doesn't?"

"Avoidance."

"Well, I don't *want* to sit here hiding, but I feel like the second I step into the Amber the wrong kind of attention will sprout up. I don't want success from infamy. And I don't want to make any big deals under that ugly umbrella. I'm just a girl from Pennsylvania who wants to live out her dreams. But I'm . . . embarrassed. There. I said it."

"You know"—he shifted a little to face her—"I've watched you working before. I've seen you in action, so to speak. You are absolutely justified in feeling what you do, but I don't think you're giving yourself enough credit to rise above it. Or to power through it."

Pierce had said much the same thing.

She flopped back into the embrace of the cushions. Slowly, slowly, they swallowed her until all she could see was the set of shelves on the opposite wall.

"I just want what I want," she said. "No matter which way I turn, I can't help feeling like I come up against huge roadblocks. And they're not something I can mentally get over. It'll take time and a completely different route that I just can't see yet."

Byrne leaned over, around the pouf of cushion, until he filled her vision. He kept licking his lips, kept shifting his eyes over to the right.

"What?" she asked. "What's that face for?"

"What if," he said carefully, "you *could* get what you want?"

Embarrassingly, she had to struggle to sit back up; the couch practically had her down its throat. "What do you mean?"

"The distillery up in Gleann."

Grinding fingers into her eyelids, she let out a huge sigh. "I told you. The cost is prohibitive right now. It would take some serious capital to even get the down payment for that place, not to mention all the remodeling and start-up costs for the distillery itself, and the fact that I couldn't even make a dime until years out. It's a pipe dream, Byrne. I thought I could do it if I stuck with the Amber and squirreled away any money I made with Whitten, and then I'd be able to *think* about shopping around for a mortgage and business loans in maybe another five years or so—"

"But what if you didn't need Whitten to get started?"

Was he not listening to her? "But I do."

"What if you didn't?" He reached over to his bag, slipped his hand between the open zipper, and pulled out a large brown envelope. One of those big ones with the flap and the string that looped around two attached cardboard circles. He looked at it for a moment, then placed it on her lap.

"What's this?" Her mouth went bone-dry.

"Open it." His knee bounced a little. His big shoulders rounded forward, and the corners of his mouth ticked up, as though the crooked smile couldn't decide if it wanted to make an appearance.

Shea's hands curled on her chest as she stared down at the heavy brown envelope. The window air-conditioning unit kicked on, spewing out a much-needed cold blast.

"Open it," he said. "Please."

Slowly she unwound the string and lifted the flap. Inside were several sheets of paper, fastened with a paperclip. She flipped through them, but they were full of tightly spaced, itty-bitty legalese.

"I don't understand. What am I looking at?"

He reached out and set the first page on top of the stack again, then tapped a finger on a line. Suddenly it became clear that she was reading an address. An address in Gleann, New Hampshire.

Her head snapped up. "What is this? What did you do?"

Oh, the smile. That brilliant, slanted smile.

He said, "I bought you the farm."

If she weren't already sitting, she might have collapsed. "*What?*"

His eyes positively twinkled, the creases deepening at their outer corners.

"I bought you the farm. The one you showed me, the one you want. The house, the barns, the fields. Everything."

"I know which one," she whispered, blinking hard at the paperwork. There it was, the address of the rural route outside of Gleann. The purchase price with all those zeros. And Byrne's name. His *full* name.

"Well, it's not final yet," he amended, "but they've accepted my bid. As of yesterday. I signed the papers overseas and put up the earnest money, and now it's in a period of attorney review. That'll end probably at the end of this coming week. Then all you have to do is set a closing date. It could be yours in another month."

"My God, Byrne." Her voice rattled like she was driving over railroad tracks. "You *bought* me all this?"

"I did. Well, I want to. There are still a couple steps to go through." He reached for her hands where they rested on top of the papers, and her reaction was immediate and instinctual.

She jumped up, the envelope and its contents sliding to the rug.

The enthusiasm and joy dissipated from his face. He drew his hands back in. "That wasn't exactly the reaction I thought I'd get."

She didn't want to know about his expectations for something this huge. Something this full of meaning. Something this one-sided. "But . . . *why*?"

With a firm nod, he looked her directly in the eye and replied, "Because I have the money. Because you deserve it. Because I know you're devastated about the mess this fucking picture-website thing made, and that makes *me* sad. Because I want to help you, and not remotely in the way Lynch has. I'm no angel investor. This is your business. I don't want a thing to do with it."

She couldn't find air. *Overwhelmed* didn't even begin to describe the way she felt.

All those zeroes . . . "You have this kind of money?"

Another nod. "I do."

Or he had it, anyway, if she actually let him go through with this.

"But that was for your land. Your parents' land and the house you wanted for them."

He stood up, too. "I have plenty more. Enough to do something else for my family when the time is right, when they let me."

She looked at the papers strewn under the coffee table. "Maybe they never let you because it's simply too much."

A deep groove divided his eyebrows.

"Byrne, I . . . I can't let you do this."

"It's done. Didn't you see my signature on the end of the bid, my initials all over? I could stop the attorney review and get back my earnest money, but I really don't want to."

Still no air came to her. Her chest pumped, her lungs worked, but it didn't feel like she was taking in any oxygen.

He inched closer, but it seemed like he crossed a great chasm to get to her. "The money is mine. I want to give this to you. I want you to have that distillery, and if you truly don't want to go into business with Whitten right now, this is the way you can begin. I don't want you to have to settle for anything. I want you to have that farm. The first step is done. You have the space. Now go out and find the capital to start everything else you said you wanted."

Pressing a hand to her forehead that felt terribly damp, she turned away and went over to the table where Willa had been working. Shea replaced and straightened the centerpiece of eclectic vases, and when that was done she went to her shelves, where she adjusted every wineglass and snifter so they were perfectly even.

"You can pay me back," Byrne said behind her. "If that's what you need, if that's what will make this all right to you. But I really do want to give it to you as a gift."

Shea choked out a laugh as she whirled around. "That kind of money?"

He opened his hands, looking so very reasonable, and shrugged. "Then don't worry about paying me back. Just take it. Start your dream. It would make me very happy, Shea. Very, very happy."

"You don't get it. I would have it hanging over my head. Every single day I went to work. Every day I slept in that house or walked across the fields to the barn. I would know what was given me and not what I earned myself."

He frowned. "Hanging over your head? No, that's not what I intended at all."

"Did you listen to anything I had to say in Gleann? Or by that lake in my hometown? After everything I went through with Marco? I got out from underneath him because I had to be responsible for myself. I wanted my own life. And while I'm grateful to Lynch for helping with that, for getting me going with the Amber, right now I feel like I'm owing yet another person. That I'm beholden to him. My immediate reaction to this is that I would be escaping that cage only to jump into another."

He came over to the table and gripped the back of an end chair. "I listened to you, Shea. To every word. And I just told you that in my eyes, it's completely different from your position with Lynch. I just thought I could help—"

"There are so, so many similarities to what happened before my divorce. And directly after. I'm having a hard time accepting this."

"Now wait a minute. I am *not* that asshole. Do *not* compare me to Marco."

"I'm not comparing you to him. Just . . . you need to stop thinking that everything can be fixed with money."

Darkness swept across his face. "That's not what I think. At all. Do not go mistaking caring for egotism."

She glanced at the pile of papers once more. When she looked back at him, his frustration had grown, not diminished.

"Good point," she said. "That's a very good point. I'm sorry."

The crunch of his shoulders relaxed some.

She pressed a hand to her chest. "But I am not your parents, Byrne. I know you're dying to help them, to know that all your hard work and saving and such added up to the thing you wanted most, but I can't be their replacement."

"You're not. You're not at all. I believe in this project. I believe in you, Shea. I think you're going to fucking kill in the whiskey world outside of New York."

She would have to leave New York. The place she'd called home for a decade. She would have to leave Byrne. A year ago, when she'd concocted the dream of Gleann and the distillery, he hadn't even been a blip on her radar screen. Now? She wasn't sure what he was, but his mere existence made her want to stay.

"Don't get me wrong, I love having you in my arms," he said, as though he were reading her mind, "but I hate seeing what I saw on your face when I walked in here. I *hated* having to leave the country when you were going through that shit. I hated watching you think it signaled the end to everything. You told me before that maybe the blow to my family was a new beginning for me, and I think you're right. It was my new beginning and it's yours, too. Because when I was overseas, it became clear what I wanted to do, and that was to help you."

Her head swam with thoughts. Only there was no surface to break, no clear revelation, just a murky, swirling, pressurized mess between her ears.

"This gift, Byrne . . . It's so much. It's *too* much."

"Not to me." His conviction spoke volumes.

"It is to me. What if I refuse it?"

His lips parted. A little sound leaked out before he asked, "You'd do that?"

"I don't know. Maybe. To be honest, it's my gut instinct."

His cheeks puffed out as he scratched the back of his head.

"You didn't even consider that," she said. "Did you?"

"My turn to be honest: no."

"What would happen, if I turned you down right now?"

"I'd get my earnest money back. The bid would die."

"And after the attorney review is over at the end of next week?"

"That money would be gone, but so would the sale."

So she had a week to make a decision, or else Byrne will have lost a good chunk of cash.

She swung out a chair and flopped into the seat. Instantly Byrne fell to his knees in front of her, and the position caused all sorts of flip-flops in her belly. All sorts of twisting in her heart.

"I know you want this, Shea. I know you do. If only you could've looked in a mirror when you were telling me about the distillery, about your dreams. I loved seeing that in you, because I recognized it. It's why I went to school, why I moved here, became what I did, so I could have my dreams. I *know* dreams. They are powerful, powerful stuff, and they don't ever go away. Not ever. I want to see that look back on your face, the one from that night in Gleann when you told me all about it. This is it. Let me do this for you. We can talk about the details later."

"I can't. I just can't."

He took her knees, rubbed them lightly. "You can. All you have to do is say yes."

"And if I don't? You just bid on a multimillion-dollar abandoned estate in the middle-of-nowhere New Hampshire."

"I'll figure it out. I'm kind of good at things like that. You know, with money and such." He grinned.

She covered her face with her hands, bowed her head. Too much. Too much . . .

"Listen." He pried her hands away. She wasn't crying, but his gorgeous face was blurred because of the buzzing in her head. "All this shit that happened with the photos? The crap that is still sticking around even after the divorce? Why don't you use this opportunity to finally get rid of Marco and that Lynch guy? Show Marco that you truly can stand on your own. Show him how much you're worth in a way that has nothing to do with revenue. Or give him a virtual 'fuck you' and just erase him from your consciousness. Show the rest of the world how resilient and strong you are. Do this. Go after your dream. Start your own distillery. Take this gift. Please."

Her hands were wrapped in his now. Big and warm and so utterly generous—

"Wait." She narrowed her eyes. "Did you do this because of Marco?"

"What do you mean?"

"I don't know. Like some sort of multimillion-dollar penis measurement thing."

"No!" He really did look horrified at that. Whereas Marco likely would've shrugged and nonverbally admitted to as much.

Byrne was absolutely right. She had to stop assuming that every guy was trying to keep her under his thumb. "I'm sorry." She gave him a wavering smile. "I didn't really think that, but I felt like I had to ask."

The papers drew her attention again, like they were doused in glowing neon paint and smelled like red velvet cake.

Lovely, soft pressure on her cheek turned her head back to him.

"I first had the crazy idea to do this," he murmured, "way back when you showed me the place. When you told me how hard it would be for you to get it and how long it would probably take. I barely knew you then, but I instantly knew that you deserved it all. And now it feels so incredibly right to me."

She was losing herself in his pale eyes again. He leaned into her, so slightly, but enough that his claiming, his desire, was evident. That hypnosis screwed with her thinking and her libido and every little impulse that existed in between. And she knew that whatever she said to him now would be affected by her feelings for him. This proposal of his required a clear heart, a clear mind. And when Byrne was this close to her, this consuming, she knew she had neither.

"I need to think it over," she finally said. "I need . . . I don't know what I need."

"I understand that. Completely." He patted her legs, then rocked to his feet. "Why don't I go out and grab us some food and then we can just sit and—you don't have a TV, do you? Well, we can just watch the wall—"

"No." She rose to her feet. "No. I meant alone."

His lips parted as he stared at her.

"I'm sorry," she said. "I need time to think about everything. To think it all through. And I don't think I can do that rationally when you're here."

He threw a grim look at her front door. The moment he finally saw his suitcase and toy train engine sitting there, his forehead scrunched up. "Of course, of course."

"I really don't want to kick you out, if that helps."

"I was hoping to spend some time with you."

Well if you hadn't sprung such a huge thing on me, she thought, *we could have.*

"That last night, in my place," he said. "Talking on the couch. Then being with you in the closet. In my bed . . ."

She had to close her eyes. "You don't know how much I've been thinking about that the whole time you were gone."

"So why can't we—"

"But you should really go."

When she opened her eyes, his jaw was clenched tight. At last he nodded. "Right. Okay."

What followed were the longest seconds in the world.

"I'm sorry," she said again.

"I understand, Shea. I understand." And he did. The trouble on his face confirmed it. "So what about Saturday night? Can we make it our first date? None of that"—he waved toward the papers on the rug—"just us."

"It's the Scottish Ball. I'm doing the tasting thing during the cocktail hour, but I thought I'd stay for the dinner and ceremony, too."

His eyes brightened. "You're up for it?"

Wrapping her arms around her waist, she nodded. "I am."

And she was, now that she'd heard what he had to say about new beginnings. Now that she'd listened to the advice she'd given him.

As he looked at her, she realized she was waiting for him to ask if he could come to the ball. But he didn't.

"Some other time, then." His eye contact was so direct, so penetrating. "Will you let me know when?"

"Yes."

Slowly, finally, he peeled away, his silent footsteps heading for the door. She exhaled, realizing she'd been scared he'd touch her again. And he'd seen that trepidation.

Hand on the doorknob, he said over his shoulder, "You asked me why I did this. Deep down, I think you know."

She sucked in a breath.

"Believe what you want," he added, "but it's for you. It's all for you."

He reached over and pulled up the long handle on his rolling suitcase. Picking up the mangled toy engine, he considered it from every angle. Then he set it on her small table next to the door.

"Do whatever you want with this," he said quietly. "I don't need it anymore."

Chapter

✳

22

*B*yrne would've hated the Scottish Ball. He would've cringed over the bagpiper playing in the corner, even though the musician was beyond skilled and the notes planted all sorts of tingling emotion inside Shea. Byrne would've made small talk with the roomful of people he didn't know, but since he had to do that all day for work, he wouldn't have enjoyed it. And he would've hated to have to put on a kilt.

Despite all that, she still wished he were here.

The gilt foyer of the posh Midtown hotel was packed shoulder to shoulder with people, some full-blooded Scottish, most only part, a few Scottish only in name. And others, like Willa, who was balancing her glass of champagne while perusing the long line of silent auction items, weren't any of the above.

Shea took a long drink of water from the bottle below her whisky tasting table. She'd been talking for nearly an hour straight, her throat burned dry, and her cheeks hurt from all the smiling. Now there was a lull in the steady stream of black tie– and evening-gown-clad partygoers, and she took the rare moment to breathe, though the tight, gold-sequined, floor-length dress seemed determined not to let her.

The two young guys she'd just given a whisky 101 to— they were just barely of drinking age, and reveling in finally being able to have a "wee dram" at this event their parents had dragged them to since they were early teenagers—now walked away, laughing. But not at her. In fact, no one that evening had.

Scanning the beautiful foyer decked out in huge sprays of flowers and dotted with tuxedoed waiters passing around hors d'oeuvres, Shea realized that not a single person had asked about or alluded to or openly joked about what had appeared on the Internet. Sure, she'd caught some knowing looks, a few wide eyes, a couple of whispered conversations with glances her way, but nothing overt.

Nothing that deterred her from what she was there to do, and that was to talk about Scotch whisky.

For an hour and a half before dinner was to be served, she poured and talked, sipped and described. She exchanged stories with enthusiastic attendees about trips to Scotland and expressed her interest in getting more involved in the Society.

She thought of her granddad every minute, seeing his face in the features of the older men who came by for a glass of single malt. She heard his laughter in the accented English that spun around the room.

The evening thus far was cathartic. It was refreshing. And, to her surprise, it was *fun*.

Willa appeared at her side, champagne fizzing in her hand. "Ugh, there is *no one* here to flirt with. When you shanghaied me into coming, you forgot to mention the whole couples thing going on."

Shea smiled and straightened the cloth Montgomery tartan flower pinned high on one strap of her dress. "You can flirt with me."

"I could, you know. You look fucking hot." She sighed. "I mean, the only unattached men here are, like, eighty."

"The things you do for your best friend."

"Right?"

A high tinkling of chimes came from the far corner of the foyer, and three sets of giant wooden doors swung open. The crowd in the foyer began to filter toward them.

"Looks like people are heading into the ballroom," Shea said.

"Are we going in?" Willa asked. "You said you were going

to see how you felt at the end of the cocktail thing before deciding if you were going to stay for dinner."

Shea surveyed the backs of the beautiful and impeccably dressed gallery and drew a deep breath. "We're staying. I made it through. I feel good. Great, actually. I feel like I've accomplished something, you know? I did it. I braved the public and I came out unscathed. And I do love all the ceremony they have during dinner. I think it might make me happy to see it."

Willa groaned exaggeratedly. "Fine. If we must, we must."

Shea reached out and squeezed her hand. "Thank you for coming."

"Well, I couldn't let you come alone. Although, if I must say, another person, someone of the male persuasion, should have been the one to come with you."

Shea busied herself with drawing out her best bottle and pouring herself a nice, healthy glass, adding the perfect amount of water. "It's not his thing."

"But trying to buy you a farm in the middle-of-nowhere New Hampshire is?"

Shea closed her eyes and took a sip, and did *not* answer Willa. Because although it had been five days since she'd seen or spoken to Byrne, she still had yet to give him an answer.

An arm lifted high above the receding crowd, beckoning to Shea.

"Ah," she said to Willa. "I'm being summoned. That's the president of the Society and we're sitting with him at the head table."

Willa perked up. "Is he flirt-able?"

Shea snorted. "I'll let you be the judge of that." And then the crowd parted to reveal the president, whose kilt was wedged underneath his gut. His white, wiry hair swept over in a spectacular comb-over.

The two women found their seats at the large round table set off to the left of the low stage where the musicians would play later. A long table spilling with flowers and greenery horizontally bisected the dance floor.

"I'm going to go blind from all the plaid in here," Willa muttered as she started to lower herself into her chair. Halfway down, she froze. Sucked in a breath.

"What?" Shea stashed her little clutch purse underneath her chair, waiting for another of Willa's snarky comments.

"Um." Willa was staring over the tables, toward the back of the room and the still-open doors. She straightened. "I think I see a hot single guy by the bar. Can't let opportunity go to waste."

"Come on. Will you just sit still for one moment and keep me company? You're like a three-year-old sometimes, I swear."

Willa was still looking toward the doors as a shit-eating grin started to spread across her face. It was then Shea realized the bar inside the ballroom was on the wall behind Willa, and not remotely where her friend was looking.

Shea swiveled in her seat. Byrne stood under the arched doorway, chest heaving like he'd just sprinted there all the way from his place on the Upper East Side.

Byrne was here. At her Scottish Ball.

Wearing formal Highland dress.

Vaguely she was aware of a light pat on her shoulder and a soft female chuckle in her ear. "I'll leave you to that fine man and go find one of my own."

The ballroom was still filling with people trying to find and take their seats. Bodies shifted like the sea between where Shea stood at the front, near the stage, and where Byrne had entered at the very back. He was squinting into the dim, candlelit ballroom, scanning the hundreds of strange faces. Looking for her.

She couldn't move. Could only stare.

He looked as spectacular as she'd known he would. Maybe even more so.

From this distance and in this low a light she couldn't tell what tartan his kilt was, but it was likely one of the universal designs meant for those who didn't belong to a clan. The black Prince Charlie jacket fit perfectly, as though it was tailored for him. As though it was bespoke. Its peaked lapels and shiny buttons on the sleeves and vest underneath made his torso look beautifully shaped. The pristine white shirt set off the deep tan of his face, and the bow tie made him look like the fanciest rugby player in existence.

She watched frustration skate across his features as he slowly ventured into the noisy ballroom. It was then that she stood up and stepped out from behind the table. It took him a few seconds to find her, but when he did, she felt the bang and zap and heat of his recognition like he was touching her all over.

She smiled nervously.

Byrne's grin, however, wasn't remotely small or hesitant. Full-on brilliant, wonderfully crooked. He started toward her immediately. When he reached the border of the parquet dance floor and broke free from the milling crowd, she was finally hit with the full brunt of his appearance. Kilt, rugby legs, and all.

The shiny silver sporran bounced on his thighs. The red flashes around the top part of his tartan kilt hose called attention to the intensity and length of his strides. The dark blues and greens of the plaid suited him to perfection.

All she could do was stand there, dumbstruck by how good he looked and absolutely soaring from his unexpected presence. When he finally reached her, the entire ballroom was swept away, noise and all.

"Surprise," he said, and he was so close she could feel his breath on her face. Feel his heat. Sense the magnetism his body created.

"Holy shit," she whispered.

The smile cracked open even wider. "You look incredible."

"That's what my 'holy shit' was for. Only about you. So ladylike, I know."

The Society president's voice crackled through the ballroom, and Shea turned to see the heavyset man leaning into a microphone onstage. "Good evening, everyone, my Scottish brothers and sisters. If you'll all take your seats, we'll begin the ceremony and festivities before dinner is served."

She swiveled back to Byrne, who was nodding at her table. "Looks like I'm staying for dinner. What're we having?"

"I brought Willa," she said dumbly, then found her friend at the edge of the ballroom, dragging a tall chair over to the bar, where a twentysomething male bartender was eagerly watching her settle in.

Byrne noticed Willa, too. "Mind if I take her place?"

"Are you kidding?"

Shea and Byrne sank into their chairs simultaneously, knees facing each other. He wouldn't stop smiling, wouldn't stop looking over her face and body in a way that made all her nerves come alive at once.

"I was wrong," he said, leaning in close, "you don't look incredible. You look delicious. I want to eat you."

She gasped just as a giant blast of bagpipes sounded from the ballroom doors. A parade of twenty pipes filed down the aisle and made a circle on the dance floor, serenading the crowd with a rousing, perfectly timed tune. She couldn't hear Byrne even if she wanted to, but he wasn't saying anything. He wasn't making a face or otherwise indicating his displeasure. He merely gave her a nod of support.

When the pipes ended, the musicians filed back out, the ensuing applause died, and a kilted man holding a giant silver platter appeared. He walked down the aisle and placed the platter in the center of the long, decorated table. Shea had to turn around in her seat to watch, and she felt Byrne move closer behind her, his chin hovering just above her shoulder.

"What in the world is that?" he whispered.

Shea had to giggle as she looked at the smooth, round, gray blob sitting ceremoniously in front of everyone. "Haggis," she whispered back, having to turn her head and finding his mouth electrifyingly close to hers. "Sheep innards cooked with a bunch of other stuff inside a sheep's stomach."

Oh, she so loved the faint choking sound that came as a reply.

At the table, the kilted man raised both hands over the haggis and closed his eyes.

"Are we about to pray to a sheep's stomach?" Byrne said in her ear. God, he was so close. So very close.

She tapped a finger to her smiling lips. "Just listen."

" 'Address to a Haggis,' " the man intoned. "By Robert Burns."

And then he recited from memory a lively poem Shea knew all too well. So did everyone else, and the whole room laughed and cheered and raised glasses during specific parts. When he was done, Byrne applauded with the rest of them and asked, "Did I hear him call that thing the 'great chieftain of the sausage race'?"

She laughed. "You did."

"Well then." He whipped his napkin off the table, stuffed

it behind his black bow tie, and took up his fork and knife.
"Let's dig in."

*T*he haggis was strange—like bland, browned ground beef.
Only not. The bagpipes were almost too loud to be properly heard, which was a good thing. The wine was divine.
And Byrne was sitting next to the most beautiful woman on
the planet.

She sparkled alone, but in that dress she was . . . hell, he
didn't know. A star? A supernova? Long and tight and gold,
the dress fit her like it had been painted on.

It had taken just about all his willpower to not grab her
when he got his first good head-to-toe. His body actually
ached from restraining himself from touching her during dinner. It had been a helpful bonus that their tablemates were
fun and interesting and were getting steadily drunk, making
them even more fun and interesting. He zeroed in on them,
setting aside, for the moment, everything he came here to tell
Shea.

But after dessert appeared on the china and two new musicians took their place onstage, he knew the night was drawing
to a close. He and Shea had gone the whole evening avoiding
the giant elephant in the room that was his bold bid on the
Gleann farm.

"There's dancing now." Shea tilted her face to him, one of
the only direct looks she'd given him all through dinner. All
that white-gold hair swung over her shimmering dress. "You
don't have to stay. I can't believe you stayed as long as you
have already." She folded her napkin and placed her fork upon
it. "I can't believe you came at all."

All he could do was smile at her because the musicians—
an older male fiddle player and a much younger female
cellist—started in on a heartrending, gorgeous tune that captured the entire ballroom's attention. Even the servers paused
in their duties. Byrne listened, rapt, enjoying it far more than
the deafening screech of the earlier pipes. A glance at Shea
revealed her eyes glistening with emotion, and even though
Byrne had never met her grandfather or had visited Scotland,
he knew the music brought back the past for her.

The second song picked up the pace considerably, with the fiddle player tapping a foot, the audience clapping in time. The first few dancers made their way to the dance floor, which had been cleared of the haggis table. Byrne rose, straightening his jacket and making sure the purse thing—the sporran?—was where the guy at the rental shop had told him it should be.

He held out a hand to Shea. "Dance with me?"

She lifted an eyebrow. "You dance?"

"No, but I seem to have found some confidence. Must be the kilt."

Her eyes flicked appreciatively downward. Then they glanced almost fearfully to each side.

Byrne frowned. "Did anyone say anything to you tonight? About the pictures?"

"No. No one."

"Will dancing with me in any way compromise the Amber or the farm or the distillery?"

Something shifted on her face as he brought up the elephant, but she wiped it away. Squared her shoulders. Good girl.

"No," she said.

He thrust his hand closer and smiled. "Then dance with me."

Silent trumpets heralded victory when her soft hand slid into his. He led her to the dance floor and pulled her body against his. She resisted for only a moment, glancing around to confirm that not a single person in the whole place cared, and then she relaxed.

The other dancers—couples and singles and little girls twirling their party dresses—were moving quickly, but Byrne chose a slow, swaying rhythm and stuck to it. Stared at Shea's beautiful face.

"Why didn't you call to tell me you were coming?" she asked.

"Didn't know I was until, oh, noon or so. And by then I knew you'd be running around getting ready, and the idea of surprising you seemed far too appealing."

"Where'd you find a kilt at the last minute? And one that fit at that?"

"It was surprisingly easy. The rental place said it's the Black Watch tartan, whatever that means."

"It means you look hot in it, is what it means."

He picked up his step and gave her a little turn, if only to disguise his grin. She felt like sunshine in his arms, and she smelled like heaven. But there was still a little bit of resistance in her, and he could feel the farm and their disagreements like a wedge between them. He had to make that wedge disappear.

Bringing their clasped hands between their bodies, he looked into her eyes and said, "I really haven't liked being apart from you these past five days."

Her brow furrowed and her body stiffened.

"And in that time," he pressed on, "I realized what I did to you that day I got back from South Carolina, after the shit with my apartment. You really were reaching out to me, trying to help me in your way—"

"Yes, I already told you that."

"—and I pushed you away. Set space between us. Well now I know how that feels and I hate it. I feel like crap for ever doing that to you. I'm very, very sorry."

Her eyes softened and her lips parted on a sigh that smelled sweetly like the chocolate torte they'd just eaten. "I'm sorry, too."

"And I was a bit of a jackass. Letting my emotions take hold like that, when my anger and frustration had nothing to do with you."

By the look on her face, he could tell she was as relieved to hear the apology as he was to say it.

"So I've decided"—he stopped dancing, stopped moving, and concentrated only on her—"that I really don't want anything to come between us again. A stupid toy train or a great big farm up north. Nothing. Everything you said to me about Alex and new beginnings was true. I was too raw to hear it before, but now I get it. It's time to let my shame go. I'll pack it away with my little brother when he goes off to jail. I won't be ashamed of my past anymore, and I'll release my dream of buying my family land or a house or anything like that, and focus on something new. I'll let that go, but I don't want to let you go. We're too good together."

"We are," she whispered. Even under the joyful, upbeat music, and the laughter and shuffling of dancing feet, he heard her.

He pulled her closer, sliding his free hand around her lower back.

"I'm not Bespoke Byrne. I'm not Rugby Byrne. I'm Shea's Byrne, and it's the best person I've been in years. Maybe ever."

She went absolutely still. But underneath his fingers where their clasped hands pressed to her breastbone, he felt her heartbeat kick up.

"The other day when I came by with the papers," he said, "I forgot to tell you something. I told you all the rational reasons why you should take the farm, but I didn't mention the most important. I should've told you then that I did it because I love you."

Her eyes shimmered again, like they had when she'd been entranced by the music.

"I'm in love with you, Shea," he repeated, because he wanted to.

Removing her hand from his, she slipped her arms around his neck and pressed herself against him. Embraced him tightly. Clung to him. Her face was a warm, teasing pressure on the side of his neck, and the silk of her skin below her ear made him dizzy. He smiled against her and clung right back.

"I love you, too," she said, and he tightened his hold.

They stayed that way for a very long time. Long enough the song changed again, to something romantic and sad at the same time, the singles drifting from the dance floor to be replaced by couples.

A whole new life opened up before him, and he shivered with the most luminous kind of contentment.

As the long, low notes of the fiddle ribboned around the ballroom, he finally allowed himself to let Shea go, stepping back to take her face in his hands.

"Is that a 'yes'?" he asked. "About the farm?"

The glow on her face faded.

"Byrne, I . . ."

He sensed her retreating again, and this time he let her go.

"I still don't know," she said. Then she looked away, and it was like someone had plunged him into shadow after having stood in the blazing desert. "I just don't know. And you're . . ."

Her words drifted off but he understood. "I'm confusing you."

"No. Not confusing. I know where you and I stand, but there's still a lot for me to sort out outside of that. But you're kind of all entwined in it, and it makes for a complicated puzzle. Like, what if the distillery fails? What would happen to us? And what if . . . what if *we* fail? How does that work with the property? It's just a lot, Byrne. A whole hell of a lot."

"I understand." The distress on her face bothered him greatly, and he leaned forward to plant a soft kiss on her forehead. "Why don't I leave? I thought my coming here, saying what I had to say, would make things a little easier, but apparently that's not the case."

How could he have thought that? Feeling love was one thing, but declaring it was something else entirely. The difference between a hill in Wisconsin and the Swiss Alps.

"No, you don't have to—"

He nodded. "Yes. I think I do. I should, anyway." As he dragged a thumb down one soft cheek, he realized that she was letting him. She was allowing him to touch her like this in front of all these people. "You know how I feel, Shea. I'll be here regardless of your decision. How about you call me when you know. Either way."

She sandwiched one of his hands between hers. The way her fingers stroked over the back and made gentle circles in his palm sent tiny shocks of happiness and worry through his system.

"Just a little more time," she said.

He sighed, disconcerted over how wobbly it sounded. "A little more time."

As he slowly backed away, he couldn't help but recall how difficult these past five silent days had been without her, and he hoped that her "a little" wasn't equivalent to his "a lot."

Chapter

⟡

23

*O*n Monday, Shea didn't even need the alarm to wake up. At five a.m. her eyelids popped open and stayed there. She hadn't been awake this early since college, and even that could be debated. She lay there for a good hour, staring at the slowly rotating ceiling fan, trying to will herself back to sleep until the eight o'clock alarm she knew was coming, but all that kept flashing across her brain were reminders of where she was supposed to be that morning.

Supposed to be, but not necessarily *wanted* to be.

The meeting at Right Hemisphere was scheduled for nine thirty at Whitten's Midtown headquarters. And she still wasn't sure if she was going.

Swinging her legs over the side of the bed, she once again took the stack of Byrne's papers from her nightstand and stared at it like it would suddenly morph into a crystal ball and give her all the answers.

Seeing Byrne's name on the papers made her think of him, of course. Made her remember his thick rugby legs in that kilt, the firmness of his broad shoulders underneath the stiff Prince Charlie jacket, the accent of the bow tie at his throat.

The sound of *I love you* on his lips.

Sinking her head into one hand, she blindly threw the

papers back onto the nightstand. The doubts about the farm she'd voiced at the Scottish Ball were still very real inside her.

Allowing him to do this for her—even without strings, without any sort of ownership in the distillery—would create a rather thick link between them when their relationship was still so new.

Then there was Whitten, whose offers had the potential to be the icing on the cake. The way to finance everything else, *if* she accepted the farm. The funds she needed . . . with the stigma of Right Hemisphere and all the bouncy-boobed, spray-tanned images that came with it.

Yawning, groggy, she padded over to the kitchen and stabbed on the coffee maker. Looked like she'd be awake for the next couple of hours as the pro-con arguments waged war inside her head, so she might as well caffeine up.

On her third cup of straight black, she sat in the deep windowsill that overlooked the street and watched her little corner of the city come alive. A little over a half hour until the window to catch a cab uptown to Right Hemisphere would close, and she still hadn't made up her mind whether or not she was going.

Her phone, sitting on the edge of the coffee table, buzzed so dramatically to life that it jumped off the wood and thunked to the rug. Her immediate thought? Byrne.

He'd done exactly as he said he would Saturday night at the ball, and had left her standing there alone in the middle of the dance floor to stew in her indecision and her want for him. In the end he'd done the right thing, because as soon as he left, she stopped thinking along the lines of an insipid Disney princess and realized that just because they felt the same way about each other, didn't mean that allowing him to buy her that farm would bring about eternal sunsets and rainbows and perfect sex and a trouble-free relationship.

On the flip side, Byrne wanted nothing to do with the distillery, unlike Lynch. Who was to say that the distillery would ever pose any kind of threat to what she and Byrne had?

When the phone hummed indicating a text message, she dove for it like she was a desperate bridesmaid at her last single friend's wedding.

The words on the screen instantly made up her mind about whether or not she was going to meet with Whitten.

In two seconds she was dashing down the hallway and throwing on the shower. In three minutes she was back out and clean—the fastest shower in the east—and wrapping her wet hair into a bun. She pulled out of her closet a pencil skirt, a fabulous top that could have been bespoke it fit her so well, and all her best jewelry.

As she did the awkward high-heeled jog to the corner to catch a cab, she realized she was only one minute late, by her previous timeline. Whitten would wait for her. He had to.

The cab pulled up in front of the black and silver mid-last-century office building, and she threw money at the driver. On the top floor she was guided by an assistant down the hallway toward the open door of the conference room. She realized she wasn't one minute late, but fifteen, and worry seeped into her system that Whitten and his staff would count her as a no-show and move on to other work.

Still, when she turned into the conference room, it was nearly filled.

Whitten was there, sitting at the far end of the table. So was Linda Watson, looking as serious as ever as she poked at a tablet computer. A couple of younger guys and another woman about Shea's age all looked up as she entered. A projector cast a square of white light on the far wall, and to the right there was a large dry-erase board set with all colors of markers. The table was filled with paper and pens and drinks and food. Fuel for a marathon brainstorming session.

When Whitten saw her, a slow smile spread across his face. He pushed back his rolling chair and stood.

It all began here.

"Here's what I want." Dispensing with opening pleasantries, Shea moved to the end of the table. She tapped a nail on the burgundy wood. Linda leaned forward, but Shea ignored her and kept her focus on Whitten. One of the younger guys scrambled to wake up his laptop, while another pulled a pad of paper close to his chest and raised a pencil. Shea ignored them, too.

"I want to do the travel series," Shea began. "To Scotland, of course, but also to other whiskey-making areas. Canada. Kentucky. Japan. Ireland."

Whitten's nostrils flared, but in a good way. He nodded once.

Shea wasn't finished. "I'll write about whiskey without being told what brands to mention or what to say about them from advertisers. I get final say on all wardrobe, regardless of media. There will be no photos of me below the shoulders without my approval. No half-dressed female models will be used for any story I do. I get final creative approval. And above all"—now she took in the wide-eyed stares of the other Right Hemisphere employees in attendance—"there will never be any mention of my current personal life, my ex-husband, or what happened in the media two weeks ago."

In the ensuing silence, Shea crossed her arms and waited.

"Well then." Pierce grabbed a pen as he slowly sat back down. He met her eyes and added, "We better get to work."

*F*our hours later, Shea wandered from the building and out onto the hot, bright Madison Avenue sidewalk. A million people surged around her, and she barely noticed.

She was flying above them all. Elated, buoyant, filled with possibility and promise. Up there, in that New York City office building, her life had turned a sharp corner. And the change in direction no longer scared her. The fact that she had smart, supportive people who shared her visions standing at her back erased most of the fear.

Taking out her phone, she opened the text message that had come through earlier that morning, the one that had made up her mind to come. She read it one final time before deleting it forever.

It was from Douglas Lynch: *Have you seen the receipts for the past 2 weeks? There's no such thing as bad publicity.*

*B*yrne hopped up the concrete steps to Shea's apartment, taking them two at a time. He was already sweating, having jogged from the far corner because of a car accident that had blocked access to her street, and because of course she'd summoned him to her on the hottest day of a New York City summer.

He'd strap on a sixty-pound pack and sprint through the Sahara if it meant she were on the other side.

The call had come through barely a half hour ago. "How soon can you get here?"

He'd had no idea how to read her tone of voice.

"If only I were magic," he'd replied, "I'd be there in an instant. As it is, I'll grab a cab in the next minute."

"I'm not taking you away from anything, am I?"

He'd looked down at the half-eaten deli sandwich his assistant had brought him for dinner and the greasy letters and numbers on his keyboard. Everything on that desk could wait. He'd had to set her aside for Switzerland because there was no way to get out of it, but the emails he was composing would wait until tomorrow.

As he'd clicked off his cell phone, the trail of her voice lingering in his ear, he realized that he'd never set aside or delayed work before, no matter how small an issue or project. For any reason.

It felt pretty damn good. It felt mighty freeing.

Now he stood on the front stoop of her building, tapping his foot, shaking his head and smiling to himself. Hoping that the reason she'd called him here was the reason he wanted.

He wanted her. He wanted *them*. Fuck the farm, if that's what it had to come to.

The door buzzed without the preamble of the intercom, and he ducked out of the hot setting sun into the only slightly cooler space of the stairwell.

Upstairs, she was standing just outside her door. The dead-bolt was engaged, keeping the door open just a hair. She was wearing these black shorts that were about an inch shy of being called underwear, and a red tank top.

"You look hot," she said.

He arched an eyebrow and growled. "Why thank you."

Swiping at beads of sweat along his temple, she grinned. "It's like Rugby Byrne is trying to bust out."

A trickle of sweat rolled down his back. "No kidding."

She cocked her head, a mischievous glint striking her blue eyes. "I think I should help him."

When he felt a tug, he looked down to see her hand pulling out his belt from the buckle. *Yes.* Good thing she was the only apartment on the top floor.

Belt loose, her hands then moved up to the buttons on his

shirt. He opened his arms to give her access while peering at her through narrowed eyes.

"I can't believe I'm questioning this, but what are you doing?" he murmured.

"Getting you ready. I have a surprise for you inside and you'll enjoy it with fewer clothes."

As she undid the final button on his shirt and parted the flaps, exposing the white cotton underneath, he realized that he hadn't seen her this way—this animated, this carefree—since before his apartment and her privacy had been snatched away.

There was evil, delicious promise in the quirk of her mouth as she turned around and opened the door to her apartment. He found himself entranced by her ass in those shorts, and the creamy length of her legs.

"Are you coming in?"

"Huh?" He grabbed at his sagging pants and hurried inside. "Yes. Definitely."

As the door snicked shut behind him, he stopped dead in his tracks and gaped at what sat before him. A huge beige dome tent took up the entire open space of her floor.

Shea moved behind him, slid her hands over his shoulders, and drew his dress shirt down his elbows and off his arms. "Surprise," she whispered in his ear.

"No fucking way." She peeled off his undershirt, and even as the cotton came off he was still staring at what she'd set up. "I get my tent."

"You get your tent."

He remembered the dome from the campground, and how tiny it had seemed beneath the canopy of the trees. Here, set up in her apartment, it felt huge. He got all giddy with excitement, and then quickly vowed never to use that word again to describe himself.

"And I get something, too," she said.

Finally he looked to her, saw how much he loved the loose, long braid sweeping over one shoulder. "Yeah? What's that?"

"Take off those pants, get inside, and I'll tell you."

Then she bent over, the shorts stretching over that gorgeous, tight ass, and unzipped the front flap.

She didn't have to tell him twice. In a hurry, he toed off his new loafers, stripped off his new socks, and let his new pants fall. He crawled into the tent just behind her, clad in only his underwear. Inside, she'd flattened out a sleeping bag.

As she knelt in the center, he walked on all fours to her, the mesh top of the tent brushing his hair. The almost painful urge to kiss her drove him forward, but her fingers on his lips stopped his progress. Torture, that's what she was.

"Sit down," she told him, as she crossed her legs in front of her. He did the same.

Placing her hands on her knees and closing her eyes, she breathed in through her nose and out through the tight circle of her mouth, like she was about to do yoga or something. When her eyelids fluttered open, her gaze fixed directly on him.

"I want the farm," she said.

He couldn't help it. He let out a whoop and some other spontaneous, indecipherable sounds of celebration. She was letting him do this for her. She was letting him help.

Thirty-plus years of hardship and shame and schooling and working grew wings and lifted off his shoulders.

"But!" She raised a hand and he settled down, though he couldn't for the life of him erase the smile. "There's a condition."

"Okay."

"My name goes on the deed. You close the deal and it's my name on the papers. I've looked into it, and if you do that, then I'm the one responsible for the taxes. Once the purchase goes through, you'll step back. That's the only way I'll let you do it."

He rubbed a thumb across his bottom lip, considering. The tax thing made sense. In case something did happen to them.

Which it wouldn't.

"And I would like to try to pay you back," she said. "It may be in small increments, and it may take forever, but that's what I want."

He bit the inside of his cheek to keep from saying, *But what if I marry you?*

"Done," he said instead. "So does this mean—"

"That I met with Whitten today. This morning." Her face cracked wide open. One of the biggest smiles he'd ever seen on her face.

"And if you're prepared to take on taxes for a good chunk of New Hampshire while starting up a new business and trying to pay me at the same time, I take it you and Pierce reached some kind of deal?"

Her head bobbed, the braid swinging. "Nothing formally contracted yet, but the salary numbers we kicked around were more than I thought. Twice as much. And today's brainstorming session . . . Byrne, I felt like I was right where I needed to be. His staff had all these ideas for me, and yes, some of them were shit, but they probably hated some of mine, too. The bottom line is, we were on the same page about the projects I want to do under his umbrella. And he gets me. He's behind me."

"Of course he is. He'd be a fool not to be." That's when he touched her, reaching out to fit his palms over her smooth knees. "And the Amber?"

The smile faltered and she looked away. "Part of me will be sad to let it go, but the other part, the larger part, will be glad to be out from under Lynch. Did you know he actually had the gall to text me this morning and tell me how wonderful my embarrassment had been for the Amber's bottom line?"

Byrne's fingers tightened as anger took over his brain. "*What*?"

Shea pushed her hands into his hair and brought his forehead to hers, instantly cooling him down. "Never mind. Forget it. It's done and I'm gone. You are not Lynch. And you're definitely not Marco. I know this and I don't fear you or what you want for me, and us. I think I was subconsciously still trying to lump you in with them, to protect myself. But I don't have to do that with you."

"No, you don't."

She smiled. "And now I have something new."

The feathers of her breath tickled his mouth, and his lips dropped open, wanting her taste. Instead his eyes closed and he just *felt*. Felt her skin beneath his hands, the heat from her body enhanced by the close quarters of the tent, and the greater meaning of her words.

"Please say you mean me," he whispered.

A finger touched the outer corner of his eye, and he opened them.

"I do. My dreams are partly made of you," she said. "But we have so much to figure out. I mean, the farm's six hours north. In New Hampshire. And your job is here."

"Well, you're not moving up there tomorrow, are you?"

She laughed. "No. But eventually . . ."

"Eventually I may be doing something else with my life, too."

She blinked several times. "What do you mean?"

Shrugging, he said, "I have no idea. But I say that from now until you move up there, we play everything by ear. See how we feel. Go for what we want, determine how to get it, all while we figure out how to be together. Piece of cake." He grinned.

She stared at him for a long second before tightening her hold on his head, and then she smashed her lips against his. The groan that vibrated in his throat came from so deep inside he felt the strain on his heart.

Felt like it had been fucking forever since they'd kissed. Really kissed. With no bullshit or worry stacked behind the action. No doubts poking at the breaths in between. Nothing but them together, and the sweet, hot taste of her tongue. The unquenchable need.

Sure her whole future had been upended and then righted with none of the original pieces left, but just one look at her told him she was doing the right thing. She had everything she needed to embark on a new life. All the new pieces, right there in front of her. All she had to do was arrange them.

Her brilliance and enthusiasm and initiative and charisma would send her sky-high. The industry was hers to do with as she pleased. And he'd be standing back, watching and loving her. There if she ever needed him again.

Breaking the kiss, he slid his hands around the backs of her knees, then yanked her legs out straight, pulling her closer. She laughed, her torso slanting backward, and she had to catch herself on her hands. Too bad he had the full intention of sending her even more off balance—both in body and in mind. He wrapped her ankles around his lower back and scooted her onto his lap. As his dick hit hard against the warm cradle of her body, the flare of desire in her eyes was almost the perfect reward.

Almost.

"It's a big deal." She was breathless. "A huge thing, what we're doing. Are we ready for it? Can we do it?"

A wave of warmth cascaded over him. "I'm convinced you can do anything."

Since he had control over her bottom half, he circled her hips one way and ground his growing erection in the opposite. He loved the feel of her body so much, the firmness of her muscles and the utter softness of her skin.

But he loved her even more naked.

"I don't really care what you do with the farm," he said against her mouth, "as long as I get my tent sex. Right here, right now."

"So I could sell it and take the money and move to North Dakota as long as you could orgasm on a sleeping bag?"

He pretended to consider that, until she broke out laughing and wrapped her arms around his neck. He'd had rugby players take him down with gentler grips, and he didn't care. Didn't care if she ever let go. They kissed hard in the heat of the tent.

"Tell me you love me," she panted.

"Gladly." His fingers dipped into the back of her shorts, his thumbs grazing the sweet dimples above her ass. "Just as soon as I'm inside you."

Chapter

24

*S*hea kicked through the fresh, powdery snow on her way back to the main house from the outbuilding that was still in the process of being renovated into her personal office. Five o'clock in the evening and it already felt late at night, dark and cold and mysterious, the shortest day of the year having recently come and gone.

The Christmas lights outlining the house's windows and every peak and valley of the roof clicked on, courtesy of a timer. Though the lights had been put up weeks ago, it was the first time she'd been standing outside to watch them come on, and part of her saw it as magic. Like the stuff in the crazy books she always caught Byrne reading. Like the portal to her own private world she'd described that first time she'd brought him here.

That had been a lifetime and four and a half months ago. So much had changed since then. And everything for the better.

Hers. This whole place was hers. The future was a bright, never-ending road.

She stopped halfway between the office building and the house, her boots settling on the shoveled stone paver pathway. From the huge barn off to her left came the whir and bang of saws and hammers as the workmen finished up another day of overhauling the space to accommodate the distillery. The mash tuns and fermentation tanks and barrel racks, and about a hundred other needed things would be delivered in the spring.

The first shipment of grains would arrive when the weather warmed, the harvests were ready, and the country roads were clear. She'd already had a horticulturist out to determine the viability of eventually growing her own rye and corn and millet in the back fields, and the outlook seemed promising.

The cold bit through her bulky fisherman's sweater, and she hurried the rest of the way down the path, then stepped through the back door that opened into the spacious, warm kitchen. Eventually this room, too, would have to be refurbished if she wanted to make an old Scottish-style manor house hotel out of the place. But . . . one thing at a time. There was the first batch of whiskey to distill and get stored in barrels. That was priority number one. Then there were all her exciting obligations to Right Hemisphere to fulfill, including the first couple of parts of the travel series that would send her back to Scotland in April.

And of course, there was Byrne.

It had been two weeks since she'd seen him. Two arduous weeks full of torture, longing, long-distance love, and physical self-gratification. She'd learned rather quickly, however, that her hand wasn't nearly as talented as any part of Byrne. And so she made herself wait, comforted by the fact that he, too, had vowed to keep his hands off himself in preparation for their reunion.

Just as she set the teakettle on the stove, her phone rang. She hadn't realized how eager she'd been to hear its sound until she fumbled getting it out of her pocket and almost shattered it on the slate floor.

"Hi, hi!"

"Were you running a marathon?" came the wonderfully familiar and terrifically sexy voice on the other end.

"Yes, as a matter of fact. About to cross the finish line. Where are you? Sounds like you're driving. Are you on your way here?"

"Almost there, actually. Took a day off work and got an earlier start than planned."

Kind of ridiculous, how the butterflies danced in her stomach upon hearing that. Usually when he came up to the farm, he left after the workday ended and didn't pull in until nearly midnight.

"You mean you took a day off the weekend before Christmas? How scandalous. How will your boss ever forgive you?"

Byrne chuckled. "He'll live. He was surprised I did it, though."

"So you haven't told him you're leaving yet, I take it."

"Nah. Not before the holidays." He paused. "Not when I have family in town."

At first she thought that was a vague reference to her, but then she heard muffled voices in the background, coming through under the hum of the car. She gasped. "You got your family to come up?"

"I did." A grand sigh full of contentment. "They let me buy them plane tickets to come up for the holidays. Couldn't be happier."

Shea had always sensed that it would only be a matter of time before his family felt more comfortable and more receptive to tiny favors once he backed off from the "Let me take care of you for the rest of your lives" angle.

"And you have them with you right now? Coming here?"

A toddler giggled in the background. "I do. All of them."

Shea squealed. "I can't wait to meet them." And that was the honest-to-God truth.

"They can't wait to meet you, either."

"I'll go turn on the heat in the extra bedrooms. It's not like I don't have enough of them."

"No, it's all good, Mom. You're not imposing," Byrne was saying. Then to Shea, "Remind me where this portal is again?"

She gave him directions from the Route 6 turnoff, even though he'd been up to the farm dozens of times over the past four months. He was great with money and numbers, terrible with directions. It was partly Shea's fault, because they spent so much time on the phone while he was on the road, catching up on what they'd missed in each other's lives while apart.

Apart. More days than together.

At first it had been hard. Damn near impossible, actually, with her zooming back and forth between New Hampshire and New York, and him flying all over the ever-loving world. The reunions were amazing, though. They erased any tidbits of doubt that had managed to wiggle into her mind during the empty space. This weekend—this Christmas—would be no different. She just knew it.

Exiting the kitchen, she walked through the grand, empty foyer and went up the sweeping, curving staircase to the third floor, where the extra bedrooms were located. Based on Byrne's location when he'd called, she had about an hour to get the place ready. She ran from room to room, adjusting the thermostats and throwing wood into the fireplaces. She stretched clean sheets over the new mattresses that, unfortunately, still lay on the floor. True beds would have to come later.

She was stuffing a pillow into a case when she saw through the front window the twin dots of light that indicated a car approaching on the access road. Leaving the pillow half-naked, she sprinted from the bedroom and almost tumbled down the main staircase to the front door. She burst outside and stood in the snow to watch as the car meandered down the narrow road. It turned to roll through the gates that would never be locked again.

Christmas lights entwined with evergreen boughs draped the length of the stone fences along the driveway. They twinkled and served as runway lights, directing the car that seemed to be taking freaking forever to get here. The boat of a rented sedan finally swerved around the front circular drive, skirting the pickup trucks and vans that belonged to the contractors, and parked beneath the porte cochere.

Shea dashed around the hood, preparing for one of her and Byrne's typical greetings.

The driver's-side door opened and Byrne stepped out. Jeans, hiking boots, sweater. Luxuriously, gorgeously casual. Shea was about two seconds away from attacking him and licking away his broad, crooked smile, when the car door behind him opened, and out stepped a dark-haired woman who could only be Caroline.

How do you properly greet the man you love more than anything after two weeks apart when his family was present? Conundrum, conundrum.

Byrne solved it without consulting her, sweeping an arm around her waist and tugging her in for a tight embrace and a long, sweet, close-lipped kiss.

"I missed you," he whispered against her lips. "So much."

She said nothing. She couldn't. Even after five months together—more if you started counting from Long Island— he still managed to do that to her.

His parents had exited the car and were staring at her, so she gently pushed Byrne away.

"Hi." Shea gave them a wave as she felt her face heat.

"Let's go inside for introductions," Byrne said with a chuckle. "My Southern family isn't built for the cold."

So Shea led them all back inside and enclosed them in the warmth of the big old house. She turned around in time to see Mr. Byrne's mouth drop open at the sight of the richly carved wooden staircase and the gleaming floors and the rooms that seemed to go on forever. Mrs. Byrne glanced around for a moment, then her face turned red and she looked at her feet. Shea knew intimidation when she saw it. Even she had felt overwhelmed during her first walk-through of this place.

Shea held out her hand to Mrs. Byrne. "I'm Shea, Mrs. Byrne. I'm so glad you're here. Merry Christmas."

Byrne had told Shea that his parents had had him when they were in high school, so even though they were thin and looked a little haggard around the eyes, dating them beyond their years, there was a gleam of resilient youthfulness in their expressions.

"Call me Betty. Please." A little of the intimidation faded as Betty shook Shea's hand.

"I suppose if I kept calling you Mrs. Byrne we might get confused," Shea added.

"Well, you could just call him Jasper," said the sister.

Byrne choked. Tried to laugh and then choked some more. Shea laughed for him. She'd seen his real name—Jasper Patrick—on the farm's paperwork, but he'd made her swear to never use it, upon pain of death. Or never giving her an orgasm again. That was an easy bargain to make.

"No," she said. "I don't think I could *ever* call him that."

"I'm Caroline," said the sister, "and this is Kristin." Kristin flopped her hand around on her wrist in a baby's attempt at

a wave. "You okay over there, Jasper?" Caroline smacked
Byrne on his back, as he still couldn't catch his breath. And
Shea noticed that the lopsided smile was a lovely family trait.

"I'm Matthew," said Byrne's dad. "And we're grateful
you're having us here over the holiday. When J.P. said it would
be a surprise . . ." As he faded away, an expression of humble-
ness overtook his face.

"He knew that I'd be ecstatic," Shea finished for him. "And
I am. Come in, come in. The only two furnished rooms right
now are the living room and the kitchen. Why don't we sit and
have some tea to warm up before I give you the grand tour?"

She led them to the front corner room, where the cushy
sofas that had made her New York apartment feel so cramped
now looked like doll furniture. As the Byrne family sat by the
lit Christmas tree and Kristin immediately lunged for the
scant few ornaments, Byrne himself wandered over to the big
reclaimed wood table and picked up one of the large sheets of
paper laid out there.

"Wow." He whistled, drawing everyone's attention. "These
are all fantastic. Have you picked one yet?"

Shea looked up from where she was dangling a cheap penguin ornament in front of Kristin's face. "Think so."

"Picked what?" Caroline asked. And just like that, Shea
knew she liked her. A woman who came right out with it.

"Logo and brand ideas for my distillery," Shea said. "My
friend Willa's a graphic designer. Really talented."

Byrne put down the sheet he was holding and picked up
another. "This one. I like this one the best. Not that I get a say
or anything."

Shea went over to him. "But I appreciate opinions. And it
must mean something, because that's the one I'm leaning
toward. Beautiful and modern, but with a sense of history."

"Exactly." Byrne was staring at her, not the artwork.

He circled around her and brought the paper over to the
couch where his parents were sitting. Willa had done an
incredible job of accurately drawing one section of the stone
wall in front of the Gleann house. The crumbled part looked
just like the walls that had swirled around Granddad's old house
back in Scotland, but since it was actually on-site of the distillery, it was decidedly American and locked in the present.

Betty touched the corner of the paper but didn't take it. "It's pretty." She peered at the writing. "Gavin Distillery. How'd you come up with the name?"

Shea stood behind the couch, admiring the way Byrne looked holding her future, standing in the house he'd bought that started it all. "Gavin was my granddad's name."

"What did your dad say when you told him the name?" Byrne asked.

"He loved it. He teared up."

It might even have managed to smooth things over between her chosen profession and her parents. After learning that, the fact that she would be producing her own liquor seemed to not make their mouths twist in unspoken discomfort. Last week her mom had even inquired about Shea's progress, and they were coming to the farm for New Year's Eve. She planned to buy them a computer so they'd be able to watch the travel series once it started airing on her new, Right Hemisphere–produced website.

Much later, after Shea made the Byrne family a dinner out of whatever was left in the fridge, and gave them a tour of the whole house, she linked her fingers with those of *her* Byrne, and together they walked slowly down the second-floor hallway. She'd deliberately chosen a bedroom as far away from anyone else's as possible. The whole north wing was pretty much hers.

"Thank you for bringing your family here," she said between their soft footfalls on the carpet.

"Thank nothing. I'm thrilled I actually got them above the Mason-Dixon Line." He stopped in the middle of the hall, tugging her around to face him.

"How'd you do it? You've been begging for years and now this Christmas they decide to come?"

He shrugged, and his eyes made an arc around the hall. "I stopped pushing, I guess. I stopped telling them I was going to do all this stuff for them, telling them I was going to set them up for the rest of their lives, blah blah blah. And then I just . . . asked. I called them a couple weeks ago and asked if I could buy them tickets to come up here and see me for the holidays. And to meet you. To see what you're building here. They accepted. So I suppose I should be the one thanking you."

All she could do was smile at him. Until he smiled back and then all she could do was get ridiculously turned on.

"Come on." She walked backward, bringing him with her. "I've made some changes to our bedroom."

"*Our* bedroom?" He resisted moving forward, like a stubborn dog on a leash. His fingers tightened around her hand, and she had to stop again.

"Were you planning on staying somewhere in town every time you came up to see me? Or maybe you wanted to borrow my tent?"

"No." That crooked grin.

Breathless. That's what he made her.

"So then this is our bedroom." She nudged her chin toward the door. "Yours and mine. I got us a real bed. A big kids' bed."

"Oh, really?"

She opened the door to reveal the massive four-poster bed that wouldn't look good anywhere but in homes like this. "You like?"

"I do. Very much. But I'd like it even more if you were in it. Naked."

She was already taking off her clothes, excitement vibrating through her. "That can be arranged."

She removed her sweater and jeans deliberately slowly, in the exact way he liked. Her bra and underwear came off millimeter by millimeter. When she climbed up onto the bed, she expected to have to do a little more wiggling, a little more teasing, before he was on her. She'd barely twitched her ass to the left before Byrne pretty much tackled her, rolling her over. Kneeling on the bed, he whipped off his sweater and undershirt.

There really were no words powerful enough to describe what she felt for him at that moment.

"Hey, I want to ask you something," she said.

"Shoot."

"It's about your parents. And your sister."

He cringed, his whole face scrunching up. Then his head tipped forward and he tapped his forehead on her shoulder twice. "You did not strip down after me not having seen you for two weeks, wave that perfect ass in my face, and then bring up my parents. Tell me you did not."

She laughed low and pushed at his shoulders so he'd look at her in the eye again. "I did. And I'm sorry, but I don't think I can wait anymore to ask."

His brow furrowed. "What is it?"

"I was thinking . . . I mean, I've been knocking the idea around for a few weeks now . . . I thought it might—"

He grabbed a throw pillow and playfully knocked it against the side of her head. "Out with it. You're naked and I'm getting hard and precious time is being wasted."

She licked her lips. "Well. I wanted to ask you if it would be all right if I asked your family to move up here and work for me. Work at the distillery, I mean."

He was so silent. So still. The only thing that moved were his eyes as they darted back and forth between hers.

"Are you serious?" he whispered.

She loved the sharp bristle of his weekend stubble. Pretty soon she would get to feel it more often. Every day, if they each got their way.

"Completely," she replied. "I mean, you've said how hard it's been to get them up here when they think they're taking handouts from you. But if you want to help them have a new life, and you want to respect the pride they feel for having a hand in their own existence, why not here? Things are really going to pick up in just a few months once I get in the grains and barrels and stills. I'll need lots of hands. Not to mention the whole back-office organization. I'll be hiring locally for sure, but I wanted to run this past you first."

More silence. More staring. So she continued on.

"I know we haven't talked about moving in together—and that's not what I'm proposing here, if that scares you—but with you leaving your company and going out on your own with a few clients, you could work more from here if you wanted. There's a local rugby team, too. And if your family worked for the distillery—even Caroline, too, now that Kristin's dad is out of the picture—you could see them a hell of a lot more. There's a lot of affordable housing in Gleann, and I'll have insurance and benefits and such. You could easily make sure they were okay. Take care of them that way. Because from what I saw tonight, I can say that they love you more than anything, and want to be near—"

He kissed her. Hard and consuming, pressing her deep, deep into the fluffy new comforter. When he finally released her, pushed to his elbows above her, and gazed down at her with smiling eyes, it was her turn to be speechless.

Sliding a hand down her side, around the curve of her breast and the dip in her waist, he took her hip in a gentle but claiming grip.

He said, "God, I love you."

She was glowing. Could feel the light and heat radiating from where those words had implanted themselves in her heart. "I love you, too," came her reply. "So is that a yes? You'd let me ask them?"

"Yes. *Yes*. You can ask them."

Shifting her head on the comforter she said, "You don't look so sure."

"I'm one hundred percent sure. I'm just—"

"Letting someone help you get what you always wanted." She let that sink in. "How does it feel?"

It took him a few moments to answer. Except he didn't do it with words. His shoulders gave a little shrug, and then his whole body shivered.

"It's okay," she murmured. "I understand."

Her turn to kiss him, to lick away his doubt.

"For the record," he said after stopping the kiss, "moving in with you does not scare me. Nothing about you scares me."

"But I still surprise you?"

One hand swept over her hair. "Absolutely. In the best possible way."